D0117859

KEVIN

"A mind-blowing thriller in the
tradition of James Rollins,
Matthew Reilly, and Preston & Child."
Ed Stackler, Thriller Editor,
www.fictioneditor.com

NEXT GENERATION
2016
WINNER
ACTION/
ADVENTURE
INDIE BOOK AWARDS

ICE

A Dr. Leah Andrews and Jack Hobson Thriller

ICE

KEVIN TINTO

Three Dog Publishing
Tiburon, California

Publisher's Note: This is a work of fiction. Names, characters, places, and incidents are fiction, except when they are not. Any resemblance to actual people, living or dead, or to businesses, companies, events, institutions, or locales is completely coincidental. ICE/ Kevin Tinto-- 1st ed. -- v1.6
ISBN 13: 9780692406373
ISBN: 0692406379

"A moment is a concentrated eternity."
Ralph Waldo Emerson

"The test of an adventure is that when you're in the middle of it, you say to yourself, 'Oh now I've got myself into an awful mess; I wish I were sitting quietly at home.' And the sign that something's wrong with you is when you sit quietly at home wishing you were out having lots of adventure."
Thornton Wilder

Author's Note

The extraordinary disappearance of the Anasazi/Mogollon cliff dwellers from the American Southwest has been well documented but never solved. Why Native Americans who lived and prospered peacefully on the mesa tops for thousands of years suddenly abandoned these villages for precarious cities lodged in the cliffs around the year 1200—and for only a period of some 200 years, before disappearing—remained a mystery, until now.

CONTENTS

PROLOGUE

K'aalógii held her *mother's hand as they wound their way through the darkened pas-sageway leading out of the remote mountain stronghold. She climbed the hand-carved steps that rose to the forest floor with her head held high, knowing—and accepting—that this would be her last time.*

Her name, which meant butterfly, had been a gift from her father. He had always said that when she was born he'd felt such joy that he could have stepped into the air from the cliff dwelling and flown like a butterfly. The happiest day of his life.

K'aalógii felt proud that she'd brought her father joy. Her people had experienced little joy during her lifetime. Now that her father was gone, she had dedicated herself to living by his warrior code, acting with honor and bravery, even during these times of terror.

She wondered whether her father might be watching her from the ancestral lands, the Navajo place of origin to which all dead returned. If so, she knew he'd be both proud of and terrified for his daughter, for she had chosen to face the others with a courageous heart and sharp spear.

Some said the others were demons with long fangs and glowing red eyes, wings like an eagle's but skin like a bat's. Some said they were the holy people or ancient, forgotten deities bent on retribution for the tribe's mistreatment of the land. Others considered them the spirits of their enemies, forbidden from their ancestral lands because of the evil in their souls, wishing to wreak only destruction and death.

There had been a time when the cliff dwellings had provided safety from their reach. But safety meant little if the remaining tribes starved to death. Those that had tried to hunt for food or sow their crops by the river had simply disappeared.

K'aalógii had even resorted to eating the deerskin tunic that her mother and father had made for her, boiling it with some leaves and shoots gathered near the secret entrance to the mountain stronghold.

Starvation alone hadn't extinguished all hope.

Some taken by the others had returned. They brought with them stones her mother had said were evil and would bring death and destruction. The returned had carried a message:

Surrender yourselves, or face the wrath of the others. The cliffs will not protect you.

The survivors had reacted violently to the message. They had killed the returned, then gathered in a council and decided to fight.

Now, climbing toward the surface of the plateau, K'aalógii grasped her mother's hand more tightly as they reached the outside. She had no need of reassurance, but she knew her mother was frightened.

Her mother stopped and knelt, pushing K'aalógii's hair away from her face.

"Now we will wait on the mesa."

K'aalógii nodded and squeezed her mother's hand again. "We will see Father again."

Her mother straightened, wiped away a tear, and handed K'aalógii the spear.

It had been the ceremonial spear of her family for many generations. Her father had been given it by his own grandfather. The handle was wrapped in well-worn rawhide and decorated with beads and feathers. The obsidian tip had been masterfully worked to razor sharpness and soundly fastened to the notched shaft with dried sinew.

K'aalógii had always thought of the spear as heavy and unwieldy. Now, as she stepped onto the mesa top, she hardly felt its weight in her hand. The hunger that had haunted her simply disappeared at the sudden sight of the stars and fresh smell of the forest.

Her mother and she joined the others making their way toward the open mesa; all had armed themselves with whatever weapons remained in the cliff city.

K'aalógii listened while the others whispered. She understood much of what was said, even the words not spoken in her Navajo language. Many clans had joined here together in fear, remnants of once-great tribes that had lived on the mesa tops for countless generations.

Tonight the survivors had resolved to leave the stronghold, put aside their fear, and fight the others rather than starve to death, waiting to be taken like mice by a hawk.

The people gathered in a circle, where two women knelt and chipped sparks into dried grass until a wisp of smoke and flame signaled the beginnings of a fire. As the fire grew, children brought dead wood from the nearby forest. A large fire would draw the others, K'aalógii knew.

An old man dressed in feathers and paint walked into the center of the circle. Wielding a spear more formidable than K'aalógii's, he thrust the weapon skyward in defiance. He then began to dance and chant, a warrior's dance passed down for generations in his tribe, K'aalógii guessed.

As the old man danced and the fire grew, K'aalógii felt her heart and spirit soar. For one last time they had become brave warriors again, joined in a defensive circle around the comforting heat of the flames.

When the old man raised his spear again, K'aalógii chanted along with him.

It didn't take long for the others to make their presence known. The plateau suddenly smelled of thunder and lightning, the very air sizzling around her.

K'aalógii stood tall, spear thrust high, her other hand held tightly by her mother, who raised her own makeshift weapon. Somehow, she stood her ground, even as the people around her dropped their weapons in terror and began running for the thin cover of trees.

Now only K'aalógii and her mother stood in the clearing, side by side, spears extended before them.

The roar grew deafening and an unnatural heat burned her skin, forcing K'aalógii to her knees. She drew upon the strength of her father, imagining him standing tall upon the mountain his scent, his bulk, his eyes, his very presence bringing forth the power of her ancestors.

K'aalógii shouted as a warrior would do, her eyes opened wider, her skin burning as the others devoured her.

CHAPTER 1

"**J**ust one more step and you're gonna get a good look at the bottom of the canyon," said Garrett Moon.

Dr. Leah Andrews pulled the binoculars away from her eyes and watched as the toe of her boot slid over the edge of the cliff. A spray of sand floated toward the green valley floor hundreds of feet below.

"I know where I'm standing."

Sand and gravel cascaded down the rocky slope behind them, followed by a giant who wore his hair in a short ponytail over a three-day-stubble beard. Only a well-placed sandstone boulder prevented his 280 pounds from barreling over the cliff.

"Delicate as ever," Leah said.

Juan Cortez wiped a mixture of sweat and dust from his face. "The coast is clear, but I'd wager those park rangers are sniffing around nearby."

"What'd you expect?" she asked, grinning despite the risk. "We are trespassing illegally in the middle of a national park."

"She smells a cliff dwelling," Garrett said.

Juan looked over the ledge and shook his head. "A monkey couldn't climb that face without modern equipment."

1

Tall, anvil-shaped clouds began rolling in from the southwest, signaling the beginnings of a late-season thunderstorm. The winds preceding the storm kicked dust up in flowing red curtains.

"That's a hint of things to come," Garrett said. "You want to be dangling from a rope when that hits?"

"Speaking of rope, where's our climbing expert?" Leah asked.

"Resting on his climbing gear near the top of the mesa, last I saw," said Juan.

"Figures." Leah hoisted her backpack into place. "I'll wake Sleeping Beauty."

Juan took another peek over the cliff. "You'd think a couple of relatively intelligent guys would have more sense than to rappel down a sheer wall in the middle of a thunderstorm."

Garrett grinned and pushed strands of black hair away from his face. "Yeah, but who else would look after her?"

"Don't let her hear that," Juan cautioned, "or we'll both be sporting black eyes."

"You two better *not* be whispering about me," Leah called back as she climbed the slope.

"We're just a pair of lowly, underpaid archeologists," Garrett answered. "Our discussions are purely of a scientific nature."

Leah was still shaking her head when she came upon Marko Kinney leaning on his climbing gear, listening to audibly heavy metal through his ear buds.

Leah poked at the shaggy young man with the toe of her boot until he killed the music. "We're checking out a wall crack."

Marko looked up and pointed toward the billowing clouds. "Mr. Thunder Bumper is headed this direction, and he's looking worked up."

"Meet me on the other side of the rock bridge with your gear."

The rock climber shook his head in disbelief, then gathered his gear and chased her across the rock arch toward a gnarled but sturdy-looking pine tree growing near the mesa's edge. He dropped the pack, pulled out a nylon-anchoring sling, and wrapped it expertly around the pine tree's trunk. Marko secured the slings, removed two 165-foot climbing lines from the backpack, and tied them together with a double fisherman's knot.

Juan and Garrett joined them while Leah fitted herself into a padded climbing harness and fastened the metal waist buckle. Marko fed the doubled line through a standard figure-eight descender, triple-checked all the connections, and patted her on the shoulder.

"You're cleared to fly," he shouted over the rising wind.

She nodded and stepped to the cliff face. As sloppy as Marko looked, he was a fanatic about safety. Because of his attention to detail, Leah felt at least some peace of mind. If her dad had enjoyed the same kind of attention, he'd have been alive today.

Marko climbed into his own harness and threaded another line through the anchoring rings. He'd feed rope as she rappelled in a classic belay technique taught at most climbing schools. If she suffered gear failure, he would serve to break her fall, at least in theory.

Garrett dug out his own harness, peeking over the edge at Leah's descent.

"I know you guys are the experts at finding cliff dwellings," Marko said, "but I'm not thrilled about roping down that cliff face with lightning cracking around my ass."

"Chances are she'll shine her flashlight into the crevice, find a dead end, and we won't be climbing down anyway," Garrett said.

The line slackened, and a moment later Marko felt three distinct tugs on the belay. "You were saying?"

Garrett glanced up at the sky. "I guess we're climbing down."

Marko yanked up the freed belay. "Okay, you're next, G."

A minute later, Marko had a hesitant Juan in his harness and ready to join the others. "They're waiting for you, Juan."

The big man hesitated, then took a deep breath and leaned over the brink of nothingness. All that separated his ample posterior from a three-hundred-foot freefall were two thin strands of high-strength climbing line.

"Down you go," said Marko.

As Juan descended, an unexpected gust of wind twisted him around, causing his face to scrape across the sandstone wall, shaving skin off his right cheek. Thunder cracked in the distance as he attempted to gain position against the rock.

"Come on, Juan," Leah shouted encouragement from the ledge below.

Juan pushed off and rappelled until his shoes touched the ledge.

"Was that so hard?" Garrett secured him to the ledge.

"Still gotta climb back up that mother."

Marko slid spider-like down the line and noted with quiet satisfaction that Leah had already inserted a removable locking-cam inside a weathered crack in the cliff. He crouched to examine the narrow opening. "It's less than a meter high. How are you gonna get inside?"

"Seriously, Marko?" Leah asked. "Lie down like you're taking a nap."

Garrett winked and patted the young climber on the back. "You're doing fine. Don't let her bully you."

Leah pushed Marko aside and dug a small flashlight out of her gear bag. "If you want something done...." She slithered quickly through the scar-like blemish in the rock cliff. Once inside, she switched on the steel penlight and crawled along on her hands and knees through the confining passageway. Ahead, the tunnel opened into a larger chamber.

"Garrett," she called back. "You got the big light?"

Garrett crawled in behind her and handed over the high-powered halogen flashlight. Leah fumbled with the switch and then lit the chamber ahead.

"Oh, my God," she whispered.

A massive subterranean cavern at least 50 meters high stretched far beyond even the powerful beam. The light did a fine job of illuminating the pristine remains of an 800-year-old Native American city hidden in the depths of the Gila National Wilderness.

CHAPTER 2

"I think you just hit the jackpot," said Juan as he joined the other three in the cavern.

Leah only managed a nod. She thought of her dad. How hard he'd worked for years in search of just such an Anasazi/Mogollon ruin that managed to survive without the plundering that had muddled the archeological record of these mysterious, cliff-dwelling Native Americans.

She quickly wiped away a tear, hoping that Juan, Garrett, and Marko hadn't noticed. The beam of the flash penetrated only a portion of the massive cavern. Even so, Leah easily identified the outline of a cliff dwelling city, with adobe structures built right up to the ceiling, easily three or four stories tall.

"Let's introduce ourselves."

Garret pulled out two more heavy-duty flashlights, handing one to Juan and the other to Marko.

Marko shook his head and declined the light. "I don't know anything about this—I'm just here to set ropes. You guys ought to use the good lights."

"Your eyes are just as good as ours," Garrett said, still holding the light out to Marko. "Everyone in this crew gets an equal shake, regardless of diplomas."

Marko glanced at Leah, who nodded. "Take it; I'll give my halogen to Garrett and use the penlight. I'm so pumped, I swear I can see in the dark."

"I don't know what to do," Marko said after taking the halogen.

Leah pointed to the rear of the cavern. "Take your light and explore."

"What should I look for?"

Leah ran her light's small beam over the wood and adobe structure before responding. "If you run into any cliff dwellers chipping away on arrowheads or painting on the walls, I'd want to know about that right away."

Marko looked so shocked that Garrett and Juan chuckled.

Leah had to restrain herself from rolling her eyes. "I'm kidding." She watched him visibly relax and look away sheepishly. "But seriously...."

Marko glanced up.

"Don't touch anything."

The climber nodded, then held the light out in front and tiptoed past Leah on his way toward the rear of the cavern.

"Light up the walls, Garrett. Juan, take a look through this mess on the floor—see if you can find something that's gonna blow me away." She slid her iPhone out of her jacket. "I want to get at least a few photos before we have to get out of here."

Garrett swung his light onto the vertical rock walls while Juan lowered his to the cavern floor.

Leah noticed right away that the cavern featured pictographs, some of them painted by highly skilled artists, others more crudely done.

"Ever seen a dwelling with this much art?" Garret asked.

"Never." Leah examined the ancient art on the walls, using her smaller light to illuminate the detail, before snapping more photos. The pictographs appeared to have been painted using ground red clay mixed with water, making a paint-like paste. The one before her featured a number of stick figures that Leah interpreted to be people. Behind them were much taller figures without defined shape, as if they'd been covered in blankets from head to toe.

"Not sure what this means, but—" Leah stopped short.

The next pictograph featured the same faceless, oversized figures that Leah could only assume were totemic creatures or some sort of holy people. In this pictograph, the figures had wings sprouting from their shoulders and what Leah interpreted as raptor-like talons serving as legs and feet.

"I have no idea what this means," Leah said. "These big, vague figures are odd enough. But wings and talons? I've never seen that before."

Garrett walked down the cavern wall, illuminating several pictographs at a time. "How many stick figures are in the pictographs you're seeing?"

"Seems to vary; some have four or five, some less. Why?"

"The ones down here, they've got a lot more, but as I work down your way, there's fewer in each picture."

"How many of yours have these big creatures or whatever?"

"Most of them." He stopped. "Damn."

"Yeah?"

"I'm sure now. Each pictograph shows fewer of the stick people—the tribe members, right?"

"Maybe it represents some kind of epidemic that hit 'em." Leah worked her way down the wall. "I've never seen something like that documented in such detail, though."

Juan spoke next. "You're gonna want to see this."

Leah walked over and knelt beside Juan, using her small light to illuminate several clay pots that had been laid carefully together.

"That's not Mogollon or Anasazi."

Juan nodded. "Simple coil and pinch construction, then fired and covered in hot piñon pitch. What does that tell you?"

"Navajo jar. Textbook."

"No shit."

"What's a Navajo jar doing in a Mogollon cliff dwelling?"

"Exactly."

"If you like that," Garrett said from a few feet away, "this is really gonna blow your skirt up."

Leah turned to join him. "What?"

"I'm scared to get too close. You'd better come over and have a look-see."

Leah stood, brushed off her jeans, and used her light to guide her through the debris-filled cavern.

She knelt beside Garrett, who held the light on the object with one hand while keeping his long hair away from his face with the other.

"I wouldn't have a clue," Garret said, "except I've had the pleasure of sitting through plenty of your lectures on ancient Native American cultures—especially the ones that disappeared."

When Leah focused on the object, she felt her heart skip a beat. Her forearms swelled with goose bumps.

"Oh my God...."

Unlike the Navajo jar, this was a large bowl made of fired-clay. The surface was smooth and had been crafted by a skilled artisan, who'd painted it with a series of bold geometric patterns in black and white.

"Well?" Garrett asked.

"Mimbres burial bowl."

"That's what I thought—but I'd only ever seen one in your slideshow, so I wasn't sure."

Leah looked up. "Where's Marko?"

"Over here," the climber replied. "I haven't found anyone yet, if that's what you want."

"Ha-ha," said Leah. "Get your butt over here."

Marko stepped cautiously around the pots and shards, making his way to where Leah, Garrett, and Juan were gathered around the artifact.

"Take a good look at this." She illuminated the bowl. "If you see anything like it, anything at all, you tell me right away."

"What is it?"

"It's a Mimbres burial bowl."

"Is it, like, really rare?"

Juan and Garrett chuckled.

Leah nodded. "The Mimbres culture consisted of several hundred small villages in southern New Mexico. Sometime around 1200 AD they completely disappeared. The only records we have of their existence are extremely rare pottery samples, like this burial bowl."

"Why was it called burial bowl?" Marko asked.

"Because it was placed over the head of the deceased when they were buried, then a hole was knocked in the bottom of the bowl."

Marko shuddered.

"Weird, right?" Leah gestured at the cavern. "Well that's nothing compared to what we're seeing here."

"Why's that?" Marko asked.

Leah stood. "So far we've found evidence of at least three distinct ancient Native American cultures all living within one cliff dwelling and enough pictographs to fill the Louvre."

"That's unusual?"

"It's unheard of."

She used her light to illuminate the structure. "Let's spread out. I want to discover as much about this dwelling as we can with the time we have remaining." She glanced at Garrett. "I'd guess there's another way in and out of here besides roping down that cliff face. How about if you and Juan see if you can locate it."

The two of them nodded.

"Marko, see if you can find more pottery near the rear of the dwelling. I'm going to search around inside the adobe houses. I want to see just how many different cultures were shoehorned into this dwelling at one time."

Within minutes, Leah had found pottery and shards indicating that Navajo, Hopi, Mogollon, Apache, Pueblo, and Mimbres Indians had lived in the cliff dwelling. She stopped for a moment to absorb what she'd just discovered. It was the discovery of a lifetime. Unprecedented. A surreal sense of elation unwound inside her, and she suddenly felt better than she had in months. It dulled the nagging pain of a marriage on the rocks and her recent and bitter divorce from her federal-government dream job. It was almost as if—

A sudden scream shattered the silence, followed by the sound of someone breaking through adobe.

CHAPTER 3

"**M**arko!"

Leah sprinted toward the rear of the cavern, frantically searching for Marko's mop of hair and goofy grin. *He wasn't that far away from me.* She illuminated the floor of the cavern ahead and found a large, round hole that had apparently swallowed the young rock climber.

"Jesus, no," she whispered, dropping to her knees and crawling toward the false floor. She reached the edge on her belly, terrified of what she might find.

To her immense relief, Marko lay on a ledge three meters below.

"Are you hurt?"

Marko rubbed his head. "That's a lump I'm gonna feel tomorrow."

Garrett placed his hand lightly on Leah's shoulder and peered down into the hole. "You probably don't want to move, my friend."

"I think he knows that." Leah reached down and scooped up a handful of the brittle adobe. "I've never heard of cliff dwellers sealing a kiva with an adobe cap."

Leah watched as Garrett ran the tips of his fingers over the edge, rubbing bits of the powdered soil. His eyes worked over every inch of the breach. "That's too deep for a kiva, and there's no reason to seal it off."

Leah nodded. One more mystery among many. No one knew why these people, who had lived on the tops of mesas and in river valleys for thousands of years, would have forced themselves into cliff caverns. She looked up into the gloom, imagining them humping their water up here from the valley, letting their children walk on ledges where one misstep meant instant death. Then, two hundred years later, these people had completely disappeared.

Like her father, Leah had devoted her life to studying the enigmatic cliff-dwellers. Her father had been a mining engineer by trade, but his passion had been archeology. Every weekend, with the blessing of her mother, who preferred tending to her award-winning gardens, he'd taken Leah out into the desert in search of the Anasazi.

She remembered sitting cross-legged inside ancient cliff dwellings while her dad taught her how these magnificent people had lived in the hostile environment of the desert Southwest hundreds of years before Columbus crossed the Atlantic.

He'd passed on his passion for archeology to Leah and he couldn't have been more proud when she'd earned her PhD from the University of New Mexico in Native American Archeology.

Her mother's death from brain cancer when she was a teen hadn't been nearly as painful as her dad's untimely demise, falling while roping down into a dwelling. His sudden and unnecessary death had served to give her a "swift kick in the ass," as Garrett called it.

The same quest that had cost her father's life had already lost Leah her job as an archeologist for the Bureau of Land Management. If she were caught today in the Gila National Wilderness, illegally searching for cliff dwellings on government land, her next address would be a federal prison.

Her dad had always felt their best chance for finding unspoiled dwellings was in the relatively unglamorous Gila National Monument and wilderness in southwestern New Mexico. Unlike well-known sites like Mesa Verde, this area was heavily forested and riddled with twisting canyons and hidden cliffs. The cliff dwellers in this area weren't called the Anasazi but the Mogollon, named after the man who'd made the original discovery.

This dwelling, with its unheard-of melding of tribes under a single roof, could well be the Rosetta Stone that finally solved the mystery of all the various cliff dwellers.

Marko had gathered himself and was preparing to climb out of the pit.

"Wait," Leah said. "While you're down there, free-climb all the way down to the floor and take a look-see for artifacts. Oh, and—"

"Yeah, I know," Marko said, sidling down the steep, rocky slope. "Don't touch anything."

"Gimme some light," he said a moment later from the bottom of the sub-cavern.

Leah and Garrett illuminated the sand and stone floor as best they could from above.

"Better." Marko bent down and then jumped back against the cliff face. "Shit! The floor's covered with bones!"

"What the hell...." Leah had joined him at the bottom of the pit, where skeletal remains lay side by side along with strips of decomposed clothing. The bones were shattered in such a way as to leave no doubt as to the reason these people had died.

Marko backed away from the remains. "I thought you said cliff dwellers were peaceful."

"This was just a child, for God's sake." Leah pulled her hand away. "Who'd do that to a child?" She slid the camera out of her jacket...and then slowly returned it. She was a hardened scientist, still, she couldn't help but feel like she was desecrating a grave site.

Garrett stood beside her now. He shook his head. "I suppose they could have been buried here, but it looks to me like they were killed down here and sealed in with adobe clay."

Marko led them down a passageway at the bottom of the pit. "I found some more of those drawings."

"Pictographs," Leah corrected.

Garrett nodded. "It's starting to make a little more sense to me."

"What is?" Leah asked.

"Think about it. What if you've got different tribes jammed into one small living space? Everyone speaking a different language...."

"They might use pictographs to communicate or pass along tribal stories, since conventional storytelling would be difficult."

Garrett shrugged. "It's as good a theory as anything else right now."

"Remind me to pay you next time I invite you to present at one of my lectures." Leah carefully stepped over the bones and walked over to where Marko shone his light on the wall. The first of the ancient drawings was in the shape of a mountain with a vertical face.

"That doesn't look like anything I've seen in this region. You've been on big walls," Leah said. "Have you seen anything like that?"

"Maybe Half Dome in Yosemite, if that's a sheer cliff like it looks." Marko took several more steps into the darkness. "More pictures here. This looks like a person holding their hands in the air, surrendering or something."

"Those are strange-looking mountains. I've got a feeling they're located a long way from New Mexico." Leah stepped carefully over the remains and lit up the drawing. It was a woman, her hands clearly outstretched over her head. The artist had intended the woman to have a look of terror on her face. "Hmm. She's not surrendering."

"What's she doing then?"

Leah winced. "Praying, or maybe even pleading." Leah backed up and shot several photos. "Looks like they painted these pictographs in a rush. They don't have the color and detail of the series in the main cavern."

Marko stepped back from the pictographs. "Okay, that's enough for me."

"Watch your step." Leah turned her flashlight in the direction of Marko's feet to make sure he didn't disturb the bones. The beam reflected back at her, revealing golf-ball-sized red rocks scattered in and among the remains.

"What the hell are those?" she breathed. The way they reflected the light, they looked almost like crystals.

Garrett knelt down and examined the stones. "Granite, I think, but I've never seen such a brilliant red coloring anywhere."

"I know you kids are having fun down there," Juan said from the top of the sub-cavern, "but the storm's getting a lot closer."

"Why don't you climb on down, scaredy-cat?" Leah shouted. "What kind of archeologist is afraid of a little rock slope?"

Juan's voice boomed back. "A fat one that's fallen on his ass one too many times."

The sound of thunder echoed throughout the cavern.

"Seriously," Juan said, "time to move or we're going to spend the night here."

Leah looked around for a moment. "I want some of these stones."

"But you said—" Marko began to protest.

"We're not touching anything else. These don't fall into the same artifact class as human remains, dwellings, or handcrafts. We'll document the rest when we return." Leah knelt and carefully picked up several of the reddish, crystal-like stones and placed them in her gear bag. "Okay, Juan, I'm coming up."

Five minutes later, Leah held her hand out for Garrett as he scrambled over the lip of the sub-cavern. "So," she said, "we climbing those ropes or what?"

"We found an entry at the rear of the cavern," Garrett said. "Sealed but not impassable...much to Juan's relief, I might add."

"I'm not too big a man to admit it," Juan said with a smile.

"Marko, use Garrett's exit. Pull up and stow the climbing lines," Leah said. "The sooner they're out of view the better."

Garrett shone his light on a large opening at the rear of the cavern, still sealed tight with adobe clay. "Guess they didn't have any plans to return."

"That's odd," Leah said. "Someone took the time to seal the cavern."

"The last one out locks the door and turns out the light?" Juan said.

"You wouldn't leave all those tools and pottery unless you thought you'd be coming back," Garrett said.

"I don't think they were coming back," Leah said.

Juan glanced over. "Why?"

"This place is a mess; did you notice? Pottery scattered, much of it shattered. If they were coming back, they'd have taken it with them or it would have been stacked neatly inside the dwelling. These finished pots were priceless in their day. It'd be like leaving home with nothing but the clothes on your back. No, I think they left in a hurry, and not because they wanted to."

"If they weren't coming back, why seal the entrance?" Marko asked.

Leah turned back toward the dwelling. "Those pictographs were painted for a reason, it's possible they wanted to seal the dwelling to preserve or record their experiences here."

Thunder boomed so loud that adobe dust fell like a fine mist from the dwelling.

"We've got all night to talk this out over beers," Juan said. "Right now, we've got to get out asses out of here in one piece."

Garrett and Juan carved away at the adobe wall with two collapsible shovels, chopping through the clay until they had an opening nearly a meter in diameter. Dim sunlight, accentuated by bolts of lightning, lit a twisting passageway that led to the top of the mesa.

"When you get to the surface, find cover right away," Garrett said. "Wicked storm clouds inbound."

Leah swung her backpack into place. "See you on top."

Garrett reached out and lightly grabbed her arm. The grin had disappeared. "I mean it, Leah. Get under a rock, a ledge—any shelter you can find."

"I understand. You just make sure Juan doesn't get stuck."

"Up you go." He watched her climb through the rock for a moment. "You ready, Juan."

"You're sure I'm gonna fit?"

"Shitty time to find out."

Juan stuck his head through, and Garrett helped him work his wide shoulders past the newly cut exit. "I'm clear," he said with more than a little relief.

"You heard what I told Leah," Garrett cautioned. "Get to cover when you reach the surface." Garrett turned and looked at Marko. "I'm sending you with most of the equipment."

"What about the rope anchor—on the tree?"

"I'll get it." Garrett grabbed his equipment bag and crawled through the narrow opening. The sounds of thunder and the smell of the ozone-rich air intensified as he climbed over the boulders toward the mesa. He looked up after a few minutes to find the surface only a few meters above. Water from the cloudburst poured into the passageway before diverting into an eroded natural culvert leading down to the cliff wall.

Leah, Juan, and Marko huddled under a wide overhanging rocky ledge near the cavern's exit point. Garrett bolted out through the opening and ran toward the cliff. He worked Marko's knots free, removed the line from the tree, and stuffed the straps and rings in his gear pack.

Suddenly air sizzled, followed by a blinding flash that obscured Leah's view of Garrett for a split second. Garrett sprinted for the rock ledge where the others had taken cover.

"Think you were toast when that bolt came down?" Juan asked.

"Let's just say I felt the hands of my ancestors for a second." He tried pulling his backpack off. "Oops, I'm hung up."

Juan chuckled. "If that's your ancestors, you pissed them off plenty." He yanked the pack off Garrett's shoulder and turned it around. The nylon still smoldered from the near lightning strike. Even the zippers had been bent and twisted into painfully unnatural shapes.

Leah glanced at the sky and then shouldered her pack while climbing out from under the rock. "Let's get out of here before we get caught in a flash flood."

CHAPTER 4

The sign hung askew over the top of the Silver City, New Mexico, store-front. The white paint, peeling off the wood, had yellowed with age and disrepair.

Jim Dixon's Precious Stones and Lucky Strike Tavern.

Leah glanced up at the sign. "Do a little rock shopping and then cel-ebrate your purchase over a cocktail...."

Juan peeked into the bar and grinned. "I like it."

The only patron was also the bartender. He sat on the customer side of the bar, sipping on a mug of draft beer. "Come on in. Beer's cold and we're not known to bite."

Leah glanced into the rock shop through a connecting door. The store appeared empty, except for the rocks and fossils displayed in glass cases or hanging from the walls. "Are you Jim?"

The bartender smiled and shook his head. "I just fill in for Jimmy when we get a load of tourists in looking at rock." He pointed down toward the end of the street. "He'll be back in a minute; walked down to the bank." He slid off the stool and walked around behind the bar.

"We'll take a look at the rock store, if that's okay," Leah told him.

"Are you folks here to buy or sell?"

Leah stiffened. "We're looking for information, that's all."

The bartender winked. "You found yourself a little stash of fossil and want to get a price?" He lowered his voice. "It's all right. Jimmy pays top dollar and he don't talk much neither."

Garrett lightly touched Leah's elbow, guiding her out of the bar and into the shop.

The bartender called after them, "Come on back and have a beer before you leave."

Leah studied the rare fossils displayed under glass. "You think he really buys fossils from the parks?"

"Possibly...." Garrett looked over a few of the pieces on display. "Doubt he'd admit it to us, though. We might be working undercover for the Park Service."

"Can I help you folks with something?" A tall, thin man with short-cut brown hair and a face worn by hours working in the desert sun removed his sunglasses and Australian-style bush hat.

Leah raised one eyebrow. "You Jimmy?"

He laid a leather briefcase down beside the glass counter and nodded. "Are you interested in fossils? Minerals? I even have a few pieces of Trinitite in the back room."

"Trinitite?"

Dixon nodded. "When they lit off that first atomic bomb back in '45' it was so hot the blast melted the sand into a blue-green glass. One old rock hound living nearby collected a whole bunch of it before they bulldozed ten feet of sand over the blast zone."

The look of disgust on Leah's face left no doubt that she was not interested in that glowing piece of history.

"Cool," Marko said. "Radioactive?"

Dixon dismissed the question with a wave of his hand.

Leah stepped forward. "What we need is help identifying a chunk of granite." She pulled one of the crystals from her pocket.

Dixon examined the stone. "Granite for sure, but I don't ever recall seeing it with this much feldspar."

"Feldspar?"

"Granite is composed of feldspar and quartz, along with a collection of other minor accessory minerals: zircon, apatite, magnetite, ilmenite, and sphene." He stared into a set of blank faces. "In plain English, that means granite from this region is whitish or gray with a speckled appearance caused by the darker crystals. Potash feldspar imparts a red or flesh color to the rock." Dixon turned the granite over in his hand. "I've never seen a sample this brilliantly colored, even for the top-quality grades like you might see on a kitchen counter." He locked eyes with Leah. "Where did you say you found this?"

"Up north," Garrett said smoothly. "I hadn't seen anything like it around here."

Dixon eyed them warily. "If you have a few minutes, I'll pull my catalogs. Why don't you step next door for a beer?"

Taking Dixon's advice, Leah bought a mug and tipped it back, letting the cool brew run down her throat. She looked over at the worn pool table just as Marko took a huge slice at the cue ball, knocking it across the room. She had to admit, the cold beer and cozy interior of the bar had a calming effect. She smiled as Marko scurried across the room, chasing the bouncing cue ball.

Dixon walked into the bar with a thick reference book under his arm and dropped it on the table in front of Leah.

Garrett, Juan, and Marko propped the cue sticks against the wall and watched Dixon find the page he'd marked with a napkin from the bar. The rock dealer paused, and then pulled his reading glasses down low on his nose. "You folks know this stone's not from around here."

Leah shrugged. "We're not geologists."

"Where did you say you found this rock?" Dixon repeated.

Leah simply shrugged, and flashed what she hoped looked like an innocent smile.

Jim Dixon eyed them suspiciously and then opened the book to a page featuring color photographs of rugged mountain peaks and snow. He tapped on the faded picture. "There's only one place on the planet you'll find granite with this feldspar content."

Leah read the entry indicated by Dixon, and her mouth dropped open in shock.

"Antarctica."

Once Dixon had left them alone in the bar, Leah shook her head. "This just keeps getting better. Now we've got granite crystal originating near the South Pole ending up in a Native American cliff dwelling?"

"Hoax?" Juan guessed.

"The adobe clay that Marko broke through was hundreds of years old; so was the adobe that blocked the entrance, for that matter."

"This is like a major archeological find," Marko said, his eyes opening wide. "Maybe the government would let you back into the national parks. You know…if you just told them what you found."

Leah's head snapped around. "Even if I didn't go to federal prison for hunting Anasazi and Mogollon cliff dwellings on government property, I wouldn't pass those nitwits one iota of information. Not after what they did."

Juan emptied his third beer. "Looks like we're in kind of a pickle; one of the most significant finds in Native American history and we can't tell a soul about it."

Garrett's eyes took on a sly cast. "Well, there's one person we could tell—and he's an expert on Antarctica." He leaned away, instinctively taking himself out of Leah's reach.

"Not a chance," said Leah.

"I'm only suggesting that if anyone will know about feldspar-rich granite, it'll be someone who's clocked weeks in Antarctica." Garrett shrugged. "I know it's a long shot, but Jack might be your only option. Do you know where he is?"

"Last I heard he was leading Alan Paulson back up Mt. Everest." She humphed. "Rich asshole's gonna get both of them killed."

Marko leaned forward. "The climber, Jack Hobson?"

Garrett and Juan exchanged glances.

"It's not amusing," she told them. "Yes, Marko. Jack Hobson."

"You know Jack Hobson?"

"Sure, she knows him," said Garrett. "What's it been, Leah? Two years now?" He nonchalantly lifted the mug to his lips.

Leah simply stared down at the mahogany table.

"Damn," Marko said. "You were dating a famous mountain climber?"

"Technically," she said, "I'm still married to him."

"Married? You have a different last name." Marko seemed to say it innocently enough. "Why's that?"

Garrett and Juan buried grins in their beer mugs.

"Would someone please educate Marko on living in the current century?"

"Wow. Jack Hobson on Mt. Everest," Marko said. "I bet he's loving every second of it."

Chapter 5

EVEREST

Jack Hobson swore under his breath as he emerged from the warm, cocoon-like, expedition sleeping bag. He zipped open the reinforced mountaineering tent and studied the storm clouds pounding the summit.

How the hell did I let Alan Paulson talk me into a late-October climb on Everest?

If the winds continued howling, they wouldn't be climbing today. The professional climbing guide and his client, billionaire New Yorker Alan Paulson, had been pinned down above 26,000 feet for nearly forty-eight hours.

Jack wiped at his wind-burned face and surveyed the tent. The floor was an appalling mess. Empty food containers, spilled powdered drinks, and fuel stains covered the tent in an unappetizing mosaic. His clothes and his body hadn't touched soap and water in more than three weeks, and that wasn't the worst of it; the body begins dying at altitudes above 18,000 feet due to lack of oxygen.

As Jack pushed himself into a sitting position, every muscle in his thirty-six-year-old body protested. He reached into his internal-framed mountaineering backpack for another thermal shirt. The one he'd worn for the past six days was rancid with the stench of a true world-class climb. Body odor, powdered soup, melted chocolate, and camp fuel competed for dominance in a miasma of disagreeable aromas.

Most world-class mountaineers are lean climbing machines. The less muscle mass, the less energy it requires to climb. Jack was an exception. When he pulled off the thermal shirt, he exposed a well-muscled torso, much of it developed on an indoor climbing wall installed at his Lake Tahoe home. His longish brown hair, flattened by the frayed Peruvian-style wool hat he'd worn almost nonstop since they'd left base camp, felt greasy to the touch—another reminder of how badly he needed a shower.

Jack gingerly touched his temporarily bearded face. The combination of high-altitude sun and hurricane-force winds had burned and cut his face to the point where it felt raw.

"What's the verdict?" Paulson asked. The billionaire client peeked out from underneath the hood of his goose-down sleeping bag. He held an oxygen mask away from his face with a mitten-covered hand and managed a weak grin.

"The weather still sucks." Jack couldn't help but be annoyed at Paulson. "That's what we get for trying to summit this mother during the fall." He winked, softening his remarks, though it made them no less true. "How are you holding up?"

Paulson drew in five deep breaths. "I haven't slept in two days; I'm breathing in a near vacuum, and haven't taken a bath in weeks. Other than that, I feel damned good."

Alan Paulson was a fifty-three-year-old corporate raider who bought control of publicly traded corporations, got rid of the high-paid executives, and either made them profitable or sold them off in pieces. Here in the tent, he hardly resembled the man who could, and did, have powerful men pissing in their two-thousand-dollar suits when he sat before them with a notepad in his hand. Paulson still had the compact, muscular frame of the fighter pilot he'd once been. He wore an oxygen mask over his salt-and-pepper beard, but his eyes still shone with energy and anticipation.

That's the beauty of mountain climbing, Jack thought. It strips away the ego. You can't tell the true measure of a human being until he's been living in a tent under squalid conditions for weeks on end. You had to admire guys like Paulson, though. For the hundred grand they spend risking their lives on Everest, you could enjoy a hell of a vacation in the Caribbean.

"You guys copy?"

Jack blinked back to reality and then searched the bottom of the tent for his Motorola handheld radio. "I'm reading you loud and clear, Kent."

"What's wrong, old buddy? Afraid we're gonna beat you to the summit?"

"How's Alex?" Jack said, not trying to hide his concern.

He was worried not about Kent Nash, his former partner and climbing guide, but about Alex Stein, an Atlanta lawyer whom Jack had tried for months to guide away from this second Everest expedition.

"Alex says he's gonna kick Paulson's ass to the top. We're bivouacked just below; when it clears, we're steamrolling all the way to the top. Alex wants to say hi to y'all."

The radio crackled with static as Nash handed it over.

"Tell Paulson, next time we drop a hundred grand, it'll include a lot more booze and blondes."

The billionaire smiled from behind his oxygen mask. "Tell Stein that he should concern his liberal ass with all the empty oxygen bottles and garbage up here. Maybe he ought to commission an Environmental Impact Study before hitting the summit."

Jack relayed Paulson's dig.

Stein replied between labored breaths. "If I know Paulson, he's probably already worked a takeover deal with the Nepalese to buy out the Hindu church."

Jack and Paulson laughed between deep breaths of their own.

When the two wealthy climbers had attacked Everest the first time, Jack had been concerned that the conservative icon Paulson and proud left-wing liberal Stein would clash. To his surprise, they'd become fast friends, sharing political barbs by way of cell phone and even dinners back in the States. Something about the shared hardships of bagging a summit, and perhaps their mutual prosperity, had bonded them beyond politics.

Jack's relationship with his ex-partner Kent Nash, however, had soured over the past months, in Jack's opinion because Nash was jealous of Jack's relationship with the well-known billionaire. Jack's insistence that Alex Stein's prior attempt at the summit of Mt. Everest be his last hadn't helped either. The partners had parted shortly after on less than amicable terms.

"I'd have Paulson jog over and shoot the breeze in person," Jack said, "but he won't climb out of his sleeping bag. How's your body, Alex?"

"I've been coughing a little blood, but my fearless guide says that's normal."

Jack winced. "Put Nash back on the radio."

Nash got on.

"It sounds to me like Alex is working into the early stages of HAPE."

At high altitude, fluids began collecting in the lungs in a potentially fatal condition known as high-altitude pulmonary disease. On Everest, it wasn't unusual to push the envelope. But this was Alex Stein, Alex with the friendly southern handshake and easy smile, not an expert climber.

"It's a high-altitude hack, that's all. We'll see you boys on top."

Jack tossed down the radio in disgust. "You've got to promise me," he told Paulson, "if you've had enough, you'll tell me."

"Don't worry about me, Jacky. I'm going to kick this mountain's butt and dance all the way back to Kathmandu."

Jack crawled back into his sleeping bag and used his expedition-style pack as a pillow. He looked at Paulson. The billionaire was wrapped in his sleeping bag, sucking deeply on bottled oxygen. Jack thought about the billionaire's twenty-eight-year-old trophy-wife.

I'd take Candice Paulson and the beach over this shit any day, he thought with twisted amusement.

Jack laid his head back and closed his eyes, letting the roar of the winds lull him to sleep.

Jack opened his eyes to the sound of gentle surf and a warm tropical sun warming his face and shoulders. I'm dreaming, he thought in that half-lucid awareness of the sleeping mind. Jack leaned back into the warm white sand. The sound of the waves crashing on the beach was wonderfully soothing.

He reached up and felt small, smooth arms surrounding him. It was a tanned and svelte Candice Paulson, rubbing suntan lotion on his back from an old-fashioned Coppertone bottle with the little girl and the dog on the label. The distinctive smell brought back memories of surfing as a kid.

"Jack, is it time?" Candice said.

"Time for what?" He felt both aroused and confused.

The salt-and-peppered beard of Paulson replaced Candice Paulson's baby-smooth face as Jack startled from the dream.

"Storm's over," Paulson said. "Time to light the stoves."

Jack opened his eyes and mouthed a silent thank you to the utter privacy of one's dream world. He emerged in a world far less inviting than his fantasy beach when he crawled through the tent's opening. It was just after eleven p.m., and the stars silhouetted the summit in a haunting silver glow. After endless hours of wind, the dead calm seemed positively unnerving.

Paulson's face looked ragged, but his eyes remained bright with expectation.

"Show time," Jack said.

Chapter 6

"**G**od Almighty," said Paulson as he looked up at the 29,028-foot summit from camp four. "This is what life is all about."

Jack simply nodded and then attached the steel-tipped crampons to Paulson's plastic climbing boots. The crampons would help anchor the climbers on the dangerously steep glaciers that led to the summit.

After getting the crampons tightened and adjusted, he fitted a full oxygen bottle onto Paulson's back and checked his headlamp.

"I'm starting you on a flow rate of two liters per hour," Jack said. "This is all you've got until we get back down to camp four." Jack locked eyes with Paulson. "If you run out, you'll have to climb without oxygen so do the best you can to conserve it."

Paulson nodded while Jack attached his own regulator and oxygen bottle. He had climbed Everest without oxygen, one of only a handful of climbers to do so, but he'd come so close to freezing to death without the supplemental oxygen, he'd sworn he'd never do it again.

Six hours, later, they'd climbed through 27,500 feet. They were ascending more slowly than planned, but that couldn't be helped. Two feet of fresh snow covered the mountain, and they were forced to "posthole" through it by lifting their legs clear of the snow with each step. It was exhausting, and even though Paulson followed Jack's steps exactly, it was still hard work for the amateur climber.

Jack stopped to give Paulson a breather and studied the sky for signs of changing weather. It remained mostly clear and calm.

"How are you holding up?"

"Kicking ass and taking names." Paulson leaned over his ice axe, breathing hard.

Jack studied the narrow ridge before them. Another five hundred vertical and they'd pass British socialite Adeline Smith. She had been part of an all-women's expedition several years before. Now her body lay frozen in the ice, a testament to climbers with the stamina to climb Mt. Everest but not make it back down.

Paulson stopped dead and then backed up several steps. Adeline Smith's body poked up through the ice like a twisted piece of modern art. Her faded parka flapped against her frozen back with each gust of wind. One leg, hideously bent and twisted, and a plastic boot also protruded from the ice.

The billionaire pulled the oxygen mask away from his face to study the corpse.

"Adeline Smith died here, on the way down," Jack said. He leaned over so his face was just inches from Paulson's. "She's warning us, Al. Getting to the summit means nothing if we can't get back down alive."

Paulson nodded, replaced his oxygen mask, and resumed his slow ascent.

At first light, Jack indicated they should stop for a breather at the base of a slight gully. He pointed with his ice axe to the southeast as the dawn illuminated Makalu, the world's fifth highest peak. "You're seeing some of God's best handiwork, right here in the Himalayas."

Paulson nodded, but didn't bother to drop the oxygen mask and respond.

After climbing for what seemed like an eternity, Jack looked up to find the Hillary Step right in front of them. He leaned against his ice axe, breathing in deep gasps.

The Hillary Step, named after Sir Edmund Hillary, the first man to summit Mt. Everest, was a seventy-foot near-vertical rock face. On a good summit day, it created a natural logjam because climbers could climb through it only one at time. No one was waiting today, partly because Jack and Paulson weren't climbing during high season and partly because the earlier storm had trapped what few climbers were on the mountain well below the summit.

"Stop here. I'll climb to the top and belay you up."

Paulson's head drooped and his eyes looked glassy. His ass is kicked, Jack thought with a tinge of uneasiness. He pulled his oxygen mask down and looked the billionaire in the face. "Are you okay?"

Paulson's voice was raspy and weak. "Never...felt...better."

Jack gave him a pat on the back. He clipped into one of the fixed ropes and climbed his way to the top of the Step. Once there, he pulled down the oxygen mask and yelled, "Make sure you don't get hung up on the lines."

Paulson clipped on to the fixed line and slowly worked up the Hillary Step. He stopped halfway up, pulled down his mask, and coughed bloody mucus onto the ice.

Christ, Jack thought. The exhilaration of the extraordinary summit weather slipped away.

"It's nothing," Paulson croaked. "Dry throat."

Paulson's coughing subsided quickly, providing Jack a temporary feeling of relief.

Once the billionaire topped the Hillary Step, they had one narrow section and then an easy slope that finished on the Summit. Jack decided not to tell Paulson how close they were to the top. No sense in allowing him to get careless. One missed step and it was 10,000 nearly vertical feet down.

After thirty more minutes of climbing, Jack slapped his client on the back. "You got this baby in the bag!"

"What?" Paulson lifted his head and shaded his eyes.

"A few more feet and you're standing on the summit of Mt. Everest."

The billionaire instantly appeared energized. A spring returned to his step, and he bounded up the slope toward the summit. At 10:26 a.m. local time, Alan Paulson stood at the highest point on planet Earth, alone in his victory. He raised the ice axe over his head and dropped to his knees.

Jack slowly inched out the final step to the summit, and the two climbers embraced. Tears ran down their cheeks. The release of emotion was nearly unbearable.

It's always the same, Jack thought. Those who didn't climb couldn't know the feeling of total release and complete satisfaction the summit brought. It was like no other emotion.

Paulson pulled from his pocket a note that Candice had written. After reading it, the billionaire let it fly with the wind. It carried off the summit, swirling up in the building breeze.

Jack reached into his pack and removed two cameras: a thirty-five millimeter automatic and a smaller digital. He snapped pictures of Paulson standing on the summit and then stowed them deep in his pack.

"We've got to go," he said, pointing down the mountain. "You know getting to the summit is just half the deal. We gotta get back to camp four and the oxygen bottles or we're both dead."

They made good time off the summit and soon found themselves at the top of the Hillary Step. "Let me check your air supply," Jack said. The needles indicating the amount of oxygen remaining in the cylinder floated well into the red. "You're running an empty bottle. I'm giving you mine, but you've got to conserve it."

Jack had the strength to make it to camp four without oxygen, but the billionaire didn't. He cranked the flow rate up to three liters per hour.

"I feel a hundred percent better," Paulson said.

"Don't waste it," urged Jack. "Get a move on."

The billionaire pointed down the slopes of Everest toward two small figures slowly making their way up from the South Summit. "We've got company."

It was Nash, climbing slowly toward the Hillary Step. To Jack's horror, he saw that Alex was "short roped." Guides used "short roping" only during emergencies. Kent worked almost like a mule hitched to a wagon, pulling Alex up the mountain.

"Pay attention and get down the Hillary Step," Jack said.

The billionaire turned around, faced the mountain and climbed slowly down the narrow pitch. He nearly made it down when one of the sharp points on his crampon caught his climbing suit, and Paulson fell the remaining ten feet to the bottom of the Step.

Jack slid down the fixed line, landing beside his client. He leaned down and pulled Paulson to his feet. "I told you to watch that footing."

"Sorry," Paulson wheezed.

Jack pointed down to the footprints in the snow they had made on the way up. "Use our footsteps exactly."

Minutes later, Jack looked up from the ice and saw Nash climbing toward them. Alex Stein's head jerked backward, like something out of a '50s black-and-white horror movie, with every step Nash made toward the summit.

"Hey, Jack," Nash said. "Did you guys bag it?"

"Turn around," Jack ordered. "He's barely conscious and you still have a long way to go."

Nash bent over and leaned against his ice axe. He shook his head before speaking. "I have to get him to the summit," he said. "It's worth an extra fifty grand."

Jack struggled to keep his anger under control. "It's not worth it. Alex isn't making it."

"Keep climbing," said a raspy voice from behind Nash. "I'm not stopping now." Alex Stein broke into a racking cough that nearly buckled his knees.

Nash smiled weakly between cracked and bleeding lips. "We're going ahead. We'll tell you all about it at base camp."

Jack pointed toward Alex. "He's your responsibility, Kent."

Nash's eyes hardened. "See you in base camp."

Paulson kept up a good pace for nearly three hours but suddenly slowed again. Jack looked down the mountain, anxiously searching for camp four. They still had nearly a thousand vertical feet to climb down, much of it on steep, treacherous ice.

"Let me check your air." Jack wiped at the gauge while Paulson bent over, his chest heaving with every breath. "Shit…. Empty."

"I haven't touched the setting," Paulson said. "I swear."

"Hose leak," Jack said, swearing under his breath. "I can see where leaking oxygen froze on the regulator, maybe when you took that fall."

"I'm tired, Jacky," Paulson said weakly. "The climb down is killing me." The billionaire used his ice axe as a crutch to help support his body weight. "I don't think I can make it without the O's."

"You're making it," Jack said. He pointed down the enormous mountain. "It's not far. Let's go."

"Okay, partner, I'm giving it my—"

Blood and sputum suddenly splattered on the ice in front of Paulson's boots. "I've got to sit down, just for a second."

"You can't do that." Jack tried to keep the panic out of his voice. "You know you can't sit down. You do and you die."

The billionaire took three more steps and coughed up more blood.

"Come on," Jack pleaded. "We're getting close. Don't give up on us now." He tried to encourage his client between deep breaths. "I can see Camp Four. We're not far away."

Paulson leaned against his ice axe. Blood dripped from between his cracked, frostbitten lips, and his eyes didn't appear to focus.

"Don't kill you and me both," Jack said, trying a different tack. "If you stop, I'm dead too."

Just as the billionaire appeared he might manage a step forward, he collapsed in a heap on the ice.

We're both dead, Jack thought. Oddly, he felt at peace. Maybe it wouldn't be all that bad to sit down. Paulson had bagged his summit; that's all he really wanted.

Jack blinked and then ripped off his wool face-mask. The biting cold cut into his face. He sucked in a deep breath and rubbed his eyes.

Don't let the mountain make you a permanent resident.

His mind raced through a list of psychological motivational tools, and he decided to use the hardline approach. "I'll tell the entire world what a pansy-ass quitter you *were*," he said, summoning up his best sneer.

Was that a glimmer in Paulson's eyes?

"Go ahead and die on the mountain like a worthless piece of shit."

Knockout punch.

"I'll miss sitting around your pool at Devil's Key; just me and Candice sipping margaritas." He paused. "Laughing about how you flew her down to propose and then got food poisoning."

The billionaire sat on the ice in a stupor, bloody drool freezing on the front of his parka.

"You won't mind if I fly down myself and give her my condolences," Jack whispered in his ear. "You were a lucky man. She's got some kind of body."

Paulson's jaw clenched tight. He reached up and grabbed Jack by the neck. "You touch my wife and I'll kick your ass."

"You're *dead*, my friend," Jack said. He shoved Paulson down onto the ice. "There's not a damn thing you can do about it."

Paulson suddenly lurched to his knees and struggled to his feet. "I know what you're trying to do. Just lead the way," he said weakly. "If a piece of shit like you can make it down, I sure as hell can."

Less than an hour later, Jack pointed down toward two tents. "Camp Four," he said softly. The billionaire nodded in recognition, and a narrow smile escaped through his cracked and bleeding lips.

Paulson pulled himself into a tent and crawled into his sleeping bag.

Jack lit the stove and heated up powdered soup. After each had consumed two cups of the hot, nourishing liquid, Jack attached the billionaire's regulator to one of several oxygen bottles the Sherpa team had stashed at the tent. He adjusted the flow rate to three liters per hour.

Jack took another oxygen bottle for himself and set the flow rate at two liters per hour. He pulled the sleeping bag up over his clothed body and fell into a deep sleep.

CHAPTER 7

Jack blinked as cold air and sunny skies met his sleep-crusted eyes. "Thank God," he said softly. Light from a new dawn streamed into the tent. He crawled to the opening and looked out at blue sky. He pushed himself back into the tent and watched as Paulson struggled to sit up.

Paulson winced and reached for his mid-section. "My ribs are killing me."

"You were hacking all night."

The billionaire dropped back down on his sleeping bag. "They're on fire."

Jack felt around Paulson's rib cage. "You might have cracked a rib while coughing last night. Do the best you can to suck it up."

"What do you think happened to Kent and Alex?"

"I tried to raise them on the radio." Jack put on an unconvincing smile. "Maybe they kicked our ass and ended up back at camp three."

"They were behind us. How could they summit and climb safely down to camp three?"

"Stranger things have happened on Everest." Jack tried to sound more confident than he felt.

Paulson attempted a smile, but the pain in his ribs turned it into a twisted grimace. "I'll forget those comments you made about my wife."

Jack nonchalantly packed his gear. "I'm surprised you remember that."

"That's just about the only part of yesterday I do remember besides standing on the summit."

Jack nodded. "Time to get out of here and back to civilization; what do you say?"

"I'm right behind you," Paulson said, grunting while wedging himself into a sitting position.

Jack pulled their gear together, leaving the tents and empty oxygen bottles in camp. He would arrange to have the Sherpa's remove the remaining gear.

By late afternoon, they were passing the first of the Australian summit teams making their way up to camp three.

"You guys see Kent Nash and Alex Stein, by any chance?" Jack asked.

The leader of the Aussie summit crew looked somber. "Sorry, not a sign and nothing on the radio."

In the late afternoon, they walked into camp two to the shouts and cheers of climbers and Sherpa teams preparing for a shot at the summit. One of the Aussies from the second team ran up, a piece of white paper flapping in his glove.

"Are you Jack Hobson?"

"I'm Hobson."

"I have a note from base camp, mate. Someone's been trying to get in touch with you." The Australian paused. "Don't you pack along the sat-phone?"

Jack shook his head. "My client is a purist. Truth is, he doesn't want to be bothered by his employees."

The Aussie smiled. "Well, this Sheila's persistent, if nothing else. She called two or three times."

Jack looked up in surprise. A woman had called?

"The info's on the paper."

Jack unfolded the stained sheet. It read:

For: Jack Hobson (Hobson/Paulson)
Please contact Dr. Leah Andrews
Call/E-Mail ASAP

He vividly remembered his last conversation with Leah. The topic had been Alan Paulson.

Paulson walked over. "What's up?"

Jack managed a weak smile. "A call from Leah."

"Uh-oh." The billionaire grinned. "Got to give her credit, plenty of spunk for someone her size." He lifted an eyebrow. "I remember you saying she was recently unemployed. Maybe she's developed a sudden taste for climbing?"

Jack chuckled. "I doubt that." He pointed down the mountain. "We should be able to climb down through the Khumbu Icefall and make it to Base Camp by tomorrow afternoon—if your ribs are up to it."

Paulson's eyes opened wide in surprise. "Damn, I was having so much fun telling anyone who'd listen about my summit experience, I forgot all about them."

"Then let's get a move on."

The next morning, Jack led the billionaire down through the collection of building-sized ice seracs known as the Khumbu Icefall. Every season, climbers died when these massive hunks of ancient ice arbitrarily shifted.

Jack always held his breath when traversing the Icefall. It just didn't seem right that one could spend weeks climbing to the top of the world's tallest mountain and then die within shouting distance of base camp.

After sliding down the last ladder leading out of the Icefall, Paulson strutted into base camp like a conquering hero. Climbers descended upon him, shaking hands and patting him on the back.

Jack worked his way toward a small grouping of tents flying a Paulson Global flag. He zipped open his tent, crawled inside, and located the Globalstar yellow Pelican case and removed the handheld satellite telephone.

Jack entered Leah's cell number in Albuquerque.

"Hello?" said a sleepy voice over the satellite connection.

"It's me," he said.

"Hey, Climber," Leah said. "You're finally returning a phone call?"

"I just got back to Base Camp."

"Well, I'm glad to hear you made it down."

Jack felt a sense of relief. He'd half expected the "did that asshole nearly get you killed again?" argument to continue.

"Paulson bagged the summit and we're both in good shape—physically."

"We found something, but I can't say a whole lot about it," Leah said.

"Well, I'd say congratulations, but—"

"Yeah, we all have our problems. That's not the reason I'm calling you."

He felt irritation welling up. "Just felt like saying, 'howdy' after nearly two years?"

"We found…unexpected things. Some I can't talk about and I don't want it on text or email." She paused. "But one thing I can tell you: red granite crystal called feldspar-rich granite."

"You're not calling halfway around the world for a rock-identification lecture."

"You only find this type of granite in Antarctica."

"Hmm. Sounds like you've got yourself a juicy mystery, Dr. Andrews."

"You've spent time in Antarctica. Have you ever seen this colored granite before?"

"Sure, you might find it running in veins on several of the interior mountain ranges."

She paused. "It probably won't come to this, but what would it cost to charter a plane down to Antarctica?"

He nearly burst out laughing. "Charter a plane to where? It's a continent, *dear*. We're not talking about New Mexico here."

"I don't need a geography lesson," she snapped. "I need your help—you know I can't go to the—"

The phone clicked, and then beeped as it lost the satellite connection. "Shit," he said. He hadn't wanted it to go like that.

He closed his eyes for a moment and then tried to call back but only got a busy signal. He thought about a text or email, but clearly Leah only wanted to talk about whatever she'd found.

Jack put the telephone back into the hard case and sat on a folding chair. Memories and feelings had flooded back with the sound of her voice.

Paulson's face poked through the tent door. "Nash is coming through the Icefall and Alex isn't with him."

"What happened?"

Paulson shook his head. "No one knows yet; it can't be good."

Jack ducked through the door and walked toward the base of the Icefall. Nash had dropped his backpack on the ground. He leaned against it, breathing heavily.

"Where's Alex?" Jack asked.

Nash drew several deep breaths. "We made the summit and—" He paused and gazed down at the ice. "You should have seen the look on his face when he stepped onto the summit."

"Where did you leave him?"

"He was doing fine on the way down," Nash said. "I told him all he had to do was sing until there was no more beer, and we'd be safe."

"You left him on the mountain?"

The smile disappeared from Nash's face. "Screw you, Jack. You know the rules. At some point, everyone's responsible for himself. I can't carry a client down the mountain."

"Where did you leave him?"

"He sat down and he wouldn't get up, no matter what I said." The guide shook his head. "He just kept singing." Nash looked up. "You understand, don't you, Al? I couldn't just sit down with him. We'd both be dead."

"Yeah, I understand," Paulson said, his voice thick with disgust, "why I paid Jack Hobson to guide my ass up Everest." He spun on his heel and walked away.

Jack was about to walk away when Nash made a fatal mistake. He flashed Jack a smile. Something inside Jack snapped. He clenched his fist and swung with all his strength. Jack felt and heard the sound of teeth breaking as his fist hit his former partner's blistered face.

Nash dropped to the ground, blood running from his nose and split bottom lip. Other climbers silently turned away as he struggled to get up.

"You guys know the rules," Nash managed to say through his injured mouth. "They have to get down themselves." Blood ran down the front of his parka and onto the ice.

Jack turned and walked toward the Australian team's communications tent. He pushed open the flap and looked inside. "Any chance we can get the hell out of here?"

The Aussie expedition leader nodded. "No worries, Jack. We've got supplies inbound by chopper in about thirty minutes. I can get you guys on the return flight to Kathmandu."

Jack nodded and then pointed back at his ex-partner, who'd just made it to his feet. "Maybe one of your medical guys could attend to Nash."

The Aussie grinned. "That's nothing, mate.... You should see what happens every night in Melbourne."

Jack turned around and walked back into the sunlight. Paulson stood near the communications tent, fiddling with a small bottle of sunscreen. "I'm sorry, Al. I know you and Alex were friends."

"He deserved better." Paulson's grin returned for a moment. "He had more heart than brains; probably why he was such a lousy lawyer."

"I've got an offer to fly out of Base Camp," Jack said. "You interested?"

The billionaire shook his head and placed an arm around Jack's shoulder. "No, thanks. I met an Adventure Travel group from the USA doing an easy trek though the countryside of Nepal."

"I'd think you'd be in a rush to get back to Candice."

"I'm meeting her in Hong Kong on the way out. She won't arrive for a few more days. Then we'll get some beach time in."

Jack felt his face blushing; he vividly remembered the smell of Coppertone and the dream he'd been having about Candice Paulson when Al had awakened him for the summit push.

"Did you get ahold of Leah?"

Jack nodded. "She's on to something but wouldn't discuss it over the sat phone."

Paulson locked eyes with Jack. "Is she staying away from those dwellings?"

Jack shook his head. "I've got a feeling Leah's not only back into those cliffs; she's gotten herself into trouble."

Paulson studied Jack's face. "You need anything at all, you let me know."

Jack quickly gathered his personal gear. He'd arranged to have the rest shipped out with the Australian teams. He was zipping his large duffel closed when the sound of the Ecureuil AS350B3 high-altitude helicopter blades echoed through the camp. As he piled into the chopper and it took off, he looked in the direction of the summit and shook his head in disgust and sadness. It was the first time he ever remembered leaving a successful summit effort not feeling elated.

Maybe Leah's right, he thought. A fat payday and bonus seemed shallow and irrelevant compared to the life of Alex Stein.

As the pilot swung the helicopter around, he wondered if this might be the last time he saw Everest Base Camp, the tent city draped in prayer flags that he'd come to feel was his second home.

An hour later, the helicopter landed at Tribhuvan International Airport, Kathmandu. Jack thanked the pilot and waved good-bye to the ground crew preparing to refuel the chopper.

He entered the small terminal building and wandered over to see what eastbound flights were available. He booked himself on a Nepal Royal Air flight leaving at 10:00 p.m. for Bangkok, Thailand. From there, he'd catch either a Cathay-Pacific flight or Air Singapore to Los Angeles.

He treated himself to an espresso and then wandered about the airport, people-watching as throngs of young trekkers and climbers traveled through the airport.

Several hours later, he strolled up to the gate and quickly boarded the Boeing and settled back into the plush business-class seat. The Everest climb and his tortured relationship with Leah played over and over in his mind. He lay back and closed his eyes. His last conscious memory was the airliner's jet turbine engines spooling up as the pilot aimed the huge aircraft down the runway for takeoff.

"Are you okay, sir?" asked the flight attendant.

Jack blinked and then smiled meekly. "Sorry, must have been dreaming." He glanced at his watch. They were already an hour into the flight. All he remembered from the dream was being frozen in a bathtub full of ice, with the rotting corpse of Adeline Smith reaching out for him, her fleshless skull inches from his face, eye sockets pitch black, mouth twisted into a wicked grin.

The flight attendant looked at his forehead then down at the folding dinner tray.

"You whacked your head good."

Jack felt a small bump rising on the center of his forehead. He must have done it during the dream.

"Lucky I hit something I don't use often."

"Were you here on a trek or mountain climbing?"

"I just got down off Everest."

She smiled. "We'll be serving dinner after cocktails."

Once the plane had landed, he breathed a sigh of relief and waited for the pilot to guide the airliner to the terminal building. Jack exited the aircraft, thanked the pilots, and strolled toward the business-class passenger lounge. He flashed his ticket to the receptionist and sat down in the lounge. His voice mail system said he had twenty-six messages. He buzzed through them quickly.

He probably had ten times that much e-mail, but when it was urgent, people still picked up the telephone or sent a text. Several clients wanted information on guided climbs, and one call was from television producer Steve Broadwin. He wanted a live remote from the top of Everest for next year's program celebrating Sir Edmund Hillary's historic first climb.

Jack saved the call from the network. They were a pain in the ass, but the pay and exposure were great. He also had several media requests for interviews regarding Paulson's Mt. Everest story, including *Time* magazine about a cover story on the new risk-takers in the world of big business.

Better to let Paulson's personal assistant Karen Miller handle this stuff. He'd been burned more than once by reporters seeking to portray the billionaire in a bad light. He took out his phone and changed his outgoing message. "Thank you for calling. Mr. Paulson and I are safely off Mt. Everest after a successful climb. For additional information on the climb, please call Paulson Global, Inc. I have no further comment."

That would redirect those calls to Karen, who dealt with such requests daily.

The next call was to Leah. He braced himself as the telephone rang and almost felt a sense of relief as it switched over to voice mail.

"I'm in Bangkok and will be flying into Los Angeles," he said. "I'll call you from LA. If you still need my help, maybe we can discuss it over the telephone." Jack hung up and leaned against the wall.

That's the way to handle it, he thought with satisfaction. No need to hop on a plane and come running every time she calls. Jack hesitated, and then the truth washed over him.

When she called, he always came running.

CHAPTER 8

The Southwest Airlines Boeing 737 touched down at Albuquerque International Airport in the early evening. Jack walked cautiously up the jet-way, through security, and looked around for Leah among the crowd of families searching for their loved ones.

He spotted her leaning against a railing. She wore her trademark faded jeans and a colored T-shirt with a denim jacket. Her long, thick auburn hair flowed down over the jacket and she brushed it back in a way that caused Jack to blink painfully with regret.

Christ, she hasn't changed a bit. Jack suppressed the sudden and unexpected urge to take her up in a hug.

"Good to see you, Climber." Leah eyed him warily with soft brown eyes.

"You're looking fit." Jack felt the warmth spread over his face and hoped it didn't show. He thought about offering a hug, but his body froze. "Well, it's been a while," he said, instantly regretting his casual tone.

She nodded, spun, and walked toward the baggage claim.

He hustled to keep up. "Where are we headed?"

"First to Maria's Restaurant for dinner; Garrett's meeting us there."

"I've got photos, Jack. I was pretty nervous and it was dark, so the photos didn't come out as well as I'd hoped. I'm hoping that you recognize something."

"And if not?"

"You're climbing down into a cliff dwelling and taking a look at some pictographs."

"In the Gila National Wilderness?" he asked. "I believe that qualifies as a felony with serious jail time attached if we're caught."

Leah stopped and turned around at the entrance to the airport. "Jackson, if you don't have the balls, say so right now and you can get right back on the airplane." She winked, then spun to hide the smile. Having Jack back in New Mexico felt like five-hundred-pounds of guilt over her stubbornness and inability to work things out, rolling off her shoulders.

CHAPTER 9

Jack was sipping on his first margarita when he felt a tap on the shoulder.

Garrett Moon stood behind Jack, a wide smile on his face. "What are you two lovebirds doing?" He shook Jack's hand with a firm shake. "Good to see you again. Leah hasn't been the same since you left."

Jack stood up. "You're still letting her drag you through every cliff and cavern in the Southwest?"

"She's one hell of an archeologist," Garrett replied, "even if she is as stubborn as a canyon mule."

"You guys haven't matured a bit," Leah said, unable to suppress a smile. She signaled to their waitress.

Jack waited until the waitress had taken their orders and walked away from the table before saying, "This granite's not uncommon around the interior mountain ranges, but," he looked to Garrett, "like I told Leah, it's a big continent. Unless you know where the rock came from, you could spend a lifetime searching." Jack glanced in Leah's direction. "Any chance your relationship with the government might thaw?"

"Not likely."

Once the waitress had delivered the steaming hot plates of spicy Mexican food and walked away, Jack said, "Pictographs?"

Leah stopped eating and set the fork down on the plate. "Nothing like I've ever seen before." Her voice fell to a whisper. "I've been thinking about it, and it occurred to me that the landmarks in the pictographs might not be local features."

Jack looked at her in disbelief. "You mean…?"

She nodded. "And if I'm correct, they could help us find the right part of Antarctica." She slid her iPhone out from her jacket and sped through the photos, while Jack looked over her shoulder. When she got to the photos down in the burial chamber, she handed the phone to Jack. "Well?"

Jack looked at the small screen, holding it close, then farther away, trying to get a better view. "Might be a good idea if you cut back on the meth when you're taking pictures. Honestly, these are out of focus, and the color's so faint, it's hard to make anything out."

Leah swore silently, then yanked the phone back, flipped to another series of photos showing the same mountain, and thrust the phone back into Jack's hands.

Jack studied the images. If anything, they were more out of focus than the first set. "There's so much light scatter, and the old drawings are so faded, I can't really make heads or tails of it."

"I was afraid of that," Leah said. "Looks like we'll have to do this the hard way."

Garrett pulled a hundred-dollar bill out of his wallet and placed it on the table. "Dinner's on me tonight." He reached out and shook Jack's hand. "Like I said, good to see you again."

Jack stood slowly, still recovering from the implications of Leah's bizarre claim. "It does kind of seem like old times—especially here at the restaurant."

Leah lifted her jacket from the chair. "You two have plenty of time to get reacquainted. I need some sleep. Tomorrow's a big day." She spun and headed for the exit.

Jack waited until she was out of hearing range and then grabbed Garrett lightly on the forearm. "What's going here, Garrett? Can this possibly be true?"

Garrett waited until Leah sped through the wooden double doors. "If I hadn't seen it myself, I'd be the first one to recommend a long rest in a padded room. The photos don't come close to doing it justice. You'll have to see it for yourself to believe it."

"I heard she'd been fired," Jack said, "Leah lived and breathed that job. I wondered if maybe the shock had gotten to her."

Garrett chuckled. "Oddly enough, she got over that pretty quick. I think the circumstances helped move her past it."

"I never heard the story."

"Leah got an invitation to some swanky event at the Smithsonian Museum in Washington, which included a cocktail party at the Secretary of the Interior's private home. Of course, she gets bored—and starts looking around."

"Snooping, you mean."

Garrett nodded. "Anyway, she opens the door to this bedroom and finds two pieces of rare pottery on a shelf. Now most people would have simply shut the door and their mouths—but not Leah. She's telling anyone who will listen that government officials, no matter what their political ranking, had no right decorating their homes with items that should be protected at the museum."

"Politically correct, as usual," Jack said. "If not politically wise."

"Exactly. So the Secretary of the Interior is forced to apologize and returns those pieces and several others back to the museum. About three months later, she's cut loose in a 'budget-tightening' effort."

Jack shook his head. "Even though she's one of the best field archeologists in the country?"

"Her boss's boss, the director of the BLM, fought like mad to keep her."

"Teresa Simpson," Jack said. "I met her once at a cocktail party in Albuquerque."

"Apparently, the Secretary needed his pound of flesh," Garrett said. "He issued an order to the Park Service: Leah is not allowed to conduct research, even on her own, within federal lands—which covers about ninety-nine percent of all Native American cliff dwellings. He dug up some dirt on her not following procedures or something and managed to make it stick."

Garrett glanced toward the restaurant exit. "Since her dad died, she's been obsessed with continuing his work, regardless of the cost."

"Don't I know it," Jack felt his knees getting weak; he looked down at the tiles, unable to meet Garrett's gaze, he still felt he bore the responsibility for her dad's death.

"The dwelling we found lends more credence to his theories," Garrett said. "Native Americans were using the caverns for more than shelter or the occasional marauding group of bandits. They were scared of something worse than that. We think."

"And this is tied to rare granite crystals taken from the most inhospitable spot on the planet?" Jack asked. "Oh, and pictographs showing the same?"

Garrett tilted his head toward the front door of the restaurant. "She's the real deal and has a nose like a bloodhound."

"How come you let her order you around half the New Mexico desert nearly every weekend?"

To Jack's surprise, Garrett's eyes softened. "Her dad, my dad, it's a long story."

"I'm listening."

"Well, Leah wasn't the first kid her dad started dragging around the desert. My dad, when he was sober, was a helluva reservation blacksmith." Garrett shook his head. "Problem was he ended up drinking most of the time. He got to roughing up my mother and me regular. It just so happened, I was sitting in my dad's old truck one day in town, when I was about twelve, and he was drunk as a skunk, screaming and yelling to beat the band. I think I'd changed the radio station or something, I can't even remember. Anyway, after about the third slap, I see the driver's door open and there's this huge man with flaming red hair, towering over my dad, holding him down on the pavement."

"Duncan Andrews," Jack said.

"Yep."

"Never a good idea to piss that man off."

Garrett chuckled. "Fortunately for Leah, she just got his Irish temper, not his looks or size." He glanced at the floor. "That was the only time I ever saw my dad scared, when Duncan had him down on the pavement. He told my dad how far down a mine shaft he might find himself if Duncan ever saw him abusing anyone again. Then he took me out and bought me a chocolate milkshake. The first one I ever had. It wasn't too much after that I started hanging out over at the Andrews house as much as I could. Leah was just three or four at the time. Duncan took me out into the desert on his archeological hunts. I hate to say it, but, as a Navajo, most of my role models, like my dad, didn't give me much pride in my own culture. Duncan made my ancestors sound like a race of kings, you know?"

"He knew how to bring them alive, that's for sure," Jack said.

"When I turned eighteen, I joined the Air Force and spent twenty years as an aircraft mechanic. I retired a couple of years ago, just about the time you two went your separate ways. I bought a little ranch outside of town. In my spare time I rebuilt an old Cessna 172 and got my pilot's license." He smiled wistfully. "Every time Leah calls, and I think about kicking back with a cold beer, I hear the old man's voice in my head. The next thing you know, we're loaded up in my Cessna and Leah's shouting directions like General Patton." Garrett looked toward the door again. "I've got a feeling about her. Especially now. She's gonna figure out those cliff dwellers. I feel it."

Jack nodded. "I remember when Leah had the temporary lecturing gig at UNM and helped out some student. I was so busy getting the climbing business profitable I wasn't paying much attention. Is that the football player I've been hearing about?"

"That's him," Garrett replied. "Juan Cortez never had anyone take an interest in him. He was always the fat kid in school with poor Mexican-American parents. The only thing he thought he had was football. That was his entire identity. After he blew out the knee, the school didn't have any use for him. Juan started hanging out in front of the student union, his leg in a cast, wondering what he was going to do next. One day Leah stopped and asked him what the hell he was doing, wasn't he supposed to be in class?"

"Just like Leah," Jack said, "always checking up on everyone."

"He told her about being a football player and blowing out the knee and how all he ever wanted was to be an NFL player. She said it sounded like he needed a swift kick in the ass, and she was just the person to do it."

Jack chuckled. "Leah and her one hundred pounds are going to give the three-hundred-pound football player a butt-whipping."

Garrett grinned. "She told him to show up at her office that afternoon. Surprisingly, he did, complete with crutches. Leah reviewed his records. He was on a full football scholarship, but because he hadn't maintained a minimum grade point average, it was being yanked."

Jack shook his head. "Odd how they always seem to do that after an injury keeps them off the football field."

Garrett nodded and then continued. "Leah gets a burr under her saddle and takes Juan on as a personal project. She raises holy hell with the school administration, says throwing away students when they're no longer making the school money is wrong. So the university agreed to extend his scholarship." Garrett laughed. "Juan instantly becomes the only former college All-American in the Native American Studies program."

"Was he interested in Native American Studies?"

"No, but every time he missed a class, Leah would show up at his dorm yelling, 'Where's Juan Cortez? I'm looking for Juan Cortez!'"

Jack laughed. "Classic Leah and her subtle motivational tools."

"It got to the point where he'd show up just to avoid the embarrassment." Garrett's eyes opened wide. "Then an amazing thing happened. Juan took a liking to Native American Studies. He was captivated by Leah's weekly lectures and slide presentations. The next thing you know, he's one of her best students; following Leah all over the desert in search of her mysterious cliff dwellings. Last year he finished his master's degree and now he teaches undergraduate Native American Studies at the local community college."

"And spends all his free time risking life, limb, and liberty for Leah."

Garrett nodded. "He's scared to death of heights and ropes, but completely devoted. Hard to imagine an odder crew of misfits: ninety pounds of fiery Irish archeologist, an old Navajo, and a Mexican-American ex-football player." He glanced at the door. "We'd better get moving or she's gonna come back in here loaded for bear."

Jack stepped out into the restaurant parking lot and looked up. The stars shone so brightly, it almost appeared you could reach up and touch them. They cast a gentle glow against Sandia Ridge, which rose nearly 6,000 feet straight up on the north side of the city. Jack had spent many a summer day riding fast-rising thermals after launching his hang glider from a small wooden ramp at the top of the Sandia Ridge.

Leah waited for them, leaning against her jeep. "About time."

"I've visited beautiful places around the world," he said. "I'm still blown away by the beauty of a clear night in New Mexico."

"You'd probably just get bored—like you did last time." Leah drove in silence up to her small adobe house nestled at the base of Sandia Ridge. She pushed open the door and flipped on the lights and shivered.

"Remember how to start a fire, Climber?"

Leah ran up the stairway and disappeared into the master bedroom. Jack placed a mix of pine and paper in the wood stove. He lit the paper and fed in pieces of oak over the pine. In minutes, he had a roaring fire.

"Not bad for a guy who warms his ass over a gas stove."

Jack turned around; she stood on the stairs wearing black leggings and a cotton nightshirt, pulling her long auburn hair away from her face with a hint of a grin.

"There's a blanket beside the couch." She stopped climbing the stairs and turned around. She watched as Jack pulled off his shirt and the light from the fire reflected off his torso. She took in a deep breath and paused. Jack thought she was about to invite him to join her in the master bedroom. No such luck.... Probably for the best, he figured.

She turned around in the bedroom doorway. "Of course, if the couch is too soft," she said with a chuckle and a wink, "you can always try the floor. Probably more like what you're used to anyway."

Jack nodded and reached for a Navajo blanket lying beside the couch.

His last thought before falling into a deep sleep was that the dwelling discovery might be more than it seemed. Complicated and, just maybe, even more treacherous than a climb up Everest.

Chapter 10

"Get a move on, Climber! You plan on sleeping away the entire day?"

Jack woke with a start as light streamed through the glass. The effects of three months on Everest and jet lag made him feel a bit unsteady. He limped toward the kitchen, where he smelled fresh coffee brewing.

He felt a tinge of vertigo and homesickness—not a welcome feeling, given the situation. Jack poured coffee into a white UNM cup and walked out onto the deck. He stood with his eyes closed, breathing the crisp, cool air for a moment.

"Shower's all yours." Leah studied his face. "Damn, you look like hell, Jackson."

He rubbed at the thick, sunburned bags under his eyes. "Just what I needed to get the new day started."

She tossed him a fresh towel. "Don't forget to brush, if you've got any teeth left after all those months living like a pig on Everest with your buddies."

Jack stepped into the shower and allowed the hot water to run down his back, hoping it might remove the taste and smell of Mt. Everest from his skin.

When he stepped out, Leah was already looking to leave. "Come on, Climber!" she shouted from outside the cabin's front door.

He dressed, grabbed his backpack, tossed it in the back of the jeep, and managed to climb in just as Leah dropped the clutch and raced out the gravel driveway.

They pulled into Albuquerque's Double Eagle II General Aviation Airport as Garrett finished a careful preflight on his fragile-looking airplane.

He looked up with a sly smile. "Did we sleep well?"

"Let's see if you can coax this heap off the ground, one more time," Leah said, stuffing her backpack into the storage compartment.

Garrett saluted while opening the passenger door. "Aye-aye, Skipper."

Leah hesitated. "You want me in the back seat as usual, I suppose?"

"If it's not too much of a bother; better for weight and balance."

Jack strapped himself into the right seat. Up in the air, Garrett banked sharply, heading due west toward the New Mexico/Arizona border.

"What did we use before GPS?" Jack was checking out the Garmin Global Positioning System Garrett had slotted on his steering yoke.

"Something even better." Garrett pointed down at the ground. "Interstate 40."

Leah woke as Garrett reduced power on the Cessna and started a descent toward the sand-and-rock landscape below. "Are we landing?"

"Garrett says we're running out of gas," Jack deadpanned. "He's praying we make it to the airport, but just in case, there's a Kmart parking lot below, and they have a blue-light special on ham sandwiches."

Garrett laughed as Leah flashed her middle finger between the two front seats. He pointed toward a deserted asphalt runway with a number of ancient hangars and a small house.

"I'm going to gas-up here before we turn south. The old man who runs the airport is a friend of mine. I like to drop in on him every now and then to make sure he's okay."

Just before they touched down, the loud squeal of the stall-warning buzzer sounded in the cockpit.

No matter how often Jack flew in small airplanes, he always jumped at the sound of the stall warning.

The main landing gear bumped, followed by the nose gear. Garrett braked and quickly exited the runway by way of a taxiway leading toward an old military-style, Quonset hut.

Except for two worn-out-looking Cessna trainers, the tarmac was deserted. The trainers displayed a frayed "Rent Me!" sign on the propellers but clearly hadn't moved for what looked like years.

The control tower, painted red and white, stood behind the Quonset hut. The steel girders were rusted and the ladder that led to the tower station had fallen free in several places.

"It's an old army airfield left over from World War II," Garrett said. "They trained bomber pilots here, so it's plenty long. You could land a 747." He brought the Cessna to a stop next to a single-pump refueling station and shut down the engine. "You two stretch your legs. We're going to be here about twenty minutes."

"Think they have any food?" Leah crawled out of the back seat and stepped onto the neglected tarmac.

"Doubt it." Jack started toward the worn building with a sign saying Pilot's Lounge hanging at an angle over the door. "Want to take a look inside?"

"I'm not standing out here in the sun."

Jack pushed open the creaky door and peeked inside. It was dusty and the air tasted of leather and aviation fuel. A couple of ancient couches worn down to the springs faced each other. A faded white Formica counter cut the room diagonally.

Flight plans and old aviation charts covered the counter. He walked toward the back of the lounge and studied the framed black-and-white photographs hanging on the wall. Jack wiped the dust off, revealing a vintage photograph of two men standing in the desert. They both wore white shirts with short sleeves, ties and 1940-style fedora hats.

"Make sure to sign the register, folks."

A white-haired man, hunched with age, limped into the lounge. He firmly planted a wooden cane with each step, and his left arm shook with the symptoms of advanced Parkinson's disease.

"You've got some interesting old photographs," Jack said.

"I'm Luke. I run the whole darn operation." He grinned, showing few remaining teeth. "At least what's left of the airport." Luke pointed his cane in the direction of the photographs. "Memories in them pictures, yes, sir. We used to get all kinds of interesting people through here." He gently clasped Leah's hand and led her toward the wall.

Luke pointed to a picture of a man wearing black pants, white shirt and a fedora. "Here is J. Robert Oppenheimer himself. He always ordered a double cheeseburger with jalapeño and a coke." He smiled faintly. "We closed the diner in 1959."

Jack blinked. "You mean the father of the atomic bomb?" He leaned closer to get a good look through the dusty glass.

"Yep," Luke said. "We had all them bomb builders in here from time to time." He stepped back and stumbled, forcing Jack to reach for his arm.

"That must have been something—given how that has changed the world."

"Yes-sirree-bob. At one time or another, they were all here."

Leah interrupted, "You mean the men who will someday be credited with destroying the world."

"Don't mind her," Jack teased. "She's got a bad case of liberalitis."

Luke sat on one of the couches and pointed a shaking finger at Leah. "Doc Oppenheimer agreed with you, once he saw the destruction it caused, the death and misery. Never saw him smile after that day; never saw any of them smiling after that."

"I couldn't agree more," Leah said. "Those weapons should be dismantled and the parts buried under a million tons of concrete."

"It's a deterrent," Jack said with a straight face. He loved to get her blood boiling when it came to her liberal politics, even though he knew he'd have to pay the price. "It keeps the world at peace."

"That's bullshit and you know it."

"You could *never* see fit to use a nuclear weapon, or any kind of weapon of mass destruction?" Jack asked innocently.

"Never in my lifetime...."

"I'd do it," Luke said. His face twisted into a grimace with the effort it took to push his failing body into a standing position. Once up, he lost his balance and stumbled toward Jack. "If it would've killed the scientists, wiped out the formulas and the laboratories, I'd have done it."

Garrett stuck his face through the open door, breaking the awkward silence. He nodded in the direction of a corroded cash register. "Do you want cash or credit card today?"

The old man looked up and wiped his hands across the white stubble covering his face. "My treat...." He winked at Leah and Jack. "It's not often I get such good conversation."

"Thanks, then. I'll catch you next time." Garrett beckoned Jack and Leah. "Okay, you two. Let's roll."

Once the Cessna was airborne and trimmed, Garrett said, "I don't know what you guys said to Luke, but it saved us about a hundred dollars in fuel."

"We were talking about the scientists who invented and built the atomic bomb," Leah said. "I guess in the 1940s they traveled through the airport on occasion."

Garrett turned around and smiled. "Luke Derringer was Oppenheimer's personal pilot. Luke has to be ninety-five if he's a day. He scouted detonation locations for the first nuclear test. He spent hundreds of hours with the scientists, flying them over every nook and cranny of the desert. Ended up, they decided to detonate it in White Sands." Garrett turned back to the windscreen. "Luke stood next to Oppenheimer when they lit the fuse on the Gadget, as it was called. He said it changed everyone who saw it; couple of the guys even committed suicide."

"Does he still fly?" Jack asked.

Garrett shook his head. "He hasn't passed a flight physical in decades. My guess is he still takes those Cessna 172 rentals up for a spin when no one's looking."

"New Mexico," Leah sighed. "The home for thousands of years to the most peaceful people on the planet, and the birthplace of the end of the world...."

Garrett lined the Cessna up on the remote dirt landing strip, lowered the flaps to the number three position and set the small airplane expertly on the runway. He taxied over near Juan's beat-up green Chevrolet Blazer and shut down the engine.

Garrett climbed out through the pilot's door and made the introductions. "Juan and Marko," he said, "meet Jack Hobson."

Jack extended a hand to the big man. "I'm glad to hear Leah's got someone to watch out for her."

Juan grabbed Jack's hand and squeezed firmly. "That's Garrett's job. I'm mainly just her sounding board."

Jack grinned. "You mean she screams a lot."

"Don't bother turning on the charm, Climber," Leah said. She pulled her backpack out of the aircraft. "All the sweet talk in the world won't get you laid out here." She swept past them toward the Blazer.

Garrett and Juan bit their lips to keep from laughing while Marko's face turned a light shade of pink. Jack ignored her comment and extended a hand toward the young rock climber.

"It's great to finally meet you," Marko gushed. "I've been a huge fan ever since they did that article on you in *Mountaineering.*"

"Leah tells me you're quite a talented rock climber," Jack said.

Marko looked down at the dirt and kicked at it with his boot. "Just weekend stuff; nothing like K2 or Everest."

"You two should get a room," Leah said. She stuffed her pack into the Blazer and climbed into the front passenger seat.

Marko pushed his blond hair away from his face. "I'd love to hear about Everest."

"I'll be happy to tell you all about it."

"Hobson.... Our deal," cautioned Leah through the open windows of the Blazer.

"What deal?" Marko asked.

"I don't tell mountaineering stories around Leah; she doesn't play Lorena Bobbitt with a kitchen knife."

Garret and Juan burst out laughing. Marko looked truly puzzled.

After twenty minutes, the jeep trail mercifully ended. Juan engaged the parking brake and shut down the engine. "This is it," he said. "Time to go from four-wheel drive to two-leg drive."

"I'm looking forward to a long hike." Leah pushed her way out the open passenger door.

"Since when did you want to strap on a backpack?" Jack asked.

"Are you kidding?" she replied. "After listening to you guys talk about motor displacements, synthetic oil, canned chili, and shaving cream, I was ready to blow my brains out."

Garrett pointed toward the wash. It narrowed significantly as it entered the rugged terrain. "We have a hidden camping area a mile or so from here," he said. "The canyon where we found the cliff dwellings are another two miles beyond that."

"Narrow in here," Jack warned. "Is this the only way in and out?"

Juan nodded. "As far as we know—and we don't want to hike along the rim of the canyon. We'd be spotted in a heartbeat."

"This wash is a bad place for an ambush," Jack said.

"The rangers don't patrol much in the wash," Juan said. "Who'd want to hike down here if you didn't have to?"

"Last hill," Juan said twenty minutes later. "After this, downhill the rest of the way...."

Once at the campsite, they dropped their packs and set up tents. Jack helped Leah assemble the fiberglass poles that created the support for her two-person dome tent. "How did you find this dwelling?" he asked as she threaded the poles through nylon.

"Research of my dad's," she replied. "Most archeologists assumed that the cliffs here are too steep for a cliff dwelling or village of any size. It's also remote and hard to navigate. Dad thought it was the last best hope for

finding virgin dwelling that hadn't been cleaned out and the pot shards sold on Ebay."

She pointed down toward the river. "The valley is quite rich, and we have plenty of evidence that Native Americans lived on top of these mesas and down near the river." Her gaze swept the canyon. "The Gila wilderness is rugged. Besides tourists coming out of Silver City to see the dwellings in the National Monument, there aren't many people tramping out here." Leah fluffed her sleeping bag, before tossing it into the tent.

"The Anasazi and the Mogollon Indians lived happily on the top of the mesa for thousands of years. They had no natural enemies from what we can tell. There was no logical reason why they abandoned the rich canyon floors and mesa tops and move entire communities into the cliffs. Can you imagine having to carry water up hundreds, if not thousands of feet, not for one person, but for an entire community? My dad understood that—and so do I. There's an answer out there and I intend to find it, even if I have to rope down every rock cliff in the Southwest."

"It's one beautiful set of canyons," Jack said, taking in the scenery. He took a step back and watched the rays of the afternoon sun weave through the canyons, making them appear to glow in shades of orange and blue.

"Make you want to give up all that ice?"

"Probably wouldn't take much after the last climb. Alex Stein died on the mountain."

Leah put her hand over her mouth. "No...."

"Who was Alex Stein?" Garrett asked from across the campsite.

"He was one of Jack's former clients." Tears welled in Leah's eyes. "He was the only one worth a damn. Alex was always helping out the poor in Atlanta with legal aid." She wiped the tears away. "What happened?"

Jack sat next to her on a sandstone boulder. "Nash had to get him to the summit, no matter what."

"What about Kent? Did he stay on the mountain with Alex?"

Jack shook his head and looked at the sand. "He left him. Left him on the mountain...."

Leah's face paled. "He left Alex on Everest?"

Jack nodded. "I couldn't believe it myself, but he did."

"How about if we get dinner started?" Juan asked. "I'd suggest you take a quick bath, but the water's getting cold this time of year." He pointed toward a grove of trees about one hundred yards away. "A little fresh water on the face probably wouldn't hurt."

"Well, this beats those sponge baths on Aconcagua," Jack said, leaning down and splashing cold water on his face.

"Being boiled in oil would've beaten those sponge baths, Climber."

After a quick dinner, they gathered around a small campfire. Leah slipped the hood of her UNM sweatshirt over her head and leaned toward the warmth. "You really mean you'd give up the ice?"

Jack put his hands up and let the fire warm his palms. "Today I'd probably give it up." He stared into the flames for a moment. "But it's my occupation. I'd have to go back sometime."

"I should have known."

Jack looked up at Marko and winked. "Leah always wanted me home for dinner, not sitting on the side of some mountain for weeks on end."

Leah picked up a rock and tossed it into the fire, scattering sparks and causing Marko to scramble away from the flame. "That's bullshit and you know it."

"Now if you kids want to argue, we can all retire to our tents," Garrett said.

Leah ignored Garrett. "I couldn't give a shit about you being gone for months on end. I couldn't stand having you underfoot every day." She pointed a finger into his face. "I never knew if you were dead or alive on one of those mountaintops." She sighed and shook her head. "I know you, Jack. Sooner than later, one of your rich mountain-climbing wannabe maggots is going to drop on the ice. You're going to say, 'I've gotta stay with him—otherwise everyone'll say I killed my client.'" She paused. "You'll end up dead. Frozen in that ice, and for what? A few lousy dollars?"

Jack bit his lip. How close had he come to that exact end with Paulson?

"I know you can't help it," she sighed. "You climbers are like salmon swimming upstream. You've got it made out in the ocean with plenty of fat anchovies to eat, but, no, suddenly you have to charge up the river. You know it's going to kick your ass and you're not coming back, but you go anyway."

Jack raised his eyebrows. "Yeah, but think of the wild salmon orgy waiting in that narrow, sandy stream bed; makes the whole deal worth it. Climbers, like salmon, just prisoners of our DNA."

Garrett looked over at Juan and they both burst out in sudden laughter, vaporizing the tension.

Leah stood and stretched. "I'm hitting the rack, Climber. Who knows what we're going to have to overcome tomorrow."

Jack stared silently at the fire, watching the flames flicker and glow. He thought about the dream he'd had about Adeline Smith on the airplane.

Leah's probably right, he thought. One of these times, you're going to check out on a peak with the client. Sit down on the ice and just go to sleep.

CHAPTER 11

"**W**e've got trouble," Garrett whispered.

Jack's eyes blinked open to the Native American's angular facial features.

"Juan spotted a couple of park rangers on four-wheeler all-terrain vehicles headed toward the canyon."

Jack forced his body into an upright sitting position. "You think someone got wind you guys are prowling these canyons?"

Garrett shook his head. "There's always a chance of running across rangers."

Jack looked around. "Wait. Where's Leah?"

"She was hell-bent-for-leather to see if the rangers had discovered the dwelling entrance. I sent Marko and Juan along with her—just in case she got any bright ideas."

Jack lay in the dirt behind a ridge with binoculars held to his eyes. "I can't believe she's sneaking up right under their noses."

In the distance, Leah ran in a crouch toward an outcropping of rocks near the natural bridge connecting the two sides of the canyon. Marko nearly stepped on her heels several times, his mop of blond hair flying in the wind as he struggled to keep up.

"I told her to stay right here and wait for you," Juan explained. "You know Leah. She's got ants in her pants and won't wait for anyone."

Jack focused on one of the two park rangers. The ranger wiped at his forehead, glanced down at a map, and indicated a new direction of travel with the wave of his arm.

"I think they're bugging out—for now, anyway." Jack set off at a run toward Leah, making sure to keep low and out of sight.

She walked out from behind the ledge where she'd huddled with Marko and nodded in relief. "They're leaving."

"Yeah? Well, what if they decide to come back?" Jack asked angrily.

"Life is full of risk. Right, Climber?"

Jack swung his gear bag over a shoulder. "Let's get this over with fast."

"Here's the entrance," Garrett said. "Hidden in the brush. Almost didn't find it again." He pulled out a couple of flashlights and handed them to Jack. "Juan and I should pack up the campsite in case we have to make a fast getaway."

"That's a good idea," Jack said. He nodded in Marko's direction. "He can stay here and serve as a lookout while Leah and I are inside."

"If I see park rangers, how should I warn you?" Marko raised his hands up to his mouth in the shape of a megaphone. "I could yell down into the entrance like this."

Leah rolled her eyes. "Yeah, that's what you should do."

"I've got an idea," Jack said. He reached for Marko's climbing gear and searched through the collection of ropes, anchoring devices, carabiners and leftover Snickers wrappers. "What have we here?" He removed several small aluminum bowls held together with a metal bar and wing nut.

"My cook kit," Marko said, looking embarrassed. "I don't think it's all that clean."

"We're not serving lunch." Jack handed Marko one end of the climbing line. "If you see or hear rangers, yank on this."

Jack and Leah slid down into the hidden entrance and slid through the maze of twisting sandstone.

"Another hundred feet," Leah said. "Do you feel a little tightness in your chest, Hobson?"

Over the years, Leah had learned most of his weaknesses—including occasional attacks of claustrophobia.

"Just a headache every time my head hits the rock," he muttered.

She switched the halogen flashlight on to its high position, illuminating the dwellings. "Not bad for an unemployed archeologist and a couple of desert rats."

Eight-hundred-year-old wooden ladders lay against the walls, providing a lattice to the top of the cavern. Thoughts of having to climb those ladders gave Jack a chill. One misstep meant a fatal fall.

"I've got to set up our alarm system." Jack pulled out a small climbing cam and jammed it into a narrow slot between two boulders. He threaded the climbing line through carabiners and clipped it to the handle on the larger cook pot, then dropped in Marko's spaghetti-crusted eating utensils and metal coffee cup.

The collection of cook gear hung like a bell in a medieval church cathedral. He gave the line a tug, and a moment later Marko tugged back. The sound of pans banging off the rock and each other echoed throughout the cavern.

"Works like a charm."

"Let's hope Marko doesn't decide to take a nap." Leah pointed down a dark alleyway separating the cavern wall from the back of the dwelling. "The vertical shaft where we found the human remains and red granite is over here."

Leah stepped across the dwelling floor, working the light back and forth. "Don't kick any of the pottery. If we had time for a lecture I could tell you stories about what we've found down here that would blow you away."

"I'll be careful, Professor."

Fifteen minutes later, Jack stepped carefully through the carnage at the bottom of the sub-cavern. "What I'm I looking for here?"

Leah dropped down right behind him. "If you're right, we know that the red stones are native to Antarctica. There's a set of extraordinary pictographs." She pointed down the narrow passageway. "They rewrite Native American history as we know it. We're not sure how far to take the story, or what it really means. That's where you come in: You've spent plenty of time in Antarctica. Some of the pictographs appear to be outlines of mountain ranges in very specific shapes. They don't look anything like the landscape around here. It's a long shot, but I thought if you saw something familiar from Antarctica, it might give us at least a clue where these stones came from. If not, we'll have to depend upon the geology—finding out where we might locate the source of this granite."

He studied the first ancient drawing, remembering what Marko had told Leah: the shape of the pictograph seemed to resemble Half Dome in Yosemite. He let his light drift above the pictograph, to the strange figures with talons. He glanced at Leah.

"I'm still working on that," she said. "It's not like anything I've seen before."

"Looks to me like they thought they'd pissed off the Gods, and the Gods weren't playing friendly."

"That occurred to me." Leah worked the lights around the interior of the sub-cavern. "If you were frightened it makes sense that you might shoehorn yourself down into this hole." She aimed the light back down the passageway. "Marko found more pictographs down this passageway."

Jack illuminated the wall, and another pictograph appeared. It featured a mountain that looked something like a bold capital I but tilted about thirty degrees to the left. He traced along the drawing, hoping it might spur something concrete from his memory.

Then it struck him. He reached up and framed his hand over the bottom of the drawing, leaving a shape that now looked more like a ragged capital T tilted forward at an angle.

Jack stepped back in stunned silence.

"You know what it is, don't you?" she whispered. "From Antarctica?"

He retraced the lines, just to be sure. "Yeah, I think so. It's a sheer granite cliff that resembles Half Dome in some respects. It's located in a remote section of the Ellsworth Range, not that far from Mt. Vincent, the tallest peak on the continent. The face juts up nearly three thousand feet above the ice; there's a thick vein of red-colored granite crystal running directly through the center resembling a big hammer. It was used as a navigation point for early aviators exploring the continent. "Thor's Hammer. I'd bet a free trip to K2, it's Thor's Hammer.

Leah opened her mouth to reply when the metallic sounds of the dinner-plate alarm system echoed frantically throughout the cavern.

CHAPTER 12

Marko crouched behind a large boulder that shielded the entryway from view. He pointed toward the mesa. "I heard the ATVs. I haven't seen them yet."

Jack scanned the desert. With the overhanging ledges, boulders, and thick pine forest, half the Chinese Army could hide from view on the mesa.

"We're sitting ducks here," he said. "Leah, I want you to run for the bridge and cross the canyon. Keep low if you can. Once you get to the other side, sprint for the campsite and tell Garrett and Juan we got company."

"What about you guys?" she asked.

"I'm sending Marko once you've cleared the arch. If we hear park rangers, we'll duck into the dwelling until it's clear."

Marko held up the end of the climbing line, still attached to his cook kit hanging where Jack had affixed it inside the dwelling. "Do you want me to climb down and unhook it?"

"Just toss the line down into the cavern. Guess you don't have to worry about cleaning that gear after all."

Leah shouldered the pack and jogged toward the rock bridge, holding the bottom so the contents didn't rattle.

"Your turn, and keep it quiet," Jack said to Marko.

The young rock climber jumped over three boulders and then tripped, nearly falling on the treacherous rock. His spill dislodged a stone about the size of a basketball. The rock's sound echoed off the sandstone walls the rock as it rolled down the slope.

"Hold up, buddy!" Two hundred meters away, standing on top of a ledge, one of the rangers waved his arms.

Marko broke into an all-out dash for the opposite side of the canyon.

"Stop running and stay right where you are!"

Jack bolted out from behind the rock and sprinted across the boulders.

"Stop!" The ranger's voice had risen two full octaves higher than his first warning.

Jack felt his heart pounding against his sternum—in an odd way, it felt good. Once an adrenalin junkie, always an adrenalin junkie, he thought. He dashed across the rock bridge, holding his breath as he jumped the larger cracks in the rock.

If he tripped here, the rangers wouldn't find much when his body, falling at near terminal velocity, slammed into the jagged rocks at the bottom of the canyon.

He slid down the sandy trail leading into the wash and found himself scarcely winded. One benefit of spending several months living at extreme altitude was a substantially higher red-blood-cell count compared to that of a person living and working at lower elevations. So Jack picked up speed but his heart rate didn't. In fact, the New Mexico high mesa air tasted thick enough to cut with a knife.

The sounds of ATV motors shifting into higher gears suddenly echoed through the wash. Those crazy idiots must have ridden the all-terrain vehicles right over the bridge, and now they're in the wash, Jack thought. There was no way they could keep ahead of the rangers on those four-wheeled machines.

The formation of cliffs featured a number of overhanging ledges anchored precariously by a sandstone base, weathered thin over hundreds of years. It wouldn't take much to block the wash, he thought, if I could break one of those ledges free.

Jack stopped and studied the near-vertical sandstone wall. He leapt upward, grabbing at the first ledge with his fingertips. Once he had a firm grip, he pulled himself up to the lower ledge.

Just above, a large and severely eroded overhang appeared nearly ready to collapse on its own. It was only a matter of time before the ledge broke free and slammed to the bottom of the wash.

Jack dropped his gear pack and dug into it for a cam. When he found the right one, he lodged the wedge-like device into a crack at eye level above the fragile ledge. He pulled out a length of climbing line and slid it through the cam. Jack looped the line around his body and tied it off in a temporary harness. He free-climbed up from the ledge, stopping every three of four feet to feed a little more line through his homemade belay. When he'd climbed eight feet above the ledge, Jack closed his eyes and jumped.

He felt the sensation of weightlessness for a moment as his feet left the safety of the rock. His eyes didn't focus on the ledge, but at the bottom of the wash. From this height, a fall would be fatal.

His feet hit the ledge and his legs instantly buckled. Jack hoped to absorb most of the impact, but the forces created when his feet hit the rock caused his knees to bend, leaving his chin headed for a violent collision with his right kneecap. At the instant the cleft of his chin touched his fragile patella, the sandstone ledge fractured and sheared cleanly away from the cliff.

Jack began to pass out as blood flowed freely from the inside of his lip. He struggled to maintain consciousness and hold on to the climbing line. If he released it, the rope would slide through the cam, and he would fall to the bottom of the wash along with several tons of sandstone.

The air rushed from his lungs as the makeshift harness tightened around his body. Jack swung over the wash in the harness several times, holding tightly to the end of the rope. When his head cleared, he allowed the line to slide though his hands, and he touched down on the sand. The former overhang now lay in the wash, forming a five-foot-high collection of boulders and rubble that would stop even the most nimble all-terrain-vehicle driver.

Now we're all on equal ground, he thought with grim satisfaction.

CHAPTER 13

"We got rangers on our ass!" Marko yelled.

"Where?" Garrett asked.

The young climber bent over, breathing hard. "I passed Leah about half a mile back." He drew in two more deep breaths. "She told me to run ahead, to warn you."

Juan shouted through the driver's side window. "Get in the truck!"

Garrett and Marko dived in just as Juan dumped the clutch, and a mixture of blue smoke and sand exploded out from behind the Blazer. The truck unexpectedly lurched sideways.

"Watch out," Garrett said. He grabbed for the dash as Juan wrestled the wheel to keep the vehicle from crashing into a three-meter-deep ravine next to the wash. Garrett pointed toward a figure running through the arroyo. "There's Leah."

Her eyes registered both fear and relief as Juan brought the Blazer to a sudden stop. Garrett jumped out and grabbed her arm. "Where's Jack?"

"I don't know," she said between breaths.

"Turn the truck around," Garrett ordered. "I'm going to look for Jack."

Jack's knee throbbed but he couldn't afford to slow down. He gritted his teeth and pushed through the pain. He ran through two more twists and turns on the wash and nearly ran smack into Garrett.

"How far behind are the rangers?" Garrett asked.

"I slowed them, but not by much," Jack gasped. He wrapped his arm around Garrett's shoulder, and they ran with his injured leg held off the ground. "How far away is the truck?"

"Just around the bend," Garrett said.

Jack looked up and saw Juan backing the Blazer up the wash, his head and shaggy ponytail visible through the driver's side window. He let go of Garrett and sprinted toward the open passenger door, ignoring the pain. He dived into the back seat, and Garrett jumped into the front seat and slammed the door shut as Juan punched the accelerator to the floor.

The two rangers rounded the corner; one raised a black object to shoulder level.

"He's going to shoot," Leah shouted. She ducked while Jack glanced out through the Blazer's rear window in time to see the ranger take aim.

Jack put his hands up in an instinctive attempt to deflect the bullets.

Juan spun the steering wheel, and the truck careened around a corner and out of view of the rangers.

"Were they shooting at us?" Juan asked incredulously.

"Kind of," Jack said. He winced as his knee hit the driver's seat. "With a camera and telephoto." He wiped stinging sweat from his eyes. "All they have to do is run the plate number."

"Unless his camera takes X-ray pictures, it won't do them much good," Juan answered. He held up a bent and rusted New Mexico State license plate. "I usually remove it when we get off road—just as a precaution."

Jack remained solemn.

"What's wrong?" Juan asked. "There's no way the feds are going to ID this old wreck. The desert's full of four-wheel trucks on their last mile."

"I'm not worried about the Blazer," Jack said. "He had a clear shot at my face."

Juan glanced into the rearview mirror. "The Blazer burns so much oil; I doubt he got any more than a huge puff of blue smoke along with a large helping of desert dust."

"Well," Garrett asked, "did you learn anything worth risking our lives for?"

"Yes, I did," Jack replied, "and it ought to scare the shit out of you."

CHAPTER 14

Juan drove toward the dirt-strip airport where Garrett's Cessna remained tied down. He pulled up next to the single-engine plane, shut off the Blazer's wheezing V8 engine, and they all piled out.

"I think that's just about enough adventure for one day," Juan said, glancing around the airport for signs they were followed out of the park. "I think we're in the clear, but Marko and I ought to get out of this area quick."

"You think the rangers will be hunting for us?" asked Marko.

"No doubt," Garrett replied. "That's the last time we'll see the inside of the dwelling." He put a hand lightly on Leah's shoulder. "I'm really sorry. I know how much that find meant to you."

Leah looked crestfallen. "That's all right. I shouldn't be putting you guys at risk anyway." She glanced back in the direction of the dwelling. "How long do you think they'll patrol the canyon?"

"I think we're all gonna be a lot grayer before we can sneak back into that series of canyons again," Garrett replied. "It's a sure bet some-one tipped them off to suspicious activity last time we were out; probably thought we were stealing artifacts." He shrugged. "I might risk it, even Marko. But if you get caught, sister, it's gonna be jail time."

"There's so much more to learn," Leah said. "All that pottery.... Those pictographs..." She leaned back against the truck. "What if someone else finds that dwelling? Someone not interested in archeology, but bent on profit?"

Garrett shook his head. "That dwelling has stayed hidden for the better part of 800 years. The only way someone's gonna find it is the same way we did and there's no chance of that with all those rangers patrolling the area. If you're worried, you can make an anonymous call to the Park Service. Even then, I really doubt they're gonna find anything without being led right to the spot."

Leah nodded, and then reached into her pocket. When she opened her hand, a piece of the rich-colored granite sparkled in the sunlight. "Here's our next clue to what happened to the people living in that cavern. It's telling us how to solve the mystery."

"How's it doing that, exactly?" Jack asked.

Leah spun and held the stone out in front of his face. "Can't you hear it, Jackson? It's calling you to Antarctica."

Jack glanced up, gauging her intentions. "I hope you're not suggesting some kind of boondoggle to the south pole."

"If Native Americans traveled to and from Antarctica 800 years ago, there could still be evidence carved into the rock somewhere near that Thor's Hammer feature you mentioned." She opened her arms wide. "Don't you get it? It'll change every history book written on Native Americans and perhaps the entire history of humankind on earth." Leah locked eyes with Jack. "It's a colossal mystery. The Super Bowl of archeology and we've been invited to the big game."

Though impressed with her enthusiasm, Jack said, "I don't have the half a million dollars it would take to pull off an expedition to central Antarctica, if that's what you're thinking."

"What about Paulson?"

Jack was genuinely surprised at the mention Paulson. "You mean the same Alan Paulson that you called—in his face—the most ecologically irresponsible person on the planet? Why, pray tell, would Paulson drop a half million dollars on your flight of fancy?"

Leah locked eyes. "He owes you big, Jack. You got his sorry ass up and down Everest alive."

Jack shook his head. "I was paid to do my job, that's all. A bunch of rocks and a pictograph faintly resembling Thor's Hammer isn't enough for me to ask my client to waste his money, toss his career away or even end up in prison."

Leah grabbed Jack by the arm, pulled him out of the truck and led him gently away from the others. When she spoke, it was in a whisper.

"Then forget about Paulson. You still owe me, Jack. You owe me for not being here when my dad was on life support and dying while you were out on a last-minute mountaineering jaunt."

Jack felt as if he'd been punched in the gut. Not only had Duncan Andrews fallen to his eventual death on a climb Jack was supposed to lead, but Leah had to suffer alone for five horrific days before her dad passed away.

Jack looked up into her eyes, now wet with tears.

"If Dad were alive," she said, "he would have sold his last pair of ragged underwear to fund the building of a reed boat to paddle to Antarctica if he thought it would lead to evidence that cliff dwellers walked on Antarctic ice."

The guilt associated with Duncan Andrew's death rolled over Jack like a tidal wave. Leah was right. Duncan would have done everything in his power to get to Antarctica, or see that Leah did.

Maybe helping her would give him some kind of relief from the guilt that swept over him with every mention of her late father.

"Okay," he said. "One way or another, I'll get you to Antarctica."

CHAPTER 15

J ack reached down under the business-class seat on the Boeing 757 as the commercial airliner descended into New York's LaGuardia Airport. He pulled out the black leather bag that held his laptop computer and opened a blank document that he titled, "Antarctic Gear."

Jack based his estimates on hosting eight to ten people for five days with an additional ten days' worth of emergency supplies. Tents, food, clothing, fuel, communications gear, climbing gear, and emergency medical equipment all ended up on the growing list. They would also need sleds to pull equipment from the aircraft's landing zone to the base of Thor's Hammer. Jack reviewed the list and then tossed the laptop into the empty seat beside him in frustration.

There's no way Paulson's buying this. Jack was tempted to tell Leah he simply couldn't arrange a meeting with the billionaire and return home to Tahoe.

Jack exited the jet and ordered a tall cup of black coffee at one of the portable espresso booths lining the airport concourse. Then he pulled out his mobile telephone and scrolled down the address book. He was looking for the phone number for Paulson's assistant Karen Miller.

If he needed to get in to see Paulson, the best way would be through Karen, who guarded the billionaire more closely than the Secret Service guarded the President. She reminded him in looks and manner of the original "Ms. Moneypenny" of James Bond fame.

Jack took a deep breath, pushed the send button, and hoped that she'd pick up her secret line.

Karen Miller was worried. When she worried, she blinked excessively, making it look like she had a grain of sand lodged in her eye.

Paulson's executive assistant blinked several more times in rapid succession, then walked toward the window of her office overlooking New York's Sixth Avenue from the 50th floor. This was the suite of offices that Paulson jokingly called "Officer Country" from his days as a naval aviator.

It served as the nerve center for his worldwide business empire, and all his top lieutenants had offices on the executive floor.

Karen studied the hazy sky—even though chances she might see a black speck shooting across the horizon were remote at best.

The sound of her mobile ringing with its familiar tune startled her. She said a quick prayer and braced for the worst.

"Karen? It's Jack Hobson."

"Oh, my God—Jack Hobson," she said.

"What's wrong?"

"Al is out flying one of those patched-together winged death machines, and if there's an accident, Mac Ridley's supposed to call me at this number."

"As long as Mac's in charge, I doubt you have much to worry about. You can bet that plane's been picked over with a fine-toothed comb."

She nodded and took a deep breath. "I know, but it doesn't keep me from wanting to wring his neck every time he goes up in one of those things."

"I understand completely." Jack paused a moment. "So…I'm in the Big Apple."

A smile crept across Karen's face. "What are you doing here? I figured after three months with Paulson you'd have found a deserted beach somewhere—besides, everyone thinks he's still in Asia."

"I called looking for him in Hong Kong. The hotel said he'd checked out early. I figured he'd get fidgety if he were away from the action too long.

Is there a chance of seeing him this week? It's important and won't take too much time."

"No problem," Karen replied. "You can meet him this afternoon at Westchester County Airport, assuming he doesn't kill himself landing that museum piece. I'll call Mac and tell him you're coming out." She paused. "Are you staying at the Waldorf-Astoria Hotel?"

"Am I really that predictable?"

"You're a creature of habit—if you stayed anywhere else, I'd start getting worried." Karen reached down and wrote herself a short note. "I'm going to have the room put on our corporate account."

"You don't need to do that, Karen."

"Shut up and enjoy it," she ordered. "With as much money as flows in here, Al can afford to put you up at the Waldorf-Astoria and buy Trump Tower to boot. I'll send a car for you."

"It's not really necessary. Al pays me plenty for his climbing tours."

"I'm in your debt," she said softly. "You got the old codger off that mountain in one piece, and I haven't heard a peep about climbing since."

"What airplane is he flying today?"

"All I know is it's an old jet fighter, Russian or something," she said. "You know how I hate when he flies those old planes. Most are antiques, and he's up there doing loop-the-loops and who knows what else...."

"I'm sure he's taking it easy," Jack assured. "Al is a very careful and conscientious pilot."

Jack clicked off the telephone and put it back in his bag. Paulson had taken him for a ride once in a restored North American P-51 fighter. Between Jack's fear of flying and Al Paulson's reckless regard for mother earth, he'd never forgotten that flight. Karen had every reason to be worried.

CHAPTER 16

The driver slowed the Paulson Global house limousine and turned onto the airport road. Corporate jets of all sizes and types were parked in neat rows behind a system of cavernous white hangars.

Jack searched for Paulson's expensive and plush long-haul business jet. The Gulfstream 550 sat parked on the airport tarmac. The aircraft registration, or 'N' number displayed prominently on the jet engine nacelle read "N111PG." The "PG" stood for Paulson Global. In the world of corporate jets, size mattered more than just about anything, except maybe range.

The limousine stopped and Jack climbed out, taking his bags and thanking the driver. He walked toward the security gate staffed by one guard standing next to a glass-windowed booth. Jack smiled and the guard nodded as he approached the gate.

"I'm here to see Mac Ridley," he said.

The guard stepped into his booth and picked up the telephone. He spoke for a moment and then said, "Mr. Ridley says to meet him at the hangar."

MacDonald "Mac" Ridley was a senior vice president and one of Paulson Global's highest-ranking executives. "One of the boys," as Karen Miller liked to say.

In a corporation as large and powerful as Paulson Global, each of Al's key lieutenants yielded tremendous power, and they were compensated with bonuses reaching seven figures.

Mac Ridley was in charge of flight operations for Paulson Global, which included a fleet of corporate charter jets and Paulson's personal collection of antique warbirds.

Jack smiled as a plump man of average height in his late fifties stepped out of the hangar. He wore greasy blue overalls and a matching blue cap with a Paulson Global logo, and he came sauntering toward Jack, wiping grease off his hands with a stained blue rag.

"Jack Hobson," Ridley said. His smiling face could have doubled for a relief map of Mount Everest, it featured so many wrinkles, thanks to thousands of hours spent out in the sun on a flight line, and his teeth hadn't seen a dentist anytime the past century. "How the hell are you?"

Jack reached out his hand. "Good to see you again, Mac."

The stories of Ridley walking into corporate headquarters dressed in his overalls with a cigar hanging out of his mouth while his Harvard and University of Chicago-educated counterparts dressed in Armani suits looked on in horror and disgust were legendary.

"Karen tells me you're making quite an impression at the monthly executive management meetings," Jack said, needling the mechanic.

"Those shit-for-brains-MBA-toting pus-nut idiots won't take a dump without spending a million dollars on a 'Trend Analysis' first." Ridley shook his head in disgust. "They most certainly don't want some dirty old aircraft mechanic saying the word *fuck* in their Ivy-League presence."

"I'm glad to see there's someone here to keep Al's ego in check."

"Hell, he doesn't need me for that." Ridley pointed up at the late afternoon sky. "Each time one of these airborne battle-wagons is about to auger-in, it serves to remind him he puts on his pants one leg at a time, just like the rest of us."

"Karen says he's flying a vintage Russian fighter."

"Chinese…. We bought three surplus MIG 15s. One to restore, the other two for spare parts." The mechanic shrugged. "I told him to let one of our pilots check it out first. Wanted to fly the thing himself—you know how stubborn he can be."

Jack pointed toward a rusting fuselage and a collection of parts near the hangar doors. "What is that pile of junk?"

"That is a *very* rare P-38 Lightning."

Ridley walked Jack over toward the hangar. "Of the thousands made during World War II, there's less than a handful in flying condition. This one crashed in New Guinea during the war. Paulson paid two million dollars in bribes to local officials, plus what it cost to remove it from the jungle."

Jack's jaw dropped. "He paid two million dollars for that wreck?"

"Believe it or not, we'll have it flying in a couple of years—after spending another couple million dollars in parts and labor for reconstruction and fabrication of non-available parts. When it's done could be worth five, even ten million dollars to the right bidder—not that Paulson would ever sell. When it comes to these antique warbirds, he gets downright obsessive."

Jack examined the rusted fuselage. "I guess these guys are serious about their hobby."

"This isn't a game, Jack. This is about big business and even bigger egos. These rare aircraft are worth millions among the real collectors, and whoever has the rarest aircraft in flying condition wins bragging rights at Oshkosh."

Ridley meant the Experimental Aircraft and Vintage Warbird air show held in Oshkosh, Wisconsin. Several hundred thousand people show up to enjoy both static and air displays of the world's most prized collectible aircraft during the middle of each summer. "We've wrapped up the summer air-show tours," Ridley said. "Now we've got to do the maintenance on all the aircraft."

Jack studied the system of hangars. "I thought Al owned more planes."

"Shit, this isn't near the whole fleet. These aircraft need maintenance or restoration. We also keep the aircraft he likes to fly handy here. We own a bunch more hangars here and one big hangar at Stewart Airfield up near Newburgh." Ridley unclipped a hand-held radio from his waist belt and tuned in the control tower's radio frequency. "He's inbound. Let's go out and see if he can land without tearing the wheels off." They trotted around the corner of the hangar and Ridley pointed out a silver speck in the sky trailing a line of black smoke. "He's coming in right there."

The wings dipped as the billionaire gently lined the aircraft up. As the MIG crossed the runway threshold, the nose lifted and Paulson gently "walked" the tricycle landing gear onto the asphalt.

"Not bad," Ridley grudgingly acknowledged. "He got a feel for the old fighter real quick."

The MIG turned off the runway and rolled toward the hangar. Each time Paulson nudged the throttle, a blast of hot gas from the jet-turbine engine blew dust and debris around the tarmac. Mac crossed his arms signaling the MIG had reached the shutdown spot. Paulson fiddled around inside the cockpit and then slid the canopy open.

"Jack Hobson," Paulson said, beaming. "Want to hop in for a ride?"

"I'll stick to ground-operated vehicles, thank you."

Ridley helped Paulson out of the narrow cockpit. "Guess it flew."

"It's a handful and primitive," the billionaire said. "Turns like a hummingbird and has a kick like battlefield artillery." Paulson studied Jack's face. "I doubt you're here to reminisce over our excellent adventure."

Jack nodded. "I heard you came back early, and I know that means you're busier than usual, but I need a half hour of your time."

"Let me take a quick shower; then we can fly downtown."

Ridley waved goodbye and left to tend to the MIG while Jack wandered about the hangar, looking over the vintage single-seat fighters. He imagined sitting in the cramped cockpit of the Spitfire during the Battle of Britain, dog-fighting with German F-190s over the English Channel.

Paulson strolled into the hangar from the offices, dressed in a custom-cut blue pinstripe suit.

"All right, Jacky, let's go." He led Jack to one of Paulson Global's Bell 430 executive helicopters. Paulson laid Jack's garment bag on one of the plush leather seats and then pointed to the rear of the aircraft, where two more seats were separated by an elegant console.

Jack sank into the hand-stitched leather. "This is a hell of a lot better than sleeping on rocks and ice."

Paulson nodded, a twinkle in his eyes. "Damn these things are expensive, but I keep telling my CFO I can't live without it."

"Are we landing on the PG building?"

"We have to set down at the Downtown Manhattan Heliport and take a car to the offices."

The pilot lifted off and flew over the airport runways, gently gaining altitude as he flew the crowded flight corridor into Manhattan.

"What's this all about?" Paulson asked, sipping on a diet Coke.

Jack pulled one of the red granite crystals out of a pocket inside his computer case and handed it over. "Leah found this in an 800-year-old Native American cliff dwelling in southern New Mexico."

Paulson studied the stone. "So these particular Native Americans were rock hounds?"

"There's only one place on Earth with this specific variety of granite, and that's Antarctica."

Paulson looked up at him. "You're sure this is genuine?"

"I saw the site. She was the first person ever inside it. It's confidential, by the way. She could go to jail for federal trespassing."

"Ha! Ms. *Straight-Arrow?*" The smile left Paulson's face. "So what do you think?"

"To be honest, I was skeptical, until I saw a pictograph that I'm pretty sure shows Thor's Hammer."

"Thor's Hammer?"

"It's a vertical granite cliff located in the Ellsworth range. A vein of reddish granite crystal runs through the face in the shape of a massive hammer."

"So you want to make a field trip to Antarctica," Paulson said. "Take a look-see for evidence Leah's Native Americans were hunting buffalo on ice?"

The helicopter bumped as the pilot landed softly on the tarmac at the heliport. They exited the Bell, ducking to avoid the rotor blast, and jumped into a waiting limousine.

Back at headquarters, Karen stood inside the plush suite, her arms crossed and a disapproving expression on her face as Paulson pushed open the doors leading into the executive offices and Jack followed him inside.

"Just wanted to make sure you're in one piece," she said.

"What'd you expect?" Paulson teased.

"With you I never know." Karen handed her boss a sheet of paper. "Paul Lever's been calling all morning about the Rockingham deal."

Paulson's demeanor darkened. "All right, get him on the telephone." He glanced at Jack. "I bought a large holding in Rockingham Home Appliance about three months ago. Thought we might try to make the company profitable. They manufacture a great line of products in American factories, and their strong brand identity positions them well within the marketplace, but the company is terribly mismanaged. They've been fighting me all the way."

Paulson led Jack into his large corner office overlooking the city and sat on the front of his desk. "You need airfare to Antarctica, and you're calling in all your Everest favors," he said bluntly.

"I guess it's pointless to bullshit you."

The billionaire grinned. "I'm paid to think one step ahead. What's your plan?"

"Fly to Thor's Hammer and see if we can locate any evidence linking cliff dwellers to the region. Leah believes petrography—ancient rock carvings—would have survived hundreds of years. Other artifacts, even human remains, could be well preserved in the ice as well. If this is true, it'll blow theories of man's migration around the planet to smithereens. Leah's obsessed with finding out if there is an Antarctic connection, and I have to confess, the evidence is compelling."

"What's this going to cost?"

Jack hesitated. "Expensive. At least half a million dollars, probably more by the time we're done."

Paulson sat in one of the leather chairs surrounding a cherry-wood conference table. "That's big money to spend on a hunch. What else have you got?"

"That's it."

The billionaire thumbed the smooth lacquered surface. "I owe you big for getting me off Everest alive. You know that."

"I'm not trying to leverage you with Everest," Jack said. "I'm doing this partly out of guilt, to be honest. It has to do with Leah and her dad and our relationship. Long story.... But in all seriousness, we could be talking about one of the greatest unsolved mysteries left on the planet."

"Why don't you just go to Leah's former employer? If you have real evidence of something extraordinary, maybe they'd overlook her digging around in a national park."

Jack shook his head. "She won't go and I can't force her. She's burned her bridges there, besides. They'd cut her out of the project, even if she managed to stay out of prison."

"Are you sure this is a good idea—you and Leah setting off on this adventure? Every time I see you with her, you end up spitting bullets. Hell, shouldn't you be planning next season's climbs on Everest instead of chasing down favors?"

"Everything you say is true," Jack said. "But just like you think you owe me? I owe Leah. Plus, I really think we're on to something. See, no one's ever been able to figure out why the Anasazi felt compelled to move into these crazy cliff dwellings or why they abandoned the cliff cities less than two hundred years later. Now, new evidence leads us to central Antarctica? It's kind of...irresistible."

Paulson whistled, shaking his head. "It makes a helluva story, I'll grant you that." He glanced up. "But I think it's about more than that for you."

Jack looked at him blankly.

"It's not guilt or science, really, is it?" Paulson gave him a sly smile. "It's the juice, isn't it, Jacky? One more high-adrenalin, action-packed adventure."

Paulson had given him an easy way out, and he took it. "I can't disagree. I guess it's just in my blood."

The billionaire stood, walked over to Jack, and sat down beside him. "You were down this road before with her, and it cost you."

"I'll keep her at arm's length this time."

Paulson glanced at his watch. "Are you staying in town?"

Jack nodded.

"If I get a chance maybe we can have lunch."

Jack reached out with his hand. "Thanks for the time, Al."

"You got me on top of Everest and down alive. That's something I won't forget." He pushed open the double doors, "That, and kicking Nash's useless ass." He walked Jack out to Karen's office.

She glanced up suspiciously. "What kind of trouble are you boys getting into now?"

Jack shrugged. "Looks like none, probably to your relief."

"Are you kidding? Take him away for six weeks. The quiet around here is fantastic."

"Watch it," Paulson said. "Otherwise I'll make you come with me next time."

"Not a chance," Karen shot back.

Paulson winked at Jack and then slipped into his office.

"You seem a little let down."

He shrugged again. "I probably shouldn't be asking Al for anything. It's—"

"Never underestimate Alan Paulson," Karen said, cutting him off. "I learned that the hard way."

Jack smiled and nodded. "I'll keep that in mind."

Karen walked him to the elevator and kissed him on the cheek. "Thanks for bringing the lug home alive."

Jack rode the elevator to the lobby and walked out onto Sixth Avenue. He grabbed a hot dog from a street vendor, and then flagged down a cab even though it wasn't that far to walk. "Waldorf-Astoria," he said.

The cabbie nodded and forced the cab out into traffic.

"Wake up, sir. We're here."

Jack looked up to find the cab parked at the curb in front of the hotel. "Sorry, it's been a long couple of days." He handed the driver a twenty-dollar bill. "Keep the change."

Jack grabbed his computer bag and garment bag and climbed out of the cab. He waved off the bellman offering to take his bags and walked through the double doors into the ornately decorated art deco lobby, complete with the wheel-of-life mosaic and thirteen priceless allegorical oil murals by French artist Louis Rigal.

"I'm Jack Hobson," he said to the well-groomed young man at the check-in counter.

The clerk smiled and tapped on the computer keyboard. His eyebrows lifted a notch, and his manner became even more attentive and animated. "I see you're here as a guest of Paulson Global, Mr. Hobson. We have you reserved in a suite."

Jack simply nodded. Karen would have had a fit if he'd downgraded to a mere executive room; the palatial suites were more accustomed to hosting heads of state than mountain climbers.

Once inside the suite, he looked at his cell phone, wondering exactly how he was going to let Leah down.

I'm too tired to do this tonight.

Instead, Jack walked over to the fully stocked mini-bar, pulled out several of the airline-style liquor bottles, and turned on the television. He dropped on the couch and downed several of the small bottles while watching CNN Headline News. Feeling completely exhausted, Jack turned off the television, closed his eyes and fell into a deep slumber.

CHAPTER 17

Jack lurched into the darkness, fumbling for the light switch and the ringing cell phone sitting on the night stand.

"Hello?" he said, feeling a nauseous combination of alcohol and exhaustion fogging his brain.

"Hobson, you lazy son-of-a-bitch, get your ass out of the rack."

"Al?" Jack rubbed his eyes. "Jesus Christ—what time is it?"

"Three-thirty in the morning. What's wrong with that?"

"Ah...." Jack looked down at the couch, where empty mini-bar liquor bottles lay scattered about. "You're still in the office?"

"I've got news for you," the billionaire said.

"If it's after three in the morning; it's either real good or really bad."

"Let me read you something off the newswire from three nights ago."

Paulson's voice faded and echoed as he flipped his phone to speaker mode. "A secret Russian expedition suffered a major setback when their Antonov 74 transport aircraft crashed while attempting to land near the wreck of a World War II B-29 bomber in a mountainous region of the Antarctic continent. Grigoriy Kryukov, a Russian industrialist and wireless telephone entrepreneur with serious ties to the Russian President, was not aboard the aircraft. However, it has been reported his son was killed, along with ten others." The billionaire's voice came closer to his phone. "Does that mean anything to you?"

"There are plenty of crashed aircraft on the continent. It's not a forgiving environment when it comes to man or machine."

"Okay, then—let me give you a little background," Paulson said. "Several World War II-era B-29 Super Fortress bombers were sold to the Chilean government after the war was over in 1945. They used the B-29s mostly for doing aerial photography of the Andes Mountains and, because of their long range, Antarctica. This particular Super Fort suddenly develops engine trouble deep in the interior of the continent.

"When the pilot can't gain enough altitude to clear the mountains, he decides to belly-land it on a flat section of ice. The crew survives the landing and, through the dogged determination of the aircraft commander, manages to stay alive for nearly two weeks until a British search aircraft locates them. The crewmembers are Chilean national heroes to this day. The name of the plane is the *Las Tortugas*: 'The Turtles,' in Spanish. The nose art on the aircraft showed a snapping turtle dropping bombs out of the belly with a, let's say, 'scantily dressed, well-developed young woman' riding suggestively on its shell."

"It has been sitting on the ice all these years? Why all the interest now?"

"Until a few years ago, nobody gave a damn," Paulson said. "They figured a wrecked B-29 sitting in temperatures reaching a hundred below zero wasn't worth the salvage effort."

"What changed?"

"A former test pilot and fellow aircraft collector named Darryl Greenamyer repaired a crashed B-29 named the *Kee Bird* and nearly managed to fly it off a frozen lake in Greenland."

"I remember," Jack said. "They flew in parts and repaired the aircraft. For some reason it burned up before takeoff."

"The APU in the rear of the aircraft spilled fuel through a broken diaphragm and ignited. Before they knew it, the *Kee Bird* burned down to the ice."

"What's that got to do with the *Las Tortugas*, and why are you calling me at three in the morning?"

"Of the more than four thousand B-29s built during the war, there's only one flying. It's the *Fifi*, and it belongs to the Confederate Air Force, a group of old farts and volunteers based in Texas. It has most of the interior stripped out and carries very little of the original equipment. The *Las Tortugas*, on the other hand, still has its machine-gun turrets, radio operator's stations—you name it. The bomber's in mint condition."

Jack suppressed an urge to say, *So what?*

"It's also a combat veteran, tons of missions over Japan. Most of the flying warbirds today were built at or near the end of the war and never saw any action. It's invaluable on the open market to any number of well-heeled collectors."

"I get it," Jack said. "That's tempting, I can tell."

Paulson chuckled. "Trust me, after the *Kee Bird* incident, I wasn't the only one who checked into salvaging the *Las Tortugas*. But given the politics, not to mention the cost, I never went past looking at it on paper. The Chileans still claim ownership of the aircraft because of the hero crew. The situation is highly complicated by the fact that it rests inside a small and generally unrecognized section of Antarctic territory claimed by the former Soviet Union—now the Russian government. The Russians are still pressing their territorial claims, probably because of national pride... and the fortune in minerals likely below the ice. Everyone finally decided the *Las Tortugas* ought to just stay where it was—except those sneaky Russians."

Jack wrote down the name *Las Tortugas* on a note pad next to the couch. "Why would the Russians want the airplane?"

"Like I said, this guy, Kryukov, has connections. He probably offered a cut of the *Las Tortugas* sale if certain high-ranking officials arranged to supply the support necessary to get it airworthy. Kryukov would have had the B-29 off the ice and on the auction block before the Chileans could say boo."

"Probably didn't thrill the Chileans," Jack said.

"They're mad as wet hens."

"This plane is where, exactly?"

"Right where you're headed."

Jack's eyes blinked as the implications washed over him. "How close?"

"Can't be more than a few kilometers; the article says, Thor's Hammer has served as guardian over the *Las Tortugas* for nearly 60 years."

Jack rose from the couch. "So you're planning to grab the *Las Tortugas*."

"I just had a little chat with the president of Chile. They'll supply as much support as we need through their Bernardo O' Higgins Ice Station located on the Antarctic Peninsula." He chuckled. "They'll do just about anything to keep it out of the hands of the Russians. I told him we had the mechanics, spare parts and skills to fly that mother right off the ice."

"I still can't believe you just called the president of Chile."

"Come on, Jack. I've got every politician in South America kissing my ass right now. They're all looking for investment capital."

"So did you have to promise them the aircraft?"

"Under my deal," said the billionaire, "Chile retains ownership of the aircraft; they simply agree to lease it back to me for one dollar a year. I provide all the funds necessary to refurbish the *Las Tortugas* and make it part of my traveling air-show collection. In essence, the B-29 becomes a Chilean ambassador of goodwill to the world. Upon my death, the vintage bomber returns to Chile permanently, as one of their national treasures."

"What about the Russian government?" Jack asked. "They're not gonna take kindly to you stealing the bomber after all the work and lives they put into the salvage."

"We'll sneak in, finish the job and fly that mother out before the Russians have a chance to regroup." Jack could tell that Paulson was nearly dancing a jig in his office. "We also get full cooperation from the Chilean government, including unlimited use of their Antarctic bases, and fuel and equipment drops from Chilean Air Force C-130 if we need them."

"You did all that in one telephone call?"

"Yep. Every time the Chilean President hesitated, like on the fuel drops, I just mentioned the Russians. I pressed him to fly us down to the ice, but he refused. He said while they would provide support, he didn't want any Chilean aircraft involved in what was already a dicey situation." Paulson cleared his throat. "He didn't want his military tangling with Russian soldiers."

"So you volunteered us for something the Chilean military deemed too dangerous for them?"

"Do you want to go to Thor's Hammer or not?" Paulson paused. "Should I just call Leah directly?"

"Thor's Hammer is one thing," Jack warned. "It doesn't sit inside Russian territory, and I doubt anyone would be inclined to start shooting at us for taking a little camping trip to Antarctica."

"I told the Chileans once the *Las Tortugas* is off the ice, I'll offer to reimburse the Russians for the parts and labor they invested in the aircraft."

"Come on, Al. You're talking about a Russian military operation under the guise of entrepreneurship. They're going to be embarrassed and really pissed off."

"It's not their aircraft to salvage. This is a legitimate Chilean national treasure." Another pause. "Besides, I need your help. You know this region like the back of your hand. I want someone running the expedition who knows how to plan and execute a trip to this godforsaken ice box."

Jack rubbed his eyes with his free hand. "All right, but I'm counting on you to know when to call it quits. Our lives are in your hands this time—just like yours was in mine on Mt. Everest. You've got to know when to turn around."

"You're in my world now, Jack. You have to trust me, like I trusted you."

Jack studied the carpet for a moment and then looked up.

"Okay. We're in."

CHAPTER 18

Gila National Monument Superintendent and Chief Ranger Glen Janssen was not happy. He'd sent two of his rangers on patrol in one of the more remote areas of Gila after receiving a tip that several suspicious individuals had been working the cliffs with high-powered binoculars.

His rangers had flushed several individuals, perhaps the same ones they'd been tipped about. The intruders had fled arrest, and one of them, an experienced climber, had intentionally dislodged a large rockslide that easily could have killed one or both of his men.

Janssen picked up a photograph lying on his desk. It was a close-up of the rear bumper of a significantly beat-up, green, mid-1980s, vintage, four-wheel-drive Chevrolet Blazer. Centered within the photograph was a rusty chrome bracket that normally framed the required license plate.

He lifted another photograph and studied the face looking out through the dusty rear window. The quality of the photo was poor, but he had the New Mexico State Police chewing on it.

Glen Janssen laid the photograph down on the steel desk and walked out of his office toward the Tourist Center Office—or, as he liked to refer to it, "Meet and Greet the Sheep." Two rangers leaned against the varnished wooden counter used during the busy tourist season. They instinctively stood erect when their boss walked through the door. He smiled to put them at ease; their egos still smarted from having lost the suspected artifact hunters.

"Something's bothering me about this thing," Janssen said.

"We shouldn't have let them get away," said Darryl Ridgeway.

"Not true, Darryl," Janssen replied with an easy smile. "An arrowhead or piece of pottery is not worth your lives. You took more risk than necessary crossing the rock bridge on those damn machines." He leaned on the counter. "What I can't figure out is what the hell they were doing in Gila."

"Probably searching for something they could sell," Ridgeway said.

Glen Janssen shook his head. "The known encampments were cleaned out years ago. Outside of a few arrowheads, pottery shards and the occasional tool, there's not much up there. Not for serious artifact hunters." He studied the faded yellow lines in the parking lot. "If I were hunting artifacts, I'd head up to Grand Gulch. Hell, you've got 100 square miles to sneak around in and a chance to find serious artifacts or maybe even a virgin dwelling."

When the word dwelling rolled off his tongue, he had a sudden thought. "What are the chances that we might find a virgin dwelling up in those cliffs?"

Ridgeway shrugged. "These canyons have been searched over hundreds of times."

Janssen tapped on the counter with fingers still bearing the burn scars from his days as a Smoke Jumper. "Tomorrow I want to take a look-see around the area where you chased that crew out of the canyon." He pointed at the younger ranger. "I want you to get into Silver City and chat with a few of the locals. See if anyone remembers seeing three or four strangers in a green Blazer—with or without plates."

"What are we searching for?" Ridgeway asked. "We combed that area good."

Janssen grinned. "People are the messiest damn animals on the planet, Darryl; there's bound to be evidence up in those cliffs."

CHAPTER 19

Jack scrolled through his phone contacts until he found Harrison Cooper.

"Cooper Arctic Air Transport. Can I help you?" said the smooth voice over the telephone.

"Harrison Cooper."

"Who is calling for Mr. Cooper?"

"Jack Hobson."

Jack endured the on-hold music for what felt like an eternity.

The music suddenly and mercifully stopped. "Jack Hobson," said a deep voice, permanently hoarse from yelling over the top of thundering turboprop engines. "You've got mountain climbers and you need a lift."

Jack liked Harrison Cooper. He was a fifty-year-old, self-made millionaire and aviation entrepreneur. Cooper had started as a primary flight instructor and then ferried stripped-down single-engine Cessna aircraft to Hawaii from the West Coast. They would remove all the seats except for the pilot's and then load the aircraft with a rubber fuel bladder and send these often inexperienced pilots nearly three thousand nautical miles toward Honolulu with no GPS and no satellite navigation—classic Charlie Lindbergh-style, seat-of-the-pants adventure flying.

Jack had chartered Cooper's airplanes for several large-scale mountaineering expeditions. His pilots were the best in the world at Arctic and Antarctic flying.

"How are things in the air-cargo business?"

"We haven't had a crash in over a month, so it's a good year," Cooper said. "What's up with you?"

"You ever heard of Alan Paulson?"

"Rich guy with a pile of warbirds and a taste for adventure. He's all over the Internet."

Jack paused. "This is strictly confidential."

"It won't go past my desk."

"Paulson received permission to salvage a crashed B-29 called the *Las Tortugas* from the Chilean government. I'm the trip planner and we need a lift down to Antarctica. A ski-equipped LC-130 Hercules."

There was a longer pause. "That's a Russian operation, and it's not going well from what I hear."

"Paulson has the blessing from the Chileans to attempt the salvage. They will supply support but won't authorize an aircraft to land on the ice."

"That makes sense," said Cooper. "Chances are; without a top pilot they'd join the Russian transport crew as a monument to aviation stupidity."

Jack bit his lip. "So you won't take the charter?"

"Knowing I could milk a billionaire like Paulson for every dollar, I'd take it in a heartbeat." He paused. "But we've gotten the word. Anyone with government contracts taking private parties into environmentally sensitive regions without the new federal eco-permit can kiss future contracts good-bye."

Jack felt a chill run down his back. "What are you talking about?"

"You know how the Fed frowns on private expeditions to Antarctica. It's even a pain in the ass dealing with them on something as non-threatening as ferrying down a group of tree-hugging mountain climbers for a shot at Mt. Vinson. The president and his new environmental czar have decided to set an example for the rest of the world: Antarctica, along with several other pristine regions of the planet, ought to be off limits to Americans and those interested in obtaining American government contracts."

"Shit," whispered Jack. "When did this come about?"

"We were sent a notice about three months ago," Cooper said. "Now that doesn't mean we couldn't do it, just means we need to get the permits, which could take six months. By then everyone will know what you're up to."

"Looks like we're screwed even before we begin," Jack said.

"If you didn't need ski-equipped aircraft, there'd probably be some options. The smaller outfits are desperate for cash and might risk it."

"What if we didn't need a ski-equipped aircraft?" Jack asked.

"You're talking about Antarctica. I don't see how you'd get down on the ice without skis."

"The Russians were planning to fly the bomber out on its tires, and so is Paulson," Jack said. "The Russians must have prepared some kind of ice runway."

"That might be true—but you said you needed the ski-equipped LC-130 Hercules. You land a loaded C-130 Hercules without skis, and it's going to slide right into the mountain—most likely on its belly."

"To get all the gear, crews and parts on the ice, yeah."

"Do you like Russian vodka and beet soup?" Cooper asked. "Because I'd bet right next to the B-29 you're going to find a large stash of Russian vodka and just about everything else you'd need to survive on the ice, not to mention repair the bomber. Assuming the Russians brought what was necessary; you could fly in with minimal equipment."

"We wouldn't know until we got down there. If the site is barren, we'd be screwed."

"Then you'd better get a look at the crash and camp—that way you know exactly what's in place."

"How would we do that?" Jack asked. "Google Earth?"

"Nope," Cooper said. "You need spy-sat-quality photos of a very specific area of Antarctica with a time stamp of yesterday. I mean you have to see cigarette butts and empty vodka bottles on the ice if you want usable intelligence on how far along the Russians got with the 29. That will tell you not only what equipment is in place but should give you some indication how much progress the Russians made with the *Las Tortugas* before the Antonov crash."

"It's a great idea," Jack agreed. "I just don't think the CIA will be open to relocating one of their satellites for a mission that violates an executive order from the president of the United States and puts them at odds with the Russians over a scrap bomber."

"Who needs the CIA? Ever heard of OrbitImaging?" asked Cooper.

"Who?"

"They're a commercial satellite company, for lack of a better term. You can order up pictures taken from their satellites for commercial purposes. We use them to shoot photos of remote locations for possible landing sites. If you get photos, you'll have a really good idea of what the Russians have stashed and the condition of the Las Tortugas."

Jack wrote the name down on a piece of paper. "What's this going to cost?"

"For Paulson, pocket change. It wouldn't surprise me if he uses them already."

"Paulson has a meeting scheduled for tomorrow morning," Jack said. "Assuming we don't need an LC-130 Hercules and there's an ice runway, can you give us any discreet leads on someone with the experience to get into and out of Antarctica?"

"There's one I think might be interested," Cooper replied. "They've got one airplane, an ancient De Havilland Caribou. It won't carry a huge load, but it has range and these guys are good on the ice. We worked with them last year on the Alaskan North Slope. They ferried equipment around for a drilling company. They put that Caribou down on ice that made my asshole pucker, and did it without skis. I hear they've had some financial trouble."

"What's the name?"

Cooper cleared his throat. "InterGalactic Air Cargo."

"*InterGalactic?*"

Cooper let out a gravelly chuckle. "Yeah. They're based out of Oakland, California. Now, if you need any help getting cargo into or out of Chile, you let me know."

Jack copied down the telephone number, thanked Harrison Cooper, and immediately redialed.

"InterGalactic Air Cargo," said a voice sounding thick with sleep.

"I'm looking for the guys who run the show here."

"That'd be me and my brother." A man with a Southern accent cleared his throat. "The name is Chase Parker."

"Everything I'm about to tell you is strictly confidential, Mr. Parker. Is that understood?"

"If this involves drugs, illegal importation of animals, minerals or people, you can forget it," Chase stated, "and no amount of money will change my mind. Beyond that, we're paid to keep our mouths shut. We wouldn't be in business long if we didn't."

Jack explained who he was and why he was calling. "It'll be a risky job," he warned. "You're going to land on an ice runway located in a valley between two mountain peaks. You're looking at a high altitude, low-density takeoff; the ice is nearly two miles deep at that point.

"We'd need fuel once we hit the continent," Chase Parker said matter-of-factly. "We won't be able to carry a full load of fuel, or cargo, due to the altitude."

Jack explained fuel was no problem. They had cooperation from the Chilean government and fuel available on the way in and out at the Chilean Antarctica base, Bernardo O' Higgins, plus a fuel drop from Chilean C-130 Hercules.

"Just one more thing," Jack said. "Harrison Cooper says anyone hauling private expeditions into Antarctica can kiss government contracts, present or future, good-bye. So if you guys want to back out, I understand." He waited for what seemed an eternity for the reply.

"We're going to need $500,000—dry," Chase said flatly.

"Dry" meant Paulson would pay all fuel costs, above the $500,000 for the charter.

"Is the plane worth that much?" Jack asked, hoping for some leverage.

"You need a lift to Antarctica, and we've got a blown engine, which means we're not getting work right now. Still, we gotta consider the risk, which will be substantial."

"I've got two hundred and fifty-thousand," Jack said, holding his breath.

"I'd want to discuss this with my brother," Parker said.

"Fine."

Chase hesitated. "Four-hundred-thousand and we throw in a box lunch on the way down."

"How many times have you flown into Antarctica, anyway?"

"Once…if you count this trip."

Jack hesitated. It was these guys or nothing.

"Start hunting down that new engine, Mr. Parker."

"Meeting with Mr. Paulson," Jack said to the security guard downstairs. "The name is Hobson." The guard handed him a pass and led him to the elevators.

The door opened to Karen's warm smile. "Back so soon?"

Jack kissed her on the cheek. "Remind me never to underestimate Paulson again."

"I think I said that yesterday," she said flatly.

Karen led him into Paulson's plush private conference room. Paulson waved him over toward his office conference table, now covered with charts.

"Were you able to line up that ski-equipped Hercules?"

"Negative. No one will touch a private charter into Antarctica. I do have a back-up. An outfit with a De Havilland Caribou will take the job."

Paulson looked up from his pile of notes. "A Caribou? Is that the best we can do?"

"Harrison Cooper said anyone landing in Antarctica without express permission of the U.S. government can and will forfeit all current and future contracts."

Paulson picked up the telephone. "Is Ridley on his way? Good." He dropped the telephone. "What's the name of our charter?"

Jack swallowed. "InterGalactic Air Cargo…."

The billionaire remained emotionless for a moment, then burst out laughing. "It fits this entire fiasco perfectly."

Paulson's chief mechanic strolled into the conference room in his usual jeans and t-shirt, although he'd attempted to smooth down his remaining gray hair, with little success.

"Mac, come on in and grab a seat," Paulson said enthusiastically. "We're going after the *Las Tortugas.*"

Ridley's mouth twisted into a grimace. "Like I *already* said, the Russians are all over that wreck. What makes you think they're going to allow us to waltz in and fly that busted-up bird out from underneath their noses, assuming we land safely and that pile of aluminum is airworthy?"

Paulson put on his best earnest expression. "The Russians have an illegitimate claim on the *Las Tortugas.* It belongs to the Chilean people."

Ridley looked down at his jeans and wiped at a spot of grease. "I doubt Russian commandos are going to have that view." He stared at the white ceiling. "If the Russians start shooting, you'll have dead employees on your hands; you want the bird that bad?"

Paulson moved to the chair next to his aircraft mechanic. "The Russians are scrambling to buy toilet paper back home. Oil prices are in the gutter and their economy's imploding. They've already lost a cargo plane and a crew and brought worldwide attention to the Super Fortress. We've got the Southern Hemisphere summer window right in front of us."

Ridley squirmed in the overstuffed chair. "This is looking to me like a real cluster." He shrugged. "If you want to hang your ass out over a cliff—"

"We're going to keep it real quiet," Paulson said.

Ridley looked at Jack. "I'd guess you're going to take care of us while we're freezing our asses off on the other end of a socket wrench."

"I'm getting your transportation down to the ice and taking care of the logistics."

"What does this piece of shit need to get off the ice?"

"Rumor says it's nearly repaired," Paulson said. "Do you have any suggestions?"

"I'd have to get a look at it. Expect we'd have to fix everything, knowing those Russian aircraft mechanics. We gotta go light, super light; the altitude at the ski-way is 9,000 feet.

Jack leaned forward. "Cooper told me about a company called OrbitImaging. They shoot commercial photographs from a satellite. If we can get digital pictures of the crash site, we'd have at least a solid picture of the situation."

"Great idea, but can this OrbitImaging keep their mouths shut?"

Jack nodded. "According to Harrison Cooper, they're discreet and like cash."

"Get them hooked up," said the billionaire. "That could save us a bundle in spare parts, and more important, time."

Ridley stood, signaling he had heard enough and wanted out of the stuffy office. "Once I see the photos, I'll know how many mechanics and what kind of gear we're going to need to get the job done."

"Meeting adjourned." Paulson looked over at Jack. "Give your crew a heads-up and get the expedition gear together. Make sure you tell Leah this is gonna be dangerous. I'm going to get this bomber, Jacky—and I won't quit till I'm flying her home."

Chapter 20

"We have Antarctica," Jack said over the telephone, in a monotone.

"It sounds to me like you're getting ready to lay out some conditions," Leah replied.

He drew in a deep breath. "Paulson's coming along."

"What's his interest in Native American archeology?"

"He's going to salvage a World War II bomber that crashed near Thor's Hammer."

"What's he planning to do, sell artifacts that we find?"

"This B-29 bomber is his only interest," Jack said. "The bomber is at the center of an international incident—involving the Russians."

"What exactly does that mean?"

"There could be soldiers in and around the area—and if the Russians decide to oppose the salvage of the B-29, there is a strong possibility of shooting or worse. The terrain has proved lethal to aircraft, even though we're in the Antarctic summer. It will still be cold, well below zero, and you'll be breathing thin air; imagine skiing in the Rockies."

"What about Garrett, Juan, and Marko?"

"They need to understand the situation. Paulson invited them along but they have to agree to provide help on the B-29 salvage if needed. You have free rein to explore around Thor's Hammer while on the ice, which in all likelihood will be only a few days."

"How far do you trust Paulson?"

"He wants the bomber badly. I'm not sure how much that will impact his decision-making."

"Jack, this is beginning to resemble an Everest climbing trip, and you know how that scares the shit out of me."

"I'd be happier if you stayed in New Mexico and let me snoop around Thor's Hammer," Jack said, tiptoeing around the issue.

"Not a chance."

"Then remember: Al Paulson's our sugar-daddy on this trip, which means he's not to be treated like the world's most dangerous criminal."

"From the sound of it," said Leah, "Al Paulson is the least of our problems."

Jack listened to the call disconnect and laid the telephone softly down. His earlier elation over the prospect of a trip to Antarctica faded. "Shit," he whispered. "What the hell are we getting into?"

CHAPTER 21

G len Janssen leaned over the horn of his saddle, staring at the endless land-scape of red sandstone canyons and scrub pine trees. He instinctively pulled the collar of his coat up against the biting north wind. Three of his rangers were spread out, combing the ground. They had found remnants of a fresh campsite; the floor imprints of several small dome-style tents were still visible in the shifting sands.

The New Mexico State Police had come up with nothing. Probably to be expected. These weren't your normal criminal types. Most likely, they weren't criminals at all, but artifact hunters caught in the act.

The ranger he'd sent into Silver City had had an interesting exchange with the proprietor of the local tavern-gem-store. Jim Dixon, who on occasion called in tips to the National Park Police, had four suspicious individuals come into the store a few days before. Dixon remembered them because they had brought in a very rare type of granite for identification. What raised red flags was Dixon's report that the strangers drove a Chevy Blazer matching the description of the one that had escaped the canyon and ended up in the photographs. When the ranger showed Dixon the photograph featuring the man's face through the rear window of the Blazer, he said the face did not belong to any of the three guys in the tavern. The woman had been referred to as "Leah." The name wasn't all that common and Janssen thought it might provide a solid lead.

What bothered Glen Janssen was the rare granite crystal they had shown to Dixon. The rock dealer said it could be found naturally only in one place: Antarctica. Once Dixon had identified the rock, he said, all four of them had seemed shaken.

Janssen had nixed use of the ATVs for today's search, deciding that horses would be more appropriate. It helped that Janssen loved horses, owning several himself, including the one he was riding.

Darryl Ridgeway tapped the flank of his horse and guided it toward his boss. "We've been all over the top of the mesa again—nothing so far. Except for footprints and tire tracks, it all looks clean."

Janssen studied the landscape. "Where exactly did you spot them?"

Ridgeway pointed toward the opposite side of the canyon. "We were motoring up that side of the mesa when we caught a glimpse of someone crossing the arch, headed for the wash." He swept his hand from left to right. "That's when we saw the second and the third one sprinting across those rocks."

"I want you guys to work back down the way they escaped." Janssen pointed up toward the archway. "I'm going to take a quick look around the mesa."

"We've combed the area three times now."

Janssen's face creased into an easy smile. "I know, Darryl. I'd like to have a look around up there myself just to be sure we haven't missed anything." He paused. "You go on ahead. I'll be along shortly, or you'll hear from me on the radio."

The rangers, with Ridgeway in the lead, turned their horses around and started back down the wash, following the escape path.

Janssen tapped the horse lightly, urging the Appaloosa up the narrow, twisting trail toward the rock bridge leading across the canyon. When he reached the edge of the mesa, he dismounted and patted the animal on the nose.

Horses were still the best way to patrol the park. They fit in with the environment, didn't make much noise, and had a sixth sense for what was happening around them. His horse Locust was especially well-suited for this terrain. He wasn't easily spooked and didn't suffer from a fear of heights, critical for working around the steep canyons. Still, Janssen knew it wasn't prudent to ride the animal over the arch connecting the two sides of the canyon. He grabbed the reins and gave the animal a gentle tug.

Janssen trotted across, making sure not to look down. Instead of climbing back onto the horse when he got to the opposite side of the canyon, the chief ranger simply dropped the reins and started walking through the boulders.

He spent nearly an hour combing the top of the mesa without finding anything out of the ordinary. His back aching, Janssen pulled his cowboy hat down over his ears, trying to ward off the afternoon chill. Locust had wandered over toward the drop-off, looking back on occasion at Janssen with bored disinterest. The horse's mood would change when he pointed the animal in the direction of the stable. Then he'd have to hold the Appaloosa back from galloping happily home.

Locust had stopped near an old pine tree and was scratching his neck against the trunk. Janssen grinned. He could trust the horse to find the only tree on the damn mesa big enough to give him a good scratch, even if it grew dangerously close to the canyon's edge.

Janssen walked over to the horse and rubbed his brown-and-white nose. "Is this whole deal boring you?"

Locust snorted in reply and backed up a step.

Janssen grabbed the reins and stepped behind the short, stumpy pine tree, hoping to catch a brief break from the cold wind. He studied the tree, wondering how old it might be, and, if it could talk, what tales it might tell from its two hundred years of living atop the mesa. He ran his hands over its trunk, feeling the thick texture of the bark, toughened by the harsh winters and hot summers. His hand suddenly stopped near the midpoint on the trunk.

The bark there had been compressed and rubbed smooth on a single narrow strip running around the backside of the tree. Something had been recently rigged around the trunk, leaving a slight but uniform indentation. Whatever it was, the pressure had been applied to the side of the pine facing away from the mesa, which meant the pull had come as someone rappelled down the cliff wall.

Janssen tiptoed toward the precipice, getting down on his hands and knees. He found clear markings where climbing lines had rubbed two distinct grooves in the sandstone; a sure sign someone rigged rope and put significant pressure on the lines.

Janssen was close to breaking one of his own rules—don't take unnecessary risks without back-up. He knew he should wait until a couple of park rangers with climbing experience rigged a safety line. He crawled forward until he could see down over the drop-off. Less than one hundred feet below, a ledge jutted out from the cliff wall.

"I'll be damned." He pushed back away from the cliff and pulled the handheld radio off his belt clip. "Darryl, you copy?"

"Yeah, but we must be nearly out of range because there's plenty of static. What's up?"

"I got a hit."

"What'd ya find?"

"Evidence that someone roped down the north side of the canyon, probably within the last week or so."

"What the hell were they doing? Those cliffs are primarily sandstone, which ain't great for safe climbing."

"Well, there's a ledge about a hundred feet down from the top," Janssen said. "They had something in mind."

"Maybe they were just plain crazy," Ridgeway replied.

"I don't think so. The evasion and escape plans were too elaborate." Janssen shivered in the coming darkness. "I want climbers out here first thing tomorrow morning; get someone down on that ledge and take a look."

"What do you think they were after?"

Janssen looked out over the New Mexico mesa. "I don't know—but it's the best unsolved mystery we have, and it's a hell of a lot better than escorting tour buses through the park."

"Copy that," said Ridgeway. "In the morning I'll have a couple of our volunteer rope jockeys take a ride down. Think we'll find an arrowhead or two glued to the side of the canyon?"

Janssen wiped dust off his cheek and drew a deep breath. "I'm beginning to wonder if we might not find a whole lot more."

CHAPTER 22

Leah scrolled down her list of contacts in search of Garrett's mobile-phone number. After her brief conversation with Jack, including the added wrinkle of Paulson tagging along, she needed to sit down with all of them, face to face.

"Hey," Garrett answered. "What's the scoop?"

"Where are the guys?"

"Juan's giving his students final exams and Marko's back in Santa Fe, probably at the climbing shop."

"I need to see everyone in person. It's important."

"When and where?"

"Meet me at Maria's, tonight at eight."

"Should I start packing?"

"We can discuss the details at Maria's." Leah dropped the telephone onto the passenger seat. She'd already made the decision; as much as it pained her, the boys were not going to Antarctica.

Chapter 23

Jack waited for Richard Breslen, the president of OrbitImaging, to pick up his telephone.

"Breslen here," the chief executive said briskly.

"I'm Jack Hobson. Harrison Cooper called you regarding my special requirements. Is that something you can do?"

"It can be done."

"That sounds like a qualified yes."

He hesitated. "I'm sure Cooper told you it's expensive to position the bird. How soon do you need these images?"

"Yesterday." Asking for and receiving Breslen's word on confidentiality, Jack filled him in on the situation. "We need to know what aircraft repairs the Russians have completed and what's yet to be finished. Do you have a cost estimate to shoot the pictures?"

"Approximately ten grand."

"Any way you can shoot the photographs any cheaper?"

"Not unless you launch your own satellite."

"Assuming Paulson agrees to pay, how long before we receive images?"

"That's the good news," Breslen said. "Once the satellite is in place, it could be a matter of hours, if necessary."

"We're going to need good pictures, Mr. Breslen. Otherwise we're wasting our time."

Breslen chuckled. "In that clear atmosphere and at that altitude, you'll damn near see footprints of the Russian soldiers who were killed working on that bomber."

CHAPTER 24

Leah glanced at the restaurant entrance for the hundredth time and then zipped the red Patagonia fleece vest up to her neck. For the first time since finding the dwelling and identifying the pictographs, she was having second thoughts, including a disturbing nightmare in which their plane had crashed on the ice and they were trapped inside, burning to death

She had no business placing Garrett, Juan, and Marko in danger. She'd given Jack plenty of headaches over putting his clients at risk. Now she had to stand up and take the heat.

Juan Cortez entered Maria's with his typical grace. He pushed open the door hard enough that it banged against the wall. Juan shrugged sheepishly at the bartender and lumbered to Leah's table.

"What's the latest from Jack?" he whispered.

Leah sighed. "This isn't a James Bond movie. Relax."

He nodded, then a smile brightened his face. "I figured it out."

"Figured out what?"

"How I'm going to sneak out of New Mexico without anyone knowing I've gone to Antarctica." Juan raised his eyebrows and leaned forward. "The semester break begins tomorrow, and school doesn't start again until after the New Year." He waited for Leah to congratulate him, but she just sat in the booth, expressionless.

"That's great," she said firmly. "But you guys aren't going to Antarctica."

Juan's face dropped. "What happened? I thought Jack talked Paulson into funding the expedition."

"It's not a simple trip in search of cliff dwellers. Paulson is paying for the trip because he wants to salvage some kind of World War II bomber." She shrugged. "Jack says that it's dangerous. I guess there are political problems with the Russians."

Juan sank into the booth's soft leather, the disappointment evident in his eyes.

"I thought you'd be relieved."

"I hadn't thought about it being dangerous and all." He looked up suddenly, his face revealing he'd been deeply hurt. "Did Jack think I'd be a hindrance?"

"This wasn't Jack's decision. I'm making this call."

"What?"

"I'm not putting you in danger, not for some wild goose chase."

Leah waved as Garrett and Marko pushed through the doors and made their way over toward the darkened booth.

Garrett looked at Juan and then Leah. "We have trouble?"

"We're not invited," Juan said. "Leah thinks it's dangerous and we'll be in the way."

"I didn't say that."

"The hell you didn't," Juan said defiantly.

Garrett held up his hands in a calming gesture. "Okay, let's start from the beginning here." He turned toward Leah. "What's the situation?"

She described the scenario exactly as Jack had laid it out. "I don't think it's fair to put you guys in this situation."

"What did Jack say about us tagging along?"

"He said you're invited if you agreed to help with the salvage of the airplane."

"So you decided to make the decision for us." Garrett's eyes bored into hers.

"What *should* I do?" She was angry but also close to tears. "Christ, what if something happens to one of you? How the hell will I live with that?"

She balled her fists. "That's what I hate about Jack sometimes. He places his clients into situations instead of having the balls to just say no."

"It's *our* lives, Leah," Garrett said. "If we're not allowed to take risks in search of what's most important to us, well, then we've already died."

"Damn straight," Juan added, winking at Marko. "Isn't that right, partner?"

"Yeah, sure," Marko said with his trademark grin.

Leah wiped away a tear, but the edge of her mouth turned up in the beginnings of a smile. "What do you know, Marko?"

"I know I've got a chance to hang out with a great mountain climber and my best friends," he said. "It can't get any better than that."

"Hear, hear," Juan chimed in.

Garrett gave Leah a solemn nod.

"Okay," she surrendered. "Either we all go—or none of us go."

Garrett stretched his hand out. First Juan, then Marko and finally Leah reached in until they'd all grasped hands.

"We're bound for Antarctica and we're gonna kick ass," Garrett announced. "If we don't come back, then we died doing what we loved."

Leah smiled but inside she wondered whether his words would come back to haunt them.

Chapter 25

Jack watched the Boeing 737 holding short on the taxiway as a single-engine Beechcraft Bonanza crossed the runway threshold and touched down at Westchester County Airport. A moment later, the commercial airliner taxied into position on the runway and "poured the coal to it," as Paulson liked to say.

It was a classic late fall in the Northeast. There were still a few brilliantly colored leaves clinging to the branches of the trees bordering the airport property. The next storm would bring snow, he thought. Not a choking blizzard common at his home in Lake Tahoe, but a soft, almost gentle dusting, as if to give notice to New Englanders it was time to pull out the sleds, but not quite time to use them.

A tap on the shoulder startled Jack. He turned around to find the grinning face of Mac Ridley.

"When I was a kid," Ridley said, "I could sit near an airport and watch those planes take off and land all day long."

"It's still a mystery to me how pilots manage to get airliners down in one piece."

"That's nothing," said Ridley, "compared to slamming a jet fighter onto the deck of a pitching aircraft carrier. Damn if I still don't get a thrill watching carrier operations, even if it's just on TV."

"Al told me he was a Navy fighter pilot and saw combat in the first gulf war, but he didn't say a lot about it."

"That's because it brings back bad memories for both of us."

"You were in the Navy?"

"That's how I met Paulson. He'd fly one of my beautiful hornets back toward the ship all shot up and then crash-land it on the deck. My guys would have to patch it up, and twelve hours later, he'd be back in the air. I was the master chief in charge of maintenance on an air wing." The old mechanic cracked a smile. "I might tease Paulson about augering-in, but he's still one of the best pilots I've ever seen, and fearless. I saw him bring that bird back aboard on a black stormy night that had squadron commanders shaking in their flight suits."

Ridley leaned against the chain-link fence providing security for the active runways and taxiways. "Two had already attempted to come aboard. Each had boltered—missed the wires that catch the airplane. They were both diverted to Saudi. Damn if Paulson didn't call the ball cool as a cucumber and ride straight down to the deck. Caught a 'Three Wire' on his first pass. You'd think he'd climb out of the cockpit and give that greasy deck a big kiss, but no, he was chatting and laughing like he'd just taken a stroll in the park."

"When did you go to work for Paulson Global?"

"I finished up my twenty years and went to work for United Airlines doing maintenance in Chicago. I happened to be at an airplane auction at the EEA show in Oshkosh and saw this familiar figure looking over a vintage North American P-51 Mustang." Ridley's face creased into a grin. "Clearly this guy doesn't know shit about what he's looking at or he'd have seen right away this P-51 had been ground-looped a few too many times. So before he writes a check for damn near a million bucks, I go over and let him know he's about to be suckered. Paulson is about to tell me to mind my own business when I pull up my cap. Damn if his eyes don't grow to the size of a Buick's hubcaps. After I give him and everyone else standing around a rundown on what's wrong with that warbird, he buys the crate for five hundred thousand. Then he tells me I'm hired to get it into shape, along with the three other junk fighters he'd already paid too much for."

"That was the beginning of Paulson's Strategic Air Command?"

"That's right," Ridley said, "and since then it's been all downhill." He laughed and Jack chuckled along with him.

"I don't like this bomber salvage idea," Ridley said in a serious tone. "I want to tell you that right up front. I agreed to take it on because I know how much Paulson wants that aircraft." The mechanic hesitated. "I need to know what the hell is going on beyond the attempted salvage of that ancient piece of shit."

Jack shrugged. "If we have time, we'll climb Thor's Hammer."

"I know a bullshit story when I hear one. I've seen the personnel manifest. You're not bringing along your wife for a second honeymoon." Ridley pointed back toward the hangar. "When I asked Paulson, he about choked himself to death with a coughing spell."

Jack hesitated and then looked at the grizzled mechanic. "Okay, Mac. Here's the deal."

After he finished telling Ridley about the Native American cliff dwelling, the granite stones, and their possible tie-in with Thor's Hammer, the mechanic leaned back against the chain link fence.

"So your trip down to Antarctica searching for Indian artifacts has turned into one hell of a mess and your wife and her buddies are smack in the middle of it."

Jack shrugged. "If our transportation can't get a new motor in place within the next few days, it's moot."

The thump of a helicopter's rotor blades closing in on the hangars turned both men's heads. The blue and gold of the Bell Jet helicopter's fuselage confirmed what they already knew. Paulson was inbound and ready to go over the details of the expedition—what few were in place.

The two men walked toward the helipad and waved as Paulson bounded out of the executive helicopter wearing a gray suit with a soft-sided bag over his shoulder. His tie whipped around his neck in the rotor blast, and he ran in a crouch out from underneath the twirling blades. He greeted them with a wide smile and placed his arms around both their shoulders.

"I hope you guys have good news, because I'm enjoying a real shitty day."

Ridley pushed through the doors and ushered them into the offices of Paulson's Strategic Air Command, where he poured cups of coal-black coffee. The office was simple compared to the suites downtown, but well-appointed for the flying environment. Pictures of vintage fighters and bombers of all types and nationalities decorated the stark white walls, and on a small conference table, several classic aircraft instruments sat inside a bowl sculpted out of aluminum aircraft skin.

"How's it going with the outfit flying us?" Paulson sipped the acid-brew coffee out of a Styrofoam cup.

"You mean InterGalactic?" Jack said dryly. "I spoke with them yesterday. They seemed to be making headway with the engine after I wired them two hundred grand."

"Ouch...." The billionaire feigned surprise. "How much more do we owe these guys?"

"Another two hundred thousand," Jack replied. "And gas...."

Paulson looked at Ridley. "Maybe you should fly out there and give them a hand. I wouldn't mind if someone I trusted had a good look-see at that flying relic."

"That's probably the only smart idea that's going to come of this meeting," Ridley said. "I'll fly one of our charters out tomorrow. Maybe I ought to pack all the tools we're gonna need and take them along. The way you guys are talking, seems we're on a tight schedule."

Paulson's eyes opened wide and he nearly spilled the half-empty cup of coffee. "Damn, that reminds me. I've got to have Karen cancel that network morning show appearance for tomorrow.

"Morning show?"

Paulson nodded. "I told 'em I'd spend five minutes regaling them with the story of our Everest climb." He grinned. "Hell, you can't buy that kind of good publicity; take a look at Trump."

Paulson slipped his smart phone out of a breast pocket. "I'll have to reschedule. Karen can make up some cock and bull story about a business deal closing or something." After speaking into the phone, he slipped it back into his coat. "How are you doing with those satellite photographs?"

Jack reached into his computer bag and pulled out several CDs. "I have them. I didn't want them sent e-mail for obvious reasons. I had the images shipped out from Denver, FedEx."

Paulson leaned forward and studied the disks. "Have you looked at the photos?"

"No, I just got them," said Jack. "I thought we might take a look here."

Jack handed the CD's to Ridley, who leaned over to his desktop computer. The mechanic cleared away several flight manuals, pushed the CD into the access slot, and selected photos listed simply as 001.jpg through 005.jpg.

"How do you know what's what?" Ridley asked, opening the files.

"I told Breslen not to label the pictures in any way, just as an additional precaution."

Ridley selected the first digital photograph and double-clicked on it. The computer chewed on it for a moment, and then a crystal-clear view of a rugged white valley appeared in brilliant resolution on the computer screen. On the right side of the photo was the outline of an aircraft sitting on the ice. On the opposite, a rugged peak jutted straight up. Thor's Hammer was clearly visible in the clear Antarctic atmosphere.

"Damn if that isn't a sight," whispered Paulson.

Ridley squinted as he studied the miniature outline of the B-29 on the ice. "I can't tell shit about the condition of the aircraft from that distance."

Jack leaned forward. "That's 16-meter resolution. There are pictures with a 1-meter resolution on those disks."

Ridley studied the area surrounding the *Las Tortugas*. "That must be the Russian camp, but I can't tell what they have in place with this lousy resolution."

Jack pointed out a thin black line. It looked strangely out of place compared to the stark whiteness of the ice. "Any idea what that might be?"

Ridley grimaced. "I know what that is." He stared at Paulson. "That's a monument to the reckless nature of this salvage."

"It's the Antonov," said Paulson.

"All that remains of an aircraft when it crashes is a thin black ribbon of debris, and the crew enjoys a flaming ride into hell."

"That's not going to happen to us," said Paulson. "We're gonna do this mission by the numbers."

Ridley shook his head sadly. "I'm sure the Russian commander promised the same. Like I said, you got cold weather, low-density take-off conditions at altitude. It's more what will go right rather than what could go wrong."

Ridley pulled the disk out of the computer and slid in another one. The photos on this disk were labeled 010.jpg through 015.jpg. "Okay, let's see what we've got here." Ridley clicked on the jpg labeled 0.10.jpg.

Instead of a white rugged landscape, the familiar shape of a B-29 Super Fortress filled the screen in razor-sharp detail.

A huge grin spread across Ridley's face. "Bingo."

He clicked on the zoom-in button and more of the *Las Tortugas* filled the screen. He pointed toward the engine nodules. "They've got new engines and props on engines one, two, three and four so that means they got the bomber on landing gear and probably have fresh wheels and tires installed."

Ridley scrolled the picture left, then right, examining the aluminum-and-fabric skin of the bomber. "Looks like they got it all patched up, at least the top of it." He scowled. "I can't vouch for what kind of job they did with the fabric—hell, it might just rip right off halfway back to Chile."

A series of metal structures stood in a circle next to the bomber. "They weren't too concerned with comfort. It looks like they converted the cargo containers to living units and probably a makeshift machine shop. They probably heated them with propane heaters while they worked on the bird."

Paulson leaned forward in anticipation. "Can you and your crew get it airworthy?"

"Provided they haven't screwed up the engine installation," Ridley said. "Boy, your Russian friends are gonna be really pissed when we fly this mother right out from under their noses."

Paulson beamed, but before he could reply, his cell phone began vibrating on the top of the cluttered desk. He picked it up. "You were able to cancel my appearance with the proper grace and decorum, I assume."

It had to be Karen.

Paulson rocked back in the chair. "You're kidding. He said that? How'd they get that?" Paulson stood and paced around the office.

Jack felt increasingly uncomfortable as Paulson's tone got angrier.

"What'd you tell them?" Paulson nodded a couple and then grinned from ear to ear. "Whatever I'm paying you, it isn't near enough." He winked at Jack. "Yeah, I know." He laid the phone back on the table.

"Let me guess," Jack said. "We got a problem."

Paulson nodded. "The word is out on our recovery of the *Tortugas*, sort of. It's just a rumor, no hard info, yet anyway. When Karen called, the producer asked if I was canceling due to the rumors that I was salvaging a 'wrecked bomber in Antarctica.' She flatly denied it, bless her heart."

"Nice," said Jack. "So that's that?"

"Not exactly. Karen told 'em I'd be happy to come on air as schedule to discuss the Everest adventure and deny any silly rumors concerning the *Las Tortugas*. She said I'd work out my scheduling conflict and be in-studio early." He gave Jack a sly smile. "Here's the best part: I'm gonna need some cover, so you're coming along."

CHAPTER 26

Glen Janssen rappelled down the rock, his jaws clenched tight. He was experienced, but rock climbing wasn't something one engaged in like tennis on a Sunday-afternoon whim. It had been a while since he'd hung from a rope.

"A couple more feet and I've got you, sir," said the part-time park ranger and expert climber.

"Break out a couple of flashlights," Janssen said.

"Yes, sir, I have them right here." The ranger pulled out two heavy-duty black flashlights and switched them on. "Care to go first, sir?"

"You can just call me Glen," Janssen said with a wink. "Stay close."

After climbing through the narrow passageway, Janssen stood on the edge of the ancient city, his flashlight working back and forth across the structures inside. He shook his head. "I can't believe what I'm seeing."

The ranger nodded in awe. "This is unbelievable. I mean, we're told to be on the lookout for undiscovered villages, but I never thought we'd find one." He pulled out his radio. "Should I make a call and get more people on the ledge?"

"We'll hold off on that for now." Janssen climbed down the first set of boulders leading to the dwelling floor.

He knew what he was looking for: pieces of red granite that had no business in an 800-year-old Native American dwelling, plus a way out of the cavern that led to the top of the mesa.

CHAPTER 27

Ridley looked out the window of the Gulfstream charter as it approached Oakland International Airport. The old mechanic woke Angus Lyon, a crack warbird mechanic he'd brought along to help with the engine replacement on InterGalactic's Caribou.

Lyon was a 40-year-old, hard-drinking Scotsman. When sober, he could take apart a large radial engine and rebuild it blindfolded. More important, he'd been checked out as a flight engineer on the B-29, critical for flying the old bomber out of Antarctica.

Ridley had learned over time that Lyon stayed rock solid and sober as long as he was on an aircraft-retrieval mission. He could work in freezing temperatures in little more than a long-sleeved T-shirt and seemed to get stronger after a series of 20-hour days out in the elements.

Get Angus home, however, and it wouldn't be long before Ridley had to bail him out of jail for drunk and disorderly conduct after getting into a scuffle at the local pub.

Next to Lyon sat Orlando Perez. Ridley had found Perez in Colombia while retrieving a downed P-51 fighter that had crashed on a ferry mission from Brazil to the United States. Paulson had bought the old fighter, which had served in the Brazilian Air Force well into the 1950s. The aircraft had been abandoned, moderately damaged, on a logging road near the top of a mountain. Paulson had sent Ridley down to see if they could get it out of the jungle.

Mac had heard that the 25-year-old Perez was a whiz at metal-forming and had hired him to help repair the aluminum skin on the downed P-51. Ridley watched in amazement as Perez, using basic tools, had formed enough aluminum skin to patch and cover large holes in the wings and fuselage in short order. Once the P-51 had been repaired and flown out of Colombia, Ridley had offered him a job as a metal fabricator and airframe mechanic.

Since the B-29 bomber had made a belly landing with the gear up, there'd be significant aluminum skin damage on the bottom of the fuselage. That was the one part of the B-29 the satellite imagery couldn't show, and although they suspected the bomber's skin had been repaired, Orlando Perez would provide insurance.

Ridley gathered his personal gear from the overhead bins, and they quickly filed off the aircraft and into the general aviation section of the airport. He expected someone dressed casually to meet them; cargo pilots weren't known for their polish.

When he spotted a man wearing a baseball style cap bearing the letters Intergalactic, AC, even Ridley was surprised. This character looked like he'd be more comfortable hanging out at a Hell's Angels motorcycle convention. He stood at least six-foot-three and from the size of his biceps spent most of his leisure time in a gym. Where the sleeves of his black tee-shirt ended, the tattoos began. They stopped only at his wrist, in what could have been a colorful long-sleeved shirt.

Ridley stopped staring at the tattoos long enough to see two large gold-loop earrings hanging from the lobe of each ear. After a moment's hesitation, he walked over and extended a hand. "I'm Mac Ridley."

"Rooster Parker," said the leather-clad biker. "Glad to meet you."

Ridley introduced him to Angus Lyon and Orlando Perez. Rooster shook hands, and then pointed toward the stairway leading away from the gates. "I've got a truck parked in short-term. From here we drive around the airport to the InterGalactic hangar and office."

Ridley nodded. "Can you point it out? I'm gonna have our pilots taxi over so we can unload our gear."

Rooster walked Mac back out of the tarmac and pointed toward a dingy set of hangers on the opposite side of the field.

Ridley walked out and instructed the pilots to taxi over and shut down. They'd unload the gear and then send the Gulfstream back to New York ASAP.

"Are you one of the mechanics?" Ridley asked.

Rooster grinned. "When I have to be…. Mostly I'm the co-owner of InterGalactic with my brother, and the copilot."

"You're kidding," said Lyon in his thick Scottish brogue.

Rooster shook his head and patted the Scotsman on the shoulder. "You know; I get that look just about every time I tell people their lives are going to be in my hands."

"Well, I've learned better than to judge a book by its cover," Ridley said with a grin. "Otherwise we'd all be out of a job."

Rooster laughed so loud that it startled the conservative business travelers walking toward the terminal exit. "We're going to have ourselves some fun on this trip," he said, patting Ridley on the shoulder. "Flying down into that frozen hell and landing on a stretch of ice about as long as a football field…. Your boss must really want that old bomber."

Ridley grimaced. "You have no idea."

CHAPTER 28

Glen Janssen stared out the window of his office. It was just after seven in the morning, little more than 48 hours after he had discovered what was going to be one of the most extraordinary finds in Native American archeology.

It hadn't taken long to find where the artifact hunters had chopped or fallen through the clay cover of the sub-cavern. Once at the bottom, after getting over the shock of seeing the human remains, he'd searched around for blood, in case one of the rogue climbers had been injured in the fall.

What he'd found were boot prints all over the bottom of the cavern, two samples of the mysterious red granite crystal, and a series of pictographs. He snapped several photos of the pictographs and the skeletal remains before pocketing the red stones and making his way back up to the main floor of the cavern. Janssen also found the makeshift alarm system and, thankfully, a hidden exit to the top of the mesa, so he'd avoided more wall-climbing.

Normally, the Park Service would have called the press and the local news stations and report a discovery of this magnitude. After all, this was the kind of find that boosted careers into the stratosphere, a park ranger diligently protecting America's best archeological treasures by doggedly pursuing artifact thieves and then finding their cache before it could be plundered.

Instead, Janssen swore his rangers to secrecy and posted several to guard the dwelling against accidental discovery. Then he had called his boss, the Director of National Parks, who immediately notified the director of the BLM in Washington.

The BLM managed more than 250,000,000 acres of nationally owned property, including national parks. The current director of the BLM, Teresa Simpson, said she wanted to fly out and assess the situation before making the discovery public. A National Guard helicopter crew was flying her directly to Gila from Kirtland Air Force Base.

The thwack of approaching helicopter blades cutting through thin air shook the windows of the park administration building, and Janssen, along with the rest of the rangers, walked over and watched the green Army Reserve Blackhawk flared onto the deserted parking lot with the sound of its rotors shaking the windows in the nearby offices. A crewmember jumped out of the open door, pointed at Janssen, and then waved him toward the helo.

Janssen pasted on his best political smile, zipped his coat up against the cold, held his signature Stetson hat, and ran in a crouch toward the helicopter.

Teresa Simpson, dressed in a standard green one-piece jumpsuit, leaned over and shook his hand. Janssen hopped into the back of the helicopter and put on the headphones handed to him by the helicopter's crew chief.

Janssen knew the BLM director was thought of as a maverick—at least in the current administration. She was African American, the former director of the Texas Department of Natural Resources, and a conservative. Her controversial views, such as being a strong proponent of drilling for oil in a number of protected locations, including the Arctic National Wildlife Refuge, hadn't made her popular among the liberal elite.

Her appointment was thought to be a political move by the president because he wanted to bring a spectrum of management ideas and styles to the administration. Placing a conservative as BLM chief would make friends with business and landowners in the West, something the president, with his Ivy-League, New-England persona, badly needed: a conservative in a position of low visibility and limited power.

Teresa Simpson hadn't stayed low-profile. She publicly clashed with her boss, the Secretary of the Interior, on any number of issues concerning the public use of lands. She had a no-nonsense attitude, and it hadn't surprised Janssen when she jumped on the next available military aircraft headed for New Mexico.

The 44-year-old director's voice came through his headphones. "I want to take a firsthand look before we decide how we're going to handle this."

Teresa was living up to her reputation, Janssen thought. "Did you travel by yourself?"

She nodded then leaned toward him. "Every time I show up with my aides the press knows every move I make, before I make it."

"What did you tell them—before heading out here?"

She grinned. "I told them if I stayed in Washington one more day I was going postal."

Janssen chuckled at her comment. It was politically incorrect, especially for a federal bureaucrat, and put him at ease.

After Janssen provided the director a courtesy air tour of the park, the Huey circled the mesa. Red dust swirled up as the pilot expertly set the helicopter down less than a hundred meters from the face of the cliff and not far from the hidden entrance to the dwelling.

Once the pilot had given the okay, Teresa Simpson bounded out of the helicopter and zipped up a nylon aviator's coat supplied by the crew. She stopped to survey the landscape and drew in several deep breaths. "Nothing like the Southwest to bring a sense of peace to mind and body." She walked over to the pilot's window on the right side of the aircraft and knocked on the plexi. The pilot opened the window, and she shouted over the thump of the slowing rotor blades, "We'll be at least an hour. You guys do what you can to stay warm."

The pilot smiled. "Yes, ma'am. We brought along plenty of hot coffee."

Teresa nodded smartly and turned around, waving with her right hand. "Okay, Glen, let's go."

Ten minutes later, she was studying the makeshift alarm system. "You guys test this for fingerprints?"

"Not yet," Janssen replied. "I didn't want to dismantle anything until someone had cleared us to move forward." Janssen led the BLM chief to the sub-cavern. "I had our rangers rig a line to serve as hand rails." He pointed out a tripod system with a Coleman lantern. "This provides plenty of light for the climb to the bottom of the cavern."

"All the comforts of home," Simpson responded dryly.

Glen lit the lantern, and the cavern glowed in the soft light. "Okay, you can climb down. It's about forty feet to the bottom."

When Teresa got her first glimpse of the city, her eyes opened wide in excitement. "This could be the archeological find of the decade, if not the century." She turned to him. "You're quite sure that our mystery guests were the first to find it?"

Janssen nodded. "If you take a look around, you'll find artifacts including pottery, tools, even clothing like I've never seen before.... Like finding King Tut, with the entire tomb intact.

"So, they took nothing?"

"We know they took samples of the granite stones. From the footprints, they only seemed interested in the remains, the stones, and maybe the pictographs. Nothing else seems obviously missing or damaged."

"So, they left a fortune in artifacts, and only take a few stones with no real value." She chewed on her knuckle. "What do we know about them?"

"At least four, maybe five, persons were involved. According to Jim Dixon, the owner of the rock store, they didn't offer him any artifacts for sale or hint they had any in their possession. They only wanted information on the red-colored granite crystal they claimed to have found while hiking in the high desert."

She nodded, but her expression remained serious. "Nothing more?"

"We believe we have a first name for one of them."

"What's his name?"

Janssen grinned. "It was a she, and the name is Leah."

Teresa blinked and stared at the pictographs for a moment. "If this Leah is Dr. Leah Andrews, she's one of our former employees, probably the best archeologist we ever fired."

Now it was Janssen's turn to blink. "Where is she now?"

"She had a run-in with the—" Teresa coughed into her hand. "Excuse me, I mean the Secretary of the Interior. Soon after, she was fired, despite my best efforts to keep her." Teresa shook her head. "She's hardheaded and tough. That's why I liked her; she reminded me of me."

Janssen smiled.

"This has Leah Andrews's signature all over it. She's a maverick and damned good at finding dwellings in places we've either walked over a thousand times or never believed were worth the effort."

Janssen leaned against one of the walls. "I'd think if someone was in that kind of trouble, they'd stay away from national parks and monuments. That's like putting a gun to your head and daring someone to pull the trigger."

"You don't know Leah Andrews."

"What's our next move?"

Teresa Simpson grimaced. "As much as it pains me, I've got to notify the Secretary. Beyond that, I can only hope I find Leah before he does."

Chapter 29

It was just before eight o'clock in the morning, and Secretary of the Interior Wick Emerson flipped through the morning news programs with a television remote. He sipped a Starbucks tall cafe latte from the recycled white paper cup with the familiar logo as he watched for political news—something he, like most politicians, did every morning.

After his near political death six months before over a mistake concerning two pieces of Native American pottery, he'd learned how fast one can get burned in Washington. He'd almost gotten past that issue, and now it had resurfaced again in spades. A report sat on his desk detailing the amazing discovery of an entire city hidden in a cavern within the national park system in southern New Mexico.

Since this would most certainly be national news, the story that nearly killed his career would certainly resurface, and in Washington, a bad story with legs could be damaging to his boss, the President. And fatal to the Secretary himself.

Compounding the issue immeasurably were suspicions that the person who'd discovered the city in the cavern was Dr. Leah Andrews, the government-employed archeologist turned pain-in-the-ass he'd summarily dismissed after the political firestorm had died down.

After she'd been caught trespassing on Federal lands, twice, he'd placed a bounty on her head: a lifetime ban from government employment and certain federal prosecution if she were caught nosing around federal lands in search of Native American sites.

Now it appeared Dr. Andrews had stumbled across a major archeological find and perhaps created an elaborate hoax designed to embarrass him along with the entire Department of the Interior.

He walked over and picked up the sample of feldspar-rich granite that Teresa Simpson had sent him from her visit to the site. The scientists who had examined the stones seemed sure it had originated in Antarctica, a conclusion the Secretary didn't quibble with, although he scoffed at the idea that a few red stones had been transported by Native Americans to cliff dwellings centuries ago.

The Secretary reached down and lifted photographs of the getaway vehicle off his desk. They'd been taken by park rangers while chasing the suspected artifact hunters out of the park. If they could positively identify the face, then by putting the screws to this person, perhaps Emerson could nail her permanently this time.

At that thought, a ghost of a smile crossed his face. He turned his attention back to the television.

Chapter 30

Jack and Paulson sat side-by-side, waiting to go live on the highest-rated network morning show in the world. Bonnie Glass, the 33-year-old co-anchor, would host the interview. She was petite, reserved, and known for lulling her victims into a false sense of security with friendly pre-show banter.

"Ten-seconds," said the director as Bonnie glanced down at her notes. When the director pointed at her, she smiled into the camera.

"I'm here with well-known New York billionaire Alan Paulson and expert mountain climber and professional adventurer Jack Hobson. They recently completed an extremely dangerous ascent of Mt. Everest." She leaned forward and engaged them with a curious but practiced expression. "What in the world makes you want to climb a mountain that," she looked at her notes, "kills one in every six climbers?"

"Because it's there, Bonnie," Paulson said. "It's as simple as that. A personal test, you could call it."

"I understand it was a grueling climb through very dangerous conditions," she said, addressing Jack. "Did you ever think Mr. Paulson might not make it?"

Jack felt her piercing eyes probing his body language and facial movements, looking for weakness. He straightened up in the chair and smiled. "Al Paulson is very determined and incredibly strong-willed. I never had any doubts he'd make the summit. It's the descent that tests the best of us."

"Apparently a former client of yours, Alex Stein, was not so lucky. Coincidentally, you were on Mt. Everest the same time he died attempting to summit the mountain. Did you see Alex Stein, and was he in trouble?"

Jack squirmed uncomfortably in the chair. "We did see Alex Stein and I recommended he turn around and return to base camp—but he was determined to continue."

"We're responsible for our own lives on a mountain like Everest," Paulson cut in. "Alex knew the risks, like every world-class climber does. He was a good man. A great man, really, and we all miss him a great deal."

Bonnie turned her attention back to Jack. "Jack you are well known to our audiences not only for guiding Alan Paulson up Mt. Everest, but also for a host of other extreme adventures." She glanced again at her notes. "I understand you're in the planning process of another trip to Mt. Everest for our show."

Jack nodded. "Much depends upon the weather and permits, but it should be quite a live broadcast for your audience."

She turned her attention back to the billionaire. "What is your next great adventure, Mr. Paulson?"

Paulson leaned back in the chair and smiled. "I think I'm done risking my neck—at least for a while."

"Oh?" Bonnie feigned surprise.

Oh is right, thought Jack. Oh shit.

"I understand you're traveling to the continent of Antarctica to repair and possibly even fly a World War II-era B-29 bomber off the ice." Bonnie smiled sweetly. "Is that true?"

CHAPTER 31

There was a rapid knock on Secretary Emerson's door. The Secretary glanced up from a stack of paperwork as the door glided open.

"Are you watching the Morning Show, sir?"

Wick Emerson looked at the flat screen in his office, now hosting a 24-hour news network.

"What have I missed?"

"That rich guy, Alan Paulson, he's planning some kind of expedition to the interior of Antarctica."

Emerson reached for his television remote and switched channels. "Have we authorized him to be in Antarctica?"

"Not that I remember, sir."

He instantly recognized the face of the host: Ms. Bonnie Glass. The White House communication director had nicknamed her the Coifed Crocodile after she'd nailed him more than once with a disarming smile and a trunkful of unnamed sources.

"I understand," Glass said as Emerson turned up the sound, "you're traveling to the continent of Antarctica to repair and possibly even fly a World War II-era B-29 bomber off the ice. Is that true?"

Emerson blinked in surprise, and then gestured toward his assistant. "Make sure we have a record of this."

"According to our reports," Glass continued, "a Russian transport aircraft crashed near the bomber during a salvage attempt." Like an Academy Award-winning actress, Bonnie Glass changed her expression to one of serious concern. "In light of the President's restrictions on Antarctica and the fact that this bomber lies in territory claimed by the former Soviet Union, doesn't this seem like a risky venture?"

Emerson bounced his pen off the top of his desk, watching it fly into the wall from the force. This was a direct slap in the face of his boss's new unilateral environmental policy on Antarctica.

"The story of the *Tortugas* is well known to aviation enthusiasts," replied Paulson, his expression conceding nothing to the crocodile. With an expression every bit as practiced and perfect as the television anchor's, Paulson continued, "As you know, I have experience in removing World War II aircraft out of rugged environments." Paulson hesitated. "I'm not sure after spending fifty years in that harsh a climate, this aircraft could be salvaged, or even should be."

Bonnie reviewed her notes. "According to certain sources, the Chilean government has given you permission to attempt the resurrection of the *Las Tortugas*, to keep one of the Chilean people's most revered treasures out of the hands of those who might steal the aircraft for profit."

Jack almost slid out of his chair at that. They'd been ambushed. The producer, who'd told Karen he didn't have any hard information, clearly knew a lot more than he'd let on. Denying it would be nearly impossible, given the specific details the network had.

Paulson chuckled and remained the picture of cool. "Your rumor mill is running overtime as usual. I'm sure the Chileans, should they want to lay claim on the *Tortugas*, have the resources to handle it." He smiled at Bonnie Glass. "If I should be asked to assist, Bonnie, you'll be the first to know."

Chapter 32

Emerson watched the morning show go to commercial. He sat on top of his desk and signaled his aides. "See if you can get me into to see the President this afternoon."

"Sir, I have the Director of the BLM on the telephone from New Mexico. She wants to speak with you."

Emerson shook his head. "Tell her I'm busy. Whatever it is, it can wait until I learn about this Paulson/Antarctica development."

"She says to tell you it's directly related to the Antarctica report."

Wick Emerson felt the first tinges of anger working up into his chest. "Remind Ms. Simpson her job is management of domestic lands. This issue will be dealt with at a higher pay grade."

The aide holding the telephone flushed as he listened to Teresa's response. "She says it has to do with a Dr. Leah Andrews and, excuse me, sir, these are her words—she said to, 'Tell the prick to pick up the telephone.'"

Emerson stopped in his tracks and his face turned crimson. "Put her through." He stomped over to his phone and picked it up, taking a deep breath as he did.

"Did you happen to catch any of the morning show?"

"Regarding this bomber retrieval in Antarctica?" he asked.

"The climbing guide who took Alan Paulson up Mt. Everest is married to Dr. Leah Andrews."

"So he made a poor choice in a life partner? I don't understand what that has to do with an apparent B-29 retrieval in Antarc—"

The telephone dropped as Emerson searched his desktop for the photographs of the mystery pickup truck. When he found the photo with the face looking out the dusty rear window, the blood drained from his face. It wasn't clear enough to use in a court of law, but Emerson had little doubt whose face stared out through the rear window. He slowly reached for the telephone, bringing it up to his ear.

"I told you Leah was going to find a way to get to Antarctica," Teresa said. "She made a connection between those granite crystals found in the dwelling and something in Antarctica. Her husband and his buddy the billionaire are funding her trip to the frozen continent of international peace."

Emerson relaxed. "I'm not sure I see the problem. There's not a chance Mr. Paulson will be allowed to pursue this project, assuming he has a real plan and we have at least circumstantial evidence Dr. Andrews and/or her spouse were involved in committing a federal crime: raiding Native American sites within a protected national monument."

"I can tell you right now, if Leah Andrews gets to Antarctica and finds evidence that Native Americans were slogging around in snow and ice, you won't be able to touch her."

"I'll have her arrested at once—that's what I'll do. Maybe as part of a plea bargain, she'll give up the information she's found."

"I doubt you could torture Leah Andrews and get a plea bargain out of her. Do you mind if I make a suggestion?"

"If you must," he said.

"Let me find her first. I'll tell her we'll forget about prosecuting her or her husband if she agrees to share information." Teresa paused. "If she provides full cooperation, we will also consider putting her back on the BLM payroll—as long as she agrees to behave."

"Absolutely not. I don't care about conspiracy theories involving Indians in Antarctica. It'll be a cold day in hell before I put that criminal back on my payroll."

"Think about it," Teresa said coolly. "She's going to get credit for making the most significant find in American archeology in well over a hundred years—forgetting about any possible Antarctica connection. You can't fight her."

CHAPTER 33

Bonnie Glass leaned back in her chair, gloating. "Best of luck to you guys, and good luck on your next adventure."

"Commercial," said the director.

One of the assistants led Jack and Paulson to the locked door leading out of the studio and into the well-furnished lobby.

"I should have known it would leak through the Chilean government," said Paulson, still seemingly unflappable. He grinned and poked Jack in the ribs. "How about that for keeping my cool under fire?"

Jack shook his head, still speechless.

As they boarded the waiting limousine, the billionaire called Karen Miller.

"I need you to get Ridley on a conference call from California." He nodded. "Yes, you can find him at InterGalactic. I want his butt on the telephone in one hour." He clicked off and looked at Jack. "If we're going to Antarctica, we're doing it in the next twenty-four hours."

Chapter 34

Stanton Fischer, the President's National Security Advisor, sat in his office across the street from the White House in the old Executive Office Building, reading the daily two-page 'threat' briefing.

Fischer was smoking as usual. It was against regulations in a federal office building, but it was one of the few pleasures he enjoyed, and no one had the guts to ask him to stop as long as he smoked out of public view. As he took another long drag on the cigarette, he flipped impatiently through the report.

He received the threat brief every morning, seven days a week. It outlined destabilizing political situations developing around the world.

Not that Stan Fischer had the patience to examine the reports in detail. His real talent was raising money for political campaigns. He'd been credited with bringing the President's campaign back from the brink of death by doggedly pursing large-money donors and organizations and then schmoozing them with every possible incentive, political or otherwise.

A plum position on the National Security Council had been his payoff, even though he was hardly qualified for the job. Before working on the president's campaign, he'd spent the previous five years teaching political science and international politics at Harvard University, the home state of the former Senator and now president of the United States.

At thirty-one, he was prematurely gray and rail thin. He was known as a bit of a recluse in the White House, but the truth was, most of the

other staffers avoided him. The President's other top advisers, especially the career military officers assigned to the NSC, kept him at arm's
length.

The military staffers thought of him as a snot-nosed liberal snoop, but
that didn't bother Fischer. After all, he had access. And in Washington, access translated to power; even the Chairman of the Joint Chiefs knew and
respected that.

Slow international news day, thought Fischer as he read through the
briefing, stopping only to highlight unfamiliar material with a yellow high-
lighter. He sat up when he found Alan Paulson's name appearing in the
report.

*Our information suggests that Russia and Chile are in conflict over a World War II
B-29 claimed by the Chilean government. This aircraft sits within a small region of the
Antarctic Ellsworth Range, claimed at one time by the former Soviet Union.*

*Mr. Alan Paulson, the CEO of Paulson Global, may serve to sharpen the conflict,
since our information suggests the Chilean government will use Mr. Paulson and his
resources to salvage the aircraft.*

"That asshole," Fisher muttered. He had met Paulson once. It was at a
summer conference of CEOs and industry leaders held in Aspen, Colorado.
Fischer had been there to make a speech and raise money for the President's
election campaign. It hadn't been a friendly crowd, given the conservative
politics of most of the participants. After his speech, he'd asked for questions and comments. Paulson had stood.

"Mr. Paulson, you have a question?"

"First I have a comment," Paulson had said. "The President suggested
he would propose new legislation requiring corporations to comply with
U.S. environmental standards no matter where they operated in the world.
This new legislation is sure to derail the free-trade agreements with coun-
tries like Mexico, where poverty and illegal emigration will escalate dramatically if American plants and factories are forced to shut down." Paulson
shrugged. "You guys have a rope around our neck. There's no way we can
compete with governments overseas when we're being held to different
standards than foreign government themselves."

Mild applause had broken out from within the ranks of the attending CEOs. Fischer struggled with the topic through three more tough questions and then gave up. The money-raising effort had been a bust. In Fischer's mind, Paulson had personally been responsible for the loss of several million dollars.

Fischer picked up the telephone. "Get me a meeting with the President," he told the chief of staff. "I think we just found an opportunity to dish out a little payback to Alan Paulson."

CHAPTER 35

Leah screamed in pain as she strained to keep the solid steel bar from crushing her larynx. She was pushing with all her might, yet the bar continued to close in on her throat.

"Come on, Leah," said the male voice from directly above her. "I'm just about to let this thing drop down and cut you in half. Give it up."

She said through a tightly clenched jaw. "I can handle anything you can dish out."

He raised his hands up off the bar. "Okay, then, show me what you've got."

"Awwww!" Leah's eyes opened wide and she showed teeth. Her arms shook and the bar wobbled, but slowly reversed direction and headed up and away from her neck. With one final scream, Leah forced the bar until her elbows locked straight.

"Nice work," said the muscular young personal trainer and gym owner. "That's a new max weight on the bench press."

"No thanks to you wanting to jump in and save me prematurely." Leah wiped sweat from her face with a towel. There were probably a hundred things more important to do while waiting for Jack to get the Antarctic trip set up, but without her workout she became even more edgy than normal. Against her better judgment, she'd decided to get a one-hour weight-training session in with her personal trainer, figuring it might be her last for some time to come.

The trainer waved his hands in front of her face. "Hello? Are we concentrating?"

"Sorry...got a lot on my mind." She glanced at her watch. They were only halfway through the hour-long workout. Something was up...she felt it. "I'm going to call it quits. I've got a schedule like you can't believe."

"Are you sure?"

She nodded while pulling off the workout gloves. "You mind doing me a big favor?"

He shrugged. "You name it."

"If anyone happens to come in looking for me or wants certain kinds of information...."

His eyes narrowed. "Are you in some kind of trouble?"

She put on a grin. "No more than usual."

The gym owner nodded and returned the smile. She leaned up and kissed him on the cheek. "Thanks a million. I owe you."

Leah pushed through the doors into the crisp air and jogged toward her jeep. She yanked open the soft-sided door, hopped in, and stared the dashboard for a moment. She picked up the mobile phone to see if she'd missed any calls from Jack.

"Our cover was blown on the Morning Show," his voicemail said. "Paulson did an Oscar Award-winning performance denying the rumors, but work of the salvage is out."

"I knew something was up," Leah whispered to herself.

"It wasn't Paulson's fault," Jack's message continued, "if that's what you're thinking. The Chileans couldn't keep quiet, so we're moving up the schedule, drastically. That means we're leaving within twenty-four hours. Drop everything, contact your crew and alert them we'll pick everyone up in Paulson's Gulfstream on short notice. I'm not sure what airport. I'll call when we figure it out. Fortunately, the gear I ordered was available to be shipped FedEx. It's going direct to the Oakland Airport. I've gotten Antarctic clothing in all sizes, so you'll need minimal gear."

Leah laid the mobile phone down in her lap. "I'll buy my own long underwear," she muttered. "No one-size-fits-all unisex junk for me."

Ten minutes later, she was running through the local outdoor store, filling a basket with piles of long underwear and other personal items she knew Jack would forget to buy. Against the far wall, mountaineering boots sat in rows on sturdy-looking shelving.

"Do I trust Jack to get me the right size?" Leah murmured. "No, I do not." Just as she pulled down a heavy-duty pair of plastic-skinned climbing boots, her mobile phone rang.

"Leah? It's Rocky."

Her trainer. "Uh-oh…. What's up?"

"I just had a visitor. The guy identified himself as a federal agent."

Leah's knees weakened and she felt sick to her stomach. "Was he looking for me?"

"He wanted to know if I'd seen you in the gym recently. You missed him by twenty minutes."

Leah held her breath. "What'd you tell him?"

"I told him you hadn't been in recently. I thought you had some kind of meeting in El Paso."

"El Paso?"

"It was the first thing that came to mind."

She sighed. "Thanks again, Rock. You're a lifesaver."

Leah clicked off the telephone and slumped on a wooden bench.

How did they found out? Had they identified Jack through the rangers' photograph?

She walked toward the cash register and paid for the thermal clothing—in cash. Once through the doors of the store, she ran to the jeep and burned out of the parking lot. The sooner she got out into the wide-open New Mexico desert, the better.

CHAPTER 36

"**O**kay, Mr. Fischer," said the secretary. He pointed toward the white-painted doors leading into the Oval Office. "Go on in."

The President stood near the middle of the Oval Office, talking quietly to his short, balding Chief of Staff.

Fischer walked toward two couches facing each other. A glass coffee table sat between the two couches, with a crystal flower vase filled with fresh flowers in the center.

"Sit," said the President. He nodded toward his Chief of Staff, who sat on a couch on the opposite side of the table.

"The Russian President called me this morning concerning this B-29 issue in Antarctica, if you can believe that."

Fischer's face registered surprise at the uncharacteristic language. "I'd think he'd have more important matters on his plate with oil prices falling through the floor. Let me guess. He's planning to fly it off the ice himself, shirtless of course."

The President shook his head wearily. "When he quit screaming, I told him that territorial claims within the Antarctic continent had no basis in international law. Then he went ballistic. You'd have thought I'd laid claim to Moscow the way he went off." The President stood, and then walked over behind his desk. "We've got enough problems with the Chinese pressing their naval strength in the South China Sea, not to mention off Taiwan. I need Beijing to believe that if they made a move, they'd face us in the Straits and have Russians running up their backside."

The President reached for a sheet of paper covered with typed paragraphs and handwritten notes in the margins. "I informed him they could, and should, remove the aircraft from Antarctica, with our support if necessary."

The Chief of Staff glanced up. "What about the Chilean claims on the aircraft?"

"How many Chilean ships will help us face down the Chinese if it comes to that?"

The Chief of Staff coughed into his hand and nodded his understanding.

"Then there's the issue of Alan Paulson," the President said. "Stan has had dealings with Paulson. Politically, he's not a benefit to us, so we have more latitude than we might otherwise."

Fischer handed out a sheet prepared with a number of bullet-pointed sentences. "This expedition requires a large cargo-carrying aircraft able to land on snow and ice," he said. "We've spent the last twenty-four hours contacting every American and international air freight carrier with lift capability and experience to handle Paulson's team. All of them assured us they will not participate in the project, excepting several small carriers, which didn't respond. We looked into those, and they all checked out clean except one." Fischer thumbed through his notes. "InterGalactic Air, which is employed by Canadian and American oil companies for work above the Arctic Circle. After some additional investigation, we found that InterGalactic very recently obtained funding for serious mechanical problems with their one aircraft. We also received information that equipment and supplies, including clothing with potential to be used in an Arctic environment, was delivered to their hangar address at Oakland International Airport, California."

"What's our best course of action?" asked the President.

Fischer looked at the President and then the Chief of Staff. "We can send over an FAA inspection crew and federal agents to inspect the aircraft and hangars. If they're involved with Paulson, we'll keep 'em on the ground."

The President stood, signaling the end of the meeting. "Shut Paulson down tight. Whatever it takes."

CHAPTER 37

Ridley crouched and studied the Caribou's flat tire. "Christ, the timing couldn't be worse."

Chase Parker nodded. "How long will it take to fix this, Rooster?"

Rooster looked briefly at his watch and then back at his brother. "Hour, maybe more.... We've got two spare tire setups, but hell if I know where they are in all this gear. I'm pretty sure we've got one handy in the hangar though."

"Paulson wants us airborne and out of here," Ridley said. "Put in layman's terms: We need to get the F off the tarmac!"

Chase Parker was the exact opposite of his brother. Tall and thin, he wore clean Levi jeans and a blue-collared shirt. No tattoos or earrings decorated his body. "You guys get this fixed," he said. "I'm gonna get the paperwork done and grab our gas cash."

Chase jogged back toward InterGalactic's hangar offices while Ridley, Angus Lyon, and Orlando Perez jacked the airplane off the ground and removed the outboard tire and wheel assembly from the set of main landing gear.

Less than an hour later, the wheel was fully installed. Rooster walked over to the jack and looked up at Ridley. "Are you ready to drop her down, Mac?"

"I want to check the air pressure." Ridley knelt down and stuck an air gauge on the wheel stem. "How long has this thing been sitting around?"

Rooster shook his head. "Ah...awhile."

"It's got about a half the pressure necessary to operate the Caribou at this weight. Do you have a compressor?"

"Same with the wheel and tires. Buried in here somewhere. Got one back in the hangar somewhere too, though," Rooster said.

Five minutes later Rooster jogged back toward the aircraft, shaking his head in frustration. "No compressor...." He pulled a handheld radio out of his vest pocket. "Chase. You copy?"

"What's up?"

"You have any idea where we put the hangar air compressor?"

"Didn't we lend that out to someone who wanted to do some painting?"

Rooster's face darkened. "Shit, that's right. I loaned it to a hydraulics mechanic because he wanted to paint his damn car."

"Hold on a second. I got a call coming in," Chase said.

Ridley gave the mechanic a look. "First-class outfit you guys run here."

"Rooster?" said Chase Parker over the radio.

"Still here...."

"Remember those calls we got warning us not to take any unauthorized charters to Antarctica?"

Rooster grinned and then keyed the handheld. "The ones we didn't return?"

"Guess the FAA took offense, because our buddy at airport security just called to give me a heads-up. They've got two carloads of guys identifying themselves as Federal Agents heading up to the gate. You'd better find a way to get that tire filled. I'm grabbing the cash and all the paperwork."

Rooster gave Ridley a pleading look. "You guys are used to working out in the boonies. Got any ideas?"

Angus Lyon pointed toward the hangar and said, "Didn't I see a barbecue inside the hangar?"

Rooster nodded. "We throw burgers on every now and then but I doubt those guys are going to stop for lunch."

Lyon looked to Ridley. "Worth a shot—don't ya think, Mac?"

Chapter 38

Jack and Paulson sat on opposite sides of the conference table, each focused on separate telephone conversations. Jack confirmed all the Antarctica equipment he ordered had arrived at InterGalactic's hangars; Paulson was closing the Rockingham Appliance deal he'd been nurturing before leaving for Antarctica.

On the table sat a detailed map of the Antarctic continent, drawn with markings and lines indicating directions and distances between southern Chile, the Antarctica Peninsula, where they would receive refueling, and Thor's Hammer, deep inside the continent.

Karen suddenly poked her head into the office. "Mac on the phone; he says Code Red."

Jack looked at Paulson who shrugged and then walked over to his desk. "What's wrong?"

"We've got big problems," Ridley said over the speaker. "Federal agents are running up our ass. Chase Parker says we have maybe five minutes before they're storming the gates."

"Get the Caribou airborne and meet us at Punta."

"Copy that. Gotta go," Ridley said. "Barbecue's here."

"What?" Paulson looked at Jack and blinked.

"See you in Chile, Al." With that, the telephone clicked with a cut connection.

Paulson put his hands on the table and studied the map of Antarctica for a moment. He looked at his watch. "You were telling me about this old Army Air Field out in the middle of the New Mexico desert. Call Leah and tell her to be there by midnight, tonight."

CHAPTER 39

Chase Parker zipped a blue gym bag containing nearly $20,000 in cash. He picked up a square, leather, pilot-style briefcase and sprinted out the rear door toward the gate leading through the series of hangars to the tie-down area. Rooster and Perez were in the process of horsing the large portable barbecue toward the Caribou.

"Jesus, what are you guys doing?" Chase said. "We've got less than five minutes before the feds are crawling all over this place."

Angus Lyon spun the valve shut on the standard five-gallon propane tank and then unhooked the clamps that held it in place. He removed the propane tank from underneath the barbecue and hefted it. "Should do the trick," he said after rolling the propane tank back and forth.

Lyon picked up the tank and carried it to the flattened tire. Ridley quickly disassembled an ordinary hand air pump that Rooster had found. He took the fill hose off and saved the strong steel clamp, then severed the propane hose where it entered the bottom of the grill. Using a steel hose mate, Ridley threaded the rubber hoses together and tightened the clamp. "Clip this on to the stem, Rooster."

"Got it," Rooster said. "What crazy bastard ever showed you guys you how to fill a tire with propane?"

"Little trick we learned bringing an aircraft out of the Congo."

"I suggest you and your brother conduct landings in an extremely gentle manner," Lyon added with a grin.

Ridley looked at Perez and said, "Take the grill and see if you can't jam the door leading out of the hangar."

"I'm getting the engines cranked up," Chase said. He bolted for the loading ramp and scrambled inside the aircraft. A moment later, he slid the side cockpit window open and stuck his head part way out. "Clear!"

Lyon and Rooster ran up the ramp while Mac waited for Perez. Once Perez had jammed the barbecue against the door, he sprinted for the loading ramp while Ridley caught the lip of the ramp with his foot, and tumbled into the back of the aircraft, bumping his head into one of the steel cargo boxes.

"We've got company!" shouted Rooster from the copilot's seat.

Several men dressed in suits and several more uniformed officers were looking out of the large hangar window facing out on the airport tarmac. When they saw the propellers spinning on the Caribou, they rushed from the windows and pushed against the door. It opened several inches and then smacked into the backside of the oversized barbecue.

Chase pushed the radio transmit button and spoke into his microphone. "They haven't notified the tower," he said. "Probably thought they had us in the bag." Chase pushed the throttles up a little more and turned the Caribou sharply to the right, chafing the left tire.

"You might want to take it a little easier on the turns," Rooster said to his brother. "If that tire gets hot, we're gonna make a big ol' hole in the runway."

Chase spoke into the microphone one more time and then goosed the throttles forward, driving the Caribou onto the active runway. "We're out of here!"

Rooster jammed both throttles to the firewall, and the Caribou roared down the runway, lifted off and immediately made a left turn, taking them in a southwesterly direction.

"Ready or not, Antarctica, here we come," Rooster said. He turned and winked at Ridley, who, despite the lunacy of it all, couldn't help but wink back.

CHAPTER 40

eah looked at her watch and shivered. It was past one o'clock in the morning, nearly an hour later than Jack said he'd arrive in Paulson's private jet. She stood with Garrett outside the familiar aluminum-and-steel Quonset hut, looking toward the star-filled eastern sky. Old Luke Derringer had trapped Juan and Marko inside, giving them the same twisted history lesson she'd heard days before.

"Where the hell are they?" Leah asked impatiently.

Garrett leaned against the wall of the Quonset hut, his eyes casually scanning the sky. "Paulson runs a huge company. I imagine he had to get a few things in order before disappearing."

"What about the airplane that's taking us to Antarctica?"

"My guess is they got the same call we did and are hustling to get off the ground with all the gear."

Leah shook her head. "What kind of plane was that again? A deer, antelope, some kind of animal man has nearly hunted to extinction?"

"A DE Havilland Caribou," Garrett said with a chuckle. "Probably a relic left over from the Vietnam war. A prop-driven Caribou is awful slow. It's going to take those guys three or four days to find their way to southern Chile—wouldn't surprise me if we have to wait for them."

Suddenly the runway lights popped on.

"What's happening?" Leah asked.

"It's Paulson." Garrett turned toward the door of the hut. "We better gather our gear. I've got a notion he won't want to stick around long."

Luke hobbled through the door behind Juan and Marko and grabbed Garrett by the shoulder. "Good luck, son, with whatever you find." The look of surprise on Garrett's face caused the old man's face to twist up in an ancient grin. "You be careful and take care of those city slickers."

Garrett opened his mouth to speak, but Luke cut him off. "I'm going to tow that beat-up Cessna of yours into the hangar the minute you get that high-priced luxury yacht off my tarmac."

"I appreciate it, Luke."

"Just make sure you get back here to pick it up."

The combination door and boarding ladder on the Gulfstream 550 dropped down after the jet rolled to a stop near the Quonset. "Paulson's Global Express, Flight 201, bound for Antarctica, now ready for boarding," Jack called through the open door.

Paulson glanced over Jack's shoulder. "Leah Andrews! What a pleasant surprise."

"Wish I could say the same, Al," she quipped but let a smile slip.

Garrett reached out and shook hands with the billionaire. "We're sure glad you could help us out, Mr. Paulson."

"The only people who call me Mr. Paulson are those who owe me money. My name is Al." The billionaire reached over and patted Garrett on the back, then introduced himself to Marko and Juan. "Get your bags aboard. I want to be gear-up in less than ten minutes."

Once the nose of the plane was lined up with the centerline of the runway, Paulson pushed the throttles forward and the twin Rolls Royce BR 710 engines delivered more than thirty-thousand pounds of thrust, powering the jet into the night sky. He piloted the Gulfstream in a southerly direction and continued to climb through the low clouds on his way to an altitude of nearly 40,000 feet.

"How are things going back there?" Paulson asked after reaching cruising altitude.

"No problem so far," Jack said while climbing into the cramped cockpit. "Where do we go from here?"

"We're going to refuel in Mexico City and then fly direct to Punta Arenas, Chile."

Leah leaned over Jack's shoulder. "I thought you needed two pilots to fly a jet like this?"

"Legally, you do," Paulson said. "This thing is so damn computerized, though, I thought I'd just handle it myself."

"Is that safe?"

Paulson glanced back at her. "Are you looking a gift horse in the mouth? Besides, what self-respecting pilot did you think you were gonna get to join this boondoggle?"

Leah tried to suppress as grin, but couldn't. "Okay," she said. "We're short a pilot and I don't see any flight attendants. You got any food on this plane?"

"We're fully stocked with all kinds of prepackaged delicacies." Paulson pointed toward the small galley. "Help yourselves."

"Mind if I sit up here for a while?" Jack asked.

Paulson nodded. "Best seat in the house."

Jack laid his head back on the high-backed seat and let the soft roar of the jet engines running at cruise lull him to sleep.

CHAPTER 41

Jack reluctantly opened his eyes and looked out through the window at the Mexican landscape below as Marko pointed toward a steep mountain jutting up from the desert floor.

"Volcano in the distance?" he asked.

Standing nearly 17,800 feet high and located one hundred miles from Mexico City, the glacier-capped volcano stood out like a gleaming jewel.

"Popocatepetl," Jack replied. "It is the fifth-highest peak in North America."

"You ever climbed it?"

Jack shaded his eyes. "Popo is a great place to get some high-altitude glacier practice when it's not erupting. Unfortunately, it's been closed to climbing for years because of eruptions. Orizaba, another volcano, is a great climb though."

"Ever gonna climb her again? I'd love to try a volcano."

Jack smiled. "It's a deal, Marko. Next time I climb Orizaba, you're on the team."

Paulson banked the Gulfstream onto final approach and prepared for landing. With a bump, the wheels touched down, and the aircraft turned off the taxiway, toward a private aviation terminal.

"All right, explorers," he said. "You can get off the plane and enter the General Aviation terminal. Then we'll cool our heels here for ten hours, maybe a little more, let the Caribou fly further south, and get some needed sleep." Paulson glanced around like a cautious parent. "Don't get lost. And don't get into any trouble."

Leah stepped down the Gulfstream boarding steps and stood briefly on the tarmac, wrinkling her nose at the brown haze on the horizon. "What should we do now?"

"Probably wouldn't hurt to brush up on your Russian," Jack said as shouldered the bag containing his laptop computer and satellite telephone.

"I'm not sure I should ask why...."

"Rumor has it that's all they speak inside the Siberian gulags."

CHAPTER 42

The President paced the Oval Office and pointed his finger at Fischer. "So our out-of-control, pain-in-the-ass, loose cannon has flown the coop. What do you propose to do next?"

"If the Chileans are working with Paulson," Fischer continued, "we won't get any help from them. The only suggestion I can make, Mr. President, would be some kind of military interdiction before they get to the continent."

"Christ, we can't shoot them down," the President said in disbelief. "For better or worse, they *are* American citizens." He glanced at his watch. "I have a luncheon scheduled with the Secretary of State in one hour." He looked up and glared at Fischer. "You wanted this job—now give me some options."

CHAPTER 43

Paulson piloted the Gulfstream into southern Chile with the light of early dawn casting a pink-and-orange glow over the Patagonian range. As the jet descended through 10,000 feet, the rocky spires of the Torres de Paine thrust up through broken cloud cover, and the Straits of Magellan spread out toward the Southern Ocean in lazy fingers.

An exhausted Jack Hobson stared out through the cockpit windows at the city of Punta Arenas. Red-and-blue tile roofs covering tin-sided homes flowed in a mosaic toward the sea. PA was a beautiful city, full of the life and spirit of Patagonia. The friendly Chilean people had always made him and his clients feel at home in this magnificently picturesque country.

The views of the city disappeared in the distance as Paulson maneuvered the Gulfstream on final approach into the international airport. He touched down on the tarmac at just after six in the morning, local time, and expertly maneuvered the private jet off the runway toward a remote part of the airport, as instructed by the control tower.

"Let's get out of this can," the billionaire said, forcing his body out of the cockpit. He walked stiffly toward the locking mechanism on the forward hatch/doorway.

Jack nudged Leah, who slept curled against the window.

"I'm sleeping," she said. "Leave me alone."

"Don't you want to get out and walk around?"

"Not one bit." She pulled a parka over her head.

"What about you guys?" Jack asked.

Garrett, Juan, and Marko were stretching and staring out the windows.

"I'm dying to get out of this thing," Garrett said.

"God...what a flight," Juan said, rubbing his neck.

Jack peeked over Paulson's shoulder. "What? No greeting committee?"

Paulson pointed. "They're headed this way."

A trio of black SUVs pulled up next to the Gulfstream. The driver of the second SUV hopped out and opened the passenger door. A short but solidly built man with cropped salt-and-pepper hair stepped out, wearing the uniform of the Chilean Air Force.

"Mr. Paulson," he said, speaking flawless English. "I'm General Martinez. Welcome to Chile."

"Good to be in Chile again, sir," Paulson said. He grasped the general's hand in a firm handshake.

The general grasped the billionaire's hand in return. "I'm looking forward to watching you fly our *Las Tortugas* off the ice—right under the nose of the Russians."

Jack couldn't help but notice the gold-capped teeth and the genuine twinkle in the general's eye.

"We'll give it our best effort," Paulson said.

"I wish we had time to provide you and your fine crew with a proper Chilean welcome," the general said with a shrug. "Unfortunately, your government has ordered us to impound your aircraft and detain its crew."

Paulson blinked in surprise. "Did they give you any reason?"

"Your President has sided with the Russians."

"But it's your aircraft!"

"Yes, of course," the general said. "You must know the United States of America carries a heavy hand around the world. It's very difficult for a small country like ours in need of assistance to resist such threats." He flashed a smile. "However, the documents were faxed in English—and we are in the process of completing the translation to Spanish, to make it legal, of course."

Paulson slumped in relief. "How long will this 'translation' take?"

"One more hour, perhaps two," the general replied with a shrug.

A young Chilean walked up to the general and spoke in soft Spanish. The general nodded twice and then turned toward Paulson.

"The other aircraft is approaching the airport." General Martinez shaded his eyes and looked out over the horizon. "They are not declaring an emergency but have requested that fire equipment stand by."

The Caribou flew down toward the runway, wings dipping slightly to one side, then the other. The pilots walked the main landing gear down on to the runway. Once the aircraft was firmly on the ground, he reversed the pitch on the propellers, and the Caribou slowed and turned off on to a taxiway.

When both engines had been shut down, the ramp at the rear of the Caribou lowered to the tarmac, and Ridley strolled out of the fuselage. He walked underneath the left wing and inspected the landing gear and tire assembly.

Paulson jogged toward his chief mechanic. "What the hell happened?"

"You know about the trouble in Oakland. It was complicated by a missing air compressor in the hangar. We've got one onboard somewhere, in all this gear." Ridley pointed toward the left landing gear. "We inflated the flat tire using propane from the hangar barbecue." He stretched. "We've been landing like an eagle with a compound fracture ever since we busted out of Oakland." Ridley wiped fatigue from his eyes. "It will take time to remove the wheel, bleed the propane out of the tire and install it. Besides," he said wearily, "we're all beat."

"The heavy hand of some State Department bureaucrat has reached clear down here. We have an hour, give or take. Sorry."

Ridley's face registered surprise and disgust. "We've been flying non-stop in that piece-of-shit tuna can for almost forty hours. We've got to have a break." He waved toward Chase and Rooster. "Get over here, guys. You won't believe this crap."

The Parker brothers looked at each other and then walked over toward Paulson. "Al says we've got a couple hours at most and then we're out of here." Ridley looked disgusted. "I told him there's no way. We've got to have some sleep."

Fatigue lines ran vertically and horizontally on Chase Parker's face. His clothes were wrinkled, and coffee stains spotted his jacket. "Give me a minute to chat with my brother." Chase nodded toward Rooster, and they walked several feet away, spoke quietly, and then returned.

"We're counting on this ferry job to get us back on our feet," Chase said. "We're willing to continue—as long as Mac's on board."

Ridley's faced twisted into a grimace. "All right, for fuck's sake." His eyes bored into Paulson. "I'm taking time off after this—lots of time."

Paulson beamed. "Whatever you want, you got it."

"Seriously, though, Al. We're pushing it with that tire. It wasn't designed to carry propane."

"Can you change the tire out on the ice?" Paulson asked.

Chase looked at his brother and nodded. "Sure, we anchor a couple of steel plates down on the ice for the jacks. We figured we might have to anyway, if that ice runway is anything but smooth."

"Great," Paulson said, clearly relieved.

Chase wiped at his eyes. "We need weather information."

The Chilean general pointed toward the Suburban. "Come with me. You can talk by radio to our scientists at Bernardo O' Higgins base."

Jack walked over to where Leah, Garrett, Juan, and Marko stood. "You all regretting you got yourselves involved in this mess now?"

Leah frowned. "What's this about the tire being filled with propane gas, making that flying wreck into a guided missile?"

"I never promised you a Caribbean cruise." Jack glanced back at the Caribou, where Chase and Rooster were busy looking over the undercarriage. "Chances are we're going to crash on landing and end up like the Russians anyway."

"Are you trying to scare me, Climber? Well, it won't work," she said. "I'm getting my gear out of Paulson's flying Mile-High Club—before the soldiers lock it up."

"Man, do you know how to push her buttons," Juan said with a chuckle.

"It's a gift," Jack replied dryly. "You guys grab your gear and get it stowed on the Caribou. If you need to use the bathroom facilities; I suggest you do it now."

"What kind of toilet do they have on the Caribou?" Leah asked suspiciously.

"A tube and a bucket," Jack replied with a straight face. "But that's gonna seem plush compared to what we have on the ice."

CHAPTER 44

The roar of the Caribou's twin engines vibrated throughout the ancient cargo plane in a manner that made Leah's teeth rattle. She sat in the cargo hold, her coat zipped up to her chin, a wool hat pulled down to her eyes and a thick set of plugs firmly inserted in each ear.

Pallets containing aircraft spare parts, tools, survival gear, clothing, food, and more were tightly packed into the aircraft's belly.

To Leah, it looked like a mountain of gear, although she'd overheard Jack telling Paulson that it was the minimum, and if they got into any real trouble, it wasn't going to be near enough.

Ridley, whom she'd instinctively liked from their first meeting at the airport, slept on blankets lying against the cargo alongside his two airplane mechanics: Angus Lyon and Orlando Perez.

The mechanics had both been polite but distant, as if having a woman along on the salvage could be bad luck. They wore insulated coveralls covered in a combination of grease and what looked like various shades of paint. Underneath wool caps, each had a full head of hair, although Leah doubted whether it had ever been washed.

Garrett, Juan, and Marko sat on aluminum nylon web seating, pointing occasionally at the pile of gear, then back at Leah, poking each other in the ribs and laughing. Leah flashed her "I'm not impressed" look while they grinned like a trio of Cheshire cats.

Leah climbed over the tied-down gear to reach the cockpit and stuck her head between the two pilots. Directly below, the glaciers of Tierra del Fuego ran like ribbons across the islands.

Jack pointed down to a small stretch of land. "Cape Horn."

"How cold will it be when we get there?"

"Probably five or ten degrees above zero. If it's any warmer, we'll have trouble."

She leaned forward. "How can warm weather be bad?"

Jack pointed toward the floor of the aircraft. "The Caribou doesn't have skis. We're counting on cold weather to keep the ice hard enough for a safe landing."

He leaned forward and shouted into Chase's ear, knowing cargo pilots suffered serious hearing loss. "How is the weather holding up?"

"I'm in contact with the Chileans at Bernardo O'Higgins Base," Chase replied. "The skies are broken and scattered at 15,000 feet with light winds."

"What about inland?"

"Forecast to be clear, but I'm more worried about Bernardo O'Higgins."

"Why?" Jack asked.

"Because if the weather goes bad at Bernardo and we're unable to land, this will be a one-way trip with an unhappy ending."

Rooster pointed out the cockpit window and down at the angry white-caps and blowing foam. "You go down in that and you can kiss your ass goodbye."

Paulson laughed and slapped him playfully on the shoulder.

Leah grimaced and crawled back out of the cockpit. "What kind of idiots joke at the thought of crash-landing in a frozen ocean?" she muttered. "I will never understand men."

CHAPTER 45

Rooster's bearded face appeared over the top of the strapped-down cargo. He signaled they should all take a seat and buckle up. The pilots were making an approach into Bernardo O' Higgins Base on the Antarctic Peninsula.

Chase brought the Caribou in low over the iceberg-filled bay toward a stretch of ice lined with empty fuel barrels painted black.

He made a low pass over the ice runway dubbed the "ski-way," searching for the windsock indicating wind direction. Once he determined the best approach, Chase piloted the Caribou into a standard left-hand pattern, aiming the nose of the Caribou for the ski-way.

Just as the wheels touched the ice, he gunned the engines and flew down the entire length of the ice strip with the tires barely kissing the surface.

Leah gripped the nylon strapping tightly.

Jack leaned over and shouted, "They're just testing the surface of the ice. It's normal. Nothing to worry about. If the ice is solid, they'll bring it to a stop next time around."

With a bang, the Caribou hit the ice on the second time around and Chase quickly reversed the pitch on the propellers as the aircraft's tires settled onto the rock-hard surface. The airplane came to a quick stop in a thick cloud of ice crystals.

"Yaaahooo!" Paulson shouted. He slapped a less-than-enthusiastic Mac Ridley on the back and shoulders.

"Get ready for a real dose of cold," Jack warned.

A blast of cold air drove through the aircraft as the hydraulics opened the cargo ramp at the rear of the aircraft. Leah's first view of Antarctica was of an overwhelming white brilliance. The sky was clear, a dazzling blue. The next sensation was of intense penetrating cold that immediately worked its way to the bone.

Each step she made on the ice created a crunching sound. In an odd way, she thought, it sounded as though she were violating it.

She looked up and saw a number of steel and aluminum buildings with British and Chilean flags cracking in the breeze from separate poles. She heard what sounded like a pair of diesel engines revving up from behind the Caribou and was shocked to see two bright, orange snowcats nearly a quarter of a mile away. In the Antarctic environment, without the distractions of city traffic, crickets, and trees rustling in the wind, either sound traveled farther or her senses craved something familiar.

The air tasted crisp, except for the tinge of aviation fuel and exhaust fumes wafting from the weary Caribou. The creaky nature of the old cargo plane was accented by the popping sounds of the engines as they cooled and the metal contracting in the subfreezing temperatures.

It served as a sobering reminder that the margins for safely in this alien environment were razor thin. All that stood between her demise in the grasp of this colossal ice monster was the Caribou and a thousand worn-out components.

A look out on the endless horizon of ice of nothingness brought the reality of Antarctica into true focus: *They* were the virus.

Antarctica, in all her vindictive glory, bristled with antibody-like defenses. Howling hurricane force winds, a penetrating bitter cold beyond human comprehension, deep icy crevasse traps, thousands of miles of desolation, and man's own insufferable arrogance.

She shivered at the realization.

Paulson apparently had no such concerns. He crawled over the cargo, his face covered in a wide grin and strutting like a barnyard rooster. "Hey, there's my gas," he said, pointing toward the snowcats approaching the Caribou.

The snowcats, towing sleds stacked with fifty-gallon fuel barrels, rolled in tandem toward the Caribou. The billionaire jumped off the ramp and walked out to meet the vehicles, Chase Parker right behind him.

When the snowcats stopped, several people wearing one-piece winter coveralls covered in grease shook Paulson's hand then worked one of the full barrels underneath the wing tanks.

"How long to fill this thing with gas?" Leah asked.

Chase pointed to what looked like a portable generator on a sled. "We'll use a portable fuel pump that runs off a generator, so not too long."

"What about when we get to Thor's Hammer?"

"Unless we have any real trouble, we should have enough to make it back here."

"If we don't?"

"We'll get a fuel drop from the Chileans."

"What if they can't make the drop or the barrels get smashed?"

"Then you've got a long walk back to O'Higgins," Chase replied flatly.

While Paulson chatted with the Chileans, Rooster, Garrett, Juan, Lyon, and Perez helped manhandled the fifty-gallon barrels of fuel while Ridley supervised the fuel transfer. Two hours later, the Chileans waved goodbye then drove the snowcats and sleds away from the ski-way.

With the two engines running wide open, Chase pulled back sharply on the control wheel and the Caribou lifted smoothly off the ice.

Ridley gave Leah a high five, and everyone cheered. For better or worse, they were on the way to Thor's Hammer—and the heart of Russian-claimed Antarctica.

Chapter 46

Chase Parker banked the aircraft in the direction of a massive granite cliff jutting straight up toward the sky. "Thor's Hammer!" he shouted while pointing out the left side of the aircraft cockpit. Everyone rushed forward, taking turns looking through the windscreen as he made two passes by the gigantic granite formation.

"Jesus H. Christ," whispered Paulson.

"Listen up," Chase said. "We'll fly down-range and check out the Russian-made ice runway."

Rooster pulled a red bandanna out of his pocket and waved it around. "If we're attempting a landing, I'll signal with this. That means it's time to strap in and hang on!"

The ice runway sliced cleanly through sastrugi, sand-dune-shaped formations of ice and snow. It appeared to be at least two miles in length and in perfect condition except for the blackened aircraft carcass and new sastrugi build-up near the *Las Tortugas*.

The green tail section, with a large Russian flag painted on the rudder, lay on its side nearly intact, in marked contrast to the burned fuselage and wings that formed a debris field on the right side of the ice runway.

"We're swinging around," Chase said. "Get strapped in. Time for us to earn our paycheck."

Jack crawled back to where Paulson appeared to be fiddling with his footwear. The billionaire glanced up and then re-laced the plastic mountaineering boots. "Don't want my shoes falling off if this heap goes in."

Leah rolled her eyes but tightened the straps on her makeshift seat belt.

Rooster slid open his side window, pulled the tape igniter on a smoke flare, and let it drop several hundred feet to the ice below. Green smoke poured out from a stream that changed direction radically every few seconds.

Rooster turned around and waved the red bandanna wildly, his signal to hang on tight or, as Rooster had put it, "Bend over, grab your ankles and prepare to kiss your ass goodbye."

The wheels touched the ice and then the roar of the engines rattled the airframe as Chase applied full power and pulled back on the steering yoke.

On the second approach, he allowed the Caribou to descend smoothly, apparently confident the crosswinds fell within an acceptable range and the surface of the ice was hard enough for a safe landing. When the wheels felt firmly down on the ice, Rooster reversed the pitch on the propellers, stopping the aircraft in a matter of several hundred feet.

"Yaaahooo!" Paulson shouted for the second time that day as the aircraft came to a stop at the bottom of the world.

CHAPTER 47

News of the InterGalactic cargo plane leaving Chile with Paulson and his crew led to an emergency meeting of the National Security Council's Crisis Planning Group.

The team included Stanton Fischer, military liaison Admiral Clay Williams, the President's Chief of Staff Don Green, and several lower-ranking members of the Department of State and Department of the Defense. This meeting also included two non-regular participants: Teresa Simpson and Secretary of the Interior Wick Emerson.

Teresa sat as directed and then studied the various high-ranking advisers and their aides who filed in, taking pre-assigned seats throughout the room. She took note of those who sat in chairs nearest the President. They were players, the staff and department heads that had the president's ear. In Washington that meant power and influence.

The aides sat in hardback wooden chairs along the wall. They were out of the line of fire, but close enough to their bosses to lean forward and whisper information that might solidify their position with the President.

Fischer walked into the room, a folder under his arm. He didn't make eye contact with any of his peers, but simply sat in one of the two power chairs.

In Teresa's mind, Fischer was the archetypal academic-trained bureaucrat piece of shit, his lips permanently stained from kissing ass. Having had a call and a meeting at his office in preparation for this evening's strategy conference, she had his shtick down cold.

After Fischer had ushered her into his office, which reeked of stale cigarette smoke, he'd tried to make her feel at ease by telling her the President was 'probably overreacting, as usual.'

Clearly, this was how he tested loyalty, but it wouldn't work with her. Teresa had put on her standard political smile and replied that if the President thought it was important, then of course she thought it must be important as well.

An aide opened the double doors to the conference room, and everyone stood. In strolled the President, dressed casually in blue jeans and a more formal white button-down shirt. He signaled for them all to sit as one of the staffers handed him a folder.

"I want to tell you I just endured another painful telephone conversation with the Russian president." The President looked at the faces, anger evident from his tone. "You can imagine he's not pleased to learn that our loose-cannon billionaire and his entourage slipped out of the United States, apparently without our knowledge." He glanced up at Don Green. "Of course he said that, in Russia, nothing of the sort could ever happen."

"Did you remind him of the Red Square incident?" Green replied, referring to the German teenager who flew a single-engine Cessna undetected into the former Soviet Union, ultimately landing it right in the middle of Red Square.

The President was unimpressed with Don Green's attempt at humor. "We're in this meeting because I gave my word we wouldn't allow our citizens to 'invade' Russian territory in an attempt to retrieve the B-29." The President shook his head. "The president even insinuated that we're secretly supporting the retrieval of the bomber." His jaw clenched momentarily. "I'm at a loss to understand why these people weren't apprehended in Chile."

Don Green tapped on the conference table. "The Chileans claim our request arrived too late to be formally translated and acted upon."

"With allies like that...." the President said.

Green gave a slight shrug of agreement.

The President glared over the top of his reading glasses at the Secretary of the Interior. "Now, I understand a Native American archeological discovery is linked to this fiasco?"

Emerson cleared his throat. "Approximately three days ago, the National Park Police, while on routine patrol, flushed out what appeared to be artifact hunters in southwestern New Mexico." He nodded toward the staffer working the slide projector. A slide of a cliff with the ledge sticking out from a long horizontal crack appeared on the screen. "This is Gila National Wilderness and the location where our rangers and we believe the artifact hunters discovered the new cliff dwelling."

The President turned toward Teresa Simpson. "Give me the short version and then let's get to the problem at hand."

She nodded and began, "Anasazi Indians—"

"Native Americans, Ms. Simpson," interrupted the President.

Teresa looked up in shock. "With all respect, sir, the people living in this region whose ancestors lived in these dwellings, refer to themselves proudly as Indians."

"That may be true; nonetheless, the proper term for these people is Native Americans or indigenous peoples."

Teresa wondered if she should just stand up, walk to the entryway, spin around, and tell him what an arrogant, politically correct nitwit he was, before slamming the doors shut.

Instead, she drew in a deep breath and started over. "Native Americans lived on the tops of the mesas and in river valleys successfully for generations. About a thousand years ago, those living in the Southwest suddenly moved into a dangerous system of cliffs and underground dwellings. They lived within these cliffs for approximately 200 years, and then, just as mysteriously, the dwellings were all abandoned. Those living in Northern New Mexico, Colorado, and Arizona are generally known as the Anasazi or as translated, the Ancient Ones. In southern New Mexico, where this particular dwelling was found, the cliff dwellers are known as the Mogollon."

KEVIN TINTO

The President leaned forward. "I thought it was drought that drove them from the cliffs."

"That's been a prevalent theory, yes."

"We've all been to Mesa Verde, Ms. Simpson," he said impatiently. "Can we get to the crux of the situation, please?"

"Yes, sir," she said. "Now, I'm not an archeologist." She glanced sharply at the Secretary of the Interior. "The Secretary fired our best Native American archeologist earlier this year, over strong objection on my part."

"That would be our wayward ex-employee, Dr. Leah Andrews," said the President.

"That's right," she said. "And we believe that she discovered this hidden cliff dwelling."

"Which," the President continued for her, "allegedly contains geologic samples found naturally only in Antarctica."

Teresa Simpson nodded. "If it's true and these Native Americans traveled to Antarctica during the Dark Ages—"

"What makes you believe that this isn't a hoax?"

"I know Leah Andrews," Teresa replied. "She's a rock-solid scientist, totally committed to her profession. I strongly believe that Leah is headed to Antarctica along with her husband and *your* out-of-control billionaire because she expects to find a connection to these Native Americans."

"Right now, all I want is Paulson and his crew taken out of Antarctica." The President turned to Fischer. "Which brings us to you, Stan."

Fischer's hands shook as he glanced down at his notes. "We believe our best option involves sending down a small contingent of Special Operators. The team will be flown directly to the region in question, where they will be inserted 'HALO' to gain the element of surprise."

Teresa held up her hand.

Fischer's face flushed with irritation. "You have a question, Ms. Simpson?"

"I'm sorry. I don't get it. Leah Andrews and her team are not enemy soldiers. They're American citizens. What's the need for all the commando hijinks?"

Fischer tossed his folder on the conference table. "They may be American citizens, but they've committed crimes, placed a vital international relationship, critical as it is at this juncture, in jeopardy."

"I have a platoon of SEALs standing by in Little Creek, Virginia," Admiral Wilson said calmly, in contrast to Fischer's outburst. "With inflight refueling by way of air tanker, we could fly them direct from their base to the insertion point in Antarctica, provided the weather cooperates. From the time we give the command, we'll have them on the ice within thirty hours."

The President leaned forward. "I don't want just anyone assigned to this mission, Clay. I want the best you've got."

The Admiral cleared his throat, glancing at Teresa Simpson. The signal to the President was clear, this is classified at the highest levels and shouldn't be discussed with low-level civilian political appointees present.

After an awkward silence, Teresa spoke to clear the tension. "And what if they resist this forced evacuation? I doubt Leah Andrews is going to welcome American commandos with open arms."

"These are SEALs, Ms. Simpson," the admiral replied smugly. "They are trained and equipped to be highly...influential."

"You mean they're armed to the teeth," she said.

"Precisely," he replied.

Chapter 48

Leah zipped up her oversized parka, pulled the wool hat around her ears, and walked down the short ramp. She drew in a deep breath and stepped onto the ice. "Damn, it's cold, Hobson," she said, stamping her feet on the ice.

"We're in the middle of a sweltering heat wave." Jack said, pushing the hood of his parka off. "It can't be less than five or ten below zero."

Marko shuffled up next to Leah and nudged her. "Yeah, but it's a dry cold so you hardly feel it."

"Dry cold, my…." Leah stopped herself and walked beyond the shadow of the Caribou, getting her first look at makeshift Russian base camp. It consisted of four steel cargo containers all painted in what looked to her like military gray. The Russians had used a tractor to push snow and ice up along the sides of the containers, trying to insulate them from the cold, no doubt. Each one had what appeared to be a stovepipe running out of the top, possibly to vent the makeshift shelters if the Russians were using gas or oil heaters.

A chill ran down her back when she saw the Russian flags flying from steel poles welded to the side of the containers. It reminded her that foreign soldiers had laid claim to this nameless hunk of ice and rock.

About fifty meters away from the circle of container huts sat the B-29. To Leah, the bomber looked ready to fly. The aluminum skin gleamed in the sunshine, the black, four-bladed propellers, and fresh tires stood out in contrast.

In the distance, the blackened wreckage of the Antonov lay scattered about and her thoughts went to the families of those men who'd perished in such a horrible way, such a long, long way from home.

It would've given her the creeps, but Jack said the Russians had mounted a mission and had recovered the bodies, or what was left of them, before abandoning the icy base.

She took a deep breath and focused on the reason she'd risked life and limb: Thor's Hammer.

She turned and shaded her eyes. Thor's Hammer looked as if she might reach out and touch it; a massive granite mountain thrusting like a belligerent fist, out of the icy depths. The vein of red granite creating the Thor's Hammer image stood out within the granite mountain like a neon-lit mega-casino in Vegas.

She understood why it had served as a beacon for aviators and why the cliff dwellers might have remembered it in this wasteland of white and gray.

"I want everyone to gather around," Jack said. "We have work to do and very little time."

Garrett, Juan, and Marko filed down the Caribou ramp, zipping up heavy parkas and applying the sunscreen necessary to protect their skin from the deadly ultraviolet rays beaming through a thin ozone layer. Ridley, Angus Lyon, and Orlando Perez followed them down the ramp.

The last to file out of the Caribou were Chase and Rooster Parker. They were both dressed in well-worn cold-weather gear and appeared calm and relaxed. Rooster set up two folding beach chairs, and the Parker brothers promptly sat down, looking around smugly.

Paulson burst out laughing. "Damn I hate it when someone thinks of something I forgot."

Rooster grinned. "Just want to make sure I'm comfortable in case this is a long-winded speech."

Jack held up his hand. "Okay, we've landed safely at our destination, which, quite frankly, I had doubts could be achieved." He turned around and pointed toward the granite mountain towering in the distance. "Right now you see the peak known as Thor's Hammer clearly. It's clear for the moment, anyway, but if the weather goes bad, you won't find your way anywhere without a rope." He paused. "No one goes anywhere alone. Is that understood?"

Heads bobbed.

"We have three missions on the ice. First is to secure the Caribou against the possibility of a storm." He looked at Chase. "What help will you need?"

"Normally, I'd say Rooster and I could handle it, but we have to change out the propane-filled tire, and we could use help jacking up the Caribou." He glanced toward Juan. "An ex-football player would come in real handy right now."

"Fine," Jack said. "He's yours until the Caribou is secured." Jack nodded toward Ridley. "Second, we're getting the *Las Tortugas* ready to fly. What do you need, Mac?"

"I think we're in good shape. We've got the three snow machines and sleds to pull the tools and spare parts. That doesn't mean I would turn down any extra help. We've got gear to set up, and with just the three of us..."

"Hey!" Paulson said in mock surprise. "I'm here to do my share."

Ridley chuckled. "Like I said—with just the three of us."

"Third, we have the archaeological aspect of the expedition," said Jack. "I think Leah, Marko, and I can get a camp set up at the base of Thor's Hammer. Garrett, how about if you give Mac an extra hand getting unloaded?"

"That's fine with me," Garrett replied, shading his eyes and pointing toward the shining aluminum skin of the *Las Tortugas*. "I'm dying to get a close-up look at that B-29."

"We're all exhausted and some of us haven't slept for forty-eight hours or, in the case of those flying down in the Caribou, even longer." Jack pulled one of the Motorola handheld radios from his parka. "We're staying in touch with mobile radios; everyone needs to have one with him or her. Make sure to keep them inside your parka because the batteries will significantly weaken when exposed to freezing temperatures."

"What if the weather gets bad and we can't take off?" Leah asked.

"We've got a sat phone, so you can arrange to call your next of kin," Jack said, showing only the trace of a smile. "No one's going to help us—even if they could. We are totally and completely on our own."

CHAPTER 49

Navy Commander Gus Beckam had grown up scuba-diving the clear and warm waters of southern California and Mexico. While his naval aviator father wanted him to attend the Naval Academy, following the family tradition of becoming an officer and a gentleman, he had decided to attend San Diego State instead, where, to his father's disapproval, he'd studied philosophy and religion.

After graduation, Gus had hung around the beach until the local dive shop told him the La Ceba Hotel in Cozumel needed a diving instructor and guide. He moved to Cozumel, taught diving, and led guided dives on Cozumel's world-class reef systems. At night, he drank heavily and often partied until dawn at Carlos and Charlie's Bar and Restaurant. Beckam wore his blond hair long and shaved only when the hotel manager requested he do so, which in Cozumel wasn't often.

One particular Saturday had started much like the rest—leading fifteen tourists on two dives. Since rules required that the first dive of the day be the deepest, Beckam had arranged to have the charter dive boat take them to Palencar Reef, a magnificent and nearly vertical coral wall running for several miles offshore from the Mexican-Caribbean Island.

During the pre-dive briefing, he had warned the divers not to exceed the maximum eighty-foot depth set for the dive. Because Palencar is a coral wall, it was easy to descend far below the maximum depth, where in a matter of minutes the standard eighty-cubic-foot aluminum tank could easily be sucked dry.

Beckam was also tasked with warning divers of a condition called nitrogen narcosis or "the rapture of the deep." The effects were similar to sudden intoxication, and divers were known to drown or, more commonly, simply disappear into deep water.

He noticed a short, balding dive tourist named Gary standing at the back of the group, not paying much attention to the pre-dive briefing. To Beckam, the oversized dive knife the young sport diver wore on his calf signaled a nervous rookie. He made a mental note to keep an eye on him.

Twenty minutes into the dive, Beckam felt a tap on his shoulder. Gary pointed down toward deep waters off the reef; Beckam wondered if he'd spotted pelagic sea life.

It wasn't fish Gary had seen. It was a series of bubbles, the kind of bubbles released when a diver exhaled a large volume of compressed air at dangerous depths.

Suddenly, Gary turned head down and kicked with his fins toward the bubbles below.

Beckam tapped on his tank with his dive knife, knowing that would alert the other divers in the group to trouble. He pointed toward the surface, which meant he wanted them to ascend for a safety stop at ten feet, surface, and climb aboard the dive boat.

Beckam turned head down and started kicking rapidly toward the two sets of bubbles working up from the depths. When he reached 110 feet, he saw the outline of two divers rising up from the dark blue of the deep water.

What he saw next had changed his entire life. Gary had the razor-sharp point of his knife nudged up underneath the other diver's chin. His oxygen regulator wasn't in his mouth, but in the mouth of the deep diver. Gary wasn't breathing in at all—he simply allowed a slow stream of bubbles to escape his mouth.

Beckam offered Gary his back-up regulator and, after a safety stop, all three safely reached the dive boat. Beckam radioed ahead to get a medical team and to prepare Cozumel's hyperbaric chamber for two incoming "guests."

"What the hell were you doing?" Beckam had shouted in anger and relief at the confused rookie deep-diver.

"You're not going to get anything from him, Mr. Beckam," Gary said calmly. "He's sky high—narced to the gills." The rookie diver shook his head. "Right now he's got no idea what planet he's on, much less how close he just came to becoming shark food." Gary patted the diver on the shoulder. "With our friend shit-faced on nitrogen, the only way I could get his attention was by giving him a little wake-up call with 'Ol' Painless' here." He pointed toward the dive knife, now safely tucked back into the rubber sheath. "He'd already sucked his tank dry, so I gave him my regulator so he'd have enough air to get to the surface."

"Who the hell are you?" Beckam asked. "Where'd you learn to do a free ascent from those kinds of depths?"

Gary looked around the deck sheepishly. "Not a whole lot to it, really, Mr. Beckam; you just have to remember to breathe out as you ascend to prevent your lungs from blowing up."

"Coast Guard!" The boat captain shouted to alert Beckam a boat was approaching at high speed.

"You guys are going to the chamber," Gus said flatly. "If everything checks out, you'll be out in a few hours. If you've got the bends, it could be more."

Gary smiled easily. "It'll give me some time to catch up on my reading."

After the CG boat had sped away, a couple of the other divers gathered around, wanting to know if the afternoon dive was cancelled. Beckam replied that the group would enjoy a shallow afternoon dive and he would instruct everyone—again—on the dangers of nitrogen narcosis. He also said the diver named Gary had probably saved the other diver's life and made a miraculous free ascent.

"I imagine he's done that before, probably more than once," said another diver in Gus's group.

How do you know that?" Gus asked.

"He's a Navy SEAL," the diver replied in admiration.

That single act of bravery and modesty had altered Gus Beckam's life path entirely.

Twelve years later, he no longer guided tourists on Caribbean tourist getaways. Instead, he served as the skipper of SEAL Team Two, a collection of fifty-six officers and enlisted men. They were motivated commandos trained to infiltrate and eliminate terrorist cells, provide intelligence, and raise hell and create mayhem, whether in a local pub in Virginia Beach or on a suspected hard target in the deserts of the Middle East.

Little Creek, Virginia, near Virginia Beach, served as the base for several SEAL Teams, including SEAL Team Two. Here Team Two trained day and night—especially at night for missions that might require their special brand of lethal skills.

Normally Beckam loved loading his men aboard a Hercules, flying hours on end, and then parachuting through the darkness into a hive of bad guys.

Lt. Danny Frantino, his Executive Officer and the number two man in the Team, watched Beckam shake his head as the C-17 Globemaster taxied to where they'd load the team and their gear.

"You got a bad feeling about this one, Skipper?" Frantino asked, his Brooklyn, accent always more discernible during a mission.

"What's not to like? We're ordered to drop into Antarctica to forcibly remove American civilians."

Frantino shook his head. "How is it we rate this special duty?"

Beckam grinned. "You're famous, Danny. Remember?"

Frantino shook his head. "Jesus—for a mission that was supposed to be top secret, it seems like everyone in freaking Washington knows about it."

"If we're lucky this one will be little easier."

"Yeah, but it sounds like a chance to snoop and scoop that Russian base. Maybe we find something good. Plus, we're out of the sand."

"Are you just trying to piss me off?" Beckam joked.

Frantino knew Beckam had expressly been ordered not to break into any of the Russian-built structures or remove anything from the site.

Beckam watched the last of his team's gear loaded aboard the C-17. It wasn't their full complement. After all, he'd been told the mission footprint was minuscule, so he'd handpicked 24 SEALs for the mission.

"Sounds like a milk run," Frantino said, shrugging. "We snatch a few civilians off the ice, plant a few American flags just to piss off the Russians. Compared to the mission in Iran, this is pure holiday."

"That's what worries me, Danny." Beckam walked slowly toward the Hercules. "In this case, 2 and 2 are adding up to more like 10. There's something going on down there we haven't been told about. There's no way there sending us down there to escort civilians off the ice unless someone is expecting serious trouble."

Coddling civilians wasn't a mission for SEALs. Like well-armed, urban street gangs, SEALs often found trouble even when they weren't looking for it. More to the point, thought Beckam, you don't send a SEAL team unless you're expecting trouble.

CHAPTER 50

Paulson stood in front of the World War II Super Fortress, admiring the weathered nose art featuring a naked blond riding a turtle. The shell housed machine gun turrets and featured bombs dropping out of the belly. The face of the turtle had been painted with an evil grin, and a pair of World War II flying goggles covered its eyes.

Ridley walked over and stood beside his boss. "Looks damned near airworthy. I might have to change my opinion about the Russians."

"Beautiful." The billionaire shaded his eyes and looked down the stretch of ice. "What about preparing the runway?"

Ridley pointed toward the Russian camp. "If we manage to get that cranky-looking Russian tractor started, we should be able to flatten a path through the sastrugi, at least enough to get you 5,000 feet of runway."

"I'll have her airborne in less than that."

Garrett walked up and nodded through the face-mask he wore to protect his skin from frostbite. "It appears we're in luck. The Russians have made decent shelters out of these containers, including some crude but functional propane heaters."

"I'm going to call Jack and rub it in," Paulson gloated. He pulled the radio from his jacket and keyed the microphone. "Hey, Jack! Do you copy?"

They had been cross-country skiing for an hour toward the base of Thor's Hammer. Jack, Leah, and Marko each towed a fiberglass sled, loaded down with tents, sleeping bags, and climbing gear, the sleds secured to their bodies with tow harnesses.

"I don't understand why we have to ski over to Thor's Hammer when we brought snowmobiles," Leah complained. She removed her cross-country skis and sat on the overloaded sled, breathing heavily, not yet acclimated to the high elevation.

"Since you enjoyed a free trip down, I wouldn't complain too much about the logistics," Jack replied. "Mac and his crew need the three snow machines way more than we do in order to haul gear to the B-29. Besides, I'm not interested in rolling along at thirty miles per hour, and suddenly finding myself dropping into a crevasse. Once we check out the route, and Paulson has the gear transferred, we may get lucky and get a lift back via snow machine."

Jack's handheld radio suddenly crackled to life.

"Hey, Jack! You copy?"

He unclipped the radio and keyed it. "I read you loud and clear, Al. What's your status?"

"We're in camp and in luck. The Russians left us a small city. We're moving in like we owned the place."

Jack glanced back at Leah. She was sipping out of a water bottle and shaking her head in disgust. "Leah's thrilled," he said dryly.

"How close are you to the hammer?"

Jack studied the towering granite wall. A mountain of snow and ice lay against the granite; it flowed down from the mountains above. They would have to climb the slope to get anywhere near the base of the mountain.

"We have some ways to go; we're going to pitch a camp well away from the slope leading up to the base, just in case it's unstable."

He glanced at Leah, who now lay across her sled. "I don't know how much farther Leah will pull her sled." He looked over at Marko and winked. "We may have to camp here until her highness gets her beauty sleep."

Leah held up her hand in response. Jack knew from experience which finger she was displaying within the thick mitten.

"Did she hear that?" Paulson asked in a stage whisper.

"I'm afraid so." Jack looked back toward the Caribou, just a speck in the distance. "Hey, Chase or Rooster, you guys got your radio handy?"

"Never thought I'd hear so much chatter this far from civilization," Chase replied.

"How are you guys doing with the Caribou?"

"We're figuring out how we're going to get the wheel off without dropping her on the ice."

"Are you setting up a campsite or gonna sack out in the airplane?"

"I'd prefer to set up camp," Chase said. "It will be a lot warmer than sleeping in this drafty old airplane, but we're shot to hell. We're sacking out for a few hours."

"We can send over one of the snow machines," said Paulson, "and you guys can take a bunk down here in Little Moscow."

"Thanks, Al. We'll stay with the airplane, just in case the weather deteriorates. I'll ask Juan if he wants to commute over. No need for him to freeze his ass off with us."

The radio crackled momentarily with static. "Juan says he's staying here with us since we've got the bottle of Jack Daniels."

"If you need any help, give a shout," Jack said. He looked at the shiny aluminum skin of the B-29 reflecting sunlight in the distance. "Al, you guys should do the same, get some rest. You'll need those eye-pillows to cover your eyes. It's daylight around here 24-7 in the Antarctic summer."

"Once we give this old beauty a once-over, we're going to do exactly that," Paulson replied.

"Let's check in again in six hours."

Jack rousted Leah and they pulled the sleds for another hour before reaching a mountain of ice leading toward the towering granite wall.

Jack looked up at the mountain and a shiver ran down his spine. Not because of the cold, but the excitement of climbing to the base of the magnificent near-vertical wall of rock. This close to Thor's Hammer, he could discern the individual red veins that made up the hammer, but that also ran in smaller, twisting lines all across the rock face.

"It's alive," he whispered to himself.

The veins of red looked like blood, coursing through the rock, reinforcing what every mountain climber believed: that mountains, especially the big ones, had a life force every bit as powerful as the oceans. They made their own weather, created paths in the ice for those they chose worthy to stand on their shoulders, and yet could kill in an instant. On Everest, it seemed even more apparent. Those who showed up in base camp arrogant and insensitive to the mountain's cultures and traditions often paid the ultimate price.

Wispy clouds cut across the top third of Thor's Hammer. For an instant, it reminded Jack of a knitted brow, the kind you saw on a powerful stranger, sizing you up for the first time and not liking what they saw. His instincts told him to be extra cautious; they weren't welcome here.

He glanced in the direction of the *Las Tortugas* and the Caribou. They were a long way from help if something bad happened.

Jack shook off the feelings of dread. "This is where we're setting up camp," he said. "We'll need shovels and saws, Marko."

Marko pulled a long nylon sack off the top of his sled, unzipped it, and pulled out three shovels and two saws designed to cut block ice. "Are we building an igloo?"

Jack made a circular motion with his mitten. "Ice wall, five feet tall to protect the tents. If we have more time, and energy, we might even try to get an igloo built. Way warmer than the tent.

Two hours later, the wall had been erected and the tents pitched within the perimeter. Jack sat down on his sled and examined his work. He'd cut blocks in the shape of steps to provide entry into and out of the small fortress. "Now all we've got to do is dig the bolt hole and a latrine and we're snug as a bug in a rug."

Leah looked fully irritated—no doubt tired and hungry. "What's a bolt hole again?"

"I've seen wind gusts over a hundred miles per hour come out of no-where," Jack said. "There's a chance we could lose the tents. We dig a hole in the ice large enough the three of us can hunker down and ride out a storm. If the tents go, we crawl into the bolt hole." He locked eyes with her and grinned. "I trust you know what a latrine is?"

"God's revenge on field archeologists."

"We'll make it first-class: a walled-in commode made out of ice blocks." Jack grinned. "With a hole in the ice couple feet deep."

"Seriously?" she asked.

"You've been to France," Jack said. "Remember those toilets—the ones that are just a hole in the floor with the cutouts that show you where to stand?" He smiled. "Normally, we'd just hand out a whiz bottle and pot—but for you, I'm going out of my way."

"I'm holding it until I get back to civilization." Leah appeared to only be half-kidding. "It's hard enough camping out in the desert—this is be-yond the pale."

"Good luck to you," Jack said while Marko hid a grin.

Leah stared up at Thor's Hammer. "When do we start exploring?"

"After we get some sack time, like I told the others."

"Maybe we should get to it right now."

Jack didn't bother to look up, knowing what he'd see in her eyes. "I'll fix a little soup, then hop into my bag for four or five hours. You two get your tents squared away while I prepare the chow."

Marko grinned and unzipped the vestibule door leading into the tent he would share with Garrett once the archaeologist finished helping with the bomber. "I wouldn't want to miss one of Jack's world-class meals."

"You wouldn't be missing much," Leah said before disappearing into the tent.

"Soup will be ready in ten minutes," Jack said. He set up a stove and minutes later had steam rising up from the aluminum pot. He opened sev-eral packs of freeze-dried soup and stirred it into the hot water until it resembled vegetable beef soup.

"Come and get it!" he shouted.

The sound of snow and ice creaking underneath mountaineering boots signaled Marko and Leah climbing out of their tents. He poured them each a large portion of the hot soup.

Marko leaned forward and grabbed a handful of crackers. "What exactly is the plan?"

"We're climbing the ice until we reach the base of Thor's Hammer," Jack replied. "After taking a good look at it, I've decided the route may have crevasses, so we'll be taking our sweet time."

"What are we looking for, Leah?"

"The one thing that might survive the last eight-hundred years."

"What's that?"

"Petrography—rock carvings."

"There's only one problem," Jack cautioned. "If Native Americans chiseled petrography in the stone, the actual carvings could lie under a hundred feet of solid ice—you know, due to the snow accumulation."

Marko shook his head. "There's no way we're going to be able to dig through that much ice."

"Well, I'm not digging," said Leah.

"How are you getting down that deep, then?" Marko asked.

Jack held his hands together and then slowly peeled one hand away from the other. "Like I said, the glacier lying against Thor's Hammer is probably riddled with crevasses. Once we get up to the actual granite, there's a chance the ice has 'walked away' from the cliff face."

"We're roping down into a crevasse?" Leah asked.

Marko nodded eagerly.

"No," said Jack. "I'm the only one going down." When she opened her mouth, Jack held up his hand. "Unless I find something significant, in which case our esteemed lead archeologist will be invited down." He scraped the last of the soup from his bowl. "These crevasses have minds of their own; they open and close without notice. If you're a hundred feet down when the ice shifts, well, you can imagine what's going to happen."

"I don't know," said Leah. "It couldn't be any more dangerous than flying your choice of airline."

Jack chuckled. "I'll grant you that." He leaned back on his gear pack. "Sack time now, kids. I'll wake you when it's ice time."

CHAPTER 51

Jack slept better than expected, zipped tightly into the cold-weather-prepared, mummy-style sleeping bag. He glanced at his watch. He'd slept six hours, two more than planned. He dragged his sore body out of the bag and did the regular post-sleep ritual: crawling through the tent's opening and looking for a change in the weather. He pulled the sleeve of his jacket up, and checked the time on his watch. Nearly 5:00 a.m. Never too early to enjoy a day on the ice....

The skies remained blue, although the winds had increased. Jack slithered back into the vestibule and began melting snow for drinking water. Once that was started, he picked up the two-way radio.

"Hey, Al, you guys copy?"

The radio cracked with static for a moment before Paulson's voice boomed through the small speaker. "Did you sleepyheads finally get out of the rack?"

"How is it going with the *Las Tortugas*?"

"We're doing an inspection now. We're got a big job of inspecting the engines and it appears they're leaking oil. The Russians have done a decent job of jacking the aircraft off the ice and replacing the tires and patching up the aluminum skin. Perez is checking the fabric they laid on the tail and Angus is checking the electrical and fuel system. Mac's going to install a new diaphragm seal in the auxiliary power unit in the rear of the aircraft.

We're going to need the APU to start the engines and we don't want to suffer the same fate as the *Kee Bird*. How are you guys doing?"

"We're beginning the climb toward the base of Thor's Hammer. Have you heard from the Caribou?"

"Yeah—they froze their asses off inside the fuselage."

Jack hooked the radio to his jacket and added more ice to the steaming pot. He was filling the second water bottle as Leah crawled through the vestibule, still wrapped in her sleeping bag.

She pushed tangled hair away from her face. "Not bad, Climber; you did a good job in selecting the sleeping bags."

"If Paulson ever finds out what I paid for those, I'll be out of a job."

"How's the weather?"

"About ten below and the winds have picked up. The sooner you two get moving, the sooner we'll be on our way to the base of Thor's Hammer."

"I'm already up," said a disembodied voice. "I'm just waiting for someone to serve up breakfast in bed."

"Get your butt over here, Marko," ordered Leah.

Two minutes later, the shaggy climber crawled into the tent, already dressed in climbing bibs.

"I'm leaving for Thor's Hammer in twenty minutes," Jack said. "I want you two chowing down and then dressed for climbing."

"If I wanted the drill-sergeant treatment, I'd be helping Paulson get that piece of shit off the ground," Leah replied.

"There's still time to send you over."

"Fat chance." She leaned back into the pile of expedition gear Jack used as a back-rest/pillow. "What's for breakfast?"

He handed her a steaming cup of instant cocoa. She wrapped her hands around the cup for warmth and sipped.

"How dangerous is this climb gonna be?"

Jack stopped mixing hot cereal. "It's serious business. That mountain of ice could tumble and it wouldn't be the first time.

CHAPTER 52

Paulson and his crew of mechanics examined the *Las Tortugas* for three straight hours, covering nearly every inch of the old bomber. The original propellers lay scattered about in sections, twisted into pretzel-like shapes from the impact of the crash landing.

Ridley pointed up toward the wing and engine cowling. "Those sneaky Russian bastards yanked the original Wright Cyclones, shipped them out, and had them rebuilt. That's the best news I've had ever since this fiasco started. I'd rather try walking across the South Atlantic rather than fly off the ice with Russian Shvetsovs."

"Why is that?" Garrett asked.

"The TU-4 bomber was the Russian rip-off of the Boeing B-29 that they reverse-engineered and copied during World War II. Their copy of the Wright 3350 Cyclone engine was called the Shvetsov ASh-73TK, and it was just as likely to burn up as get you home. The Wrights are damn good engines." Ridley glanced over at Angus Lyon, who smoked a cigarette as he admired the old bomber. "What do you say?"

The red-bearded Scotsman took a deep drag off the cigarette before responding. "Knowing those Russian mechanics, I'd rather stand outside a pub in Glasgow in my underwear for the whole bloody winter than risk my arse in that bucket of bolts. I think we have our work cut out, Wright engines or no."

Ridley walked over to where Orlando Perez examined the recently re-placed aluminum skin running the full length of the bottom of the fuse-lage. "How does it look?"

The Colombian shrugged. "Is a poor job, but I think it will hold until Chile." He pointed back toward the fabric-lined tail. "The fabric on the tail, it is torn."

"Can you patch it?"

Perez nodded.

Ridley pointed toward the black oil sprayed on the ice. "If we can't get the oil leaks fixed…"

"Yeah, I know," Paulson said. "Our Antarctic vacation was a wasted trip."

"Just as long as you understand," Ridley cautioned.

"How are we fixed for fuel?"

Ridley turned around and surveyed a mountain of fifty-gallon fuel drums, many of them clearly empty. "Looks like the Russians have enough for the maximum ferry range of 5,000 miles. If they pumped in as much fuel as I see in those empty barrels, we're probably close to what we need to limp 2,000 nautical miles to Punta Arenas."

"What can I do, Al?" Garrett asked.

Paulson looked over at Ridley and grinned. "He's the boss."

"I've got a list about a mile long." Ridley nodded toward the ice runway. "We'll have to pull the old girl through the sastrugi. We need that tractor running."

"I already got a good look at it. All the instructions are in Russian."

Ridley wiped grease from his hands and then stuck them in his pockets before they froze. "Never saw a machine in any language that refused to start without a shot of Quick-Start in the carburetors, a hot battery, and fresh gas in the tank." He looked at Lyon and nodded in the direction of the radial engines.

"What the hell," Lyon said with a belly laugh. "Let's see if we can get one of those Wrights fired up."

Ridley nodded. "Check and see if you can get fuel to engine number two and pull the pre-heater over here and let's get the portable APU out of the Caribou." He paused and spun around and pointed at Paulson. "Wait a minute! Al, you drag the preheater over." He nodded toward one of the overloaded sleds being pulled by a snow machine. "It's on that sled."

"Yes, sir," replied Paulson.

Thirty minutes later, Ridley yelled over the roar of the preheater blowing hot air into the engine. "We need to spin through the prop." Garrett and Paulson jogged over and pushed on one of the massive blades. As the huge propeller came around, Ridley, Perez, and Garrett grabbed the next blade and pushed it through.

"Okay, that should do it," Ridley said.

Lyon climbed into the belly of the aircraft and slid into the flight engineer's station. It was the heart of the old bomber and contained all the instruments and throttles necessary to start and monitor the B-29's engines. He scanned the complicated instrument panel and set the throttles to start position.

Paulson climbed into the cockpit and opened the side window. "Clear!" he yelled, letting the mechanics know he was prepared for ignition.

Garrett gunned the APU connected to the aircraft through a plug near the nose gear. Ridley waved his hand in a circle outside the left side cockpit window.

"Crank it up," said the mechanic.

The propeller spun slowly as the starter motor strained to turn several thousand pounds of steel. A puff of black smoke suddenly belched from the cowling.

"Come on, you SOB!" screamed Ridley, willing the engine to life.

The engine coughed black smoke, backfired, and then caught with a vengeance.

Lyon let it warm up for a minute and then nudged the throttle forward, bringing the big radial motor up to high idle speed. Paulson and his raiders raised their fists in the air and shouted in delight.

CHAPTER 53

"We're going to rope up right here," Jack said.

"Even I can get up that puny slope," Leah said.

Jack dropped his fifty-pound expedition pack to the ground. "I want ropes and crampons, right here." He removed a set of telescoping poles out of his gear pack that, when fully extended, resembled a set of downhill ski poles.

"You're not using your ice axe?" Marko pointed toward Jack's axe, still secured to the rear of his gear pack.

"I'm going to probe for crevasses as we ascend the slope."

"What happens if we fall?"

"You'd better be able to arrest yourself, or we'll all be eaten up by a crevasse in what will be an unhappy conclusion to this climb."

"We're not a couple of your clients," Leah said, a sparkle in her eye. "I don't think we need the 'you're on the edge of death' speech."

After climbing several hundred meters, Jack's crevasse pole broke through soft snow, and a narrow strip of darkness appeared.

"Jump over and don't waste time looking down," Jack instructed. "This isn't much of a crevasse, but it doesn't bode well for the rest of the climb." He dropped his pack and pulled out another coil of climbing line. "I want more rope between the three of us." He pointed at Marko, who held the anchor position. "If Leah and I go in, you've got to get the head of your axe jammed into the ice. You'll only have a few seconds to get us anchored. Do you understand?"

Marko nodded.

Jack drew in a deep breath after climbing another 300 meters. Even to his high-altitude-trained lungs, the air felt thin. He turned to admire the view without saying anything.

In every direction, rocky peaks jutted through crystal-white glacier. A continuous range of mountains, not the infinite fields of snow and ice he'd imagined it'd look like before making his first trip onto the ice. The sky was a deep shade of blue with wispy clouds cutting across the sky like a series of razor-sharp knives. In the distance, he could plainly make out the *Las Tortugas*, the burned hulk of the Russian transport, the small dots representing the Russian base camp, and the Caribou sitting quiet, a stark contrast to the earsplitting rumble he'd come to associate with the Caribou while flying to Thor's Hammer.

While sound could travel long distances over the ice, it always seemed quiet in Antarctica, as if the ice itself were different down here. It could smother sound; during a storm, when visibility dropped to near zero, you couldn't hear someone screaming your name from ten feet away.

The air always tasted odd, as well. After a couple of trips to Antarctica, he'd realized that was because the continent was void of everything familiar, an almost sterile environment.

"What's on your mind, Jack?"

He pointed out at the horizon. "How much bullshit we deal with every day, instead of taking time to look at beauty like this."

Leah admired the view. "I have to hand it to you, when it comes to scenery, you know how to pick it."

A throaty roar in the distance broke the moment. It echoed off the granite walls and shook the entire valley.

"If you want evidence of your cliff dwellers, you'd better get a move on," Jack said.

Leah shaded her eyes. "Is that what I think it is?"

"It's the *Las Tortugas*, breathing fire again. If I know Paulson, the bomber will be ready to fly long before we get tired of this view."

Jack took five steps forward, and suddenly the ice fractured with an audible crack. Before he could shout a warning, Jack disappeared into the blackness.

CHAPTER 54

Ridley trotted toward the front of the *Las Tortugas* and signaled Paulson with the classic hand-under-the-throat motion to shut the engine down. The billionaire climbed out of the cockpit and met his mechanic under the engine cowling while Lyon turned off the aircraft's electrical systems.

"What's the prognosis?" Paulson asked.

Ridley nodded toward the warm liquid dripping down onto the ice. "These engines are leaking oil like a sieve."

Paulson bent over and dipped his fingertips into the viscous brown liquid. "Can you repair them?"

Ridley shook his head. "Don't know. Could be they weren't rebuilt properly. We might nursemaid them to Punta Arenas, but then again they might burn up a hundred miles out to sea. In that case, we're headed for a cold swim."

Garrett walked over and examined the oil dripping down on to ice. "They stripped the battery out of the tractor. We haven't found it yet."

Paulson swore under his breath. "Christ, what else can go wrong?" He spun around and shaded his eyes. "I sure as hell hope Jack is having better luck than we are."

CHAPTER 55

Marko slammed his axe into the ice, burying the tip nearly four inches deep. He watched helplessly as the rope snapped tight, pulling Leah over onto her stomach and dragging her toward the gaping black hole. The young climber gritted his teeth, leaned on the axe, and held tight.

The force of several hundred pounds slamming against his harness knocked his breath away. He prayed the tip of the hardened steel axe would hold. If it didn't, they were all in for a ride toward the bottom.

Marko's ice axe held the weight for several seconds, then pulled out of the ice with such ferocity that the axe tore away from his hands. Marko felt himself being yanked away with Leah toward the crevasse.

When Leah had been pulled off her feet, she'd repeatedly slammed the axe down on the frozen surface, desperately trying to get a bite. Each time the axe simply bounced off the rock-hard surface, showering her with an explosion of ice crystals.

While Marko's axe held them out of the crevasse, she'd swung at the ice once more, hard. Miraculously, the tip sunk several inches into the ice and held, even after Marko's axe slipped, leaving her mere feet from the crevasse.

Marko, sensing the reprieve, had slammed his axe into the ice and then began digging furiously into his pack.

She lay on top of the axe, her arms shaking with the strain. It wouldn't be long before the ice axe popped out of the ice and she was pulled into the crevasse.

"I can't hold it much longer," she yelled.

"Few seconds," Marko replied calmly.

"What the hell are you doing?"

"I'm sinking an ice screw. It should be enough to anchor the line."

"This harness feels like it's cutting me in half!"

"Almost got it." Marko clipped a carabiner into a knot loop in the line and secured it to the ice screw. "You're going to slide forward a little," he said. "Don't worry. It's just the ice screw taking up the slack."

"Come on, Marko—"

Marko pounded the tip of another screw into the ice and spun it down. He secured a line and freed Leah. She rolled away from the line, breathing heavily.

"Check on Jack," she panted.

Marko clipped a safety line to the anchoring screw and crawled toward the lip of the crevasse.

"Jack! Are you okay?"

Someone was shouting, but it sounded miles away. Jack blinked, and then felt a throbbing lump growing on the right side of his head. After falling into the crevasse, his momentum had swung his head against the ice wall.

"You okay?" Marko repeated.

Jack looked up and saw Marko staring down at him from the surface, some fifteen feet above. "Watch that first step," he croaked. "It's a doozy."

Marko turned to Leah. "He's conscious."

She crawled toward the lip of the crevasse. "Are you hurt?"

"I'm not sure yet," Jack replied. "Send me down a rope with a carabiner on the end."

Marko scrambled back toward his own pack and pulled out a length of line. He dropped it down into the crevasse, and Jack secured his gear pack.

"Do you want me to pull it up?" Marko asked.

"Just hold the weight for now. I want to get my spare axe." Jack removed his ice axe from the rear of the gear pack, making sure to put the safety lanyard around his wrist in case he dropped it. "Okay, take the gear."

Jack pushed off the wall and swung himself toward an ice shelf protruding two meters out from the wall. The second push brought him close enough that he jammed his axe into the ice and pulled himself on to the ledge. "Do you have me secured?"

"I sunk two screws deep in the ice. Are you going to use a jumar to climb out?"

"Give me a second to catch my breath," he said. "I thought for sure I was headed for the bottom."

"Don't thank me," Marko called down. "Leah saved both our asses. My axe slipped and she got a solid bite. Otherwise we'd have all gone down."

"It's getting cold up here, Climber. Move your butt," shouted Leah.

A bead of sweat ran down his nose and hit his glove with an audible splat. Jack stopped and felt his forehead. It was damp with sweat. He peered down into the darkness for a moment. "There's a flashlight in my pack. Get it out and sling it down to me."

A moment later, a small flashlight clipped to Jack's line slid down to his position. Jack fumbled with the switch and aimed the powerful beam down into the crevasse. He saw what appeared to be the bottom at least fifty meters below. A glint in depths caught his eye.

"Something's reflective, could be coming from the bottom of the crevasse." He removed his glove and held his hand out, palm down. "There's definitely heat rising up."

"How can that be?" Leah pushed herself further over the ledge.

"I don't know." He swung the light up and looked around the walls of the crevasse. "I'm coming up."

"We should check it out," she said bluntly when Jack climbed out of the crevasse. "It might be a kind of clue."

"I figured you'd say that," Jack said. "I want to secure a couple more ropes first. We'll use the ice ledge as a staging area. Marko, I'm sending you down first. Secure two ice screw anchor points on the wall."

Marko climbed into a harness and set up a rappel system. He eased himself down into the opening of the crevasse and within a minute stood on the ledge. Jack sent down a small gear bag, from which Marko pulled out several stainless steel ice screws resembling regular household wood screws, except they were nearly a foot long and three-fourths of an inch in diameter.

"Got it," said Marko.

Jack double-checked Leah's harness and then grabbed her arm. "Go down and wait with Marko for me on the ledge. I'm securing a couple of back-up lines first. Then I'm gonna give Paulson a call."

Leah rappelled down the steep, icy walls, pushing off every few feet with the steel-tipped crampons.

Marko helped swing her onto the ice ledge. "Nicely done."

"Let's get to the bottom."

"Shouldn't we wait for Jack?"

"Let him have all the fun?" Without another word, she rappelled off the ledge, pushing off the ice every five feet. She hit the bottom with a thud and slacked off the line.

"I'm down."

The bottom of the crevasse felt flat and relatively wide. She unhooked and stood clear of the dangling line, then pulled a flashlight from inside her parka and lit up the nearest ice wall. When she turned the beam to the far side of the crevasse, her mouth dropped open in shock.

Chapter 56

"**C**ome in, Tortugas base," Jack called.

Garrett stepped out from under the wing of the *Las Tortugas* and pulled the radio from his coat, fumbling with it through thick gloves. He held the radio up and pressed the transmit button.

"How are you guys doing over there?"

"We're only about a third of the way up to the base of Thor's Hammer, but we've found a crevasse."

"A big one?"

"Deep and I don't think it's due to shifting ice. There's warmth coming up from the bottom."

"Can you work around it?"

"We're climbing down to take a look."

"Be careful. Even I know those ice crevasses open and close in a flash."

"What's happening with the plane? We heard the engines rumbling."

"We found out why the Russians didn't get the B-29 out of here. The test engine blew oil all over the ice, and us. The mechanics have the inspection ports open but if they have to remove the cowlings we're not going anywhere. How's Leah? Giving you any trouble?"

"I've got her occupied," Jack replied. "Right now she's dying to rappel into the crevasse."

"When do we get to join the adventure?"

"Get your release note from Paulson and come on over."

"You'd better check up on Leah. It sounds like she's been on her own for at least five minutes—and you know that spells trouble."

CHAPTER 57

When Leah illuminated the ice wall, she found out to her surprise that it wasn't ice, but a metallic surface. The exposed portion extended up from the floor for three meters and appeared to measure three meters in width.

"What's happening?" Marko asked.

"I found something; maybe an old plane crash," Leah replied between deep breaths.

"I thought Jack said it only snowed like two inches a year. How can there be an airplane under a hundred feet of ice?"

"Get your butt down here and see for yourself."

Jack crawled to the edge of the crevasse and looked over, expecting to find Leah and Marko standing on the ledge. Instead, all he saw were ice-screw anchors and two ropes leading toward the bottom of the crevasse.

"What the hell are you two doing?" he shouted.

Leah said, "I found what looks like an airplane wreck, a big one."

"Stay right where you are; don't move." Jack swung himself over the lip of the crevasse and fast-rappelled.

"Something's melting the ice," Leah said when Jack hit the bottom of the crevasse. "It's coming from down here; feel the warmth." She pulled his ungloved hand down to a six-inch gap between the slush and the bottom of what appeared to be a sliding door that remained partially open. More of the opening appeared to be hidden below feet of semi-soft ice.

Jack instinctively recoiled as warm air brushed up and over his hand. He hesitated and then began digging through the slush with gloved hands. In less than a minute, he had increased the six-inch gap between the bottom of the door and the ice by half a meter.

"Give me a hand here," he said.

Five minutes later, they had cleared away enough snow and ice to crawl through the doorway and examine the interior of whatever structure stood before them. Jack dropped to his stomach, pulled himself underneath. He illuminated the space with his flashlight.

He expected to find a mountain of twisted and broken aluminum like he'd seen at other remote mountain crash sites.

Instead, the beam reflected off a small rectangular compartment. The only recognizable feature was another doorway leading further into the structure. The second door was sealed tight and appeared to be made of the same smooth, silvery metallic substance. Its only marking was a triangle-shaped depression in its center, about six inches long on each side.

Jack shoved his way back out. "It's not a commercial jet airliner. This looks more like an airlock than something you'd see on an aircraft."

"What then?" Leah asked.

"I don't know. There's an undamaged compartment inside, with another doorway, although it looks sealed. The floor is covered with water and something is generating enough heat to melt snow and carve out this deep crevasse."

He glanced up toward the surface. "I'm headed topside to call Paulson. He's the expert on plane crashes."

"What do you want us to do?" Marko asked.

"It'll take energy to jumar up the ice wall," Jack said. "You two sit tight." He stared at Leah. "Stay out of there until I get back."

Jack disappeared over the lip of the crevasse; Leah dropped to her knees. "Come on, Marko, let's go inside."

CHAPTER 58

J ack pulled himself over the lip of the crevasse and crawled to solid ground before standing. He zipped up his parka against the cold and searched the pockets for his handheld radio. He checked to make sure the Motorola communicator was tuned to the proper channel.

"Las Tortugas base, do you copy?"

Paulson's voice bellowed through the radio's speaker. "Go ahead, Jack."

"We found something at the bottom of the ice. It could be aircraft wreckage."

"What kind of wreck? Military?"

"I was only able to gain access to a small section of the fuselage, or whatever it is"

"Jesus, did you find any bodies?"

"That's the strange part; no, and I don't see much damage either." Jack paused. "I know you guys are working on the *Las Tortugas*, but—"

"Stand by...."

Jack paced the ice, stomping his feet to warm his toes.

"Okay, here's what we're gonna do," Paulson said. "I'm coming over with Garrett since Ridley says it'll be a cold day in hell before he climbs down into a hole in the ice."

"I've got Leah and Marko standing at the bottom of the crevasse. How soon will you be here?"

"Twenty minutes' tops on the snow machine," Paulson replied. "A much shorter trip than you had pulling those sleds."

CHAPTER 59

"Come on," Leah said from her prone position on the ice. "Don't be such a baby."

Marko paced the slushy ice floor of the crevasse. "I'm waiting for Jack. He told us not to poke around inside until he returned." He backed away from the doorway. "You go on ahead."

"Have it your way." Leah picked up the flashlight and slid under the lip of the entry. "I'm standing up in here," she called back to him.

A moment later, the young climber forced his way after her through the narrow opening.

"There are a couple inches of water, so watch out." She patted his shoulder when he stood up. "See, no bogeyman." She pulled off her glove and felt around the inner door's seal. "I wonder how we open this second door."

"Sure you want to? Jack said that could be an airlock."

"You're nervous as a cat, and you're making me jumpy. Nothing's gonna bite you in here...I'm pretty sure." She placed her palm against the wall and pulled it away. "This wall feels warm."

Marko took two steps back. "Whatever you say."

Leah let her fingers trace along the triangular indentation in the door's surface. "There's got to be an opening mechanism of some kind."

Leah jerked her hand away. "Whoa. I got a little shock right here in the middle of this triangle." She looked to Marko. "Maybe this is how you gain entry; some kind of identification system, fingerprints or something."

"Obviously you don't know the right code. So it sent you a warning."

"Only the military would think up this kind of draconian security system," Leah said. "I wonder if this is some kind of CIA base, designed to spy on the Russians or something."

"Watch out, Leah...that wall already bit you once."

"Hold the light so I can see what I'm doing."

She opened her hand and placed it against the wall, sliding her palm around in an attempt to relocate the sensitive spot inside the triangle. She spread her palm as wide as she could and leaned against the door.

Without warning, the door slid open vertically, disappearing into the wall. Replacing the smooth surface was a cavernous blackness, into which Leah fell more than stepped. As Marko rushed forward to pull her back, the door slammed down at lightning speed, trapping her inside.

CHAPTER 60

"Leah, can you hear me?" Marko beat the door with his fists, then kicked at it in frustration. He felt around the center of the entry with his hand and got no response. "I've got to find Jack," he said to himself in desperation. He started crawling through the partially open entryway, only to have his face sprayed with ice crystals.

It was Jack, rappelling down the wall at high speed.

"She wouldn't wait," Marko said breathlessly. "She started messing with the second doorway inside the thing, and somehow it opened and sucked her inside."

Jack landed heavily on the ice floor. "Relax and tell me as best you can exactly what happened."

"We crawled under the door," Marko paused. "Then she starts feeling around the center of the inner door. There was a mark on the middle of the door. It gave her a shock."

"A shock?" Jack dropped down on his stomach, preparing to pull himself under the doorway.

"A small electric shock, that's what she said anyway. She wasn't hurt, so—"

"She decided to give it one more test."

"That's when the door opened." Marko shook his head in disbelief. "I swear to God, it sucked her inside and slammed shut."

Jack pushed his way through the gap, and Marko followed.

"Show me exactly where she touched the door."

"Right here." The beam of the flashlight shook as Marko tried to hold it steady.

Jack reached out and let his fingertips brush against the entry. "You said she felt some kind of shock."

"She jerked her hand back real fast. It scared the crap out of me."

Jack allowed his fingers to roam over the center of the triangle shape. Every time he moved his hand, Marko flinched. "I'm not feeling anything at all. You sure it was in this area?"

"Right there."

Jack stood and stared at the doorway for several minutes, his jaw clenching tight as he analyzed the problem. "Stay here. If you hear or see anything, give a good shout."

Forty minutes later, Paulson and Garrett rolled up to the crevasse and shut down the snow machine. Jack glanced at his watch. "What took you guys?"

"We got about ten minutes out of camp and Garrett's radio caught fire in his hand. Looks like something overloaded it to such a degree that the lithium battery literally cooked off. We went back to camp to get another one but it turns out every handheld radio we had turned on at the time fried. Better check yours. If you had it on, it's likely in the same condition."

"I had mine off to save battery," Jack said, checking the radio after pulling it from his parka. He switched it on, and the LED screen lit up. "I'm good here. What do you think caused it?"

"Don't know," said Paulson. "Lucky we had the aircraft comms shut down. If I was the paranoid type, I'd think maybe our government had a hand in it."

"Well, just because you're paranoid," said Jack, "doesn't mean somebody's not after you."

CHAPTER 61

W hen Leah tried to stand, she slipped, falling hard onto the smooth surface. She felt a thin layer of liquid covering the floor, water that probably entered when the door shot open. She couldn't see the water—or anything else. It was dark inside. Pitch-black.

She sat up and took several deep breaths. The air tasted thick and putrid; breathable, but barely. She felt her heart rate increase and, with a tinge of irony, realized how Jack felt when he suffered a bout of claustrophobia.

Same as crawling through darkened caverns in New Mexico, Leah thought. Simply take a deep breath, stand up calmly, find the door, hope it opens from the inside, and exit posthaste.

Leah drew in a breath and pushed herself to a standing position. She reached out and realized the doorway wasn't within reach. It reminded her of having a power failure at home when you least expected it. Suddenly you're completely disoriented, using your sense of touch exclusively in an environment that you know well but that suddenly seems terrifyingly alien. She took two tentative steps with hands extended, finding only empty air.

"Marko!" Her voice echoed within the structure, but she received no response. That didn't surprise her.

The jammed door leading into the structure had been about half an inch thick. Made sense. You'd need something like that to survive in Antarctica.

Leah turned and faced the opposite direction, or at least what she thought was the opposite direction. She extended her arms, hoping within two or three steps she'd touch the familiar smooth surface. She took three steps forward, two more than she'd taken facing the other direction. At the end of the third step, Leah reached out but found nothing but stale air.

"Marko, open the door!" she shouted in anger and desperation.

Instead of turning 180 degrees, she turned 90 degrees. This way she'd make three steps at all points of the compass. If the wall were within three steps, she would have to run into it, so long as she continued scientifically.

Leah put her hands out in front and took one step. When her hands touched only air, she stepped forward one more step.

On the third step, her left boot struck something. She fell more out of surprise than lack of balance, hitting her forehead directly on the wet floor.

CHAPTER 62

Beckam did a re-count just to make sure all the SEALs had boarded the Globemaster while the pilots and crew readied the aircraft for flight.

"We're good to go, Skipper," Frantino said.

Beckam studied the body language of his crew as they settled into the nylon web seating for the long flight. He read excitement in their posture. They'd all been around long enough to know the mission was more than some training sortie. Any chance of seeing real action tended to bring Navy SEALs to life.

As if reading Beckam's mind, Frantino gave him a wicked grin. "It's about time we got back into the shit."

CHAPTER 63

"It's not an aircraft," Paulson said, feeling the surface with his ungloved hand.

"How can you tell?" asked Jack.

"The fuselage has no curvature. If it was an airplane, even a huge one, we'd see some curvature to the surface." Paulson shrugged. "My guess is a weather or science station."

"Well, whatever it is, Leah's trapped in it." Jack pointed to the hole dug underneath the partially opened doorway. "Follow me." Inside, he showed Paulson the second door. "So she touches the middle part here, and the thing slides open and she falls in." Jack said. "You give it a shot. It all feels about the same to me."

Paulson placed his bare palms near the center of the triangle-shaped indentation and felt around the smooth metal surface. "If Miss Smarty-pants got her butt in there, we can too. Let's figure out what she did."

Leah rolled over on to her back, her head pounding. She reached up and felt around her forehead while cold water dripped down her face.

She had tripped over something. If the object had been solid, she might have caught her balance. Instead it gave way, like kicking a rolled-up carpet. It had caught the toe of her boot, and she'd fallen over it.

Leah realized her hands were running across a rather thin but distinctly recognizable shape: that of a human face. She bolted to her feet and ran without regard to direction. On the fourth step, she slammed directly into the wall.

Paulson turned to Marko. "You sure that's the spot she touched?"

"That's right where she held her hand."

"If it's some kind of fingerprint detector, I guess it's possible or even likely Leah's hand has the necessary parameters needed to engage the mechanism." He shrugged. "Actually, that makes no sense at all." Frustrated, Paulson went back to studying the triangular impression that apparently had engaged the opening mechanism.

Suddenly the door flashed open, and Leah fell into the room with them. As she crossed the threshold, the door slammed shut.

Garrett, Jack, Marko, and Paulson stood in shock as Leah lay prone on the wet deck, breathing heavily.

Jack knelt to her side. "Are you okay?"

She nodded and after three more breaths pushed herself up to her knees.

Garrett reached down and lifted one arm while Jack lifted the other.

"There's a body inside," she said matter-of-factly.

"Body?" Jack said. Paulson's eyebrows raised, and even Garrett, always Mr. calm and collected, looked shocked.

Jack glanced at Paulson, then at Garrett and sighed. "What else?"

Leah pushed wet hair out of her face. "I don't know because it's completely dark." She paused and then spun around to face Marko. "Thanks for opening the door. Were you guys planning to leave me in there to teach me a lesson?"

"We all tried to get through the door with zero luck," said Jack.

"Looks like you're the only one with the magic touch," Paulson added.

"Yeah, well, I've been telling Hobson that for years." She looked at the three of them. "If you boys can scrounge up a couple of flashlights, I'd be willing to go back inside and check it out."

Jack studied the doorway and felt along its edges with his fingers. "We've got no idea what this place is—for all we know, it's some kind of secret military operation."

Paulson examined the walls. "I'm not sure it's a good idea to go back inside. It could be emitting radiation. It might be the source of whatever burned out our radios."

"Why do you say that?" Jack asked.

"Because it's still generating enough heat to melt a hole in the ice," Paulson said. "That means it's got a helluva power system. The fact that somehow Leah can open the door makes it even more mysterious. That'd make no sense if it were a military creation."

. "And… you've already found at least *one* dead body," Garrett said.

"Did you happen to notice if your hands were glowing while you strolled around inside?" Jack asked, deadpan.

"Thanks for your concern, Climber."

"What was the temperature in there?" Paulson asked.

She shrugged. "I didn't notice. It didn't smell good, though."

"If there's a serious radiation leak, then we're all cooked already anyway," said Paulson. "I vote for going in if she can get the door back open."

"What if we all get trapped?" Jack asked.

"Why don't we try to block the door open before going in," Paulson suggested.

Jack looked over at Garrett, who'd been standing by quietly. "What do you think?"

"I'd say let's take a risk."

Jack studied the sealed entry. "Marko, grab a couple ice axes."

When Marko returned with the axes, Jack said, "So Leah works her magic, and when the door flashes open…." He showed how he would hold the axe vertically under the door. "When it drops, we'll see if the axe can handle the pressure."

"If so, do we all go inside?" asked the billionaire.

"Marko, I want to you stay here." Jack said.

"Why?"

"Because if anything happens and we can't escape, you're to drive the snow machine back to the *Las Tortugas* and tell Ridley to return here with cutting torches." Jack crouched down in front of the door. "Okay, Leah, see if you can open the door."

Leah stepped up and laid her palm flat on the smooth surface. She slid her hand around in a circular motion, feeling for the right spot within the triangle.

"This is it." She leaned forward, pressing her palm out flat.

The door flashed upward and Jack jammed the axe into the darkness, hoping he had it centered. He felt the shock of the door slamming down on the head of the axe with tremendous force. Far too fast for him to get his hand out of the way.

CHAPTER 64

Juan listened to the roar of the B-29's engines in the distance. The last time he'd spoken to Ridley, the mechanic was attempting to get a handle on the oil leaks. That required cranking the engines up one at a time, identifying the leaks, and then shutting it down and repairing it while the Wright radial engine remained warm enough to restart it.

Rooster shambled over in his greasy overalls. "What's happening, partner?"

"Can't reach Jack on the radio," Juan said, pointing over toward the *Las Tortugas*.

Suddenly the roar died, and after a mild backfire, the *Las Tortugas* went silent. Juan pulled the radio back out of his pocket, turned it on and pushed the transmit button. "Hey, Mac, you copy?"

"I read you loud and clear. I'm guessing you didn't have your radio on a few minutes ago."

Juan shrugged. "No, just turned it on."

"Mine got hot as hell and quit working."

"What's the status on the bomber?" Juan asked after examining his radio.

"We're lucky so far. We've been able to fix most of the leaks without having to remove the cowlings. I'd say we're running ahead of schedule."

"Have you heard from Jack or Leah?"

"Jack called in and said he'd found a crevasse and what appeared to be an aircraft wreck. Al and Garrett drove over to take a look-see. How are you coming along with changing out that tire?"

Juan handed the radio to Rooster.

"We managed to remove it, but we need to pull the stem and empty the propane. Then we can dig a spare out and install it.

"How long?"

Rooster looked over at Juan and shrugged. "Twenty or thirty minutes to empty the tire."

"You guys aren't going to empty that propane anywhere near the Caribou, are you?"

"Hell, no," Rooster said with a chuckle. "We're gonna use Juan here to muscle it on to a sled and then pull it onto open ice and run like hell."

"We're cooking up hot chow," Ridley said. "How about I send Perez over with the snow machine, and instead of pulling that thing by hand, we can tow it out on open ice and drain it while we have some hot soup."

Rooster stomped his feet on the ice. "That's the best idea I've heard all day.

CHAPTER 65

When the axe didn't shatter and Jack's hands remained intact, he opened his eyes cautiously. The axe remained trapped under the door, held by such pressure that he couldn't budge it, even by yanking on the climbing tool with both hands.

"It's holding," he said cautiously, "for now."

"What would happen if the axe broke while someone was crawling underneath the door?" Paulson asked.

"You'd be cut cleanly in half." Jack reached for the second axe and wedged it under the door. "Since Leah was able to open the door from the inside, we probably don't need to do this, but I'm not leaving anything to chance."

Jack dropped to the wet floor and examined the cavernous interior. His flashlight illuminated the shriveled figure, curled up in the fetal position. "I see the body. Otherwise it appears empty."

One by one, Leah, Paulson, Garrett, and he slid under the wedged door and stood inside the darkened chamber, leaving Marko in the outer room. Jack's narrow flashlight beam cut through the darkness, reaching up toward a domed ceiling, apparently made of the same smooth, silvery metallic surface as the outside walls and the small entry room.

The vertical walls blending into the symmetrical domed ceiling reminded Jack of visiting a planetarium. The chamber was otherwise empty, except for three table-shaped structures, set in a triangle at equal distances from the walls.

Jack knelt next to the small, shriveled shape. "This body appears mummified."

Leah joined him but didn't touch the blackened skin. "It looks old, possibly hundreds of years."

"Wonder how it got here," Garrett asked. "You think someone else has been on to this story?"

She bent down and examined the long black hair streaming off the skull. "It's a good bet this is the body of a woman."

CHAPTER 66

The pilot-in-command nodded to Gus Beckam. They were lining up on the jump at 20,000 feet AGL—20,000 feet over the ice. The nod from the pilot indicated that Beckam should make final preparations before the air force crew cracked and depressurized the C-17 cargo ramp.

Beckam climbed down the ladder from the cockpit into the cargo bay. His four teams of six commandos each checked and rechecked each other's gear while the load-master, wearing an oxygen mask and electrically warmed flight suit, hit the switch to open the loading ramp at the rear of the Globemaster.

Beckam's first impression was that of a giant clam opening; something out of the 1960s TV show "Voyage to the Bottom of the Sea." His second impression was of sudden and intense cold as the heat sucked out of the fuselage.

Breathing wasn't a problem. He wore an oxygen mask, O2 bottle and Nomex flight coveralls over an arctic-white combat suit. He waddled toward the back of the aircraft, weighed down with a hundred pounds of combat gear, including a Beretta 92-SF in a thigh holster and a Heckler & Koch MP5 machine gun, along with 600 rounds of ammo, plastic explosives, a second parachute, and a host of other necessary and mostly lethal goodies.

Beckam adjusted his oxygen mask, necessary at this altitude to keep him and his men from passing out, then waited in anticipation of a green light signaling they were over the drop zone.

When the twin green jump indicator lights came on, the teams flung their heavily loaded bodies off the ramp and into an atmosphere so thin and cold that exposed skin would freeze instantly.

Commander Beckam spread his arms and legs out like a flattened crab's in the same way he'd done nearly a thousand times before. He looked through his jump goggles at the landscape and, more important, his altimeter. He'd calculated they'd have approximately ninety seconds of free fall at 130 miles per hour before they opened their parachutes at the leisurely altitude of 1,800 feet above the frozen surface.

When he passed through 1,900 feet, he released a small pilot chute from his parachute pack. As the pilot chute pulled his main parachute out of its container, he dropped one shoulder just in case the chute caught in the vacuum—called a "burble"—forming at the small of his back.

When he felt the lines tighten as the main chute inflated, he snapped his knees into the airborne version of a deep knee bend. The overwhelming air pressure on his outstretched arms and the sudden reduced pressure on his lower body caused Beckam to pivot into a vertical position.

He reached up and grabbed the risers a millisecond before the chute snapped open and his airspeed dropped from 130 to only 20 miles per hour in a bone-cracking 1.5 seconds.

Beckam looked up and counted the open panels on the parachute. Called "squares," the chutes were more rectangular than square and allowed a jumper to glide down with more directional mobility and forward speed than the old round chutes made famous by paratroopers in World War II. All his panels were open and inflated, so he cleared the steering toggles and pulled hard on the right one to initiate a high-speed spiral toward the ice.

The massive granite cliff known as Thor's Hammer overlooking the valley stood a short distance away. Beckam made note to stay away from the dangerous downdrafts created by the mountain cliffs and ridges, especially in the prevailing twenty-knot winds.

As he spun toward the ground, Beckam caught a glimpse of the *Las Tortugas*, its gleaming aluminum skin contrasting sharply with the more recent, blackened carcass of the Russian aircraft.

The ice came up fast. Beckam held his breath, released his gear bag, and pulled on both steering toggles, hoping to slow his descent by flaring the canopy directly above the frozen surface.

He hit the ice hard. The parachute, now powered by the surface winds, dragged him and his gear horizontally across the coarse surface. Beckam pulled a ring that cut away his parachute on one side, allowing the air to escape.

He took several deep breaths before standing. Quickly and quietly, he gathered the SEALs and assessed the success of the jump with one simple question.

"Everybody in one piece?"

The nods and professional manner told him the team was on the ice safely and ready to go.

Frantino produced a compact pair of high-powered binoculars. Beckam studied Thor's Hammer, then turned the glasses in the direction of the B-29.

Bodies wearing brightly colored cold-weather overalls scattered like ants from a kicked anthill. They clearly knew Beckam and his platoon had dropped in for an unscheduled visit.

"I want everyone to remember that these are not combatants." Beckam looked several of his SEALs directly in the eye. "That, gentleman, means you will use restraint. I don't have to remind you this mission is a pet project of the President. Unless you want to spend the rest of your career advising the Botswanan military, I suggest you think twice and open your mouth once."

The Senior Chief Reynolds raised his hand. "So if someone starts taking pot shots at us, should we return fire or shout soft poetry?"

Beckam grinned. "I don't believe we will be shot at. That said, there's shit we haven't been told, so report anything out of the ordinary." His expression hardened. "Everything I just said goes out the window if we meet up with Russians or anyone else packing weapons and hostile intent."

Beckam shouldered his pack. "I'm buying the booze when we get back to Virginia. Now, let's get this done quick and clean."

CHAPTER 67

Chase Parker stood in front of the Caribou, allowing himself a rare treat: sight-seeing. They had decided to put the spare tire on the Caribou first, to avoid having the airplane up on jacks and stands any longer than necessary. The only remaining task was towing the propane-laden wheel out onto the ice, clearing the propane and loading it back into the cargo bay for the trip home.

"Hey," shouted Rooster to his brother. "We've got the sled hooked up and the tire strapped down. Let's get a move on."

Chase suddenly held up his hand, signaling he needed a moment of silence.

"What's he doing?" Juan stamped his feet around the ice, trying to keep warm.

"Hell if I know." Rooster jogged toward the nose of the Caribou. "We're all freezing our asses off back here."

"I heard something."

Rooster looked at his brother warily. "Like what?"

"I'm not sure but it sounded like a parachute opening at terminal velocity."

"What?"

Chase pointed toward a white canopy spiraling downward. "Shit, we're about to have company." He spun and sprinted toward the snow machine. "Get it cranked up!"

"What the hell's happening?" Juan asked.

"Paratroopers are dropping in, and I'd bet it's not a social call."

Juan jumped on the snow machine behind Perez. Rooster and Chase hopped on top of the propane-filled tire, now secured on the equipment sled.

"Go!" shouted Chase.

Perez let the clutch out and slammed the throttle open. The snow machine's rubber and steel tread spun just long enough to cover the Parkers with ice before it got a bite and roared toward the Russian base and the *Las Tortugas*.

CHAPTER 68

"Let's assume for argument's sake that this is one of your Native American travelers. Could this body be 800 years old, based on its appearance?"

"I can't say for sure," Leah replied.

"You guys okay in there?"

"We're fine, Marko," Jack said, "but we've found another door and we're going to jam it open."

"Can I come take a look?"

Jack hesitated and then said, "Okay, bring a couple more axes with you."

Jack crouched down in front of the second sealed doorway, axes held at the ready.

"Okay, Leah. Open it."

When the door flashed open, instead of thrusting the axe, Jack flew back across the smooth floor in an explosion of compressed gas.

Leah skidded across the floor with visions of a commercial airliner suffering explosive decompression. She ended up lying near the opposite side of the rounded room with Jack sprawled on top of her.

Paulson was the first to his feet; he rushed over to Jack. "You okay?"

Jack nodded, and Paulson helped him into a sitting position as Garrett and Marko checked out Leah.

"Where's the axe?"

"I don't know. All I remember is a hammer hitting me in the chest and not much else."

"Over here." Marko walked cautiously across the wet floor and retrieved it.

"That explains those airtight doors," Paulson noted.

Jack pushed to his feet. "Why would the military pressurize a science station?"

Paulson shrugged. "If we hadn't found the body, I'd say this was a test model for a habitat to be used on the moon, or maybe a trip to Mars. Likely wasn't pure oxygen, or it probably would have exploded with the first spark and we'd be toast. Clearly a mixed gas with enough oxygen to breath, and not blended with something else that would kill us. There's no need for pressurization unless you needed to breath a richer mix of gas, or, in case of a containment breach, like we created, the outside atmosphere stays outside." Paulson eyes opened wide. "You said this appeared to be the site of an avalanche. If that kind of decompression happened at the entrance, the shock might be enough to trigger off unstable ice."

"That would explain the location." Jack rubbed his head, where now he had two lumps: one from falling into the crevasse and the other from being tossed across the room. "You'd need to isolate the inhabitants in an environment resembling a hostile planet's surface." He paused. "The slide that covered this has been here a while, a long while. I didn't happen yesterday, or for decades I'd wager."

"Pressurize the inside of the structure," said Paulson thoughtfully.

"It's not pressurized anymore," Leah said hopefully.

Jack nodded. "It could be that the small outside compartment served as an airlock." He wiped water from his face. "That matches up with your theory, Al."

"Think so?"

Jack nodded. "If both doors leading outside were opened at the same time, the explosive decompression would could a massive shock wave into the ice. Thor's Hammer would serve to magnify it."

"If 'someone' were still inside...." Garrett began.

"They'd be buried under a million tons of ice," said Jack.

Paulson glanced at the sealed doorway. "Stands to reason why we got just a little puff of air on door number one. Probably be the same with door number two, now that we've all had our bell rung with the first attempt."

"This time everyone stands clear of the door before we plant the axe." Jack knelt to the right of the door, making sure to position himself behind the solid wall.

"Okay, Leah."

She reached up and pressed her palm against the familiar triangle. A millisecond later, the door flashed open and Jack thrust the axe underneath, letting it slam down into position. Only a light puff of warm air flowed from the door, signaling that the interior had depressurized itself completely during the explosive decompression.

"Okay, same drill," said Jack. "You guys follow unless I start shouting." He dropped to the floor and pulled himself underneath and into the darkness.

Leah peeked through behind him. The hair on the back of her neck stood up as Jack's beam traveled around the interior; even the powerful halogen beam couldn't cut through to the opposite wall.

"It looks okay," he said. "Come on through."

It was a much larger room, reminding Leah of an oversized wine cellar. Instead of wine bottles, massive racks contained bottle-shaped units, appearing to be three or four meters in length. The bottom half of each tube seemed to be made of the same silvery metallic substance as the rest of the structure. The top halves were semitransparent, a soft, yellow glow emanating from their glass-like surface.

Leah headed straight for the system of racks and tube units and looked at the first container she reached.

Inside, lay a perfectly preserved human body.

CHAPTER 69

Ridley stood with his arms held high as soldiers dressed in arctic combat garb pointed short-barreled automatic weapons at his chest. Each carried a large, white backpack and wore communications gear. The soldiers' eyes were concealed by ski-style goggles with yellow tinted lenses.

"Please remove your headgear," said one of the commandos.

Ridley glanced from side to side and nodded, indicating they should all pull down their hoods or remove their wool hats.

"I'm Commander Gus Beckam. Our orders are to evacuate Mr. Paulson and his party to a secure location within the United States. I'm looking for Mr. Paulson."

Ridley stepped forward, a sign he knew from experience would identify him as the man in charge. He kept his hands up. "Paulson's not here." He turned in the direction of Thor's Hammer. "Others in our party are over near the mountain called Thor's Hammer, examining an apparent plane crash."

"How many of your team is located at the base of the mountain?"

"Five others, including Paulson."

Several SEALs appeared from around the wing of the *Las Tortugas*. They walked up to the commander and conferred quietly.

The SEAL commander turned again to Ridley. "We'd like to use your snow machines and sleds to secure Mr. Paulson and the second group."

Ridley nodded. The request had been made politely, but Ridley knew if he refused, they'd take the vehicles anyway.

"Are you in radio communication with Paulson?"

"We think they roped down into a crevasse because we can't raise them on the radio." Ridley looked at the SEAL before continuing. "Our radios burned up like 4th of July sparklers. You wouldn't know anything about that, I suppose?"

Beckam paused for a moment to consider what Ridley said. "No, I don't." He pointed toward the sled-snow-machine combination parked next to the B-29. "Clear the wheel and tire off the sled."

Two SEALs lifted the wheel and propane-filled tire off the sled and rolled it over to the nearest Russian building, one that had been used as a makeshift machine shop.

Rooster glanced at his brother and then at Ridley as the SEALs leaned the tire against the wall. Ridley shook his head in a clear signal to keep their mouths shut. No reason to complicate the situation by trying to explain that the commandos were handling a potential bomb.

The SEAL pointed toward the snow machine. "Check it out."

"It's warmed up and in good shape, Skipper."

Ridley heard someone call the leader by the name of Beckam.

"Danny," Beckam said back to the man, "you take a crew over to that crevasse and find and secure the five climbers. We should have transportation here within twelve hours, provided weather isn't a problem. Make sure you collect all radios and satellite phones from the civilians. We don't want or need any unauthorized 911 calls."

"Kind of like killing a spider with a howitzer, ain't it," Ridley said in an offhand manner.

"Gather your men," he ordered Ridley, "and follow me."

CHAPTER 70

Each three-meter, semi-clear tube contained one human body lying on spongy material that molded itself to the shape of the occupant.

Jack touched the smooth surface that made up the top half of the tube and jerked his hand away. It felt icy cold to the touch in comparison with the warm temperature of the room. The body inside looked ghostly white, with a metallic-looking cloth covering the torso; a clear glassy tube about a half an inch in diameter running the length of the tube entered the body at what appeared to be the inner thigh.

"Did you notice...?" he said aloud.

Leah nodded.

The occupants looked very much like ethnic Native Americans.

"They're alive," Leah said.

"How do you know? I don't see any movement, no sign of breathing, no moisture on the glass."

"They look frozen," said Marko.

Paulson stood over the viewing port on the bottom tube and examined the body inside. "It might be some kind of cryonics experiment."

"Cry-what?" asked Marko.

"Cryonics. The science of placing a body in a deep freeze for months, years, even centuries, then reviving them later." Paulson touched the smooth surface of the tube. "I've invested in several companies experimenting with cryonics. The problem they can't overcome is repairing the damage to human cells and organs after they've been frozen at liquid nitrogen temperatures."

"What happens when the cells freeze?" asked Marko.

"They suffer irreparable damage."

Marko shivered and took a step back. "What is that tube running into their leg?"

"Don't know," Paulson replied, "could be a way to circulate the cryonics fluids throughout the body during the freezing process—and maybe other chemicals that are necessary during the reanimation process."

"Then it's a laboratory," Leah said. "What if these people have been frozen for 800 years or more?"

"Hey, now," said Jack. "This is modern technology."

"*More* than modern, wouldn't you say? Think about it," she said. "This is the answer we've been searching for; why these people hid in caves and cliffs. They had to hide. From *this*."

"You're not suggesting this place is the result of an extraterrestrial snatch-and-grab program some 800 years ago, are you?"

"That's exactly what I'm suggesting." She gestured around them. "All the evidence fits. We've got granite crystals from this site, a damn-near perfect pictograph of Thor's Hammer, and a bunch of frozen Native Americans."

"Why the hell would someone travel all the way here," Paulson said, "and build a lab in the most inhospitable place on the planet?"

Leah shrugged. "It's one way to conduct science in a sterile or controlled environment. That's first rule of scientific research. Antarctica is cold, so cold it's sterile. Whatever you experiment on, it can't be affected by something in the local environment."

"Or maybe what you're experimenting with," said Garrett, "is so dangerous you wouldn't work with it on your own—planet."

Paulson shook his head. "I don't buy it. There's got to be a simpler explanation. This raises too many questions."

Leah turned to him. "Such as?"

"If these 'visitors' were so advanced; how come you can open their doors?"

"It could be her skin chemistry, or the size of her hand, or the perfume she put on last week," Jack said. "She also happens to be the only woman here."

"Thank goodness at least one person noticed," Leah said.

"And if Jack's theory is correct," Garrett added, "the owners might've been caught outside when the door somehow malfunctioned and the resulting avalanche buried this place. Even the most advanced technology doesn't mean you can't make a bonehead mistake."

Leah wandered past the pods, examining each carefully. She ran the tips of her fingers over the smooth clear surfaces as if tracing imaginary lines across the occupants' faces. Suddenly she stopped and examined one of the ground-level tubes.

"Oh, my God, this one's just a child," she said softly.

Jack flooded the tube with harsh light. Inside, a small, frail body, unmistakably a girl, perhaps ten years of age, lay as if in a coma. Her eyes were closed and her expression tranquil, likely belying the terrible circumstances in which she'd been taken.

"She's beautiful and just a baby," Leah said, a tear rolling down her cheek. "How could they take a child, such a beautiful child?"

"I'll climb out and contact Ridley on the radio," Paulson said. "Whatever we've found is way beyond my level of expertise."

"Don't get into details." Jack pointed at Marko and Garrett. "You two follow him up; everyone, keep this information under your hat for now."

CHAPTER 71

Jack gently gripped Leah's arm with the intention of leading her away from the child. "We've got to go."

She yanked free. "You go. I'm getting these people out of these tubes."

"We don't have a clue how to do that." Jack softened his approach. "Anything that we do might kill them, even if they are alive."

"I'm taking them out of here, with or without your help," she said stubbornly.

"Let's climb out of this hole, and then we can discuss what happens next."

"You can discuss all you want. I know what I'm here to do."

Jack felt anger building in his chest. "Sometimes you can be—"

"Stand where you are and do not move," said an unfamiliar voice from outside the structure.

Jack swung the light around toward the blocked entrance. "Who was that?"

As if anticipating the question, the disembodied voice shouted back. "Please return at once to the point of entry."

A powerful light swept underneath the door, and a second later a white shape slithered under the door and knelt in a firing position.

Chapter 72

Mac Ridley and the others sat glumly on the steel floor of the shipping container that the Russians had used as a machine shop. They'd rolled the Caribou tire inside to use as seating, but it had proven to be less comfortable than sitting on a pile of rags to soften and insulate them from the cold steel floor.

"Waste of time and money, if you ask me," said Rooster, glaring at Beckam, who stood at the door. "Scare the shit out of a few airplane mechanics. Is that the best you can do these days?"

Beckam glanced at Rooster and then spoke softly into the microphone. He nodded once, then stepped back out of the machine shop and locked the two doors with a cable the SEALs had clearly brought along for just such an occasion.

Chase's face broke into a wide grin. "Think he's ordering a pizza?"

Rooster laughed despite himself and slapped his brother on the back.

Chapter 73

Outside, Beckam could scarcely believe what Frantino was telling him.

"It must be a Russian laboratory or something, Skip. We didn't find any weapons, but it's generating heat and there's a shitload of these glass coffins."

"With bodies in them?" Beckam remained incredulous.

"Yeah. I counted thirty, plus one."

"What does that mean?"

"There's an extra one lying in the first room Paulson breached. It's... ah, been there a while."

Beckam swore under his breath. "I'll bet a case of gin this is the little secret we weren't supposed to find out about. I'll phone this in and see if I can't shake a few trees. For now, the mission stays the same. We get the civilians secured and prepare to evacuate."

"So, bring 'em on down?"

"Yeah, secure them in their tents down here. Leave one guard and one of the snow machines in case we need to move in a hurry." He paused. "Oh, and make sure to search the campsite again; just to make sure we've secured any communication devices and weapons before letting them back into those tents."

CHAPTER 74

"I know the way to camp, General," snapped Leah.

"I'm a Navy lieutenant, ma'am," replied Frantino. "But I appreciate the temporary promotion. And change in services."

That was the last word any of them spoke for an hour, when they were all huddled in Jack's tent, sipping hot soup. One SEAL guard stood out in the cold, his machine gun slung in a semi-ready position.

Leah lifted the cup of hot liquid to her lips. "So what do we do now?"

"I wouldn't RSVP to any Christmas parties," Jack replied.

Leah rolled her eyes. "Did you hear the guy in charge—Frantino? He thinks it's a Russian military base, for Christ's sake."

"They'll figure it out," Garret said.

Leah shook her head in frustration. "If we're right, this will change how we think about our world, our universe, forever. There's no way the government can keep this a secret."

"Oh, sure they can keep it a secret," Paulson said, spooning more soup into his cup, "and they won't be thinking of the philosophical, cultural, or spiritual consequences."

"What can be more important than that?"

"Technology and power," Jack said, after sitting quiet. "If that structure has a power source that's been cooking for nearly eight hundred years...." He didn't bother to finish.

"Plus they've tapped the key to cryonics," Paulson said, "if the poor souls in those tubes are really alive."

"They're right," Garrett said. "No government would dare share technology like that."

Marko asked, "So are we dealing with a—a flying saucer or something?"

Paulson shook his head. "I don't think what we found was meant to fly. The shape's not conducive to flight and I didn't see anything that resembles flight control systems. My guess, as unreal as it sounds, is that this was some kind of transfer station. You'd bring your victims, or patients, or whatever here. Maybe they were checked out for diseases and then put into those stasis tubes for transport."

"Like the first astronauts that went to the moon," Garrett added. "They had to spend weeks in some isolation trailer to make sure they hadn't brought back any moon bugs."

Paulson nodded. "When pressure blew and the avalanche covered the station, either they couldn't get to it or decided it had been destroyed. Given the fact that it was buried under hundreds of feet of ice in the middle of Antarctica they had good reason to assume that it'd never be found in the future."

Marko cleared his throat. "Have you guys forgotten something? What happens if these aliens or whoever come looking for their property?"

Paulson grinned. "If Leah's right, I'd like to be around for that."

Jack dropped his spoon into the empty cup. "We need a plan to get out of here."

"Why?" Leah asked.

"I've got a bad feeling about this."

"You always say that."

"Look," Jack said. "We're sitting on what will be the biggest discovery in the history of man. If what we've seen is true, it's gonna push the discovery of fire right out of the history books. Think about it. An endless power supply, cryonics technology, and who-knows-what other advanced technology percolating inside that lab."

"So it'll change humankind for the better." Leah shrugged. "I for one can't wait to get the word out. It could bring relief to so many suffering around the world."

"That's my point," Jack said. "If this is exposed, there'll be tremendous pressure to share this technology and, knowing how government works, they're not going to do that willingly. After all, it could offer the military an entirely new generation of weaponry; it could change the balance of power forever. No, this is a secret the government will mean to keep, and that bodes ill for the likes of us."

"That sounds like acute paranoia, Climber."

"I don't think so," Paulson said. "Once this gets to the White House, issues of national security are going to be raised, and national security trumps all. For all I know, we might end up in Guantanamo Bay permanently if we don't agree to keep our mouths shut."

Leah's expression changed to one of concern. "So what are you suggesting we do?"

"We need a plan to get out of here on our own, not in custody. That means getting to the Caribou and getting off the ice on our own terms."

Chapter 75

Jack woke with a start and glanced at his watch. He'd been asleep for six hours. He glanced around the tent; everyone else remained stretched out in their sleeping bags. Paulson was even snoring softly.

They'd worked every angle of escape for more than two hours but no one could come up with anything that remotely sounded realistic, given the two armed guards stationed outside the tent. The fact that they were all bone-tired hadn't helped. After several arguments had broken out, Jack called a time out. They all needed sleep; otherwise, they'd be in no shape to carry out an escape, even if the opportunity presented itself.

Jack leaned over and unzipped the vestibule on the tent. His eyes opened wide in surprise. Only one SEAL seemed to be standing guard. Given that they'd been sleeping, maybe the SEALs had assumed they were secured.

He leaned back into the tent, scratching at three-day stubble. Only one guard remained, but how to overcome him was still a puzzle. With his brain fresh from sleep, ideas flashed through his head, one after the other.

Suddenly his eyes opened wide. "Jesus, that might work," he murmured. The others woke as Jack began digging through his gear bag.

"What's happening?" Leah asked, pulling hair away from her face.

"I've got an idea," he whispered. He couldn't believe he hadn't thought of it sooner.

"If I can find the magic box, we might have a ticket out of here well ahead of that."

"What's the magic box?" Marko asked.

"I always bring a heavy-duty medical kit along." Jack replied. "As a trained EMT," Jack pulled a rectangular-shaped nylon bag, filled to near bursting, from his gear bag, "I have access to some potent and—depending upon which country you happen to be in— illegal pharmaceuticals."

Marko's entire face lit up. "Better living through chemistry."

"I doubt they're your brand of chemicals," Leah said dryly.

"Just a little bit of morphine," Jack said.

"What's your plan?" Paulson asked.

Jack looked up at Leah and raised his eyebrows.

"No way, not doing it," she said flatly.

"Oh, yes you are," he said, "and I'm going to show you how."

Chapter 76

Beckam stared at the bodies lying within the tubes, not shocked at the sight—he had seen plenty of bodies during his SEAL career, most shot to death or worse—but slightly shaken.

This is no Russian installation.

Beckam had seen Russian technology, and this wasn't even close.

"I don't think the brass have a clue about any of this," Beckam told Frantino. "What did Dr. Andrews think about this place?"

"She didn't say a word."

"I need to speak with her, right now."

"Aye, aye, Skipper. I'll get you transportation down to the camp." Frantino turned and issued orders to a SEAL standing near the entryway.

The vestibule opening to the expedition tent shook as the guard unzipped the flap. Jack stuffed the medical kit under a sleeping bag and Paulson quickly sat against it, covering the bag with his body.

"Commander Beckam is inbound, and he'd like to have a word with you," said their SEAL guard before zipping the flap shut.

Ten minutes later, the growl of a snow machine increased in intensity, finally shutting down near the tent.

"Listen up," Leah called out. "I'm not interested in speaking to anyone with a machine gun pointed at my chest."

The flap unzipped and a tanned face poked through the vestibule, sans goggles. "I'm Lt. Commander Gus Beckam." He smiled as he looked from one member of the group to the next. "I understand you've met Lieutenant Frantino."

Leah found herself staring at the whitest, most perfect teeth she'd ever seen. Beckam's short-cut, bleach-blond hair looked anything but SEAL-like. When Beckam smiled, his blue eyes twinkled; he managed to appear confident and completely relaxed at the same time.

"I want to commend whoever designed and built this camp."

"I'm glad someone's paying attention to my efforts," Jack said.

"What the hell is going on here, Commander?" Paulson asked.

"We've been ordered to remove your expedition from Antarctica, Mr. Paulson."

"How is it that you know our names?" Paulson asked.

"When we were briefed, I received files on Mr. Paulson, Dr. Andrews, and Mr. Hobson."

"Know your enemy," said Leah. "Right, Commander?"

Beckam ignored the comment. "I'd like to have your analysis of the structure back there, Dr. Andrews."

She shrugged, staring him down. "Didn't you talk to Admiral Frantino? He says it's a secret Russian military base."

"I've heard Lt. Frantino's analysis. Now I want yours."

"You're not going to like it."

"Indulge me."

"Well, it's not Russian," she said.

"I figured that much. So what do you think it *is*?"

"I'm not sure there's any point in us having this discussion." Leah leaned forward and crossed her legs. "What would a machine-gun-toting Neanderthal know about Native American archeology anyway?"

Beckam raised his eyebrows. "If it helps, I majored in philosophy and religion with a minor in physical anthropology, so...a fair amount."

"Okay," she said. "You asked for it."

Twenty minutes later, Leah breathed out a sigh of relief. The truth was out in the open, and it actually felt good to get it off her chest. "My concern," she concluded, "aside from our personal safety, is that this whole thing will be covered up, and these captive people, if they can be revived, will be the next generation of lab rats. That after they've already suffered so much."

"Let's assume your hypothesis is true," Beckam said. "Why would these people have been returned to New Mexico by whoever brought them here? And why bring rocks with them?"

"We don't know," Leah said simply. "Clearly it didn't turn out well for the returnees, who were apparently butchered by their fearful fellow tribe members. I have no way of knowing what these...visitors intended, or expected."

"Maybe these visitors weren't that friendly."

"Maybe...but do you really think they'd go to all the trouble of transporting captive humans back and forth, only to have them killed by their own kind? I don't picture them as pulling-the-wings-off-flies types. Perhaps they returned people after running whatever god-awful experiments they had planned. The red crystal granite is rare. Within the Native American cultures, the samples would be highly prized valuables. It might have been a misguided attempt to reward the abductees with something of value. From what we saw in the cliff dwelling, it didn't go as planned." Leah rolled her eyes. "These aliens, or whoever, clearly weren't the sharpest knives in the block."

Beckam nodded. "Sometimes the simplest answer's the best. Maybe this was an alien version of what we call a cluster-fuck. Sometimes things just don't go as planned." He looked down at the bottom of the tent for several moments, his jaw working as he crunched through the problem. "Back to the present.... We're sitting on a find that has massive cultural, scientific, and spiritual consequences." He studied Leah's face. "As I'm sure you already know, militarily, politically, and tactically, it's a much more difficult situation." Beckam turned around and zipped open the vestibule doorway. "For now, I need you to sit tight."

Beckam spoke quietly to the guard. "Have there been any problems?"

"They were doing quite a bit of grumbling at first...."

Beckam patted his SEAL on the shoulder. "You stay sharp; it could get interesting around here real quick. There's a security issue here. Given what they've seen, I need to keep them separated from the rest of the crew down in camp."

He pulled out the secure sat phone. The command structure, right up to the President, was in for a very big and unpleasant surprise. Unless they'd already knew the civilians had stumbled upon something extraordinary. Either way, the importance of this mission, and its potential danger, had just shot off the scale.

CHAPTER 77

T he secure satellite call, along with the photos Beckam sent, had the same effect as knocking down a hornet's nest. The extraction-of-civilians-milk-
run had morphed into a secret operation that made the Glomar Explorer's
raising of the Russian nuclear ballistic missile sub in the 1970's pale in comparison. Unfortunately, for Beckam, most of the behind-the-scenes scrambling was on a top secret need-to-know basis, and even though he was the
senior commander on station, he apparently didn't have a need to know.

He been ordered to keep the civilians on ice, literally, for thirty-six
hours. Command was flying down a black-operation Hercules transport.
He'd wanted to consolidate the civilians, including Dr. Leah Andrews,
down in the main camp where they had better security and heaters inside
the containers, but he was ordered to keep them in the tent camp to avoid,
"further contamination." In other words, they didn't want Leah and crew
filling in everyone on what they'd found.

After freezing their asses off hour after hour, and working to avoid a civilian mutiny, the next act was about to begin. Beckam watched as the unmarked, ski-equipped Hercules painted flat black roared over the mountain
ridges, dropping down low into the valley. The four-engine turboprop flew
down the length of the makeshift ice runway not once, but twice.

When the Hercules reached the end of the valley for the second time,
the pilot stood the airplane on its wing tip and turned 180 degrees, aiming

the nose for the threshold of the runway, which was marked by the sharp line of sastrugi. When all three sets of landing gear/skis were planted, the pilots reversed pitch on the massive propellers, and the cargo plane came to a stop in a huge cloud of blowing ice and snow.

Mac Ridley and Rooster Parker peeked out through a gap between the two wooden doors of the machine shop. The SEALs had opened the doors slightly, allowing fresh air inside; the heavy smell of oil and other chemicals stored by the Russian crew was unbearable with the doors shut.

Rooster leaned over Ridley's shoulder, trying to catch a glimpse of the new arrival. "What's happening? More joining our party?"

"I sure as hell hope that's our transportation out of here." Ridley glanced at his watch. "It's about time. Christ, if I had to spend another 24 hours in this crate, I'd just request the SEALs shoot me and get it the hell over with." He shook his head. "We still don't know what the fuck happened to Jack and Leah."

Angus Lyon joined him, looking out to where the Hercules was turning around and preparing to taxi back toward the camp. "Would you look at that...."

Ridley nodded. "I know." It was no regular military Hercules. It had been painted black for night operations and lacked any tail number.

"Looks like some kind of special-operations Herc," Rooster said from behind Ridley.

"Something else is happening besides escorting us off the ice," Ridley said. "Something to do with that plane crash, or whatever it really was."

"Maybe if we waltz out there and smile they'll fill us in," Chase said sarcastically.

Ridley chuckled. "You don't want to know anything about it. It might just get you out of here alive. Wait a minute.... There's armed guys running off the back of the Hercules. They're forming a perimeter around the aircraft." Ridley swore under his breath. "Now I know they found something they should've left alone in that damn crevasse."

Rooster sighed. "If we'd known we were getting involved in a national-security-type mess, we would have demanded more money."

Chase Parker chuckled. "No shit."

"Hold on," said Ridley. "They're driving something off the Hercules."

Rooster, Chase, Lyon, and Perez pressed themselves against door, peering over the top of Ridley's gray head.

A white snowcat, the size of a small bus rolled out of the belly of the cargo plane. A cargo trailer followed the snowcat out, complete with skis. It sported white cylindrical tanks strapped down to the roof. A series of tubes and hoses ran from the tanks into the trailer.

"Damn if that doesn't look like an oversized travel-trailer without any windows."

"What do you think those tanks are for, Mac?"

Ridley shrugged.

Another snowcat, this one smaller, rolled down the ramp, pulling a trailer loaded with equipment and steel cylinders. Four high-powered snow machines followed the smaller snowcat down the ramp. The drivers parked them near the rear of the aircraft.

"There's your answer. They've got enough acetylene there to cut a submarine in half," Ridley said. "Whatever's under that ice, they're planning to cut it up like a birthday cake."

CHAPTER 78

Beckam waited for the turbines to spool down and the cargo ramp to open before approaching the Special Ops aircraft.

Frantino leaned over and whispered in Beckam's ear. *"Citizens-In-disArray."* The XO put a special emphasis on the 'A' in disarray.

It was one of a cluster of derogatory terms the military used for their clandestine counterparts in the Central Intelligence Agency.

"You think the spooks want to play soldier, Danny?"

"Take a look. They're acting like they're preparing to storm the beaches at Normandy."

After a number of commando-dressed guards set up a perimeter around the Hercules, a lone figure exited the rear of the aircraft, trailing a stream of cigarette smoke.

"I can't wait to meet the Woody that's in command of this cluster," Beckam said softly. He walked forward and when he got within three meters of the man, he stopped. "I'm Commander Beckam."

The man hesitated and then reached out with his hand. "Stanton Fischer, National Security Advisor to the President of the United States."

Beckam opened his mouth in surprise. Some shit-for-brains civilian was in charge? He'd expected surprises, but not like this.

"Commander, I need to brief you on a matter of critical national security. Is there a place we can get out of the cold?"

Beckam nodded, but his posture signaled his displeasure at the turn of events. "I'd suggest one of the Russian containers, but as I recall, we're not allowed to enter them."

"That may be the least of your problems, Commander."

"Well, that's good." Beckam glanced at Frantino. "Because we've got the civilians in the machine shop and we're using the storage facility as HQ."

Fischer gritted his teeth and simply waited for Beckam to point the direction. Once inside, Fischer sat next to a Russian-made portable propane heater, similar to one Beckam had authorized for Ridley and his crew. Frantino and Beckam sat across from him.

"The tactical and strategic situation is fluid." Fischer reached into his pocket for another cigarette, his hands pale and shaking. "We had reason to assume, even before your first communication, that Mr. Hobson and Dr. Andrews had stumbled upon a secret Russian research or communication system." He lit the cigarette. "You know we've been having communication problems. We believe the source of those problems is the 'facility' under the ice."

"Their handhelds were cooked." Beckam said.

Fischer nodded. "Well, here's what you don't know: This facility suddenly and without warning sent a massive burst of high energy out into space."

"What type of energy?"

Fischer shook his head. "Like nothing we've ever seen before."

"Think it's a homing beacon from the structure?"

"Could be—but our problems are far worse than that. It took down a number of communication and navigation satellites. Ours, as well as others'."

"Let me guess. Our Russian friends got wind of the same signal."

"There was an exchange between the President and the Russian President. To say it was unpleasant is an understatement. At first, they condemned us for testing some type of new particle beam weapon in

Antarctica, on Russian territory no less. The President's denials only served to inflame the situation. At some point, the Russians came to the same conclusion that we did; something extraordinary is under the ice."

Beckam felt the anger starting to rise into his throat. "What exactly is our situation, Mr. Fischer?"

"We're expecting elements of the Russian Spetsnaz here within hours." He stubbed out the cigarette. "Under no circumstances can we allow the Russians access to whatever is buried under the ice."

Beckam started at the mention of Russian commandos inbound. "If we have Russian Spec Ops on the way, then I suggest we get your mission accomplished and get out of here ASAP."

Fisher stared at Beckam. "Our orders are to secure as much of the contents of this under-ice structure as possible and then destroy it. Your orders are to hold the Russians at bay until our two missions are accomplished."

Beckam blinked. "What kind of support can we expect—especially air support?"

"None. Insertion of additional assets could result in an uncontrolled escalation."

"We'll need time to lay explosives. Should I order my men to start?"

A radio in Fischer's pocket beeped, indicating an incoming transmission.

"Resurrection, this is Steel Point," Fischer said. "Do you copy?"

"We are prepared to begin evacuation and dissection."

"Set up sling and stand by," Fischer replied.

"You mind telling me who or what 'Resurrection' is and what you're planning to do?" Beckam spit out the words.

Fischer hands shook as he fumbled with the radio. "Have you ever seen an auto dismantler, Commander? They start with an old car and within hours it's been cut into a hundred different pieces, and the balance is crushed into a recycling cube."

"Well, this car has bodies inside. What about them?" Beckam asked.

"My orders are to remove them on a priority basis. We think the occupants, if they are still alive, may lead us toward powerful advancements in the science of cryonics."

"Break glass only in case of war," muttered Frantino.

Fischer blinked. "I don't follow you, Lieutenant."

Frantino shrugged. "You maintain an army frozen solid in some salt mine, and when it's time to fight, just add water or whatever."

Fischer ignored Frantino's response and turned back toward Beckam. "We're also to collect any equipment that might have space travel, medical, or military applications. What about the civilians? Have you gotten any useful information?"

Beckam nodded. "It appears that Dr. Andrews was the key to breaching the installation. When she placed the palm of her hand within the triangular shaped depression on the center of the hatch it engaged the opening mechanism."

Fischer froze for a second, then nodded as he filed away the information.

"Who are your friends with guns?" Frantino asked.

"A collection of CIA and NSA field agents and a selection of our best research scientists."

"We couldn't help but notice they're heavily armed," Beckam said. "Will they be available for perimeter defense, should it be necessary?"

Fischer shook his head. "Negative, Commander. Their mission is strictly to secure the contents of the facility and the LC-130. They will not be detailed to you, nor do they report to you." He looked up. "Do not interfere with them. They are highly motivated in their mission and told to execute it all costs."

"What about our civilian guests?"

"They're not a priority in this mission. I've been given strict instructions as to their disposition."

"What the fuck does that mean?" Beckam asked, nearly reaching for his weapon.

His honeymoon with Fischer was over before it began.

CHAPTER 79

The two snowcats motored up a steep incline, coming to a stop a hundred meters from the edge of the crevasse. Men dressed in white arctic jumpsuits climbed out of the cabs and unloaded gear from the larger snowcat, including cutting equipment and an array of scientific tools, all crated within sealed boxes.

They unloaded several sections of aluminum piping and assembled a tripod over the crevasse, anchoring it to the ice on three different points. They ran a steel cable from a winch on the front of the smaller snowcat to a pulley system at the top of the tripod.

After making sure the pulley system ran freely, the men swiftly assembled a basket designed to carry ten or more people and a large amount of cargo. When they had the basket hanging over the crevasse from underneath the tripod, two men connected an aluminum "bridge" to the side of the basket and anchored it in the ice, providing a walkway between the ice and the makeshift freight elevator. After the system had been tested, one of the men radioed Fischer.

"Steel Point, we are on site and prepared to begin dissection."

Chapter 80

"Okay, we're all agreed then." Jack looked at Leah, who stared at the bottom of the tent and nodded. They'd been cooling their heels for nearly two days, and even Leah finally agreed they had to make a break for it.

Marko squirmed uncomfortably. "I don't know. It seems crazy to try an escape with the Caribou." He pointed in the direction of the B-29. "What about Juan and the rest of the guys?"

"They'll figure out what we're trying to do and will be cheering us on."

"I just don't like violence, that's all," Marko said softly. He took a deep breath. "If you think it's the only way…."

"Let's go over this one more time," Jack whispered. "Leah will disable the SEAL guard. Once that happens, we grab the snow machine."

Garrett glanced through the vestibule and then back at Jack. "I hate to throw darts at your plan, but there's no way we're all gonna fit on one snow machine."

Jack nodded at Paulson. "You two are riding in the sled while Leah, Marko, and I ride up front. Then we make for the Caribou." He glanced at Paulson. "You're sure you can fly it?"

"Got wings, don't it?"

"Okay, Leah…. Showtime."

Leah peeked out through the vestibule doorway and smiled at the SEAL guard. "I need to use the facilities, again." She pointed toward the ice latrine.

The guard lifted his eyebrows. "Okay, ma'am. Come on out."

Leah pulled herself out of the mountaineering tent and then walked over toward the guard. "How long do we have to stay cooped up inside that tent? I mean, aren't you all freezing?"

The guard remained stiff. "I have to ask you to use the head or return to the tent."

"You've got to give a woman a chance to stretch her legs first." Leah looked up at the young SEAL, and then reached out with her hand. "My name's Leah. You are…?"

CHAPTER 81

Fischer had made the trip inside the buried installation, where he immediately felt claustrophobic. He struggled to keep his hands from trembling. He'd seen the photos, and had been briefed on what to expect. Still, the desire to simply order the Herc off the ice and hope this was all a Russian practical joke was overwhelming.

Are they alive?" he asked a middle-aged, balding scientist who looked to Fischer as if he could have been Woody Allen's long-lost, older brother.

The scientist looked at Fischer nervously. "I believe they are held in cryonic suspension." He smiled. "My name is Dr. Gordon—I'm not sure we've been properly introduced.

"How are you going to get them out of here?" asked Fischer without a hint that he'd even heard Gordon's introduction.

Dr. Gordon walked over to one of the life-support tubes, touching it lightly. "It appears that each one of these habitats operates on a self-sufficient power source, perhaps designed that way in the event of a power failure in the larger structure." He shrugged. "We don't know how long the tubes will continue to operate once removed from the installation. In truth, we don't know anything about any of this." Dr. Gordon led Fischer to the door into the room. "I understand Dr. Andrews opened the doors by placing her hand just so. Perhaps she also holds the key to cycling open these tubes."

"Dr. Andrews has been less than cooperative," Fischer said, "but that's about to change."

CHAPTER 82

Leah's smile was Academy-Award caliber. When she held out her right hand, the SEAL seemed reluctant to take it, but that smile must have won him over, because his hand met hers. She gripped his hand tightly; when he smiled, Leah knew she had him.

Without warning, she yanked herself toward the SEAL, using his outstretched hand as leverage. Her left hand came up, and in a flash, she jammed the needle into his neck and pushed the plunger to the stop. The SEAL pushed her away, and Leah stumbled backward into the snow.

The SEAL reached up to his neck, where the needle and syringe dangled. He took one step forward and fell into the snow.

Jack and Paulson dragged the unconscious SEAL into the tent.

"He's going to be okay, right?" asked Marko nervously. "You didn't kill him or anything, did you?"

"How's he doing?" Leah asked anxiously.

Jack felt for his pulse. "He's fine. I just hope he doesn't have some kind of reaction to the morphine."

"What type of reaction?"

"If he's allergic, it could be a problem."

"Why the hell didn't you tell me that?"

Jack glared back at her. "Would you have done it?"

"No!"

"That's your answer." Jack reached into the medical kit and pulled out a syringe. "I'll give him a shot of adrenaline, just in case. By the time he's able to stand, we'll be long gone."

"You sure this is a good plan?" Paulson asked.

"You got a better one?"

"Nope."

Chapter 83

Beckam glanced inside the rear of the LC-130 Hercules as the crew scurried to load the contents of the trailer.

"What are the spooks doing inside that structure?" Beckam asked Frantino over the secure communicator.

"Don't have a clue, Skipper. We're not allowed any closer than about a hundred or so meters from the snowcats. From what we can tell, they're using a lift system to take stuff out—but most of it is covered with thermal blankets, so we can't really tell. Whatever they're doing, that damn snowcat with the covered trailer's already made five or six trips, each time loaded to the gills."

"What's the status of the civilians at the mountain camp?

"Getting restless, to say the least. They keep asking why they have to stay in the tents instead of being shuttled down to the main camp. Any indication when we're gonna be wheels up? I want to be as far away as possible if the Russians make an appearance."

"I've been riding Fischer's ass on that, including what his so-called plan is for the civilians. I'm not overly concerned about the Russians. Fischer would be shitting his pants if he thought we had contact inbound. I don't think anyone wants to be the one to pull the trigger on World War III. Unless the Russians know what's under the ice, they'll think twice, maybe three times before they roll in weapons hot."

"What's your plan, Boss?"

"Keep the guys ready, Danny. Assume Fischer has some surprises concerning the civilians, and us. Be ready to move in a moment's notice."

"Copy that. Hope for the best. Assume we're fucked. Standard sit-rep."

Beckam stole another glance at the rear of the LC-130. "Stand by, Danny I'm going to do a little recon."

Beckam moseyed over toward the rear of the LC-130 until he caught the attention of one of the perimeter guards, who waved him away. Before he turned back around, he got a solid view of the Hercules cargo hold, already packed solid with a collection of gear surrounded by thermal blankets and a variety of other equipment.

He did a silent head count and tallied up twenty-six SEALs, ten civilians, and maybe thirty spooks and scientists. If they continued to load cargo at the current rate, there wouldn't be room for the SEAL Team, much less the civilians. Beckam decided it was time to have a chat with the civilian mechanics held in the machine shop.

If Fischer intended to double-cross them, he wanted to make sure they could get out on the Caribou before the Russians decided they'd been patient enough.

CHAPTER 84

"**S**omething's going down," Juan told Ridley.

Ridley jammed his face through the crack in the door. The armed LC-130 security commandos spread out in every direction. Ridley noted their SEAL guard seemed confused by the hubbub, and to his credit, hadn't left his station.

"What's the fuss?" Ridley asked the SEAL guard outside the door.

"Your friends aren't too smart. They're trying to make a run for it."

Juan slapped Ridley on the back so hard the older mechanic nearly fell to the ground. "I knew they couldn't keep Leah tied down!"

"If they've got the snow machines, it might give them enough time to get the Caribou cranked up." Ridley's thick eyebrows lifted. "Probably help if they had some kind of diversion. Otherwise I doubt they'll make it."

"If you've got something in mind, now would be a good time." Rooster pointed at their guard, who was moving farther away from the building, trying to see the action out on the ice.

"There's no way we can jump him before he turns around and opens up with that grease-gun," Chase cautioned.

"I've got a better idea." Ridley walked over to where the propane-filled tire had been left for seating. "Help me flip this thing over."

Juan and Perez manhandled the propane-filled Caribou tire into the middle of the shed and laid it on its side. "Find me a screwdriver or something like it."

"Wait," Rooster said. "You start filling this place with gas...one spark and we're headed for the moon."

Ridley grinned. "Can't wait."

Chapter 85

Jack held the throttle wide open as the snow machine-sled combo flew over imperfections in the ice. Leah hung on to Jack and Marko clung to Leah. Paulson and Garrett lay in the sled, holding on for dear life, their eyes closed against the stinging ice thrown up by the tracks. Jack caught a flash of sunlight gleaming off a metal surface. It was the Caribou, and it still seemed a million miles away.

To say it didn't sit well with him to leave Juan and the others behind, was an understatement. He silently hoped somehow they might make their own escape when they saw the snow machine tearing down the mountain.

We'll need five minutes, he thought. Our entire lives are coming down to five lousy minutes.

Beckam ran from his position near the rear of the LC-130 Hercules, past the B-29 and toward the Russian camp. In the distance, he saw a speck flying across the ice toward the Caribou parked 2,000 meters in the distance. The snowcats are too slow to catch them, he thought, but the snow machines are a different story.

Several of the CIA guards armed with automatic weapons suddenly sprinted away from the LC-130 and hopped aboard the high-performance sleds.

"That asshole Fischer will kill them," Beckam muttered, his normally cool SEAL temperament boiling over. He bolted toward a snow machine, weapon in hand, shouting into his headset as he did. "Get weapons around the civilians! Fischer's gonna send rounds down range and I don't want him ordering anyone else shot in the process!"

Jack skidded to a stop next to the Caribou; Paulson rolled out of the sled and ran for the switch that opened the loading ramp from outside the aircraft.

"How much time do we have?" Leah asked.

"Less than we need," said Jack.

Paulson dashed into the empty cargo hold of the Caribou, headed for the cockpit. Twenty long seconds later, the sliding cockpit side window slammed open.

"Clear!" he shouted.

Jack yanked Leah away from the propeller as the Number One engine belched black smoke twice and then settled into a reciprocating roar. He unfastened the steel wire tie-downs and then pointed toward the rear of the Caribou.

"Run for the loading ramp!"

CHAPTER 86

Ridley knelt on the tire and worked at the oversized stem with a flathead screwdriver. "One more turn and this place will be flooded with propane in less than thirty seconds. I want everyone to stand near the door. After we blow it, run for the Hercules, and let's see if we can grab a couple of those weapons."

Ridley glanced up. When Rooster nodded, he pulled out the sealing mechanism and ice-cold propane streamed out into the shed in a thick, white mist.

"One, two, three, four—go!" he shouted.

With Juan and Rooster in the lead, they burst through the door. The SEAL guard instantly spun and raised his weapon.

Rooster and Juan stopped and raised their hands in the air. "Don't shoot!" they both shouted simultaneously.

The sound of automatic gunfire in the distance distracted the SEAL for a millisecond. Rooster casually opened a Zippo lighter, gave it a flick with his fingers and it popped alight. He turned around and in a single motion, tossed the lighter through the open door.

"Gentlemen, now would be a good time to hit the ground," he said.

In a blink, the building exploded, sending wood and metal shrapnel in every direction and blowing the SEAL backward onto the ice.

"It'll be close," Paulson shouted. His eyes worked over the instruments, and he cranked around the nose wheel, orienting the Caribou into a direction offering them the best possibility of making a successful takeoff. "If they decide to open up with any of that artillery, we're never getting off the ground."

Jack was unable to reply because armor-piercing rounds suddenly cut through the wings and the tail section of the aircraft, filling the old Caribou with the sounds of ripping and tearing metal.

A second later, one of the white-hot rounds pierced the fuel tank, and the aircraft erupted into flame.

"Get out!" he cried to Paulson.

Toxic smoke burned deep in his lungs as he blindly felt his way back to the last spot he remembered seeing Leah. He felt an arm grabbing for his and turned to find Leah with a hand over her nose and mouth. Taking her hand, he searched frantically for a way to exit the burning aircraft. He spotted a combination of flames and natural light piercing the skin of the Caribou. He dived for the opening, pulling her through the tattered aluminum toward the snow and ice.

CHAPTER 87

Beckam sprinted past the *Las Tortugas* and toward one of the snow machines. The civilians were standing outside of the machine shop, their hands held high in the air. The young SEAL standing guard swung his weapon toward the civilians, and for an instant, Beckam feared he might fire on them.

When he didn't, Beckam felt an intense flash of relief. As he opened his mouth to order the civilians back into the machine shop, one of them spun and tossed a silver object toward the opened door.

He stopped running and just managed to get his hands up to chest level when the blast knocked him backward. The last thing he remembered before losing consciousness was the sound of automatic gunfire—and screaming.

CHAPTER 88

Fischer stood at the lip of the crevasse, watching black smoke billowing up from the Caribou in the distance. The sound of automatic gunfire had erupted within seconds of his issuing the command to abort the takeoff by any means necessary.

Just when he thought the situation was under control, another huge explosion rocked the valley. Fischer's eyes darted back toward the Russian camp, where a plume of black smoke burst from one of the Russian buildings.

Fischer pulled out his handheld radio and keyed the transmitter. "This is Steel Point. What the hell is going on down there?"

"The civilians detonated something in one of the huts and assaulted our position."

"What's your status?"

"Several of the civilians are down, but our aircraft is secure."

"I see the civilian aircraft burning," Fisher said. "Are there any survivors?"

"I doubt anyone could survive that fire."

Fischer's eyes narrowed as he issued the order. "We are in final phase. Repeat—we are in final phase."

The voice over the transmitter paused. "Are you ready for the package?"

Fischer wiped a drop of sweat from his brow despite the freezing cold. "Send over the package."

"Headed your way."

CHAPTER 89

Jack and Leah slid on blackened ice as Jack led her away from the burning aircraft. A minute later, Leah lay gagging as her lungs purged themselves of lethal smoke and fumes.

"I'll be forced to shoot if you move," said a steely voice from behind them.

"There are others," Jack said. He struggled to his feet, spun, and faced the CIA field agent and his automatic weapon. "I've got to get them out."

"If they're not out, they're not getting out."

"I can't leave them," Leah said. She pointed her finger at the combat-gear-clad agent-soldier, her eyes blazing. "You're nothing more than a cold-blooded murderer."

She reached out, but Jack held a firm grip on her jacket.

Three figures suddenly appeared through the smoke. Two of the agent-soldiers, also armed with automatic weapons, escorted them away from the inferno.

Leah yanked free of Jack's grasp and ran for the trio. Jack turned and held his hand up, blocking the automatic weapon from getting a clear shot. He stared into the man's eyes and the message was clear.

If you want to shoot her, it'll have to be through me.

Fischer's commando leveled the barrel at Jack's chest for a moment, then lifted it up and away.

Leah dropped down to her knees and looked into Garrett's soot-covered face. "Are you okay?"

Garrett coughed once and nodded. "We saw you guys go out—by the time I found Marko, fire had filled the exit." He nodded toward the billionaire. "Al grabbed and flung us both to the floor of the airplane, or we'd have been dead."

"We got out through a hole in the fuselage." Paulson wiped soot off his lips and looked up at the machine guns pointed down at them. "Guess we screwed up big."

"Get into the sleds," ordered one of the armed men.

"And if we don't?" asked Leah.

"Several of your expedition members are already dead, ma'am. I suggest you don't make it any worse for yourselves."

CHAPTER 90

Leah looked down at Juan Cortez's lifeless body. Next to him lay Rooster and Chase Parker. Dark-red blood stained the ice around their bodies.

Leah dropped on her knees next to Juan. "What happened?" she cried, rage threatening to blind her as she blinked away tears.

"They tried to give you more time to get the Caribou airborne," Ridley said softly. Angus Lyon and Orlando Perez stood behind Ridley, their grease-covered overalls stained red with blood from trying to save their friends. "The SEAL guarding us got knocked down, but he's okay. He could have shot us but he didn't. The SEAL commander got chopped up by flying debris." Ridley nodded toward a storage building. "He's inside—unconscious."

"Who ordered deadly force?" Jack demanded.

Ridley pointed to a thin figure walking quickly toward the rear of the Hercules. "That's the guy in charge—from what we hear."

"You're a murderer," Leah shouted.

The figure turned, hesitated, and then walked toward them. When he got within ten feet, he stopped and flipped down his hood. "My name is Stanton Fischer." He pointed toward the bodies, now covered with the tarps. "I'm sorry about your friends, but they shouldn't have—"

"Do you know what you've done?" Leah raged. "These aren't soldiers. They never hurt anyone!"

"Dr. Andrews, I presume," Fischer said. "You have no idea what you're dealing with, and the implications for our national security are incalculable."

"Screw your national security, and screw *you*!" She lunged toward him, and he stepped backward in shock. Ridley held her back with a gentle hand.

"Do you know what you stumbled upon?" Fischer asked.

With visible effort, Leah controlled her voice. "We found real people whose lives were already a living hell—people who deserve to be taken back to their homes and allowed to live in peace."

"The President has a more realistic view of the situation." He signaled his commandos. "Give them two minutes to pay their respects and then lock them in one of the remaining Russian shacks where they can't get themselves into any more trouble."

"You can't keep this a secret," Leah said. "When I get out of here, I'm calling every television network and telling them what we found and what you've done."

Fischer simply turned and, without another word, jogged toward the black Hercules.

"We're not getting out of here," Paulson said flatly.

Ridley chuckled. "You figure that out all by yourself?"

Paulson looked down at the ice and blinked. "Damn, it looks like I did it this time, Mac. I really fucked up."

"Yeah, you sure as hell did," the mechanic replied. "Now you'd better figure out how to get us out of this mess."

Leah squeezed her eyes tightly shut. Even so, the tears flowed down her cheeks. Jack reached out and held her.

"Juan worshiped the ground I walked on. It's my fault that he's dead—and we're in this debacle."

"We all knew what we were getting into," Jack said, "including Juan."

She pulled back and wiped away a tear. "If I could just take it all back."

Jack looked at her and then at Paulson. They were in deep trouble. After what they had discovered and what happened to Juan and Rooster, they'd never be allowed to speak to the media. Paulson was right: *We're not getting out of here alive.*

The billionaire nodded, acknowledging Jack's understanding, but also seeming to urge Jack to do something.

As he held Leah through her wracking sobs, Jack thought back to Paulson on Everest. To get them out of this, he'd have to go deep—deep and personal.

I need to motivate her—motivate all of us.

"Juan's gone, Leah. You can't help him but you still have an important job."

She looked up, her brow wrinkled in confusion, bordering on anger. "Juan and Rooster and Chase are dead. What possibly could be more important?"

"What about that little Native American girl we found?"

Her face went blank for a second.

Time to push her hard.

"While you're here feeling sorry for yourself, she and her people are being loaded into a scientific meat wagon."

"What the hell can I do, Hobson?" she snapped. "You want me to charge the Hercules—like Juan?"

"It'd be a better ending than crying in your soup." Jack softened his tone. "As long as we're alive, there's hope for them. If we can find a way out of this, you'll have a chance to tell your story to the world."

"How the hell are we going to get out of this?"

Jack glanced over at the billionaire. "Got any ideas, Al?"

"I doubt they got the balls to execute us." He looked up at Stanton's commandos surrounding the LC-130. "We'll probably be held at some secure facility outside the United States until someone decides our fate." He shrugged. "We're like enemy combatants. We'll have to be warehoused at some CIA black site."

"So we play ball like good little boys and girls," Garrett whispered. "For now. Then make a break for it when we get a chance."

"Exactly," Jack said.

Chapter 91

BLM Chief Teresa Simpson sat in her Washington office, watching the first snowfall of the year drift down over the city. Six inches of fresh powder had snarled traffic and shut down the federal government, a situation that seemed patently ridiculous to Teresa, who had grown up in Denver, Colorado.

The serene picture was in stark contrast to the reality of the situation, at least for the handful of people who knew what was going on. And she unfortunately knew precious little. After her rare appearance at the National Security Council, she'd heard nothing regarding the civilian extraction.

The forest is too damned quiet.

That's what her dad had often said when he took her deer hunting in the Rockies. If the forest got too quiet, it meant the animals had been spooked.

Teresa opened her desk and pulled out the notebook in which she kept personal notes jotted down during telephone conversations. She flipped backward through the pages until she found a name written near the bottom of one page with a phone number directly above it. She hesitated for a moment; making this call would mean breaking the chain of command.

"Screw it," she muttered. "I've had about enough of this job anyway."

She picked up the phone and dialed it herself.

The phone rang twice, then a crisp military voice answered. "This is Major Richards speaking."

"I'm Teresa Simpson, Director of the BLM. Stan Fischer gave me this number since I'm involved with the mission to remove the Americans from Antarctica. Is he available?"

"I'm sorry, Ms. Simpson. Mr. Fischer is not in the office."

Teresa could tell from the pitch of his voice that the staffer was under incredible pressure.

"Where can I locate him?"

The voice hesitated. "He's on a classified mission—"

Teresa felt a twinge of anger and frustration. "I'm a member of the NSC staff working on this mission. Check Mr. Fischer's own records to confirm I was present at the NSC meeting."

"I'm sorry, Ms. Simpson. This mission is highly classified." The staffer paused, stress even more evident in his voice now. "I have to conclude the call. We're very busy here."

Teresa bit down on her lip. "Thank you, Major." She dialed her secretary. "Get me Emerson on the phone."

She tapped her fingers, waiting for a return call that would either be Emerson or one of Emerson's staffers making some kind of ass-kissing excuse about why he couldn't come to the phone.

She was shocked when Jeanie walked into her office, her face void of color and her eyes wide with fear.

"What's up?"

"This is off the record, Ms. Simpson. I got this from a friend."

She fidgeted until Teresa asked her to sit on the office couch. Teresa sat beside her.

The secretary turned to Teresa, her hands rubbing her skirt. "The entire senior staff, the cabinet and Vice President were ordered out to Andrews about three hours ago."

"Why?" Andrews Air Force base, located in nearby Maryland was a central hub for secure government travel and the home base for Air Force One.

"I don't know. If you're around long enough, you learn to pick up things." She leaned forward. "It sounds crazy, but my friend at the White

House, he said that Air Force One and Air Force Two and several refueling aircraft had been summoned and put on high alert. People are being told this is some kind of preparedness drill, but schedules were cleared and everyone—I mean *everyone*—is supposed to be rushing the cabinet and staff out to the airport."

"What?"

"They're putting everyone into airborne command centers and spreading out the cabinet and their staff. With the refueling aircraft, my friend said Air Force One can fly almost indefinitely."

"There's only one reason for that—the possibility of a nuclear exchange."

The secretary burst into tears when Teresa said it.

"What about congress? Are they being evacuated?"

The secretary wiped at her face. "No, that's why everyone thinks this is a drill of some kind."

"What makes you think it's not?"

"Because," the secretary said, pushing herself off the couch, "my contact, well he's more than a friend, and he begged me to get out of Washington. Get out fast."

Teresa walked over to her desk, maintaining as calm a demeanor as possible. "I'm going to need your help." She looked her secretary in the eye.

"What do you want me to do?"

Teresa smiled. "First, we're in this together, so you might as well call me Teresa."

"Okay, Teresa."

"Get me a telephone number for McMurdo base in Antarctica."

Teresa understood from the NSC meeting that the Navy was to pick Paulson's party up and transport them off the ice. If the plan had been executed, Navy personnel at Murdo would have the details.

Two minutes later, the secretary walked into her office, and handed Teresa a piece of paper with several phone numbers listed, including Flight Operations for the American Antarctic base.

"Good work," Teresa said. "Now, get on the phone and do your best snooping. I want to know exactly what's going on around here."

The secretary spun and flew from the office.

Teresa picked up the phone and dialed. After several delaying clicks, the phone went dead. For some reason, the satellite communications were down.

Pacing around her office, Teresa formed a picture of Paulson's Gulfstream jet in her mind, the same jet that she knew from her last briefing was parked in Punta Arenas. The Gulfstream was fast and had worldwide range. If Paulson and the others had gotten the *Las Tortugas* airborne before the SEALs arrived, they'd be headed for Chile.

Teresa sat again and worked through the scenario. Leah had found something of extreme importance and sensitivity, something that might lead to nuclear conflict.

A satellite picture of the Antarctic base formed in her mind, including the container shelters, the B-29, and the wrecked Antonov.

Teresa's eyes opened wide.

The Russians. It had to be some kind of impending conflict with the Russians, something so secret that only the President and his immediate staff knew anything about.

"Leah Andrews found something all right," she muttered, "something so off the charts, it might pass the next cold war and go direct to World War Three."

Clearly, whatever Leah Andrews had found, something had gone desperately wrong. Hell, the government had locked itself down.

"This is crazy," she muttered while shaking her head. "Even for me."

She walked from her office and scanned the office for her secretary, who had managed to paste a smile so as not to alert the other staffers something was wrong.

"Can I see you in my office?" Teresa smiled sweetly.

The secretary nodded, and scurried toward Teresa's office. Teresa shut the door.

"I'm going to Chile," Teresa said plainly.

"Why?"

"This is strictly between you and me." Teresa stopped long enough to solicit a nod from the secretary.

"I think the sudden and unexplained evacuation has something to do with an ex-employee of the BLM. Someone I hired and Secretary Emerson fired."

"Dr. Andrews."

Teresa was going to ask how she knew, and then remembered that Leah's termination had grabbed headlines within the Beltway.

She nodded. "I'm not going into details since that is still classified information. However, if this is what I think it is, I believe Washington is safe from nuclear attack, at least for now. Antarctica, of all places, is the flashpoint."

The secretary opened her mouth, but Teresa anticipated the question. "Don't ask, Jeanie, because I can't tell you—partly because I don't know all the facts myself and partly, like I said, because this is still highly classified."

"What are you planning?"

Teresa pulled out a world atlas from a shelf behind her desk. She flipped to a map of Chile, her fingers resting on the southern tip of the country. "I'm going to a place called Punta Arenas."

"That sounds crazy. I mean, what can you do?"

Teresa looked up, her eyes steely. "Leah Andrews was my employee and my responsibility. It's partly my fault we're in this mess because I didn't have the guts to buck Secretary Emerson when he fired her. I can't sit here and twiddle my thumbs." She shrugged. "It's not in my nature."

"What do you want me to do?"

"Book me on a commercial flight to Punta Arenas, or anywhere close. In fact, just get me out of the country. Mexico City or, better yet, anywhere in South America. After what happened on 911, you can bet the airlines could be grounded at any minute." She opened a draw on her desk and pulled out a black Gucci purse. From it, she produced an American Express credit card and handed to the secretary, who looked at the front of the card.

"This is your personal card. Shouldn't we book this through the travel office?"

"This is a personal trip, *not* government authorized travel, and it's not to be discussed with anyone. As far as you're concerned, I've left Washington to inspect beetle infestation in California or whatever. Email me so I know what story I'm supposed to use when I get back."

"And when you get to Chile?"

"There's a chance I might cross paths with Leah Andrews there. If so, she might need my help, and this time, unlike last time, I intend to provide it."

CHAPTER 92

Gus Beckam lay on a cot in the Russian bunkhouse, in pain and angry. Not at the civilians for nearly blowing him and the SEAL he'd assigned to guard them away, but at his inattention to detail, which had caused the entire catastrophe.

He should have handcuffed the civilians to guarantee their safety. Now, three of the civilians had been killed, he'd been injured, and Fischer had taken command of his SEAL team.

When Frantino had come to check out his wounds, Beckam had been too dazed to order him to draw weapons on Fischer and his crew and hold them at bay until he contacted the Pentagon, specifically Admiral Reins. The Admiral was a Spec Force vet now driving a desk who would have put a stop to this lunacy, even if it cost him his career.

Never underestimate the ability of a motivated guerrilla to overcome superior numbers and firepower.

One of the first rules of unconventional warfare, it was beat into every SEAL candidate from basic BUDS training through advanced counter-terrorism. In this case, ragged groups of what he thought were little more than adventure seekers had rendered one-man unconscious through a drug injection and cut up another with a machine-shop blast.

Without Fischer's maniacs present, it would have been a successful escape. Beckam wouldn't have allowed his men to fire on the Caribou—regardless of the cost to his career.

He wore the results of the explosion on his face and upper body. Wood fragments propelled like shrapnel had cut his face and penetrated his upper body, shredding his Arctic combat suit like so much confetti; only his goggles had kept him from being blinded.

Beckam reached down next to the cot, where Frantino had placed a walkie-talkie in case he recovered enough to communicate. He felt around for a moment and then rolled over far enough to see the primitive wooden floor.

Fischer had taken the radio. The prick was taking command of his team and apparently intended to keep it that way. Beckam struggled to stand, took one unsteady step, and fell to the wooden floor.

CHAPTER 93

The door to the Russian equipment shed rattled as the chain and lock were removed. When the door opened, Fischer and three of his armed guards looked in at the prisoners.

"Is it time to leave this lovely locale?" Jack asked.

"We're moving you for your own safety." Fischer pointed toward the larger of the two snowcats, which towed the heated trailer that Fischer's people had used to ferry the pods from the structure to the LC-130.

"Into the trailer, all of you, and make it quick."

"Exactly where are you taking us?" Leah asked.

"Shut up," Fischer snapped. "Climb into the trailer, or I'll have you subdued and thrown in."

"Think they're going to shoot us?" Leah said much less boldly, once secured within the trailer.

"It's a sure bet we're not going to a health spa," said Paulson.

The snowcat motored at its top speed of thirty miles per hour over the icy plain separating the *Las Tortugas* from the mountains, then made a turn toward Thor's Hammer.

Ten minutes later the engine on the snowcat strained with the increased slope angle, and the driver shifted into a lower gear. They passed the small crevasse Jack originally roped off and three minutes later stopped near the smaller snowcat. Fischer and his men got out of the snowcat and walked to the rear of the trailer, where they physically manhandled Jack and Leah out onto the ice.

"Over to the crevasse," he ordered.

Jack yanked his arms free from one of the guards. "You're going to push us into the crevasse?"

"Don't be ridiculous, Mr. Hobson," Fischer replied. "We're expecting the arrival of Russian commandos in the valley at any moment. Since our aircraft is an obvious target, this will be the safest place for you." He pointed toward the lift system and the heavy-duty aluminum basket. "If you please—I don't have much time."

Fischer's guards herded Jack, Leah, Paulson, Ridley, Garrett, Lyon, and Perez toward the makeshift elevator.

"I believe we can take you all down in one load." One of the guards suddenly moved forward, cutting Leah away from the others. "Unfortunately, I must ask Dr. Andrews to accompany us in the LC-130."

"What?" Jack forced his way out of the basket, only to have one of the guards use the butt of his assault rifle knock him back into the makeshift elevator.

"Why me?" she asked calmly.

"You were the key to breaching the structure, Dr. Andrews. We're hoping your magic palm might free these people from their cryonic freeze."

"Forget it, Fischer. I won't go without them."

"Remember our discussion," Jack cautioned Leah. "You're the only one who can help these people now."

"I'm not leaving you behind."

Fischer signaled toward one of the men. He grabbed Leah by the back of the jacket and dragged her toward the snowcat.

"Back in the basket," said Fischer. "I'm sure you all understand this isn't personal—it's for the national security of the United States."

"Why don't you just execute us right here?"

"We don't execute American citizens." Fischer nodded toward one of the men who ran back to the smaller snowcat and set the winch system to "lower." The basket descended quickly into the crevasse, hitting the bottom and spilling its occupants onto the ice.

Fischer gave the winch operator thumbs-up and wound his hand in a cranking motion, indicating the operator should lift the basket up to the base of the tripod.

Fischer jumped up on the track of the larger snowcat, opened the glass-and-metal door and climbed into the heated cab. He nodded and the driver put the snowcat in gear and jammed the accelerator to the floor.

"How much time do we have?" asked the snowcat driver anxiously.

Fischer glanced at his watch. "Less than an hour."

CHAPTER 94

"**Can you free-climb** out of this hole with a couple of ice axes?" Jack pointed up the steep ice walls of the crevasse.

Marko shook his head. "Not without crampons."

"I thought you're some kind of hotshot climber."

Marko pushed the blond hair out of his face. "That's over a hundred feet to the top.... I don't know...without rope, harness and screws?"

"Well, if you don't think you can do it...." Jack peered up at the sliver of light above them.

"I didn't say that," Marko said.

"It sure as hell isn't going to be me," Ridley said, staring up at the surface.

"We still need to find ice axes," Garrett said. "Maybe we can fashion some crampons as well, if they left enough cut metal inside."

Jack turned and looked at the two gaping black holes where Fischer's people had managed to cut away the doors. He stepped through the entryway chamber and into the room where they'd found the first body. The body had been removed, and cutting torches and gas cylinders littered the floor.

Ridley let his hands rub across the smooth metal walls. "What I wouldn't give to get my hands on the engineering schematics. Can you imagine what we might learn from this?"

Jack nodded and pointed toward the second chamber. "Mac, you take Marko, Orlando, and Angus, clear the debris away and search around inside for climbing gear." He paused. "Marko, you've already been inside. Check and see if Fischer's men removed all the bodies."

Marko led the others into the cavernous second room. Equipment lay strewn in piles, exactly like in the first room. Marko aimed his flashlight on the huge system of racks that had held the tubes just hours before. Now the racks stood empty with wiring intertwined among the alien machinery like strands of spaghetti.

"Found one!" Garrett shouted. He came in and showed Jack a red-handled ice axe.

Jack stopped digging through the debris for a moment. "We need at least one more," he called back, wiping a bead of sweat from his brow.

"Hey, Jack?"

"What's up, Marko?"

"There's something here I think you should see."

Jack stood and turned around. "What is it?"

"Some things I found under the debris. Like mini beer kegs, but a lot scarier, with flashing panels and stuff. I don't remember seeing them before."

"I'm coming to take a look." Jack stepped over a small pile of debris and then stopped. "Don't touch them."

"Don't worry." Ridley's coarse voice echoed off the metallic walls. "The last thing we're gonna do is touch 'em."

CHAPTER 95

Gus Beckam regained consciousness on the floor when the shed began to vibrate to the whine of turbine-driven jet engines and variable-pitch propellers. His face felt raw, and the wood splinters lodged under the skin made their presence known, but most of the dizziness had gone. Gus walked stiffly toward the door and pushed. It gave two inches and then stopped. They locked me in, he thought.

Why would they lock me in?

Beckam shoved his shoulder into the door with all the strength he could muster. It moved, but not enough to break away the chain. He searched around the bunkhouse, picking up a hammer that had been used to nail the bunks together.

Instead of pounding against the door, he slammed the hammer against the metal hinges. On the third strike, the screws holding the hinges in place moved out several millimeters. Beckam stopped to take several deep breaths; he still felt weak and disoriented from the blast concussion. He lifted the mallet with both hands and this time struck the door with an overhand arcing swing. The sound of metal twisting followed the mallet strike.

Beckam dropped the mallet and slammed into the door with his shoulder, breaking it free of the hinges and creating an opening large enough to slide through.

Beckam held his hands up to his eyes; the intensity of the light after the relative darkness of the shed was blinding. As his eyes adjusted, he watched the unmarked LC-130 Hercules lift off the ice with four lines of light-gray jet exhaust trailing each of the powerful turbo prop engines.

After the Hercules climbed several hundred feet, it made a sharp 180-degree turn and flew directly overhead at low altitude in what Beckam assumed was a radar-avoiding tactic.

He dropped to his knees and pushed a small pile of ice together with his hands. Beckam brought the ice up to his face, and then, holding his breath, pushed the freezing-cold slush into the bleeding wounds on his face.

CHAPTER 96

Fischer held on while the Hercules bounced over the ice before finally getting airborne. When the skis lifted off the ice after what seemed like an eternity, he felt tempted to breathe a sigh of relief. But he knew that Phase II of his mission still lay ahead.

Officially, Phase I included recovery of as much of the structure and its contents as possible. The President had given him virtual carte blanche with regard to completing both Phase I (recovery) and Phase II: plausible deniability.

To accomplish the latter, there would soon be a detonation. Since they hadn't been able to gain access to the lower levels of the structure, they'd had to use a device that would destroy everything within a reasonable distance, plus ensure any technology inadvertently left intact would be unusable by humans.

For this job, one device stood out: a top-secret nuclear weapon codenamed 'Copenhagen.' Its Hafnium-Iso warhead provided a massive detonation, followed by an equally massive release of gamma-ray radiation, but zero fallout.

The Russians still didn't know exactly what they'd stumbled upon, or they'd have already been knee deep in Russian commandos. Fischer's job was to make sure they never found out.

Fischer glanced up to see Leah Andrews staring at him. He had no doubt that if she managed to free herself from her hand and ankle cuffs and find a weapon, she'd make good use of it. Dangerous as she might be, however, Dr. Andrews still had a significant role to play when they reached their destination.

Chapter 97

Jack knelt beside the three metallic canisters. Each stood about meter high and measured fifteen or so inches in diameter and had a lighted control panel and touchpad on top.

"You're the engineer, Mac. What do you think?"

The old mechanic sucked air through his teeth for a moment as he studied the objects from all sides. "I think Fischer left us a going-away present of high-explosives."

"They look pretty high-tech for TNT. Think they're nuclear?"

"Well, I'm no expert on nuclear weapons, but I suppose it is possible. That seems crazy to me, though; there's no way you're going to get away with detonating a nuclear weapon in Antarctica." Ridley scratched at his stubble. "No doubt they're on a timer; could be set for any time."

Jack nodded and stood. "We've got one ice axe; we need one more, and then at least we've got a chance to get out of here. Everyone fan out and dig though this place until we come up with another axe."

Three minutes later, Paulson shouted, "Got one." He yanked the blue-handed axe from a pile of debris.

"Bring it over here." Jack studied the handle—it still had its safety lanyard attached. "Okay, Marko. It's time to get us out of here."

"You'll have to free-climb it, hand-over-hand." Jack demonstrated by slamming one axe into the wall of the crevasse, pulling himself up using the strap to hold on, and then stabbing the other axe into the ice.

"That's a long way, hand over hand without crampons," Marko said tentatively.

"Sorry, Marko. We're fresh out of crampons. You're our only chance." Jack tried to instill more confidence than he felt himself. "No one else is going to have the strength or the skill to get to the top."

"It's too far without crampons, Jack. Even I can't climb that much ice on arm strength alone."

"Give me five minutes, Kid," Ridley said. "I'll patch together something. It's hard enough walking around down here without cutting yourself to ribbons with the mess they made. I'm sure we can make something that's gonna work."

More like ten minutes later, the toes of Marko's climbing boots sported drill bits designed to cut through metal. Ridley had fastened two to the sole of each boot in the shape of a "V," thrusting out like a set of reverse spurs from hell.

Ridley slapped the young climber on the back. "Hell, I could almost climb out with this set-up."

Marko glanced around. "Well, I wouldn't suggest anyone be standing underneath, in case I fall."

"You're not going to fall," Jack said.

"What do I do if…. When I get to the top?"

"Get to the snowcat, if they left it behind. It should have a winch still connecting a cable to the pulley above the crevasse. There'll be a brake release on the winch. Run the cable down to us and we'll get in the basket. If you can't operate it or it's not there, hopefully you'll find a rope or something. If you can set any sort of line, I'll climb out." Jack gripped his shoulders. "You can do it, but you've got to hurry."

Marko slammed the axe into the ice and pulled himself up. Then he reached up and hammered the other axe into the ice a foot higher. He looked down, and slammed one of his boots into the ice. Just as Mac had said, they held almost better than traditional crampons, although, his boots were wrapped with so much duct tape, he wondered if he'd ever get then off. With renewed confidence, Marko rested for a second and then pulled himself up and punctured the ice, showering the bottom of the crevasse with ice crystals.

They didn't dare say a word while Marko climbed through the first thirty feet. Then Paulson shouted, "You're looking good! Just keep moving!" A chorus of shouts and cheers followed Marko as he plunged the axe, time after time, into the vertical wall.

Marko couldn't ignore the sweat running out of his gloves and down his palms and onto the handle of the axe then dripping into his eyes every time he slammed the ace in the ice to secure it. The axes had become increasingly difficult to hold on to the slippery steel, even with the straps securing his hands to the axe. Worse, the drill bits had worked loose underneath the tape, and were unusable the last brutal twenty feet. As he neared the top of the crevasse, the shouts and cheers got even louder.

Marko gritted his teeth and worked around a ledge, where the ice formed an overhang, and with the last of his strength, he swung the axe over the lip of the crevasse, pulling his fatigued body up, kicking with his knees as he climbed to solid ice.

Exhausted, panting, Marko simply lay on the ice for a moment. Then, remembering the blinking panels on the bombs in the lab, he stood and followed the cable from the pulley across the ice. *Thank god.* The snowcat was still there.

A quick search revealed a remote control unit that controlled the winch. Marko pushed one of its three buttons. The winch cable snapped taut and the basket slammed into the top of the tripod. Marko reversed the winch, allowing the basket to swing back and forth like a bell in a church tower. Every time the heavy metal basket hit the legs of the tripod, it clanged loud enough to echo off Thor's Hammer and into the valley.

Nearly tearful with relief, Marko held the second button down and watched as the swinging basket lowered down and out of sight.

CHAPTER 98

Frantino watched the LC-130 Hercules lift off the ski-way, make a sharp turn, and then fly out of sight. He'd been ordered to secure the valley, a near impossibility with only twenty-four uninjured SEALs. Instead, he'd set up a perimeter with four teams of six each.

If Russian commandos parachuted into the valley, the best they could hope to do was lay down enough suppressing fire to give the spooks' Hercules a chance of getting off the ice. Now, with the cargo plane gone, their mission was effectively over, and his only concern was the safe evacuation of the team.

"You think the Skipper's gonna be okay?" asked the Senior Chief.

Frantino nodded. "He just got his bell rung and a few cuts." He scratched at the three-day beard. "That asshole Fischer said one of their top priorities was to 'med-evac' him and the civilians to safety in the Hercules."

"So when you think we're getting out of here, Danny?"

An unexpected clang rang through the valley, echoing off sharp canyon walls. Frantino glanced over at the Senior Chief. With the second clang, he spun around. "What the fuck now?"

Frantino swept the horizon. He saw nothing moving on the valley floor, so he focused the glasses toward Thor's Hammer. He panned over the snowcat, the piles of equipment left by the CIA crew, and the steel lift basket hanging from the tripod.

It swung from side to side several times and then abruptly dropped into the crevasse. "What the hell?"

Frantino turned the binoculars back toward the snowcat. Standing in front of the cat with a remote control in hand was one of Paulson's crew. He could tell by the colorful red parka, which stood out on the ice like a beacon. "It's one of the civilians."

"I thought they were all being flown out along with the Skipper."

"That's what that puke Fischer said." Frantino searched the area around the crevasse but spotted only the one civilian. He swept the glasses down toward the Russian camp, where the old B-29 bomber still glistened in the sunlight.

"We've got someone moving through the camp," he said. "I need your shoulder to steady the glasses."

He steadied the glasses on the Chief's shoulders, allowing him a better view of the figure walking in front of the B-29. At this distance, he couldn't identify the man, but the clothing was unmistakable. The bloody streaks darkening the normally arctic-white combat-issue suit.

That goddamn, lying Fischer....

Frantino spoke into a communicator, ordering the SEAL team closest to the Russian camp to use its snow machine and pick up their skipper.

"Get him and meet me up at the crevasse." Frantino turned to the Chief. "You're coming with me. We're going to find out why we still have people in a hot LZ."

CHAPTER 99

When the basket cleared the crevasse, everyone aboard let out a loud cheer. Marko pushed the aluminum docking bridge out, and Jack connected and locked it on the basket. One by one, they skittered across the bridge, slapping Marko on the back as they passed.

"We're getting out of here on the snowcat," Jack said. "Everyone get inside the cab or pile on top."

"Looks like we've got company, again," Paulson said. He pointed toward two snow machines, one climbing toward the crevasse and the other still a speck on the valley floor.

"I'm not waiting around," Jack said.

He pulled at the glass-and-metal door of the vehicle, found the starter button, and pushed it. The snowcat struggled to turn over its cold engine.

The first of the two snow machines arrived in a hurry, skidding to a stop in a spray of ice.

Frantino jumped off and shouted, "I want everyone over here."

One of the SEALs jumped on the snowcat and aimed his weapon. The message was clear; Jack should immediately shut down the snowcat. He swore under his breath, climbed down to the ice, and jogged over to where Frantino had his weapon trained loosely on everyone else.

"What are you guys doing here?" Frantino said. "You're supposed to be on the Hercules."

"Fischer dumped us all in the crevasse." Jack replied. "Except for Leah."

"Dr. Andrews?" Frantino shook his head. "Asshole."

"He also rigged the structure with explosives," Jack said. "They could be nukes. We don't know. But they're certainly high-tech, and no doubt on a timer. We need to get out of here now."

"Everyone down slope," Frantino said. "We'll hook up with the Skipper and find out what the hell's happening."

Chapter 100

Even from a distance, Jack could see that Beckam's face was cut up bad and his clothing had been shredded in places by flying shrapnel. Up close, the SEAL Commander looked worse. Jack winced. "Sorry about that—"

Beckam shrugged it off. "I'd have tried the same myself…if I'd known what a cluster this was."

"So as far as I understand it," Jack said, "Stanton Fischer tried to kill us and lied his ass off to you and your men."

Beckam looked at Frantino, and both men nodded.

Jack and his crew had joined up with Frantino, Chief Reynolds and Commander Beckam near the *Las Tortugas*. The remaining SEALs remained at their perimeter posts around the valley, waiting for the arrival of the Russians.

"So you boys don't think help's coming, do you?" asked Paulson.

Beckam shook his head. "We're hung out to dry." He looked over at the *Las Tortugas*. "Think it'll fly?"

Paulson turned to his mechanic. "Mac, it's our only way out. What do you think?"

"The Number Four engine is still blowing oil, and I don't have a clue how the control cables look." Ridley spit on the ice and scowled. "It has fuel, at least. We'd have to pump some of the fifty gallon barrels into her just to be sure."

"So you're saying you can get it flying?" asked Jack.

Ridley barked out a mirthless laugh. "Sure—but I can't guarantee we're gonna fly it real far."

"Well," Paulson said with a glance at the SEALs, "we're not in a position to be real choosey. How much time will you need to get us up?"

"Two days would be the usual. But as this is an emergency and all, an hour or so."

Jack asked Beckam, "Do we have that much time?"

"I doubt it," said Beckam, "between the Russians and the timed explosives." He thought for a moment. "There's nothing we can do to stop the Russians from coming, but the bombs.... About how big are they?"

Jack described in detail what they'd found.

"Shit, Gus," said Frantino. "That sounds a lot like Shoe-Goo."

Beckam nodded in agreement. "If this is what we've dealt with before, maybe I can shut them down."

"What *are* we dealing with?" Jack asked, feeling the hairs on the back of his neck tingle.

Rather than answer, Beckam sighed. "Why is it that scary things always come in small packages?"

"They're nuclear, aren't they?"

"Not like you've seen on the Discovery Channel. These will reduce every living thing for half a mile into what we refer to as 'Shoe-Goo,' not to mention roast the structure." He scanned the horizon. "I want the platoon back into a closer defensive perimeter." He pointed toward Jack. "You're coming with me."

Jack nodded. "We'll need someone to run the lift system."

"Take someone who's not gonna help working on that old bomber."

"Marko."

Marko swallowed, then nodded.

"You're coming with me."

Chapter 101

Every time Leah tried to lean into the web seating, the handcuffs binding her hands behind her back bit into her wrists, cutting off the blood flow so that her fingers felt cold and numb. She tried to ignore them. Now that the plane had been in the air for a while, she'd begun thinking through the realities of her situation with a renewed calm. She ran scenarios through her mind on ways she might escape and get help for Jack, all of which seemed lame given her current dilemma.

She sat near the front of the C-130's cargo compartment, facing the rear of the aircraft. Fischer's goons lay slumped around the web seating, most sleeping soundly. Leah had no doubt that upon landing they'd be ordered back under whatever rock they'd crawled from under until Fischer required their particular brand of sleazy skills again.

Not everyone on the aircraft slept, however. Several men, older than Fischer's armed thugs, scurried about the cargo, taking notes and conversing among themselves like kids on Christmas morning comparing gifts left by Santa—the "cargo" being the tubes containing the cliff dwellers still held in suspended animation, from what Leah could tell.

As a scientist, she couldn't help but be fascinated with the possibilities of having a face-to-face conversation with the inhabitants of the tubes. She mentally went through a sampling of the questions she'd ask, beginning with how they'd ended up in Antarctica. Before she got far, though, thoughts of her father rose, unbidden. He'd long rejected the theories about why these people had built entire cities in cliffs all around the Southwest. She wondered what he'd make of this new, outlandish explanation: Eight hundred years ago, the planet had extra-terrestrial visitors who'd started abducting members of these peaceful tribes.

Once you got over the crazy premise, it all made fairly good sense. The alien visitors had arrived with technologies out of a science-fiction movie, setting up a lab in Antarctica, probably for some type of research. The same kind of study a scientist like Leah might have carried out in a similar situation. They'd chosen Antarctica's relatively sterile environment to avoid contaminating the research—and perhaps themselves. Maybe, if they were altruistic, they even chose the remote location to avoid disrupting more of earth's inhabitants than necessary.

Once the abductions had ended, perhaps a hundred years later, those who'd moved to defensive positions in the cliffs had fled again, into dif-ferent regions of the Southwest, creating entirely new Native American cultures and languages along the way.

The Anasazi or, Ancient Ones, as they had become known by other tribes, had disappeared without a trace, it seemed. And now Leah thought she knew why.

An accident had occurred, destroying the visitors' lab or ship or what-ever with an avalanche of snow and ice. Leah thought of the woman lying dead on the floor of the structure, the red granite in her grasp, the outer door still opened and jammed with ice.

She wished at that moment she could examine her own palm. Something about her chemistry had allowed Leah to open the door between the rooms. It was reasonable to assume that the Anasazi woman had been able to do the same thing, hundreds of years in the past.

Maybe the dead woman had seen the visitors open the door and, hop-ing for an avenue of escape, copied what she'd seen them do, somehow breaching the outer airlock.

The resulting shock wave from the rapid change in air pressure could have triggered the avalanche, sealing the structure. If any of the visitors had been caught just outside of the structure, they might have been buried under tons of snow and ice.

Anger replaced wonder when she saw Fischer climbing down from the cockpit. He glanced in her direction and smiled in that condescending manner that so ignited her temper. It was probably a good thing she remained handcuffed; otherwise, she'd have bolted from the seat, grabbed Fischer around his pencil neck, and squeezed with all her might.

Fischer, apparently oblivious to her wishful thinking, worked his way toward her through the sleeping commandos and equipment. He stopped and pulled a thermos from an army-green canvas bag, along with two plain ceramic cups, and then slid down beside her and poured a cup of coffee.

He shouted over the roar and vibration. "If you behave, Dr. Andrews, I'd be happy to offer you a hot cup of coffee."

"You can take your coffee and shove it up your ass."

Fischer appeared to ignore the comment completely.

"You have a historic responsibility here." He sipped the hot coffee. "Do you mind if I call you Leah?"

Leah leaned toward Fischer, making sure he heard every word. "Can I call you Prick and/or Cold-Blooded Killer?"

Fischer bristled momentarily, then regained his calm demeanor. "You still have a very important role to fulfill. Our experts believe that you hold the key to safely releasing the inhabitants."

Leah's eyes narrowed.

"You were able to access the structure with nothing more than the palm of your hand. It seems you're the only person within our team who has that ability."

"So?"

"You noticed, no doubt, the environmental tubes containing the Native Americans feature a similar triangular pattern. It's our belief that the process to cycle them out of their stasis could be initiated with your hand."

Leah started to speak, but before she was able to spit out a string of four-letter words describing various parts of Fischer's substandard anatomy, he held up a hand and his expression hardened.

"Let me say what I've got to say, Dr. Andrews, and then you can respond positively, or I can arrange for you to spend the balance of your life locked down in some secure underground facility where no one will ever hear from you again."

Leah clenched her jaw and waited.

"Our scientists believe that the viability of the tubes' life-support systems, once disconnected from the structure, will be limited. How long they'll last, we can't say. That means that you—"

"Forget it, Fischer. I'd rather see these people dead than living in some kind of glass-encased prison, being tested like rats in laboratory."

"You speak a collection of Native American languages—is that correct?"

"Enough to have your ass kicked on most reservations."

Fischer smiled despite himself. "You could work with us gathering information."

Leah reared back. "You don't give a shit about these people, do you? All you care about is finding more about whoever built the laboratory."

Fischer shrugged. "The items we recovered could offer the United States an opportunity to lead the world for generations in advanced technologies spanning every application thinkable."

"You mean weapons."

"Defense, medical technologies, power supplies spanning centuries, transportation—the opportunities are infinite."

"Forget it, Fischer. Not interested."

Before Fischer was able to reply, one of the scientists shouted and then clambered over the equipment.

Fischer jumped up as the scientist waved his hands wildly, while pointing back toward the life-support tubes. Fischer nodded several times and his face paled visibly.

He turned and grabbed Leah by her parka and yanked her to her feet. "You talk quite a game, Dr. Andrews. Let's see just how callous you are."

"What's happening?"

"Apparently, the pods' power systems are beginning to fail." He nodded toward the scientists, who were busy ripping the insulation off the tubes. "One of the inhabitants is suffering a seizure—a young female."

Leah felt her face going numb with the realization that it must be the little girl she'd seen when they first found the tubes and the cliff dwellers.

She wheeled around, turning her back to Fischer. "Get these cuffs off and let me get to work."

CHAPTER 102

Jack led Beckam through the jumbled mess of cutting tools and equipment containers left behind by the science crew, past both doors, and into the second chamber, where the three metallic barrels sat side by side.

Beckam knelt and didn't touch them but studied each with the practiced precision of a weapons expert.

To Jack, they seemed much too small to release a mushroom cloud like he'd seen on television hundreds of time before. "Are they...?"

Beckam didn't respond. He was busy examining the casings on the black canisters.

Jack crouched down and studied the cases. He resisted the urge to reach out and touch the metallic surface of the barrels. "Nukes?"

"No." He glanced at Jack and offered a faint smile. "If I tell you what they are, I'm supposed to kill you."

Jack found himself amused in spite of the situation. "You've killed me already. What are they?"

"Hafnium-isomer warheads." His fingertips worked over the control panel as he talked. "These are the next-generation tactical weapons. Super-secret, James Bond."

"How do they work?"

"Each one of these contains about twenty pounds of charged Hafnium," Beckam said.

Jack shrugged.

"You ever take physics? Hafnium is a metal, atomic number 72 on the periodic scale. To make a bomb you bombard it with a super-high-energy source. Think of it like a charged battery from hell. You heat the Hafnium with a short burst of X-rays and this mother explodes with a force ten-thousand times as strong as TNT. It'll sterilize a half-mile radius with enough gamma radiation to—"

"To turn all living tissue to shoe-goo," Jack said, feeling a chill run down his spine.

"Since there's no fission, it leaves no trace radiation like a nuclear detonation. Most people think these are just theoretical weapons. So they can be used with what we call plausible deniability. Each of these will detonate with the force of about 500 tons of TNT. That barely nudges the needle on a scale when it comes to tactical nukes, but for this kind of job, they happen to be perfect."

"Jesus," Jack whispered. "I bet you never thought you'd see one of these in action."

Beckam glanced up from the control panel, locking his gaze on Jack for a second. "How do you think we blew up that nuclear weapons facility in Iran last year and got away with it?"

"You did that?"

Beckam nodded, wincing slightly. "Destroyed the facility and fried every Iranian scientist and quite a few Russian and French scientists and technicians to boot. With weapons that supposedly don't exist." He turned back to the three bombs.

"Can you disarm them?"

On the top of each canister sat a raised, lit panel six inches long by three inches wide. Next to the panel were two buttons. Beckam reached down and depressed both buttons at the same time. The panel flipped open, exposing a series of keys. Then he slid one of the canisters clear of the other two and began scanning the side.

"What are you looking for?" Jack asked.

"Serial numbers on the casing. I want to see if these are the same weapons we trained on for the Iranian mission." He glanced at Jack. "There are only a handful of these warheads in existence. It is possible once these went back into storage that the codes weren't changed."

"Wouldn't you need a code book, or something?"

"Yeah, you'd need a codebook to arm and disarm the weapon while in the field. The codes are two strings of nine digits consisting of letters and numbers. In addition, each warhead had a specific time delay required between entering of the first string and second. If the book said to enter the strings ten seconds apart, the arming mechanism would lock out if you didn't hit the first digit of the second string within two seconds of the set delay."

Jack felt his heart sink as Beckam continued to feel along the side of the casing.

"Bingo." Beckam crouched sideways and examined the serial number cut into the case.

"Without the code books, what can you do?"

Beckam favored him with a Buddha-like smile. "Never underestimate resourcefulness of a SEAL."

CHAPTER 103

Ridley shouted over the roar of the propane preheater. "How much fuel have you put into the wing tanks?"

Garrett pulled back the hood off his jacket. "Five hundred gallons; how much more do you want?"

"That's going to get you from here to the end of the runway, Son."

Garrett nodded and pointed toward Perez and Lyon as they loaded additional fifty-gallon barrels of high-octane fuel onto sleds attached to the snow machines. "We have more on the way."

"That and what the Russians already pumped into the tanks will have to do." Ridley pointed toward the Russian tractor. "I found a battery in the equipment shed. We're going to drag this old war horse through the sastrugi and onto smooth ice with the tractor."

Paulson stuck his head out the side cockpit window and shouted. "You about got this thing patched up, Mac?"

"I sure as hell hope you know what you're doing, because this bomber doesn't fly itself like that overpowered pimp wagon sitting back in Chile."

Paulson winked. "You just get those engines cranked up."

"One hour," Ridley shouted, "and we're out of here—for better or worse."

CHAPTER 104

"**G**et me to the surface!"

Marko jumped at the sound of Gus Beckam's voice coming from the bottom of the crevasse. His hands moved over the elevator controls almost like it was Beckam operating them himself. When the basket hit the tripod, Beckam had to hang on to avoid being thrown from the basket.

Marko cringed. For a second, he wondered if the SEAL would pull out that oversized pistol he wore and shoot Marko between the eyes for mishandling the lift.

Instead, Beckam opened the gate and waited as Marko slid the bridge and locked it in place. He jumped out onto the ice and spoke into the microphone headset he wore.

"Danny—it's definitely Shoe-Goo. We've got three in the oven ready to pop. We caught a break. The series read: Charlie, Oscar, Papa, Echo, November and three digits, nine series."

Beckam pressed the headset against his ear to hear the response. Then he nodded. "I sure as hell hope you haven't burned too many brain cells after all that post-mission party time in Little Creek."

Beckam nodded and then returned to the lift. He pointed at Marko. "After you drop me, raise the lift. You're gonna see a SEAL coming this way hell-bent-for-election. You're not gonna breathe until he gets here. If you have to piss, I expect you to wet your pants because I don't want your hands off those controls. You understand you're not to move for any reason?"

Marko nodded quickly, wondering how long he could actually hold his breath.

"Now get me back down into this hole, pronto."

The basket dropped so fast that Beckam had to hold on to avoid getting thrown out.

CHAPTER 105

Beckam ducked back into the structure. He reached into his jacket and pulled out a pen and a small pad of paper.

"You guys come prepared," Jack said, amazed that Beckam would have pen and paper in a combat zone.

"Yeah. It's hard to remember everything with RPGs exploding around your ass."

"What is your plan?"

"These are the COPEN series warheads, like I thought; I recognized the serial numbers right away. COPEN is short for Copenhagen. Hafnium is the Latin translation for Copenhagen—a little inside joke from the bomb-builders at Los Alamos."

He glanced up. "Normally that wouldn't help us worth shit without the codes, but Danny, bless his heart, happens to have an eidetic memory." Beckam looked at Jack. "Photographic. He's got a photographic memory. It's bailed us out of shit on more times that I can count. He says if the serials match up to what we'd trained on, he'd remember the code for each of the weapons." Beckam glanced at his watch. "It'd be just our luck to have 'em detonate before Danny gets down here." Beckam copied the serial numbers onto his pad.

Once finished, he sat and, for the first time, appeared to relax. "Take a load off, Jack. We've got five, maybe ten minutes on our hands with nothing to do but wait."

"You don't look real nervous," Jack said.

"If it's our time to go, at least it's gonna be fast. And what the hell: we did everything we could do." Beckam glanced around the inside of the structure. "I just can't get out of my mind what Fischer told me."

Jack sat on a used aluminum equipment case. "What's that?"

"How the Russians knew we'd found this place." Beckam leaned forward. "He said that something you did down here triggered off a high-energy beam, like a microwave signal used for communications, but thousands of times stronger. It was aimed out into space, and Fischer said it cooked half the satellites operating in the southern hemisphere."

"It must have been when Leah opened that first door," Jack said. "It fried all our handheld radios and GPS units that were operating at the time."

Beckam chuckled. "I got a feeling Dr. Andrews is gonna have the last laugh when all this is over. Seems to me when she got those power systems running again, this mother phoned home. Whoever set up this little chamber of horrors might have reason to return."

Jack was interrupted by the sound of the aluminum basket hitting the ice.

"Skipper!"

"Here!" Beckam called back.

Jack turned as Frantino worked his tall frame through the entryway. "Jesus," he said. "They made a mess out of this place."

"That's nothing compared to what's in store if you can't remember the codes and sequence for these little honeys."

Frantino grimaced when he saw the canisters lined up side by side.

Beckam read off the serial number for the first canister. "Any chance you happen to remember the codes?"

Frantino took a deep breath. "I'm gonna have to see the PALs in reverse order, since I always remember the arming codes first in sequence, then the disarming code—not to mention the sequence."

"PALs?" Jack asked.

Beckam nodded. "Permissive Arming Links. Lingo generally used for traditional nukes, but these warheads use similar arming procedures, not quite as complicated since they have to be battlefield-armed. He glanced over at Frantino. "I'll read off the serial numbers and you've got to match the codes."

"What would happen if you fed in the wrong code?" Jack asked.

"They'd cook-off with a one-minute delay unless the proper code was entered on a second attempt."

"Then it was good we didn't mess with them."

Beckam glanced up. "Chances are, one of the warheads will blow before we get them all disarmed anyway."

Jack decided then that his best contribution to this enterprise was to remain silent. As he watched, Beckam scribbled down the ten-digit code, repeating each letter and number in sequence while Frantino, eyes shut tight, recited the numbers from memory. He also told Beckam the time delay required between entering the two sets of digits.

"That's it," Frantino said, taking a deep breath. "Unless I had a brain fart and didn't match the right set of codes with the right warhead, you should be good to go."

Beckam hovered over the first warhead. He quickly entered the numbers into the keypad while Jacked watched over him.

"Get ready on your watch, Danny."

Frantino pushed the sleeve of his jacket up, making his wristwatch visible. "Ready."

"First sequence: Charlie-9er-2-1-Echo-4-Alpha-5-Fox-0."

Beckam entered each digit as Jack watched on in fascination. When finished with the last digit he said, "Mark."

Frantino counted down the required 15-second delay sequence between strings for the first warhead.

When Frantino hit zero, Beckam began entering the second string.

When the final digits had been entered, the LED readout on the panel flashed remaining time on a counter and then went blank. Jack couldn't help but notice that the warheads had less than eleven minutes remaining on their timers.

Within minutes, Beckam had successfully disarmed all three warheads.

He tossed the notepad to Frantino. "Copy down the arming codes, delays and sequence for each warhead."

Frantino's eyes opened wide.

"We have Russians on the way, Danny. No time for explanations."

Frantino nodded and then began to scribble the codes on the torn pieces of paper.

"Why three?" Jack asked. "If what you say is right about the blast, one of these would vaporize a good part of the valley."

"Redundancy is standard procedure for nuclear-tactical combat. Plus, we don't know what this structure's made of. Fischer obviously wants to make sure it's useless to the Russians."

"Could those be detonated now?" Jack eyed the bombs.

Beckam shook his head. "Unless the arming codes are inserted, they are as safe as Aunt Millie's Strawberry Preserves. You could toss them off a cliff and they wouldn't detonate—although I wouldn't test my theory in a populated zone." He glanced up. "Danny, get back into position. I've got to finish down here. I'll join up with you in twenty minutes."

Frantino nodded and slipped out through the doorway.

Beckam's expression hardened. He knelt and, using the codes that Frantino had scribbled on the pad, entered the arming codes back into the first canister.

"What are you doing?" Jack asked, alarmed.

"I'm still a United States Navy SEAL, and although misguided in its execution, Mr. Fischer's plan was essentially the correct one." He looked up at Jack. "We have no idea what remains in the lab that could be converted into weaponry by the Russians." He nodded toward the ceiling. "They've hardly touched the interior of this place. We've got no idea what else is buried under that ice. If your theory is right about extraterrestrials, there could be all kinds of nasty things buried in the ice."

"This was a science lab, not a military platform. Think of the power systems that continued to operate for nearly 800 years."

"It creates an entirely new set of problems," said Beckam. "This technology wasn't meant for us, Jack. It's like one of those philosophical questions we used to argue about back in school." He nodded toward the Hafnium warheads. "Imagine if Hitler had ten of these in, let's say, 1935. We'd all be speaking German today. If anything remained of the United States at all. The technologies found in this lab could create that exact imbalance in power. While Fischer's a major prick, I'd much rather whatever came out of this nightmare be on our side."

"Think they'd trade Leah and the cliff dwellers for one of these warheads?" Jack asked suddenly.

"Would you trade a million lives for Leah?"

"No," Jack conceded.

"I think that answers your question." Beckam smiled. "A weapon of terror is no good if you don't intend to use it."

Frantino's voice echoed from above throughout the structure. "Skipper! Showtime! We got chutes!"

Jack watched as Beckam finished entering the codes into the first warhead. The menu prompted him to enter time-to-detonation. Jack was shocked by the simplicity of the device, once you had the arming codes.

"Thirty minutes, Mr. Hobson. That's how long you and your friends have to get the B-29 off the ice. We should be able to hold off the Russians for thirty minutes, but I won't guarantee more." He tore up the notepad containing the codes and tossed the pieces into the debris. Then he glanced at Jack. "Twenty-nine minutes—I don't think you want to spend it standing here."

"We're not leaving without you and your men...."

"You can't have it both ways, Jack. If we make a run for the B-29, the Russians will shoot it down before we got airborne. The only way you get off the ice, and we make sure this place goes up, is if we're able to pin them down for a while."

Jack couldn't believe what he was hearing. "That's a suicide mission."

Beckam simply stared at Jack. "The Russians will have orders to make for the structure so they can secure it. If these weapons malfunction, you can bet that the next thing you'll see is the gloves coming off and twenty US nuclear-tipped cruise missiles headed for the valley. Then it's all going to a hell-in-a-hand-basket when the Russians launch on Washington." Beckam sighed, shaking his head. "I'd hoped that was the last I'd ever see of these weapons." He glanced up. "Let's get out of here."

Jack nodded, and they both sprinted through the doors and into the bottom of the crevasse.

"Marko, get us out of here!" Jack shouted toward the surface.

Jack Hobson and Gus Beckam climbed into the basket, closed the gate, and waited for what seemed like an eternity for Marko to run to the snowcat and engage the remote control.

When it reached the surface, Marko slid the steel gate toward the basket and Beckam locked it down as the sound of small arms automatic gunfire echoed off Thor's Hammer in raucous waves.

Beckam shook Jack's hand firmly "You'd have made a hell of a Navy SEAL."

Jack opened his mouth to respond, but Beckam held up his hand.

"I'd have been tempted to take the warheads. She's a hell of a woman." Beckam's expression darkened. "If you ever bump into Fischer, you make sure and give him my regards." He started toward the snow machine and then stopped and turned. "White Sands, Jack."

"White Sands?"

Beckam nodded. "Danny overheard the flight crew from the LC-130 say something about White Sands, New Mexico. If you get out of here, that'd be the first place I'd look for Leah."

Before Jack could respond, Beckam climbed aboard the snow machine. He started it and threw a rooster tail of snow and ice when he hammered the throttle.

Jack sprinted toward the snowcat and hopped up on the cab. "Come on, Marko. We're getting out of here."

"What about the basket?" Marko asked. "It's still connected to the snowcat."

"Were gonna back up, yank the tripod over and drag it to solid ice. Then I'm going to disconnect the basket, and we're making a beeline for the *Las Tortugas.*" Jack suddenly stopped. His eyes narrowed. "White Sands," he whispered his eyes opening wide for just a moment.

"What's wrong?"

"I'm going back down into the crevasse," Jack said.

"What?" Marko's eyes opened wide and he pointed down-valley. "They're shooting; in case you hadn't noticed." Marko ran after him, shouting. "Wait! What can be down there that's worth anything to us?"

Jack jumped into the basket, and Marko pulled the bridge clear. "Once I'm at the bottom, you give me five minutes and then lift the basket."

The basket descended quickly into the icy gloom. When it hit the bottom, Jack stepped clear, ducked into the opening, and ran through the debris into the second chamber.

He scrambled to the debris pile where Beckam had torn up the codes. Jack dropped to his knees and began gathering the pieces of paper. With shaking hands, he assembled the pieces on the smooth floor, until he had the arming and disarming codes staring back at him in Beckam's precise handwriting.

"Okay, let's hope I've got this right."

He repeated what he'd seen Beckam do, using entering the codes into the rectangular keypad of the first canister after triple-checking that the serial number matched. He held his breath until the LED screen blinked three times. Jack entered the right code and sequence. Now it was unarmed.

The number two canister remained armed, the LED blinking as it counted down the seconds to detonation. He entered the de-arming codes for the third canister, because he could more easily read the code through the tears in the note paper.

Jack hastily gathered up the pieces of paper and jammed them into an inside pocket in his parka, making sure to zip it tight.

Beckam was right. Scary things did come in small packages. Now Jack had a plan to get Leah back alive. If it required using two of these weapons-from-hell, so be it.

He rolled the warhead to the basket and set it down inside. He returned for the third Hafnium warhead and loaded it into the basket.

Jack shouted up toward surface and had just closed the gate when the lift cable snapped tight and the basket jumped off the ice, banging into the frozen walls as Marko brought it up faster than it was designed to move.

When it reached the surface, Marko shoved the aluminum bridge out so Jack could secure it to the basket.

"What are you doing with those?"

"I don't have time to explain," Jack said. "Just set the bridge so we can get the hell out of here."

Marko secured the aluminum bridge to solid ice, and Jack walked across, balancing the canisters with one arm held out over the abyss. "Take it to the snowcat," he ordered. Marko nodded, his eyes open wide with fear and his body pumped full of adrenalin.

Marko lifted the device clear of the ice and sprinted with it toward the snowcat.

The sound of gunfire had increased and included the loud boom of an occasional mortar shell, as the SEALs attempted to keep the Russian commandos pinned down a thousand meters away from the *Las Tortugas*. Jack picked up the second warhead and carried it toward the snowcat.

"Help me get these into the cab," Jack said.

Marko hopped up on the snowcat and hoisted each warhead into place as Jack pushed up from beneath. Jack climbed into the driver's seat and pushed the starter button as Marko piled in beside him.

They had twenty minutes to get to the bomber and off the ice before detonation.

Chapter 106

Paulson waited in the command seat while Ridley connected the Russian tractor to the nose wheel. All four radial engines roared at idle speed, with just a note of whine as the superchargers came up to speed.

Angus Lyon sat at the flight engineer's station, adjusting the engine throttles, cowling positions, and fuel mixtures for a high-altitude, low-density takeoff.

The Scotsman noted, with more than casual interest, the hot cylinder-head temperatures in the Number Three engine. He looked through the view port and studied the radial engine for telltale signs of smoke. From the flight engineer's station, the engines appeared to be running normally and Lyon breathed a sigh of relief. At this density and altitude, even without a bomb load, there was no way they could lift off with only three engines.

Ridley ran out in front of the cockpit windows and waved wildly at Paulson. He pointed with his hands in a left-hand direction, meaning he wanted Paulson to turn the nose wheel to the left.

Paulson nodded that he understood as Ridley climbed into the tractor alongside Garrett. The tractor and *Las Tortugas* combo rolled smoothly over the ice, pulling the bomber 180 degrees, almost within its own radius.

Garrett lowered the blade on the tractor to cut a path through the sastrugi for the fragile nose gear. The main gear would have to roll over the unplowed ice.

When they neared the worst of the icy dunes, Ridley stood up on the tractor and wound his hand in the air several times.

Paulson nodded and nudged the four throttles. Ridley had told him that when they reached the larger sastrugi, he should give the engines more throttle to help drive the bomber through the ice. The roar of the engines increased, as did the clouds of snow and ice blowing up behind the Super Fortress as the Soviet-era tractor plowed through the ice and snow.

"Yaaahooo!" Paulson shouted as the *Las Tortugas* cleared the sastrugi field and all three wheels rolled onto smooth ice.

Ridley crossed his fists: a signal to Paulson to pull the throttles down to idle. He disconnected the tow bar, and Garrett steered the tractor out of the path of the *Las Tortugas*.

Ridley opened the hatch at the bottom of the fuselage and climbed into the belly, past Lyon and Perez, and into the cockpit.

"We're all set," he shouted to Paulson over the roar of the engines. "I'm going back out and look for Jack and the SEALs."

The billionaire nodded and Ridley dropped down out of the bomber. He ran toward Garrett, who stood on the ice with a pair of binoculars at his eyes, working the high-powered glasses between the ice valley that separated them from Thor's Hammer and the intense firefight three kilometers distant.

"See anything?" Ridley shouted.

Garrett pulled his eyes away from the glasses. "Negative." He pointed toward the plumes of snow and ice where mortar shells rained down on both sides. "How long are we waiting?"

Ridley shook his head.

Garrett lifted the binoculars and swung them out onto the ice. "There!" He pointed with one hand while holding the binoculars with the other. "It's the snowcat."

Sure enough, a snowcat glistened in the distance as its tracks threw up dual rooster tails of snow and ice.

Ridley tapped Garrett on the shoulder and spoke into his ear. "Tell Paulson to hold his horses for about two minutes."

CHAPTER 107

The snowcat flew twice while crossing the steeper sastrugi, but Jack never let up on the throttle. He and Marko bounced around inside the cab, banging their heads against the roof and seat backs. The *Las Tortugas* lay directly in front of him, its four engines spewing blackened exhaust and the huge propellers spinning in a blur of high energy.

Jack maneuvered the snowcat to within fifty feet of the bomber's nose and jammed on the brakes. "Roll one of these to the airplane."

Marko nodded and jumped out his door. Jack climbed out into the track and pulled the first of the two warheads out from behind the seat.

Marko stood at the bottom as Jack slid it down to him and he rolled it toward the *Las Tortugas* while Jack fished the second canister out from behind the seat.

When he rounded the snowcat with the heavy cargo in tow, he nearly ran into Ridley, who pointed toward the raging firefight.

"If those SEALs are coming, they'd better get a move on."

"They're not coming," Jack shouted over the combined roar of the four thundering engines.

Even the normally gruff Ridley looked stunned. "What?"

"I said they're not coming." Jack nodded toward the bomber. "If we don't get out of here within the next few minutes, we won't be leaving, either."

Ridley's eyes dropped to the bomb in Jack's hands. "What in the hell are you doing with that?"

"I can't explain right now." Jack looked away from the mechanic toward the fuselage of the bomber. Marko stood at the bottom of the hatch with the barrel-warhead. He was attempting to wedge the device up into the bomber, with no success.

"You get inside and I'll heave them up to you," he shouted. Marko nodded, climbed into the aircraft's belly and pulled up on warhead number one while Jack pushed from the bottom. When they had the first canister aboard, Jack pushed the second inside with the climber's help.

Jack waved toward Ridley to climb aboard the *Las Tortugas*, even as plumes of ice exploded less than three hundred meters away.

The Russians were advancing their position against Beckam's outnumbered and outgunned SEAL team.

Jack climbed into the belly of the roaring bomber and frog-walked into the cockpit. Paulson sat in the left command pilot's seat and Garrett in the right, methodically reading off pre-take-off commands over the roar of the engines to Paulson from the B-29's flight manual.

He shouted, "Wing flaps 25 degrees—switch auto pilot to off position—propellers at high RPM, turbos set for takeoff."

Paulson's hands stopped sweeping across the instrument panel long enough for him to flash a grin and shout, "Damn, Garrett, I'm going to make a four-engine bomber pilot out of you yet."

Jack tapped Paulson on the shoulder and gave a karate-chop move with his hand indicating they should go.

"What about the SEALs?" Paulson shouted over the roar of the engines.

Jack shook his head vigorously. "They're not coming!"

"Are you sure?" Paulson caught Jack's expression and immediately understood. He nodded once.

A fountain of snow and ice erupted into a geyser not more than two-hundred feet away.

"It's now or never, Al."

Paulson let Garrett lead him through the final few items on the pre-takeoff checklist. Then he glanced left and right out of habit to make sure they were clear of any obstacles and smoothly fed throttle to the 18-cylinder radial engines until they were roaring away with a combined 8,800 horsepower.

The *Las Tortugas*, rolling on its tires and under its own power for the first time in more than fifty years, rattled and vibrated as it picked up speed over the ice runway.

The billionaire went against his instinct to pull the yoke back and get the Super Fortress off the ice. The only chance was gaining as much ground speed as possible and then physically yanking the heavy bomber off the runway. After that, he'd have to fly less than fifty feet above the ice in ground-effect to stay airborne in the thin atmosphere until he built up enough airspeed to climb out of the valley.

Ridley tripped and fell into Marko, who sat jammed into the radio operator's station behind the cockpit. "Is it going to fly?" the young climber asked, his face pale with fear.

Ridley grinned. "Like a homesick angel." He winked and patted Marko on the shoulder. "You just hang on."

Paulson struggled to keep control of the bomber as it bounced off the ice and crashed down on the landing gear once, then twice. "Just a couple more seconds," he whispered, jaw clenched tight. Suddenly he jerked back on the yoke with both hands. "We're out of here!"

The *Las Tortugas* leapt off the ice and Paulson held it aloft feet above the tops of the sastrugi. When the billionaire-pilot nodded, Garrett flipped up a lever, raising the landing gear.

Ridley crawled back into the cockpit and struggled to hold on between the two pilots. "Angus says the cylinder head temperature gauges are pegged. You got to pull back on them throttles."

Paulson nodded, but his eyes didn't leave the horizon as he fought to keep the bomber airborne.

"I think you got it," the old mechanic said. "Pull her nose up a bit more."

"You want to fly, Mac?" Paulson snapped while struggling to cross-control the heavy bomber in the erratic drafts created by the jagged mountains surrounding them.

"No—you're doing just fine."

Jack turned around and fought his way back to the radio operator's station to check on Marko and the two warheads.

The interior was incredibly cramped for a large aircraft. As Paulson had said, "It was designed to be a flying gas tank and bomb platform—nothing more, nothing less."

He patted Marko on the shoulder and studied the two metallic canisters now securely jammed behind the cockpit. The irony of the situation seemed overwhelming. Here he was, flying in the same type of aircraft that ended World War II by dropping two nuclear bombs on Japan. By doing so, he'd probably started a new and deadlier world war—one in which these two weapons of mass destruction would play a pivotal role.

Jack worked his way back toward the cockpit. "How far behind is Thor's Hammer?"

"Maybe four or five miles." Paulson glanced over at him. "We're out of range of the Russian soldiers if that's what you mean."

"I'm thinking of the blast that's coming," Jack said. "Those bombs are something else. Not standard nukes, according to Beckam, but enough to turn anyone in range to Shoe-Goo with a massive dose of gamma ray radiation."

Ridley's eyes opened wide, and real anger replaced the normally gruff but yielding personality. "Then what the hell are you doing bringing those aboard?"

"Bringing what aboard?" Paulson asked.

"Christ! Jack brought two of those bombs along, and he says they'll make old-school nukes seem like Fourth-of-July fireworks!"

"They're safe as long as you don't set the code sequence," Jack said.

"Have you lost your mind?" cried Paulson. He looked every bit as enraged as his chief mechanic. "If we crash, and chances are we will, we sure as hell don't need any help making an explosion bigger!"

"Maybe." Jack fought to control his temper, his anger fed by stress and fatigue. "All I know is that unless we have a bargaining chip, Leah's going to be held captive for life. Or worse."

The two men gave him doubtful looks. Now Jack felt real rage building in his chest—and it felt good. "What do you think we're gonna do, Al? Waltz back into the States and take up where we left off?" He wanted that to sink in for a moment before using his closer. "We're all dead men and you know it."

Suddenly the sky flashed brilliant white.

"I've got to have a look." Paulson turned the yoke hard left, and the B-29 banked sharply over.

"Don't get any closer," Jack warned. "Beckam said this thing not only would make a hell of a fireball, but it's going to release a dose of radiation that will wipe out every living thing in the valley."

Although the old bomber made the turn with agonizing slowness, within seconds a small mushroom cloud could be seen rising in the distance. The base of the deadly cloud sparkled with colors: yellows, reds and hues of blue and even purple. A massive rainbow wrapped the cloud like ribbons on a gift; a million tons of ice instantly flashed into white-hot steam.

"My God," said Jack softly. "It's gone."

The magnificent vertical wall and the granite vein that had identified it for millions of years lay in ruins; portions of jagged granite peaks cut up through the mist and vapor-looking more like a worn set of molars than the massive granite cathedral that once guarded the valley. What couldn't be seen was the gamma ray radiation that had cooked everything within a mile of the explosion.

"You think the SEALs survived?" Paulson asked.

Jack shook his head. "Not the way Beckam described what was going to happen at ground zero…. Rest in peace, fellas."

Paulson nodded and swung the bomber back on to a northwesterly course, guiding the Super Fortress over the Antarctica Peninsula and toward Punta Arenas, with O'Higgins as the emergency landing designate. "God bless 'em," he whispered

Jack murmured a prayer for the SEAL and his men. He saw Ridley was doing the same.

"Now, Jack, I gotta know what your plan is for those warheads," Paulson said. "If I don't like it, I dump them into the ocean."

Jack leaned over Paulson's right shoulder. "We're going to play a game of high-stakes poker. Think you've got the stomach for it?"

Paulson kept his eyes focused on the B-29's instrument panel. "What do you have in mind?"

CHAPTER 108

Leah wiped the sweat from her forehead, even though the interior of the LC-130 had felt cold just minutes before. She had the palm of her hand pressed firmly down against the panel as the girl in the tube convulsed repeatedly.

She didn't hear Fischer and the scientists shouting at each other or feel the aircraft lurch as the pilots pushed the throttles forward to speed their descent into the White Sands Missile Test Range.

Leah's sole focus was the Native American child, who was flailing her arms and legs as if in severe pain.

Leah turned her head but didn't remove her palm. Her gaze darted about the rear of the aircraft until she saw Fischer's pencil neck and pale skin. She indicated the tube with her free hand and shouted, "She's dying! Get something and break open this damn tube!"

Fischer nodded and, seconds later, a soldier stood over the tube with a fire axe that he'd yanked off the side of the fuselage.

When he raised the axe over his head, Leah instinctively shielded her eyes from what she was sure would be a shower of shards when the axe hit the clear, glass-like material.

Instead, the axe head simply bounced off the surface like it had struck solid granite, not glass.

"Again!" she shouted.

The soldier raised the axe over his head and swung it down, this time bending his knees as he brought his muscle and body-weight into the swing.

The axe bounced off the clear material and flew from the soldier's hands, causing the others who'd gathered around to cover their heads and duck for cover. Leah beat on the tube with both palms, then laid her palm on to a panel with similar characteristics to the door she'd opened, praying that whatever had given her the ability to open the entry on the alien station in Antarctica would be enough to free these people before they died.

Suddenly, blue liquid filled one of the clear tubes inserted into the thigh of the girl. Within seconds, her mouth opened and chest swelled as the interior surface of the tube fogged.

"Oxygen," Leah said breathless. "The tube is being filled with oxygen!"

The fogging cleared and the chest of the girl began expanding at decreasing intervals. At first, it looked like one breath every five seconds, then once every three seconds, and then she appeared to be breathing normally. The skin on her cheeks and chest went from the color of ash to bright pink.

The top half of the tube retracted seamlessly into the bottom half, leaving the girl exposed to the pressurized air within the aircraft.

"Get me a blanket!" Leah shouted.

An army-green blanket was pressed into Leah's hands, and she laid it over girl's body. As she did so, she felt breath on her face. The girl opened her eyes. She blinked several times, and then opened her mouth, but no words came out.

Leah reached down to the girl's hand and held it, hoping that it would comfort her.

The girl blinked several more times then opened her mouth, appearing, to Leah, determined to speak this time.

"Anihiilaaigii," she whispered just loud enough Leah could hear inside the noisy interior of the LC-130.

Leah jerked her hand back in shock. The last thing she expected was to hear the Navajo language.

Fischer bent over the tube. "It's talking?"

"It's a girl, Fischer. She's speaking Navajo."

"Anihiilaaigii," the girl repeated in a stronger voice.

"What's she saying?" Fischer asked.

"I think she wants to know if we are her...Creator."

Before Leah could reply, there was a shout. "Another one of these tubes is gonna go bad!"

"Shit." Leah pressed the little girl's hand and whispered softly in Navajo, "Adahayoiyi T'aadoo t'oo nihi."

The girl blinked in understanding and the muscles in her face relaxed.

One of the scientist looked up from another tube. "It's going into convulsions! You'd better get over here!"

Leah turned to Fischer. "You stay away from her."

Fischer's eyes remained cold, but he smiled. "I knew you'd be helpful, Ms. Andrews."

Leah pushed Fischer out of her way, knelt, placed both palms on the next tube, and pressed hard, silently commanding it to safely release its captive.

Chapter 109

Teresa Simpson tried unsuccessfully to fight her encroaching fatigue while sipping espresso out of a small porcelain cup. From her vantage point at the airport terminal, she enjoyed a clear view of Paulson's Gulfstream. The private jet sat on the tarmac near military hangars, gleaming white with blue striping.

Armed men wearing green fatigues strolled causally around the aircraft but paid it no particular attention.

Guards ordered to watch the multimillion-dollar jet, she thought.

Teresa had booked a room at the Hotel Terra Del Fuego in downtown Punta Arenas near the town square. It was a twenty-minute cab ride to the airport, but most hotels were located in town and she'd had a difficult time even getting a room because it was the southern hemisphere summer and Punta Arenas was filled with tourists.

She'd set up a special arrangement with the hotel's assistant manager to allow her to get a few hours of badly needed sleep. Without offering any details, she told him she had interest in a large private jet parked on the military side of the airport. She'd then pulled out a stack of American bills and asked if he could arrange to have one of the hotel staff watch the Gulfstream and call her the instant anyone appeared to be ready to use it. She'd been surprised, and more than a little alarmed, when he asked why she wanted Señor Paulson's private plane watched?

"How do you know Al Paulson owns that jet?" she'd asked.

"He's bringing back our *Las Tortugas*," replied the assistant hotel manager. He smiled widely. "You must be with CNN—or perhaps a *diario*? Do you want an interview when he returns?"

Teresa Simpson opened her mouth—and then shut it. "Yes," she said with her best "you got me" facial expression. "I'm writing a major story about the recovery of the *Las Tortugas*, and I'm desperate to get the first interview." She'd even pulled a digital camera out of her handbag, hoping it made her look more authentic.

Apparently, no one had approached the jet while she slept. Upon waking, she'd left a message for the Assistant Manager, saying she was headed for the airport to keep an eye on Paulson's plane herself.

Teresa now stood at the window, fighting off the effects of stress, fatigue, and bone-numbing jet lag. She sat for a moment, and her eyelids felt as if they might reach down and touch the collar on her denim jacket.

"This is a waste of time," she muttered in frustration. She emptied the last of the espresso and set the cup back on the counter. After one last glance out the window, she hoisted her bag over her shoulder and headed for the exit.

Teresa walked up to the cab line and was about to enter a minivan when a beat-up yellow Toyota Corolla careened around the corner and screeched to a stop. The driver missed the reverse gear on his first attempt to back up, and the worn transmission whined in distress.

"Señora Simpson!" shouted the front-seat passenger after the Toyota backed into the curb.

Teresa looked up to see the familiar face of the hotel's Assistant Manager. "The *Las Tortugas*—it approaches the airport!"

She joined him in the Toyota, and his young driver stomped the accelerator.

"Miguel's cousin works in the control tower," said the Assistant Manager pointing toward the driver. "He says the *Las Tortugas* will land in less than ten minutes." He leaned forward, speaking rapid-fire Spanish to Miguel. "The pilot has declared an emergency, apparently due to engine trouble."

The driver swung the steering wheel, and the cab turned onto an access road that cut around the perimeter of the airport.

"But to enter the aviation area...." He shrugged. "We will need more—"

"You just get me to the gate," Teresa cut in. "I have what's necessary."

They drove down the access road for two miles, where it dead-ended at a series of hangars. In front of the hangars stood a tall chain-link fence with razor wire wrapped around the top.

The driver stopped near the guard tower. "You wait here a minute," said the Assistant Hotel Manager.

He spoke to the guard, who glanced toward the car on several occasions. The guard nodded and the Manager ran back toward the Toyota.

"I have told him you are an American reporter covering the return of the *Las Tortugas*." He glanced around nervously. "He won't allow us to drive through, but for one-hundred dollars he will allow you to pass."

Teresa opened her bag and pulled out three crisp one-hundred-dollar bills. "One for him and one for you and one for Miguel," she said with a smile.

The Manager nodded. "We should go now." He smiled. "Best of luck to you."

The guard at the gate pointed her ahead between two hangars and then nodded toward the right, where he waved a finger as if to say, 'Don't walk that way.' Teresa got the message.

She jogged through the first series of hangars. After making sure the coast was clear, she ran toward the second set of hangars and caught a glimpse of asphalt-covered runways and taxiways. As she approached the open tarmac, the sharp nose of Paulson's Gulfstream appeared around the edge of the last hangar. As she rounded the corner, a loud noise came from beyond and above the private jet. Through the mist, she saw the *Las Tortugas* descending steeply toward the runway. The bomber rocked from side to side, clearly having trouble controlling it.

Then she saw it. One of the massive propellers on the right wing wasn't spinning. The four-blade prop stood frozen in contrast to the blur of the other three. Beneath the bomber, three full sets of landing gear appeared to be down, although she couldn't tell if they were locked into position.

They've got a chance, at least.

The nose of the bomber flared, and the main landing gear slammed down hard enough that the B-29's wings appeared to shudder and flex. The pilot, who Teresa assumed was Paulson himself, did a masterful job of keeping the Super Fortress headed straight down the runway. When the bomber braked to an abrupt stop, Chilean emergency vehicles quickly surrounded the B-29. But instead of shutting down the engines, the crew inside the *Las Tortugas* waved wildly.

Their message was clear: "Get the hell out of our way."

Teresa felt a tear running down one cheek. Goddamn if they hadn't pulled it off, against all odds. They were bringing the grand lady home and bringing her home the right way. Alan J. Paulson was going to drive that battlewagon right up to the hangar with engines roaring hot, just like the old days. There was going to be no embarrassing runway shutdown followed by an anti-climactic tow to some secluded spot.

The emergency vehicles cleared away, and the bomber's three functioning engines increased in RPM while the bomber followed a trio of military trucks toward a shutdown area near the Gulfstream. The aluminum skin on the *Las Tortugas* appeared smooth, but repaired sections gave the bomber a quilted look. Several of the rivet lines ran contrary to the rest of the airplane, where aluminum skin had been cut free and replaced with a temporary patch.

Black was the other defining feature—heavy black lines where oil and smoke flowed freely from the engines and had painted the wings and fuselage with wicked black stripes.

The *Las Tortugas* pulled up within a couple hundred feet of Paulson's Gulfstream, and the engines shut down one by one. Teresa pulled out her digital camera and snapped photographs of the magnificent aircraft.

Military vehicles surrounded the bomber and heavily armed soldiers dressed in green fatigues fanned out around the *Las Tortugas*. Another trio of vehicles pulled up, this time black SUVs that Teresa recognized as armored transport vehicles built for VIPs. She'd ridden in the same type around Washington on many occasions. A soldier sprinted toward the middle Suburban and opened the rear door.

A short, but stout middle-aged soldier dressed in an impeccable and high-ranking uniform stepped out and adjusted his cap. He walked over to the ragged crew exiting the Super Fortress.

When everyone seemed to have disembarked onto the tarmac, Teresa realized that Leah Andrews wasn't among them. She dashed toward the B-29 until one of the Chilean guards cut her off some fifty feet away. She thought she recognized the face of Jack Hobson but couldn't be sure. The man staring at her wore a week's worth of beard, and his face had been badly sunburned to the point of blistering. Two oval-shaped white circles highlighted his eyes where glacier-style sunglasses had protected him from the ultraviolet rays of the Antarctic sun.

She struggled against the soldier, her digital camera swinging by its wrist cord, banging against her face and shoulder. "I'm looking for Dr. Leah Andrews," she called out. "I'm Teresa Simpson, Director of the Bureau of Land Management."

Jack nodded but didn't reach out to shake her hand. "I recognize you, Ms. Simpson."

"Dr. Andrews worked for my department." She glanced toward the B-29. "Where is she?"

Jack blinked and waited a beat. "I'm exhausted and probably not thinking clearly. But if you don't know where Leah's been taken, what are you doing here?"

"I'm here because Dr. Andrews was a damned good archeologist and I let the Secretary of the Interior screw her over. I didn't have the balls to protect her then—but I'm not going to make that mistake twice. Now, did you just say she was 'taken?'"

Paulson limped over and stood beside Jack. "Who's this?"

Jack nodded toward Teresa. "This is Teresa Simpson, Director of the Bureau of Land Management."

His eyes narrowed. "What are you doing here, if I might ask?"

"Looking for Leah, she says," Jack said. "Ms. Simpson claims she doesn't know where Leah's being held. But I find that hard to believe."

Paulson nodded in agreement.

"Look," Teresa said, "the last I heard, SEALs were removing you from Antarctica. When I asked for an update, the President and his staff had fled Washington. Whatever happened down there seems to have created a geopolitical crisis. Why don't you fill me in on what you know—and what happened to Leah Andrews."

Despite his obvious fatigue, Jack Hobson smiled broadly. "You remind me of Leah. Impulsive, determined, and stubborn as hell. Why else would you jump on a plane and fly to southern Chile?"

Teresa simply stared at him, refusing to answer the rhetorical question.

"What do you think?" Jack said, glancing at Paulson.

Paulson glanced over at Teresa and studied her face for a moment. "She'll do."

Jack turned back to Teresa. "You wouldn't happen to have some clear tape, would you? I've got to reassemble a few torn pieces of paper."

CHAPTER 110

Teresa Simpson stared in shock at Jack and Paulson. "I knew Fischer was a prick," she said, shaking her head in disbelief. "And the President's an arrogant ass. But I can't believe he sanctioned this."

"Believe it," said Jack. "Now I'm prepared to do anything necessary to obtain the release of Leah Andrews."

Teresa shook her head again. "Look, if I speak with the President, I'm sure he'll—"

They stood inside the hangar facing the *Las Tortugas*. Jack closed the space between them, keeping his voice low but resolute. "No. This is what you're going to do. You will transmit this message to the President of the United States." He handed her a sheet of yellow notepaper.

Teresa Simpson eyes grew wide. She looked up at Jack. "You have possession of *this*?"

"Right behind you." Jack nodded at an oversized, red climbing-gear bag. "I want you to remember every detail of what you're about to examine." He unzipped the bag until the top of a metallic canister peeked out.

"Commander Beckam told me it is called a Hafnium-Iso warhead. Just mentioning the name will get the President's attention." He nodded toward Paulson. "We've seen what they can do. We were fortunate to be out of range, but we still caught a glimpse. Now imagine it detonating in a populated area." He watched her blink several times. "Are you with me, Ms. Simpson?"

She nodded but didn't reply.

"Feel free to take all the photos you want." Jack pointed toward the bag. "Inside, how many devices do you count?"

"One."

"Very good," Jack said. He pointed toward the top of the casing. "Please note the panel." He reached down and pushed on the two buttons, causing the metal top to spring up. Jack's expression hardened. "This is very important, Ms. Simpson. I have all the codes necessary to set this device back on timer, detonating at my convenience."

"What are your terms?" she asked.

"I'll be flying back to the United States with the Hafnium warhead tucked right between my legs."

"In the Gulfstream?"

"Negative. The Chilean military has agreed to provide us transportation over South America and ultimately into the United States. Flying the Gulfstream, the minute we got into international airspace, we'd be tracked, targeted and shot down."

"Do the Chileans know you have this—warhead?"

"The general who authorized the Chilean military aircraft knows that we're wanted men because of the *Las Tortugas* incident but nothing more. He and his people have been advised that it could be a dangerous trip and to expect trouble, but they're providing us an aircraft in return for bringing their bomber home safely." Jack nodded in the direction of the warhead. "You can see it's important that we fly back into the United States—if nothing else, to secure the warhead, given the Permissive Arming Procedures."

"I just don't think the President would—"

"Ms. Simpson," Jack interrupted. "The government has murdered three of our crew and attempted to kill me on two different occasions. Not to mention sacrificed an entire SEAL team."

"So I tell the President what you have and what you want. He's to allow the Chilean aircraft free entry into US airspace without harassment." She glanced at the paper. "The final destination is Holloman Air Force Base, New Mexico?"

Jack nodded.

"In exchange for Leah and the President's personal guarantee of no further prosecution of this case, you and your people agree to hand over the device and keep quiet."

Jack nodded again. "Perfect."

CHAPTER 111

"**O**h my God, Ms. Simpson!" Teresa's secretary's voice made a tinny echo through her mobile phone. "I've been so worried about you!"

"I'm in Punta Arenas, Chile, with Jack Hobson. This is directly related to the problem that we discussed while I was in Washington, remember?" Teresa paused and took a deep breath while Jeanie acknowledged. "I need to speak directly with the President. Right now. Is your friend still working at the White House?"

"Yes, Ma'am," she said.

"Call him and relay what I've just told you. Tell him I expect the President to call me at this number. Do you understand?"

Teresa clicked off and glanced over at Jack Hobson. "I expect to get a call from the President within an hour."

"How do you know the message will get to him?"

"Trust me, I have my ways."

Before she could continue, her phone rang, but the number was blocked. She glanced at her watch. "That's a record, even for Washington."

She answered the phone, nodded twice, and then switched her cell phone to speaker.

"Ms. Simpson? Are you there?" The smooth baritone was instantly recognizable.

"Is Fischer with you, Mr. President?" she asked.

"No, he's not present."

"When this is all done, Mr. President, I'm going to tell you and your lapdog exactly what you can do with yourselves. For now, my only concern is the safe return of an armed Hafnium warhead. And Dr. Leah Andrews." Teresa passed along Jack Hobson's simple list of demands and a detailed description of the warhead.

"I'm shocked at what you're telling me, Ms. Simpson," said the President. "The civilians were to be extracted safely; the same for the SEAL platoon. I have absolutely no knowledge, nor would I ever authorize the use of such weapons, even if they existed."

Jack had heard better from used car sales representatives, but he kept his mouth shut, for the moment.

"Is Mr. Hobson available?" asked the President, his voice wavering slightly.

"He's been standing here the entire time," Teresa said.

"I'd like to have a private conversation with him."

Teresa handed the phone to Jack and stepped away.

"Jack Hobson here."

"This is the President. Now, I'm sure you understand that this is an extremely dangerous game you're playing, and—"

"Shut up and listen," Jack said. "My only interest is the safe return of Dr. Leah Andrews. For that I'm willing to exchange the Hafnium warhead and the codes." Jack fished the taped-together pieces of paper with the arming codes and sequence from his jacket. "This is proof that I have the information necessary to arm and detonate the warhead, thanks to SEAL Commander Gus Beckam." He read off the codes. "Are we clear?"

"What exactly are *your* terms?" The President's tone had changed dramatically.

"After Dr. Andrews is safe and secure with me, you'll have our complete silence. Or we'll affirm whatever story you're dreaming up to avoid the next world war."

"We agree," said the President.

Jack drew a deep breath to calm himself, letting the President wait. "I understand that you're agreeing to my terms. Unconditionally."

"Yes, however, you are *not* to enter the air space of the continental United States. We'll arrange to have you divert to Diego Garcia. It's a remote British military base located in the South Indian Ocean. I'm sure you understand our safety concerns."

"No deal," Jack said flatly. "I'm coming right up the coast of South America, and then we're continuing across along the Baja peninsula and across northern Mexico, entering the United States over El Paso, Texas, and landing at Holloman Air Force base in Alamogordo. You will notify the Mexican government that we are on a drug interdiction mission and provide us whatever clearances we need, including air traffic control codes allowing us safe passage. Do you understand?"

It was the President's turn to pause. "It sounds like you're running the show, for now."

"I have just one word of caution, Mr. President. Commander Beckam, a real American hero, not only showed me how to arm the warheads. He also filled me in on that little job you ordered done in Iran using similar warheads."

"I'm listening," said the President.

"If you're thinking of shooting us down with air-to-air missiles, you'd better kill me instantly because I will enter all but the last digit of the field code and set the warhead's timer on zero. That'll give you a little something to explain to the American people. Furthermore, I've already arranged for this full story—and the details of the Iran operation—to be relayed to media outlets around the world in the case of my death."

Jack breathed a sigh, when the President said, "Understood. You have my word that you will be free to enter American air space as you have requested."

"Expect to find us on the ground at Holloman Air Force Base in thirty-six hours." Jack ended the call and handed Teresa Simpson her phone.

"The President isn't one of my favorite people," she said, "but I expect that he will hold up his end of the bargain."

"I highly doubt he plans to hold up his end of the deal, Ms. Simpson. Regardless, I'm prepared to continue in good faith." Jack walked over to Paulson and reached out for his hand. "Thanks for getting us off the ice."

Paulson nodded solemnly. "We'll be waiting for your call, Jacky."

Jack followed Garrett and Marko, who each carried one strap of the giant red bag, struggling to hold it off the tarmac as they walked toward the loading ramp of a Chilean Military C-130 Hercules.

"You sure we can't tag along?" asked Garrett over his shoulder.

"You two have gotten yourselves in enough trouble on Leah's account. It's about time I took on that responsibility myself."

Ridley joined him next to the C-130, followed by Angus Lyon and Orlando Perez. "I understand what you're doing, Jack, but it still doesn't sit right with me. We're all in this together."

Jack reached out grabbed the older mechanic's hand. "Someone's got to tell the story if we don't make it. I'm counting on you guys to do it."

Teresa Simpson had also followed him. "I'm coming with you. I'm responsible for this mess."

Jack thought for a moment. "You're right, you are responsible. Get aboard and stay out of my way."

Paulson stood by as the Chilean Air Force crew spooled up the four turboprop engines and taxied the transport aircraft out to the edge of the runway. When the tower offered clearance, the pilots throttled up the C-130 Hercules, and its four turboprops bit the air with 13,000 combined horsepower.

Half a minute later, Paulson watched the C-130 disappear into the low-lying cloud cover. "What do you think, Mac?"

"I think his chances of reaching American airspace are about the same as you passing through the Pearly Gates."

Paulson nodded grimly and glanced over at the two aircraft still on the tarmac. "Come on. We've got work to do."

CHAPTER 112

The two Chilean pilots spoke perfect English. They updated Jack as to their slow but steady progress up the coast of South and Central America. They stopped twice for refueling, once in Lima, Peru, and the second time in San Jose, Costa Rica.

During the long flight north, Teresa Simpson had tried to engage Jack in conversation, but he'd avoided her with an unbending expression that invited no discussion.

She ended up spending much of the flight walking around the cold, cavernous interior of the Hercules, adjusting her earplugs, eating prepackaged foods, and drinking instant coffee.

For his part, Jack spent most of his time on the flight deck, looking out through the windscreens. He had no doubt they were being tracked, probably by Air Force and/or Navy AWACS planes, and by satellite as well. They were sitting ducks, for anyone who wanted to shoot them down.

Thirty hours into their journey, as they flew off the coast of southern Mexico, Teresa slid cautiously into the oversized cockpit. She nodded to the command pilot, who nodded in return as he pulled a pair of shaded aviator glasses out of his flight suit, flipped them open, and fed them between the headphones and his close-cropped black hair.

Jack glanced in her direction, and a rare smile flashed across his weathered face.

Probably something about the dawn of a new day, she thought. It always seemed to put things in perspective, make them feel more manageable.

"Maybe you were right," Jack shouted over the roar of the engines. "Maybe the President will keep his word."

She was about to respond when the needle-nose and glass-bubble cockpit of a jet fighter filled the windscreen in what Teresa could only assume was going to be a head-on collision.

CHAPTER 113

The Chilean flight crew instinctively ducked when the carrier-based Navy FA-18 Hornet fighter jet screamed over the top of the much slower and less maneuverable C-130 Hercules.

The pilot in command swore loudly in Spanish while at the same time disengaging the autopilot. Both pilots craned their necks, scanning the sky, searching for the jet fighter. Seconds later, a second Hornet over flew the Hercules, this one making his approach from the six o'clock position, high and from behind. When the Hornet was directly over the top of the Hercules, the pilot pulled the fighter vertically and kicked in the afterburner. The resulting concussion shook the C-130 right down to its wing roots, tossing the crew around the cockpit like so much confetti.

"What the hell is he doing?" Teresa asked.

The pilot turned around and shouted, and Jack nodded in understanding.

"It's called thumping," Jack said. Clearly, the President intended to call his bluff after all. "They're forcing us down to a lower altitude."

A third Hornet swooped in underneath the Hercules, pulling up directly in the cargo carrier's flight path and lighting off the burners as it passed not more than a handful of feet in front of the nose.

"Hang on!" shouted Jack as the cargo plane pitched and rolled violently through the turbulence. Jack grabbed Teresa, keeping her from banging into the side of the cockpit.

"Get down on the deck and head toward the coast," Jack shouted to the pilots.

The pilot swore again, clearly questioning whether a couple of Americans were worth their lives.

The pilot pushed down on the yoke with such force that Jack felt his stomach rising right into his throat. He watched in amazement as a collection of debris, including pens and pencils, floated up from the floor of the cockpit and bounced off the ceiling. The dark blue of the Pacific Ocean filled the windscreen as the Chilean pilot held the nose of the Hercules in a steep dive.

He held tight to Teresa Simpson, who'd covered her face with her hands in a futile attempt to prevent the white capped waves below from breaking through the windscreen.

Jack closed his eyes in anticipation of the impact, but instead felt intense positive G-forces as the pilots struggled to pull the reluctant C-130 out of its terminal dive.

His body crushed the thin padding of the jump seat as the G-forces made his hundred and eighty pounds feel more like five tons.

Jack opened his eyes to find the C-130 flying just above the water. The whitecaps rushed underneath the cargo plane in a blur of white and blue that changed direction each time the pilot jerked the yoke in a well-intentioned but ineffective attempt to keep the fighters off his tail.

"The beach," he shouted. He pointed to the white sands and green mountainous jungle of the Mexican coast.

"Are they going to follow us into Mexico?" Teresa asked.

"I'm counting on it," Jack said.

Jack leaned forward and engaged the command pilot in an animated conversation as one of the Hornets flashed overhead and then turned sharply in an attempt to gain a firing position from behind the Hercules.

"What's happening?"

"The bastards are trying to run us out of fuel," Jack said. "The Hercules burns a ton of fuel flying at low altitude. The Navy pilots radioed ours and said they'd be forced to shoot us down if we climb above 3,000 feet."

Teresa leaned over and grabbed his hand, glancing at the red bags containing the Hafnium warhead. "The President knows you can't do it, even for Leah."

Jack Hobson stared at the BLM chief for a moment and then grinned. "I've told the pilots I have something in the red bags that our fighter-jet friends want badly. I'm sure, if we give it to them, they'll be forced to stop the attack."

Teresa leaned back slightly, assessing the expression on Jack's face. "What on earth are you planning?"

Chapter 114

Paulson sat in the command seat of the Gulfstream, Garrett to his right, and Mac Ridley crouched behind the two of them, looking anxiously through the windscreen. Marko and the mechanics were sleeping in the rich leather seats in the rear of the aircraft, dead to the world.

Paulson had the Gulfstream holding short of the active runway and had just finished speaking with the control tower.

"Okay," he said. "Let's put the spurs to it."

"About time," said Ridley.

Before Paulson let off the brakes and allowed the Gulfstream to roll out onto the runway, he looked through the side window and stared long and hard at the shiny aluminum skin of the old B-29.

"You think we're gonna see her again, Mac?"

"After what we've been through, you still want that damned bomber?"

Paulson shrugged. "It's one beautiful airplane."

"I'm sure whatever federal prison were doing time at will give you all the illustrations of B-29s you want—and crayons to color them with too."

Paulson glanced at his watch. "We're ahead of schedule, for once."

"You think we're going to beat Jack home?" Garrett asked.

"We'd better," Paulson replied, "Or, this crazy plan will never work."

Ridley swore under his breath and shook his head. "God*damn*. Here we go again."

Chapter 115

The trio of volcanoes reached toward the sky in magnificent contrast to the gentle farmland. Like three giant ice-capped trolls, they dominated the Mexican countryside in every direction.

For high-altitude mountain climbers, the volcanoes ranged in personality from the mild-mannered Iztaccihuatl to the exceedingly dangerous Pico De Orizaba. The Aztecs had named the volcanoes for their magnificence—hundreds of years later, nothing about that had changed.

To Jack Hobson they looked like a trio of old friends welcoming him back after a long absence—and Jack was glad to be home.

Orizaba lay to the south and Iztaccihuatl north of the aircraft. Dead in the middle and directly ahead through the windscreen stood Popocatepetl.

Named 'The Smoking Mountain' in the native Nahuatl language, Popocatepetl rose nearly 17,800 feet above sea level, a perfectly round cone covered in black from a recent eruption. Out of the cone rose a thin wisp of sulfur gas—just enough to remind anyone climbing her flanks that she wasn't yet ready to be tamed or controlled.

Jack pointed toward the mountain, indicating they should begin to climb around its base. When the C-130 Hercules flew through 3,000 feet AGL, the Hornets didn't shoot, but they thumped the Hercules repeatedly, forcing the Chilean pilots to manhandle the controls.

Jack's head slammed into the jump-seat backrest each time the Hornets disrupted the Herc's airflow; it was clear that his pilots were exhausted, while the Hornets' pilots were only emboldened by the bigger airplane's struggle to climb higher.

A black oily substance had built up on the windscreen. The exhaust from the Hornets' twin jet engines, fogging the windshield. Despite the dark haze, Jack noticed during the next attack that the tail markings on the jets had changed.

They're tag-teaming us, flying in with full fuel tanks after in-flight refueling.

Suddenly the summit of Popocatepetl poked through a break in the clouds, like a closed fist thrust in defiance. The pilots stood the big Hercules on a wingtip while Jack directed them with hand motions.

Jack looked down into the crater and caught a familiar glimpse of the black cauldron along with the lazy strings of sulfur-rich steam lofting up and flowing over the top of the cone in lazy circles.

Suddenly, one of the Hornets made an especially close and dangerous pass, so near that the C-130 Hercules nearly rolled inverted.

"What are you going to do?" Teresa shouted.

Jack unhooked the harnesses and seat belts securing him into the jump seat. He stood and unclipped an oxygen mask off the rear wall of the cockpit and fitted it over Teresa's face. The pilots grabbed their own masks and worked them into position over their faces.

Jack patted the copilot on the shoulder and then worked his way out of the cockpit and into the cargo hold. He pulled a harness out of equipment webbing and fastened it around his shoulders and waist, then attached himself by way of carabiner system to a cable running the length of the cargo area along the fuselage. When Jack stood near the rear of the cargo bay, he spoke to the pilots through an intercom system.

They dropped the Hercules's speed to just under 130 knots. Jack pushed a switch that lowered the ramp in mid-flight. Moments later, brilliant white sunlight and thin freezing air flooded the Hercules. Jack reached down and grasped the straps on the red bag. He tugged at it once, then twice before it slid along the floor of the cargo bay. As he approached the open ramp, the roar of the engines and the winds collided in a deafening howl.

The Hornets flew in sloppy formation not more than the length of a football field behind the Hercules, curious as to what Jack was attempting. One flew under and behind the left wing, and the other flew above the right wing. Air-to-air missiles hung menacingly under both their wings and fuselages. The slower speed had dropped the Hornets close to stall speed. The wings rocked back and forth as the American pilots watched and waited.

Jack stood on the loading ramp, his hair blowing madly in the wind, his legs spread wide for support. He looked over and made eye contact with the Hornet pilot flying at the ten o'clock low position. Jack nodded toward the pilot, who nodded in return, Jack's intention now apparent. He pulled the bag farther out onto the ramp, then waited until the massive black cauldron of Popo's crater was clearly visible. Then, with all his strength, he rolled the silver warhead rearward until the air caught the cylinder and sucked it out the back of the aircraft.

The wings on the two Hornets rocked as the pilots decided what they should do. An instant later, they both broke formation to the outside. Jack watched as they circled back toward the volcano's crater, searching for the warhead falling at near terminal velocity.

Jack worked his way back into the cargo bay and closed the ramp. He spoke with the pilot, who beamed in return.

Jack sat down and turned to face Teresa. "We're making a short fuel stop in Mexico City and then we're headed home."

"Does it matter now?" she asked angrily. "If you were going to drop the warhead, why put our lives at risk?"

"I needed to know how desperate the President had become." Jack studied her face. "Desperate people do desperate things." He smiled sadly. "A Navy SEAL told me that once. I didn't think it was worth your life, the lives of the pilots, or the innocent people on the ground so I dumped it."

"You'll be arrested on terrorism charges, or worse, won't you? Wait! What are you going to do now?"

He shrugged. "I'm exhausted, Ms. Simpson. I'm going to get some sleep."

Chapter 116

Jack woke with a start to find the copilot pointing out through the windscreen toward the pitch-black deserts of southern Baja Mexico 25,000 feet below.

Teresa Simpson slept in the jump seat beside him, covered in an army-green blanket. He wiped at his eyes, but that didn't remove the feeling someone had rubbed sand into his corneas the entire time he'd slept.

"How far to Holloman Air Force Base?"

"Less than one hour," replied the pilot.

"How is your fuel?"

"We can fly for three hours, no more."

Cutting it close, Jack thought as he calculated time.

"We're not headed to Holloman," he shouted over the engine roar.

The pilot's expression relayed his alarm.

"Not to worry." He reached into his blue jeans and pulled out a set of GPS coordinates. "This is an abandoned Army Air field. It has a long paved runway, and it's not more than a hundred miles northwest of Holloman."

The command pilot fed the coordinates into the onboard navigation system. "Okay," he said, "but once we land, we cannot continue without fuel."

"You won't need to. That's the end of the road."

Chapter 117

Leah leaned back against the fuselage and let the vibration of the changing pitch of the turboprop engines work into her stiff neck and sore shoulders. She'd been so pumped up during the resuscitation of the Native Americans that she'd forgotten she hadn't slept in more than two days. Of the thirty souls within the stasis tubes, they had been able to resuscitate twenty-eight, including the Navajo girl who'd asked Leah if she were a God.

Once it had been determined their vital signs remained within acceptable limits, all twenty-eight had been sedated to avoid subjecting them to any more trauma than necessary.

Fischer said they were headed for the White Sands Missile Test Facility, where much of the equipment cut from the alien laboratory, or whatever it was, would be off-loaded. Leah and the Native Americans were to be kept in isolation at White Sands for an undetermined amount of time.

Leah felt a bump as the wheels kissed the runway and the pilots reversed pitch on the huge propellers to slow the LC-130.

She wanted to stand and stretch but Fischer had immediately handcuffed her to her seat once the Native Americans were removed from the tubes.

Fischer climbed down from the flight deck, looking pale but confident. Leah noted that he was now wearing a military-looking black metallic pistol in a holster on his waist. The contrast of the bureaucrat sporting a designer haircut and polished fingernails toting a handgun was almost enough to make her break out in laughter.

"You should be proud, Dr. Andrews. Thanks to you, nearly all of them remain alive." He shook his head. "Imagine it, after how many years?"

"Eight-hundred years, maybe more."

"What a fantastic opportunity."

"So they can become your next generation of lab rats?" Leah shifted away from Fischer. "Now that I've had time to think about it, I wished I'd just let them die in peace."

"You never would've done that."

Now that they'd landed, concern for Jack washed over her in a wave of panic. "Where's Hobson and the rest of my crew?"

Fischer's eyes remained cold, although he did put on a smile. "I believe I told you I had plans to take care of them. I'm sure they're resting soundly as we speak."

Again, Leah looked away. *God, I hope you outsmarted this clown, Jack.*

The flight crew had assembled gurneys that Leah was told were used to transfer wounded soldiers to hospitals from combat zones. Many of the Native Americans lay in those racks, while others occupied makeshift stretchers on the floor of the aircraft. All were covered in blankets and were being attended to by Fischer's cloak-and-dagger scientists and doctors.

"What now?" she asked.

"Everyone who has had contact with these people will remain in isolation. We've cordoned off a section of the White Sands Missile Test range." He smiled sweetly, adding, "Home sweet home for you and our guests for now."

"And what exactly do I have to do now?"

He sat down next to Leah and clasped his hands together.

"I'm glad you asked. It's vital that we find out from our 'guests' if there are more laboratories like the one we just vacated."

"You think you missed one?"

"You must understand the nature of what we have already discovered. In the wrong hands this technology could be—"

"I can't imagine it being any worse than in your hands," Leah blurted against her better judgment.

"Nonetheless, your life, Jack's life, and the lives of your Indian friends are based upon your cooperation."

"Doing what?"

"We're planning to bring one of the subjects out of sedation. We need you to ask questions in their native language regarding the source of this technology and if there are more of these facilities that we haven't discovered."

Leah took a deep breath and thought for a moment. As much as she didn't want to disturb them, she had to admit that she was probably more anxious than Fischer to speak with a living cliff dweller. "The girl was speaking a Navajo dialect. I might be able to communicate with her—given the proper environment. The other languages sounded like Apache, and a strange mix of Pueblo and Navajo. She I can understand."

"A proper environment? Which would be...?"

"A private one, without you or your goons present."

Fischer's jaw clenched for a moment; Leah felt a flash of satisfaction.

"We have a secluded section of the base, including medical facilities and—"

One of the pilots jumped down from the flight deck and spoke directly to Fischer. "The President needs to communicate. He says it's critical that you contact him on a secure phone at once."

Leah had to laugh at Fischer's pained expression and feigned nonchalance.

"I guess I'm not the only one on a short leash."

CHAPTER 118

Jack leaned over and shook Teresa Simpson. She bolted awake, kicking and clawing the blanket away from her face.

"We're in New Mexico," he said.

She tried to stand but apparently had forgotten about the restraints and slumped back into the jump seat.

"Uh, Holloman Air Force Base is it?"

"We over flew it ten minutes ago."

Even in her tired state, she managed to look startled. "I thought that's where you planned to land."

"No," Jack said. "That's where I told your boss we planned to land."

"Then where the hell are we? Even I know this bucket can't stay airborne forever, and you know they're tracking us on radar."

"We're meeting friends," was Jack's reply.

The light from a million stars cast a soft silvery glow over the desert. It wasn't enough for Jack to make out any geographical features below, but he could picture the hills and valleys and desert flora.

He felt his jaw clenching tight.

I'm wound tight, he thought. Who wouldn't be after what's happened?

Jack watched as the copilot flipped the lever that dropped the landing gear; the hydraulic sounds ended with an audible 'thunk', and a series of red lights turned green, indicating the gear were down and locked into position.

As the Hercules passed over the runway threshold, the pilot pulled the nose gently up, and the landing lights illuminated two military-style hangars and a Quonset Hut.

Jack tapped the Chilean command pilot on the shoulder and pointed in the direction of the two hangars. The pilot nodded, taxied the big plane over, and shut down all four engines.

"Let's go," Jack said. "We don't have much time." He pulled himself out of the jump seat and climbed through the cockpit door into the cargo hold with Teresa close behind.

They walked down the loading ramp and stepped onto the tarmac, where Teresa shivered visibly. It was cold; their breath flowed out in smoky white patterns.

"Follow me," Jack said.

Teresa walked alongside him toward the first of the two deserted hangars. The huge hangar door was being rolled back on its rusty track by three individuals dressed in heavy coats and hats.

Inside, two overhead fluorescent panels illuminated Paulson's Gulfstream jet.

CHAPTER 119

L eah stood outside the rear of the C-130 on the tarmac at White Sands Missile Test Range, the scent and sounds of the southern New Mexico desert pumping her with nervous energy. In the distance, she could see the familiar crystal-white gypsum sand dunes that had given the place its name.

The Native Americans had already been transferred inside what to Leah looked like a huge hangar. She guessed that the tall structure had been used for testing weather balloons during the 1950s, when White Sands had regularly sent hundred-meter-tall balloons into the stratosphere.

Leah had played on the dunes that bordered the southern part of White Sands as a child when her parents had traveled through on vacation and during her dad's exploration of Mogollon dwellings in the Gila National Monument.

She'd even visited Trinity Site, ground zero for the first nuclear test conducted in 1945. Her dad, a devoted anti-nuclear-weapon advocate, had made sure she'd seen it. It was perhaps no surprise, then, that Leah had adopted his views on nuclear weapons and the military.

A cool breeze blowing across the desert brought Leah back to reality. She might have even considered it cold, were it not for her recent excursion into Antarctica. Still, puddles of water on the tarmac here had frozen solid.

"Dr. Andrews?"

Leah turned to find one of the flight crew standing behind her.

"You're needed in the hangar."

Leah nodded, and then turned toward the huge doors that had been shut once the transfer of the Native Americans had been complete. The containers of alien hardware were being unloaded to another building next to the hangar.

Fischer's armed crew was still present. Now they stood in a perimeter around the aircraft, weapons at the ready. Not that they'd meet any resistance out here.

She put her head down against the breeze and walked toward the hangar. A guard standing with legs spread and weapon at the ready in front of the door gave no ground.

"Are you gonna let me in?"

The guard stepped aside and opened the normal-sized door located near the huge hangar doors.

When Leah entered the hangar, she couldn't have been any more surprised. The interior of the hangar had been transformed from a dusty relic to a modern looking hospital with ten-foot-tall partitions. Huge electric heaters blew warm air from several locations and rows of standing klieg lamps had been set up. The only things missing were the hundreds of people you'd expect to see in a field hospital of this size.

A few moments later, one of Fischer's scientists walked around the partition. Leah remembered seeing him on the LC-130. The balding man had skin so pale and soft that Leah had wondered whether he'd ever seen sunlight.

"We're conducting some medical tests," he told her without any formal greeting. "An hour or two, we'll need you."

"Where's Fischer?"

He blinked several times before answering. "In conference with the President."

"The President is here?"

"Teleconference. The President's aboard the Airborne Command Center."

Leah's eyes narrowed. "You have a name?"

The man nervously adjusted his black-rim glasses. He seemed to realize he'd told her more than he should have. "Dr. Alfred Gordon."

"Look, Gordo. I'm not an expert, but even I know that if the President's in the Airborne Command Center, something bad is gonna happened."

Dr. Gordon, to his credit, didn't react, although his face paled significantly, something a few minutes ago Leah wouldn't have thought possible.

Chapter 120

"How was your flight?" Paulson asked. His face was creased with fatigue, but his eyes shone bright with anticipation.

"I've had better," Jack replied. "Since you're here, I'm assuming you didn't have any trouble."

The billionaire nodded and took a sip of hot coffee. "With the entire military tracking one Chilean C-130 Hercules, no one bothered to keep an eye on my unimportant corporate jet." He glanced up at the sky. "How much time do we have?"

"A few minutes," Jack replied. "I'm sure they tracked us on radar over-flying Holloman. So...did the old man agree to do it?"

Paulson nodded. "He said after years of regret, he was happy to do some good." He shook his head. "Goddamn crazy as hell, but still sharp. He scared the crap out of me and Garrett, dropping down into those canyons. Damn if he doesn't know every inch of that desert. He landed the Cessna down in a canyon so narrow I thought we'd scrape the paint off the wings."

"Where are Garrett and Marko?"

Paulson pointed back toward the hangar. "They are securing the old boy's Cessna. Ridley and Lyon are swapping war stories inside the FBO." The billionaire suddenly grimaced and nodded toward the coal-black liquid staining his Styrofoam coffee cup. "The old coot makes the worst damn coffee I've *ever* tasted."

The corners of Jack's mouth turned up in a faint smile. "How'd the pictures turn out?"

"Excellent, we even had time to pose for a group photo. Let's get that poker game you were talking about started."

Teresa approached them from behind, hands on her hips. An icy glare shifted from Jack Hobson to the billionaire and back. "You guys mind filling me in on just what the hell is going on here?"

"I'd love to Ms. Simpson, but right now I believe we're a little short on time," Jack said.

"Look," she said, "if you're up to something, I think I should be—"

The sound of helicopter blades chopping through thin New Mexico night air cut Teresa off in mid-sentence.

Jack recognized it as an Army Blackhawk helicopter sweeping low over the runway. The chopper dropped to the tarmac, and soldiers jumped out and spread out toward the C-130 and the hangars. Two more helicopters swooped down, and at least twenty more soldiers flooded the tarmac, all using what looked to Jack like night-vision equipment and carrying what he assumed were military assault rifles.

After the soldiers flooded out of the last helicopter, one man wearing civilian clothes dropped to the tarmac. He looked over the operation as the soldiers gathered up Garrett and Marko from the hangar and Ridley, Lyon, Perez, and a stooped but proud Luke Derringer from inside the Quonset hut.

"I would suggest that you don't move," Jack told Teresa Simpson. "Just raise your hands slowly."

CHAPTER 121

D r. Gordon led Leah through a maze of medical equipment, some of it set up, much of it still packaged from transport. Whatever thought had been given to the disposition of the Native Americans, it had clearly been done in a rush.

Given the ad hoc nature of this endeavor, Leah kept a sharp eye out for a stray cell phone or other communication device—not that she'd have any good options if she did find an opportunity to make a call.

She shook her head at the entire situation, which might never have come about if not for her own rash decisions and stubborn determination. Jumping into situations without thinking through the consequences had gotten Leah in trouble before, but never on this scale.

In retrospect, she supposed she could have announced the dwelling discovery anonymously from a pay phone and been done with it. The government archeologists wouldn't have had the balls (or probably the smarts) to reach the Antarctica conclusion, though. It all would have remained another undiscovered mystery.

How ironic was it that poor Juan had suggested that very solution?

Suddenly, she had a taste of what Jack must have been feeling all these years about her dad...the deep, endless guilt.

"Jesus what an ass I've been," she whispered. How many times had she held her dad's death over Jack's head? Now, she was going to pay the price for that in some karmic way. Her smart-ass comments weren't to be taken literally—most of the time, anyway. But now she'd have no chance to tell it to Jack.

Well, if they did somehow manage to get out of this mess alive, her relationship with Jack was headed a whole new direction. If he wanted to climb mountains with Paulson, so be it. All that time and energy she'd spent trying to keep him alive, and in the end, she'd likely been the one to kill him.

"This way," the doctor said, pointing through a curtain.

Leah peeked inside, shocked to find the Native American girl in the open, lying unconscious on a steel gurney, covered in a thermal blanket and with two IV's running under the blanket.

She stepped back and whispered, "These people have been in suspended animation for eight-hundred years. Bad breath might be enough to kill them; never mind all the modern diseases they were never exposed to. There's no way I'm going in there without a mask, gloves, and surgical gown."

Dr. Gordon nodded. "Our first thoughts, of course. However, the results of the initial blood work have been stunning. Their immune systems are hyperactive, possibly a result of the cryonic procedure itself. We believe it's safe to continue."

Leah stared at him for a second, then pushed through curtain.

There was another man inside with the girl, dressed in the same operating-room garb. He nodded to Dr. Gordon and left through the curtain without a word.

"How is she?" Leah asked.

"Her vital signs are stable. We're feeding and hydrating intravenously. She was suffering from malnutrition. Starving, really."

"Is that because of the cryonic freeze?"

"We doubt it. From what we could gather, they were for all practical purposes frozen from the moment they were placed in the tubes. We don't think there was any metabolic activity at all from that point on."

"So they were starving before they were put in this state of suspended animation?"

He nodded. "Ironic that, if they hadn't been taken and placed into stasis, they would have all been dead in a matter of days, or weeks."

Leah glanced around; only the little girl was present in the room. "There were twenty-seven others. Where are they?"

"In separate cubicles, all getting proper treatment."

"You can't keep them here," Leah said. "It's a hangar, for God's sake."

"Our orders are to stabilize them here. It's not like we can ship them to Bethesda for treatment."

"Did Fischer issue talking points to you guys? You all sound the same."

Dr. Gordon stared at the little girl, seeming not to have heard Leah's comment. "So…you speak her language?"

Leah nodded. "I told Fischer I'd do it, but not with his flunkies standing around. Waking her will be frightening enough as it is."

Dr. Gordon nodded.

Leah glanced around at the lights, medical equipment, all the shiny chrome and polished steel. How was she going to bond with this eight-hundred-year-old Navajo with all this modern equipment around?

"Can you turn down the lights? Maybe turn off some of this medical equipment?"

He nodded and began following her instructions.

"You wouldn't happen to have a deerskin lying around here."

His eyes widened. "No, I don't believe we would."

CHAPTER 122

"**A**má," the girl said in a soft voice.

Her eyelids flickered immediately after Gordon administered a mild stimulant via the IV. Gordon now waited on the other side of the curtain in case of a medical emergency.

Leah leaned close to the girl and placed a hand on the blanket covering her shoulder.

The girl opened her eyes slightly and moaned, but she didn't appear to see Leah over her. Suddenly, her eyes locked on Leah. The girl flung the blanket aside with surprising speed and grasped Leah's forearm.

"Amá."

Leah felt goosebumps running up her arm, emanating from where the little girl touched her. The girl was asking for her mother.

Leah answered in Navajo that she didn't know where her mother was but that she'd be okay.

"Haado'one'e nili?"

"A tribe like yours, but not those who took you," Leah replied in Navajo.

When the girl unexpectedly smiled, Leah felt bolt of joy that she hadn't expected and couldn't name. "Who are you?"

"K'aalógii," the girl replied in whisper.

"K'aalógii," Leah repeated. "Butterfly."

Leah felt the small fingers squeezing her arm. She placed her hand over the girl's, deciding what to say next. Should she make up a Navajo name, something K'aalógii might understand? In a moment of clarity, she decided that these people had had enough deception.

"Yinishye' 'Leah.'" She hoped what she'd said translated as, "My name is Leah."

"Láiish" the girl repeated softly.

Leah smiled and nodded. Láiish translated as something covering your hands, like a glove or mitten. It was close enough.

In the most exhilarating ten minutes of Leah's life, she managed to understand much of what the little girl was saying, but not all. Some of the language she used was unfamiliar, while other phrases Leah recognized as Navajo.

Much of what she could translate made sense, given what she'd discovered about the cliff dwellers in the hidden stronghold.

The girl used the Navajo word for "suffering" several times: ti'hoo'niih.

Leah did her best to convince her that she and the doctors weren't the "Others" and that K'aalógii had been asleep for a very long time and Leah hoped to return her to her home soon.

Before she could ask her any more questions, the exhausted girl's eyelids flickered and shut; it appeared that she had fallen asleep.

"Damn," Leah whispered. She turned and walked to the curtain, where she expected to find Gordo peeking through the curtain watching the exchange. She wanted to make sure the girl was just sleeping and hadn't fallen unconscious because of her medical condition.

Leah parted the curtain and, to her surprise, found no one present.

She shook her head. "This is worse than an HMO."

Back bedside, K'aalógii appeared to be sleeping soundly.

Voices rose outside the curtain—hardly more than whispers. Leah crept forward and peeked through a gap between the partitions.

Stanton Fischer was doing all the talking. He had a group of armed security men with him. Dr. Gordon and several others scientists simply stood silent as Fischer filled them on the gravity of the geo-political freefall.

"The situation is fluid and deteriorating," Fischer said, his voice hoarse and strained. "The Russians are deploying armed forces to Antarctica in rapid fashion. It's our belief there are more of these 'facilities.' The Indians weren't building cities on cliffs for two-hundred years because thirty individuals disappeared. Think of all the cliff-dwelling cultures around the world. We got to this one first, but the next one? We cannot allow the Russians, or anyone else, access to this technology under any circumstance. It's now a matter of the highest national security, and no assets will be spared in order to ensure our technologic supremacy."

"What you're saying, then," Gordon said, "is we could be on our way to the next World War."

Fischer glanced nervously in Leah's direction, catching her off guard. He didn't seem to see her through the narrow slit in the partition.

"That's why it's extremely important that Dr. Andrews communicate with your guests," Fischer told the doctor. "If there are more facilities, the Russians might get the same opportunity we have. We need to get what we can, then dispose of the subjects. As important as gleaning the information about other facilities is sweeping up our footprints here."

To his credit, Dr. Gordon refused. "I won't do it. That's murder, and we won't cooperate with that."

Fischer lit a cigarette and casually dropped the match after blowing it out. "Dr. Gordon, your family has already been evacuated to safety. Did I mention this?"

Gordon swore beneath his breath and turned away.

"I assume then that I can expect your full cooperation in this manner regarding the final disposition of the survivors—and Dr. Andrews." Fischer glanced at his watch. "Unfortunately, another developing problem requires my attention."

CHAPTER 123

Leah let herself believe that Fischer's other pressing "problem" had been caused by Jack and the others. It seemed a long shot, but it was the first remotely positive development she'd heard. By believing it, even for a moment, it helped her clear her mind and focus on how she might negotiate for the safety of the Native Americans at White Sands.

Escape.

That was the first step. She couldn't save them all, not while a captive here.

She quietly turned and tiptoed back through the piles of medical equipment to where K'aalógii still slept. She peeked through the curtain; the girl remained unattended.

She could hear Fischer's scientists talking in low tones, the shock of what he'd told them still sinking in. Leah pushed through the curtain, checking to see if anyone had followed her; the coast remained clear.

"We've got to get out of here, Baby," she whispered.

K'aalógii couldn't have weighed more than forty or fifty pounds; Leah could carry her if necessary. She calculated how far from the facility she'd seen the dunes of White Sands. *Was it four, maybe five miles?*

If she got to the dunes, she might be able to make it to the road. A small section of White Sands was accessible to the public. The White Sands National Monument was a site well attended by the public, even during the winter. There was a good chance she'd find visitors walking the dunes, or perhaps a park ranger.

It was opportunity to make a frantic phone call to someone, anyone she knew, in nearby Alamogordo, or to academic colleagues in Albuquerque.

Leah looked around the room. K'aalógii was nude underneath the thermal blanket that covered her body. If she kept her wrapped in the thermal blanket, it might keep her warm enough for the journey through the dunes.

She tried not to think about whether she would have the strength to carry the child the entire way. She'd climbed on three of Jack's moderate mountaineering expeditions, humping a forty-pound, internal-framed backpack with no problem, although sprinting across desert and dunes with a child in her arms would be completely different.

You're kidding yourself. Chances of getting outside the hangar and away from Fischer's security detachment in one piece are slim to none.

Leah slipped back into a flight jacket that the crew had given her on the C-130, but froze at the sight of the two IV's streaming clear liquid into K'aalógii's veins.

She grabbed a handful of sterile gauze and tape from the medical supply tray. After taking a deep breath, Leah removed the tape that held the needles in place. She placed her finger near the edge of the penetration and pulled the needle deliberately and smoothly out of K'aalógii's fragile arm.

K'aalógii blinked, but didn't seem to regain consciousness during the procedure. Leah applied the sterile gauze and wrapped the arm in a bandage that would keep the gauze in place. She was relieved to see very little bleeding when removing pressure from the puncture.

One more needle to go.

Leah had the tape removed and was preparing to slide the needle out when she heard the sound of the curtain being swept aside. Gordo's face peeked through the curtain.

"Just what do you think you're doing?" he said in a whisper.

Leah froze, and then continued on with the removal of the second needle. "I'm getting her the hell of out here."

Gordon didn't respond. Didn't move.

"I overheard Fischer," she said.

Gordon instinctively glanced at the girl.

Leah said, "She spoke to me. Not much, but enough that I have a good idea what happened to these people."

"What about other facilities? Did you ask—"

"Sorry, Gordo. Wasn't on my top-twenty."

"You understand the seriousness of our situation and how important it is that we learn if there are more of these alien installations."

"Get real." She struggled to keep her voice low. "When I heard about Fischer's disposal plan, I lost all interest in alien labs and nuclear war. I'm sure you feel the same way."

Gordon simply stared at her.

"I also heard about your family," Leah said. "I'm in the same boat. What can we do?"

Gordon's shoulders slumped and he looked away. "I don't know. But I can't do what Fischer said."

"Good," Leah said. "Then you'd better grab yourself a coat."

Chapter 124

"Mr. Hobson, welcome back to the United States," said Stanton Fischer. Fischer removed a pack of cigarettes out of his coat pocket and lit one, then walked toward the group until he stood less than a meter away from Jack's face. "You're a lousy poker player, Jack. I expected more out of you than a cheap bluff."

"From what we're hearing," Jack said, "the Russians already called yours." Before Fischer could respond, he continued. "I want Leah Andrews released. I'm reasonably sure since you're here, Leah is not far away."

Fischer almost looked amused. "What makes you think you can bargain for anything?"

Jack lunged with lightning quickness at Fischer, catching him and the soldiers off guard. Before they could grab him, Jack swung up from his waist, tensing his stomach muscles as he did. His uppercut caught Fischer on the bottom of the chin, the force of the blow lifting him off the tarmac. Fischer fell to the pavement, motionless.

Before Jack had time to reach down after him, the group of soldiers mobbed him and wrestled him to the ground. One smashed him across the face with his automatic weapon, splitting Jack's lip. Fischer moved a bit on the tarmac, then tried to get up. Every time he sat, he toppled to his side, until two soldiers grabbed him and helped him to his feet.

"Did that make you feel better?" Fischer managed through a mis-aligned lower jaw.

Jack wiped blood off his face. "I didn't do it for me. I did it for Navy Commander Gus Beckam, whose last request on this earth was to pass along his regards. I haven't yet begun to make you pay for what you did to us on the ice. Yeah, for the record, it made me feel a whole lot better."

Fischer tried to free himself from the soldiers, but couldn't lock his knees well enough to stand on his own. "She's dead anyway. So are you. When—"

"You know," Paulson interrupted loudly, "it's times like these when pictures can mean so much." He reached into his jacket and pulled out his smart phone.

"What are you talking about?" Fischer finally stood on his own and walked unsteadily toward Paulson.

"I'd love to sit here and chat all night, but with the world sliding dangerously close to all-out war. I think we ought to get down to business." Paulson nodded toward the soldiers guarding them with the automatic weapons. "Since I don't know what security clearances your soldiers carry; I suggest we retire to the Quonset hut for a short presentation."

"You're not going anywhere," said Fischer.

"I'm not asking," the billionaire snapped back in an authoritative voice. "I'm telling you: you're walking to the Quonset hut, or I promise, what the Russians have in mind will seem like a picnic compared to what we dish out."

Fischer blinked, nodded to his soldiers, and pointed Paulson toward the Quonset hut.

Chapter 125

Leah had K'aalógii, wrapped in the thermal blanket and nestled in her arms. She was a heavy load, carried that way, but Leah's adrenaline level seemed to compensate.

"Her vitals are stable," Dr. Gordon whispered. "Should you successfully escape; you must seek medical care at once." He reached over and slipped a medical form off the clipboard, into Leah's pocket. Gordon had declined to leave, though he had decided to accept whatever consequences came with enabling her escape. "Present this to the emergency room physician. It's a record of her treatment. There will be things you can't explain, certain chemical traces that remain from the cryonic state." Gordon shrugged. "I'm sure a person of your tenacity will overcome any issues that arise."

"Thank you," Leah said.

"I'll call the guard watching the door, the perimeter guards, and our medical staff in to discuss—I don't know. I'll make it up as I go. It'll buy you several minutes, no more. You'll need to be out of sight of the hangar before the security detail returns to their positions outside."

"How long will we have until someone finds out we're missing?"

"I can cordon off the partition for the sake of the girl's health…maybe an hour."

Leah leaned over and kissed Dr. Gordon on the cheek. His cheeks blushed but he quickly regained his composure.

"Give me three minutes."

He ducked through the curtain and was gone.

Leah glanced at her watch, counting the seconds while her heart thrummed a much quicker beat. It felt as if she were carrying only the thermal blanket in her arms, now, K'aalógii's body seemingly as light as a feather.

In exactly three minutes, Leah pushed through the curtain with the child in her arms and made a beeline for the hangar door. She heard Dr. Gordon telling the security and medical staff that he had drawn up a preliminary plan for disposing of the subjects. He wanted to review the events that were to follow and needed their undivided attention.

When Fischer's security personnel complained that their orders came directly from Fischer, not the medical and science staff, Dr. Gordon let loose a string of profanity that made Leah grin as she reached the door. The force of his statement served both to quiet the guards and cover the sound of fifty-year-old hinges squeaking as Leah swung open the door and slipped into the frigid air.

CHAPTER 126

"It is show-and-tell time," Paulson said, downloading his smart-phone's photos into a laptop.

Luke Derringer, his bearded face twitching in anticipation, sat on the couch, along with Garrett and Marko and Teresa Simpson. Jack stood next to the counter with Paulson. Fischer paced near the door. Two soldiers stood next to him, their weapons in the ready position.

Paulson opened the software and selected 'Slide Show' from a number of choices. "Okay—we're ready to go. I'm setting the slides on a thirty-second timer so you can get a *real* good look at each one."

Fischer stepped up to the counter, his eyes darting back and forth. When the computer flashed the first photo on the screen, his injured jaw dropped open and he grabbed the counter with both hands.

Paulson pointed toward the photo, which had been taken in the late afternoon in front of the hangar where the Gulfstream now rested. It was a group photo, as he'd promised. In the rear stood Garrett and Marko who had his arm around old Luke; down in front knelt Paulson himself, along with Ridley. Between them sat the familiar round metallic canister of a genuine Hafnium bomb. The only other defining features were Ridley's prominently displayed middle fingers.

"Hobson tossed the device in the volcano," Fischer said in near panic. "Our pilots confirmed they saw it leave the back of the aircraft." He reached into his jacket and fumbled for the cigarettes.

"Well…." Paulson began theatrically. "This is what you call…. What did Commander Beckam call it?" he asked Jack

"Redundancy," Jack said on cue, leaning against the counter.

Fischer swallowed. "So while we were chasing Hobson through Mexico, you were—"

"Just wandering home like we had all the time in the world," Paulson replied. "Well, we did drop down onto the deck for the last five-hundred nautical or so, just to keep under the radar." He nodded toward the hangar. "That Gulfstream is fast when it needs to be. Gave us plenty of time to get our chubby little friend hidden out in the desert."

"Ask your boys here to step outside," Jack said. "The next part of our discussion is confidential." Fischer nodded, and the two soldiers stepped back out through the door, weapons still at the ready the entire way out.

Paulson pulled a flash drive from the laptop. "Here is a complete set of color photos. I suggest you send them to your boss right away, along with our modest list of demands."

"What are they?"

"Dr. Leah Andrews delivered to me within twelve hours," Jack said. "If any of us disappear or have an unfortunate accident, no one will prevent the bomb from detonating."

"That would mean you already armed it and set the detonation timer."

"You know I had the codes. Oh, and I got quite a briefing from Commander Beckam regarding their 'use' on the Iranian nuclear facilities, and a rundown on the bombs themselves. I'm generally not known to be blabby, but I'll have to make an exception here."

"It'll take time," Fischer said weakly.

"That's the thing about those bombs," Paulson interrupted. "You know you can set the timer to detonate with a ninety-day delay? Any moron who can operate a microwave oven could program that thing. I guess that explains why they gave 'em to you. As an FYI, you don't have anything like ninety days. I suggest you get your ass in gear unless you want this part of New Mexico glowing in the dark for some time to come."

Fischer started to speak, but Paulson cut him off.

"Time is short. Which is all the more reason for you to shut up and get your ass in gear. When my buddies in the Senate and Congressional Oversight committees get a classified briefing *from me* on how your boss got us into this mess with the Russians, not to mention what could be coming down the road…well, let's just say your boss is going to be resigning office for medical reasons. I'd suggest that he call the Russian President, ASAP, and promise to share the alien technology."

"I think it might be too late for that," Fischer said. "The Russians have been flying assets into Antarctica. We think they intend to occupy the continent. In fact, just about every world power is activating their forces. It didn't take long for rumors of what we found to spread around the globe."

"Let's let your boss worry about that. Now, about Leah and the Native Americans…."

"I'm not sure I can help with Dr. Andrews," Fischer said, slumping against the counter.

"That's no good." Jack moved closer to Fischer, who shrank back in fear despite the guns behind him. "What have you done with her?"

"It's what she's done," Fischer said quickly. "Your wife is extremely resourceful, it seems. With help, she managed to slip out of the facility at White Sands." Fischer hesitated, obviously fearful of what Jack might do if he went on. "I ordered two helicopters to search for her. If she resists, they're authorized to use deadly force. They had to pause the search to re-fuel, but I believe they're searching again now."

Jack felt himself wanting to rip Fischer's head off with his bare hands; instead he took a deep, calming breath and said, "Then I think you have a call to make. Pronto."

CHAPTER 127

The first hour after escaping, Leah made good progress across the desert, passing several ancient-looking missile-test stands and a variety of broken-down equipment. She guessed this part of range hadn't seen active testing for years, probably why Fischer had been given use of it.

At first she'd glanced back toward the hangar at least once a minute, expecting to see a cloud of dust and a series of headlights rushing across the desert in search of their two missing guests. Fortunately, heading toward the dunes led her out into the desert; no vehicles could follow in the direction she was going.

K'aalógii continued to sleep soundly despite Leah having nearly fallen several times while sliding down the steep banks of a wash. Leah paused once every five minutes to rest her arms and make sure that the girl was still breathing normally with a strong pulse. Not that Leah could do anything if her condition deteriorated.

The glistening dunes of White Sands were now half a mile away. The going would get tougher through the dunes and the travel more exhausting, slogging up steep slopes of frosty sand.

When she reached the first dune, Leah's heart soared. Not only had she crossed what she thought was the most dangerous part of the journey, but the winter rains had frozen, solidifying the surface of the sand. She was able to move across without sinking in.

"We're almost home, baby," she said, between deep breaths. Her legs were beginning to wear and her tongue felt like the entire Russian Army had marched across it in their socks. There had been cases of bottled water lying among the mounds of medical equipment. She'd have given up her house in Albuquerque for a single liter right now.

They were crossing the crest of the third set of dunes, when Leah heard the heavy thud of attack helicopters as they began sweeping the desert. They must have assumed she'd stick close to the paved road, since most of their efforts seemed to be in that direction, at least for the moment.

"Got to keep going," she said, willing her aching legs to continue carrying them across the dunes.

To Leah's dismay, when she reached the summit of the next mountainous dune, the sea of sand seemed to stretch right to the horizon. The fantasy of crossing two or three sets of dunes before running into national park facilities or personnel had been only that—a fantasy. These dunes ran for what looked like at least twenty miles in each direction, with nothing but barren sand beyond.

Forty minutes later, she'd crossed three more dune summits and—working in her favor—the helicopters had suddenly ceased their search, disappearing into the distance. She couldn't believe they'd give up that easily.

It seemed like she'd only made it across two more dunes when her worst fears were realized: the choppers returned, sweeping in low over the desert and banking toward the dune sea. She couldn't escape the helicopters; they'd be on top of her in minutes.

Leah looked every direction, hoping to find some cover, any cover. The green flight jacket would stand out like a beacon, identifying her and K'aalógii from miles away.

Leah stood with her legs spread wide, breathing heavily, wondering which of the two helicopters would spot them first.

She was so focused on the weaving helicopters that at first she didn't feel the tug on her jacket. It was only after she heard, "Anihiilaaigii!" repeated for the second time that she looked down.

K'aalógii's eyes were opened wide and she was pointing toward the deadly ballet as the helicopters worked up one set of dunes and down another.

"Anihiilaaigii," she repeated pushing herself out of Leah's grasp and falling to the sand.

Leah had to think for a moment.

Anihiilaaigii.

That's what she'd asked Leah when she'd been revived.

Gods, or the Creators—her abductors. To K'aalógii these were no mere flying machines; they were the "Others," reborn above her.

Before Leah could explain, K'aalógii squirmed out of her arms and began digging a hole in the sand with energy that a minute before Leah would have thought impossible.

The girl stopped for a moment, turned toward Leah, and said something in rapid Navajo that Leah couldn't understand. But the message was clear. If she wanted to live, Leah should help K'aalógii dig a hole deep enough that they could hide.

Leah nodded and then began digging furiously alongside the girl. When the hole appeared halfway done, K'aalógii tugged on the thermal blanket.

Leah looked at the child in amazement. She'd figured out the thermal blanket matched the color of the shimmering white sand.

If they got into the half-dug hole and covered themselves with the blanket, they'd have a chance.

Leah dropped down and drew her legs up, pulling K'aalógii in beside her. Just as the helicopters were flying up the backside of the nearest dune, Leah flung the blanket over their bodies.

The ruse would have worked, except the lead helicopter was flying so low over the sand, intense rotor blast lifted the thermal blanket and swept it away, even though Leah was holding it with all her strength.

Leah didn't see the second helicopter as it flared and hovered, the sand from the first had blown into her eyes, momentarily blinding her. The sound of the blades cutting air deafened her and the sand whipped up by the rotors abraded the skin on her face.

Leah half covered her eyes and watched as the helicopter landed in the valley between the dunes.

K'aalógii tried to flee, but Leah held her tight. Leah whispered in Navajo that she should not be afraid. It was a mother's instinct, a mother's words, useless in the extreme.

It was over.

Crew exited the aircraft and waited. A moment later, Stanton Fischer jumped clear of the helicopter's door.

To Leah, he didn't resemble in anyway the arrogant jerk she'd first met with in Antarctica. This man looked beaten, literally and emotionally. His jaw was swollen, blackened, and off-kilter, his lower lip cut and still bleeding. He looked down at the sand as he walked; he wore the emotional exhaustion in huge creases that crisscrossed his face.

Leah looked for the thermal blanket. It had come to rest perhaps fifty feet away. She held K'aalógii's hand while retrieving the blanket, then wrapped the child.

The excitement of trying to hide from the helicopters had taken its toll. The girl's eyes were glassy; as her body shut down, she struggled to remain conscious. As soon as Leah had her rewrapped in the blanket, she passed out; Leah scooped her up into her weary arms and held her tight.

Fischer stopped when he was about ten feet away. "It's over, Dr. Andrews."

"You're going to have to kill us right here, Fischer. I'm not getting aboard that helicopter."

Fischer looked momentarily shocked, before regaining his composure. "No, you don't understand. Your husband has negotiated your release."

"Bullshit. You're not getting me that easily."

Fischer slowly reached into his jacket.

Leah expected to see the black barrel of a handgun pointed at her chest, but when he removed his hand, Fischer was armed only with a sheet of white paper.

"Mr. Hobson said you'd resist. He asked that I give you this." He walked over and laid the note on the sand five feet in front of Leah, and backed away.

She bent down, keeping her eyes on Fischer the entire time. The note was handwritten in Jack's unmistakable chicken-scratch:

Leah,
>   First, I want to let you know that I love you, and that we are safe.
>   It's critical you accompany Fischer; as much as I'm sure it pains you.
>   I'm at the old man's airport.
>   Time is short.
Love,
Jackson

She felt the tears flowing down her cheek. Jack hated his given name of Jackson. She only ever used it to get under his skin. It was a sure sign that he had sent the note out of his own free will.

Leah wiped at the tears without much success and clutched the girl more tightly to her body. "Okay, Fischer, let's go.

Without another word, Fischer turned and walked back toward the helicopter.

The crew offered to take K'aalógii from her, but Leah refused. She climbed aboard with the child in her arms.

Fischer was preparing to get back aboard the chopper when the crew chief held out his gloved hand. "I'm sorry, sir. The second helo will pick you up and secure the area."

Fischer looked at Leah, then nodded and stepped back away from the door.

The crew chief spoke into his microphone.

Seconds later, Leah heard the turbine engine spooling up and the helicopter took off. She looked out the opened door, K'aalógii still wrapped in the thermal blanket and held tightly in her arms, and watched Fischer until he became an insignificant black speck on the dune.

Leah looked out a side window and had to smile. The second helicopter, now in tight formation with hers, hadn't stopped to pick up Fischer at all.

Chapter 128

The Blackhawk circled the airport once and hovered over the tarmac before setting down. Jack, Garrett, and Marko stood together in front of the Quonset hut, watching the helicopter land. A woman who looked remarkably similar to Teresa Simpson paced behind them, phone to her ear as she barked orders.

Jack ran for the back of the Blackhawk, closely followed by Garrett and Marko, as Leah exited the helicopter, carrying her precious cargo in the silver blanket.

Leah approached the trio. "What took you so long, Climber?"

"You know I can't pass up a high-altitude adventure."

She smiled and beckoned the trio closer. "I want you to meet someone."

The men craned their necks as Leah pulled the thermal blanket away from the girl's face. She slept soundly in Leah's arms.

"Her name is K'aalógii." Leah glanced at Garrett, knowing there'd be a reaction.

"She's Navajo?" Garrett said, both shocked and delighted.

Leah nodded.

"How many more are alive?" Garrett asked.

"Twenty-seven."

"You know her name—you've spoken with her," Jack said.

Leah nodded.

Jack stared at her expectantly. When she didn't say anything more, he had to ask. "Well, what did she say?"

Leah's fatigue was clearly getting the better of her. "The Anasazi weren't a single people. They were a number of tribes, all fleeing those extraterrestrial visitors and the abductions. K'aalógii, her mother, and a few dozen other survivors were starving to death in the cavern we discovered. They decided they wouldn't be picked off one by one—they'd go out in one final battle." She glanced down. "You'll never find a fiercer warrior that the one I'm holding right here."

"Leah Andrews—it's so good to see you again."

As Leah turned to face Teresa Simpson, Jack spoke quickly: "She came looking for you. To help. She found us in Chile."

Teresa held up both hands. "No time for tearful reunions. I just got off the horn with Washington. I've been put in charge of this recovery and research operation, and we've got work to do."

Leah looked at her with only minimal comprehension.

"I'll fill you in when you're fully conscious, Leah. I need someone to head up this operation, and you've got the job, whether you want it or not."

Just then, Simpson's cell phone rang. "Look," she told the caller, "you people need to learn how to wipe your own ass without calling me every time you've got a problem." She rolled her eyes. "I've just appointed someone to honcho this entire deal."

Teresa reached out and handed the phone to Leah.

"This is Leah Andrews," Leah said, giving Teresa a questioning look.

"Dr. Andrews? You're the person in charge?"

It was Leah's turn to laugh as she recognized the voice. "You heard right, Gordo. I'm your man."

"I'm...I'm glad you made it. It looks like we have our work cut out for us."

"We sure do." Leah took a breath, thinking. "Okay, here's the plan. I need experts to work out protocols for handling our guests. Start with a calm environment: low lights, consistent personnel, low noise level, all that."

"Anything you need."

"I'm going to give you a list of names. They'll be tribal leaders located on reservations all over New Mexico and Arizona. Hopi, Pueblo, Apache, Navajo, and more. Tell them I won't take no for an answer and that cost is no object." Leah looked over to Teresa Simpson, who nodded agreement without hesitation. "One more thing, I want them to bring along traditional dress."

"I'll form a team right away."

"And Gordo? I want this handled by you personally."

"What do I tell them?"

"You'll figure it out." Leah ended the call and returned Simpson's phone. "When the refugees are healthy, I want to transfer them back to the mesa tops in Gila National Forest. It's only fair, after what they've been through."

Teresa nodded thoughtfully. "We will need to close off the Gila National Forest to public use and access for the indefinite future." She smiled. "And I've got just the man for the job." She dialed her mobile phone. "Get me Glenn Janssen." She nodded and then snapped her fingers at Marko.

The young climber jumped as if he'd been shocked with a cattle prod.

"Come on, Marko. I've got a feeling I'm gonna need someone who knows his way around those cliffs."

"But—"

"Don't *but* me, Mister. I'm bringing you aboard under the same arrangement as Dr. Andrews. You're drafted."

Garrett Moon stepped forward. "Since you're looking for native speakers, I got some Navajo."

"You sure, Garrett?" Leah asked. "After all I've put you through? This could be tough sledding."

"Actually," he said, "I think I've been waiting for this my whole life."

"You remember what my dad used to say?"

Garrett nodded. "That the Navajo were a race of kings and warriors."

"When you see them up close and out of those pods," Leah said, "it's gonna blow you away."

When Simpson, Marko, and Garrett had left them, Jack came over to Leah and kissed her.

"Why am I not surprised you already have this totally under control?"

Leah stepped back and wiped away a tear. "I don't know. I hope you're right. They'll need help. Lots of help."

"They've got the best in you." Jack glanced toward the sky. "This isn't the end of it, you know. Beckam told me that when we breached the lab, or whatever it was, the structure beamed some kind of high-powered signal into the sky. Apparently, it roasted satellites in the Southern Hemisphere on its way out into space. The Russians have moved to occupy Antarctica, and everyone, including the Chinese, have itchy trigger fingers."

"No surprise there," Leah said. "Fischer believes there are likely more than one of these alien labs, or transfer stations. After all, the visitors abducted a hell of a lot more than the 30 cliff dwellers we found. He was dying to find out if the Native Americans knew about any other facilities in Antarctica."

"Well?" Jack asked in anticipation.

"I haven't had a chance to ask; she's been sleeping for the most part since we got on the helicopter. It seems like common sense they wouldn't know anything...." Leah paused. "Still...the red granite stones, the returnees to the cliff dwellings. I'd bet Paulson's plane collection there's a lot more we don't know." She flinched. "It just gets worse, doesn't it, Jack?"

Jack nodded. "Unless you knew where to look, it's a mighty big continent. If she tells you something of value, we'll have a whole lot more leverage with the government. Then again, if those 'visitors' come back looking for their property...."

Leah glanced up at the sky, then down at the girl in her arms. "We whipped their sorry asses once, and our spears are a lot sharper now."

Jack looked at her in surprise. "You're advocating the use of weapons of mass destruction?"

"Only if I find someone worth using them on." She glanced around. "Speaking of...where's Paulson?"

"Washington. If you want all hell to break loose, Paulson's your man. But our leverage isn't going to last forever."

"What?"

Jack shook his head. "It's a long story."

"Ah," Leah said, working it out in her head. "Of course Fischer wouldn't just release us because he had a kind heart."

"You're right. Fortunately for you, Paulson's a much better poker player than I am. We 'obtained' a super-secret weapon, the same type that wiped out Gus Beckam, the SEALs, and a small army of Russian Special Operations Commandos. It also destroyed the alien lab and Thor's Hammer. For the moment, at least, we've got another one of those bombs positioned to insure cooperation at the highest levels."

Leah put her hand to her mouth. "So you're saying Beckam and all his men...?"

Jack nodded. "He saved us. He and his SEALs gave their lives so we could escape."

Leah stood silent, wiping away a few tears, working to regain her composure.

Jack's mobile phone sounded. He glanced down at the screen. "Paulson's calling me from Washington."

Leah watched as Jack said something about *top secret*, before he walked away a few steps and continued the call. She knew from experience that it wasn't a conversation Jack was enjoying from the way his jaw clenched while he nodded in agreement with what Paulson was saying.

When he disconnected the call, he let out a long sigh before returning to face Leah.

"I've been drafted too."

Leah's mouth dropped open. "No.... Don't even, Jackson."

Jack stuffed the phone in his pocket, unable to hide the grin creasing his sunburned face. "If I'd let Paulson continue talking, I likely would be. Like you said, the government's hot to find more of these facilities, if any exist." He walked over and wrapped his arm around Leah. "Are you as tired as I am?"

She nodded so that he could feel it.

"Man, I've had all the excitement I can handle for a while."

Leah pulled back. "What? No new summits to climb? No rich tourists to guide? Do you really think you'll be sticking around a while this time, Climber?"

Jack looked down at K'aalógii, then nodded. "Watching a sunrise over an amazing mesa, populated by former cliff dwellers, free from fear? Can it get any better than that?"

Leah pulled him closer. "Not from where I'm standing."

The End

EPILOGUE

Antarctica—1259 AD
She awoke on a hard, smooth surface that felt like polished stone. Fear competed with anger in her breast. Her last memories were of standing with her daughter K'aalógii, their spears brandished at the brilliant white light of the demon-gods—and the heat—and then nothing.

The rest had been like a dream. The faceless bodies of the creatures standing over her. She unable to move even a finger to resist. She had watched them move about without seeming to touch the smooth floor.

She rolled off the strange surface with one fierce desire: to find K'aalógii and escape.

They seemed to be gone, at least for the moment. She recalled seeing them approach the smooth wall, just so, and place their small, delicate hands against the shape in the center. It had opened some sort of doorway, and then they'd left the chamber.

Approaching the wall, she tested the air, which felt thick and hot. Now that she was standing, her ears ached strangely, and she felt intense pressure at the front of her head. She glanced down—she was nude, the reed skirt gone. No matter. She had to find K'aalógii.

Now.

She looked around the empty room, then back at the wall before her. Perhaps her daughter lay beyond the magic door. She reached forward, her hands shaking, flattened her palm, and pressed her hand against the smooth warm wall.

The door disappeared upward, just as it had done for her abductors, and she stepped into the smaller room beyond. When the door slammed, her ears popped and she felt faint as the crushing pressure against her body lifted, along with the hiss of compressed gas.

She shivered with the change in air pressure, as cooler air replaced the hot thick air of the larger cavern. In front of her lay another doorway, like the one she had just passed through. She hesitated and then reached forward again with her flattened palm. When the door flashed open, the shock of seeing the brilliant white of the snow and ice against the blue of the sky overcame the intense cold that flooded the smaller room. She stood with her mouth opened in awe, staring at the frozen world.

She stared for what seemed like forever, never feeling the biting cold as it penetrated her skin and worked its way to her core. She might have simply frozen to death—except the demons appeared first.

She tried to scream but no sound escaped her throat.

She spun and ran back to the other door, put her hand over the symbol, and willed the door to open, but in her panic, her hands missed the mark. She turned once and caught a glimpse of the creatures as they sped toward her in their smooth white skins. Just as they reached the threshold, she felt a shock run through her arm and down into her body.

She turned away from them, facing the inner door again, and pressed her palm against the symbol with all her might. The door flashed upward along with the crack of an explosion as the pressure from inside rushed to fill the low-pressure void outside the room. Her pursuers were blown backward as they reached her.

She would have been thrown back with them into the whiteness, except that she'd slipped and fallen to the side of the doorway when the blast came. She tried to stand, but her feet slipped again on the frozen surface, and she fell anew. The inner door closed before she could get through it. A noise drew her attention to the outer door. The sound was deep, a loud rumble, as a cloud of white snow and ice roaring down the mountain. The avalanche piled through the outer door, trapping her on the floor. A million tons of snow and ice buried the doorway—and trapped her in place.

The soft blue glow lighting the inside of the cavern flickered twice, and then there was nothing but blackness—and the stones. K'aalógii's mother curled into a ball on the smooth floor and cried for her daughter....

AFTERWORD

Thank you for reading ICE! I would love to know what you think of it. Please stop by my website www.writingthrillers.com and send me an email or drop in at Kevin Tinto on Facebook. If you enjoyed ICE, please tell a friend or two. And please help out by rating ICE and writing a short review at Amazon. REVIEWS ARE EVERYTHING!

The next book in the Leah and Jack series is ICE GENESIS. If have questions about what happened to the Native Americans, what that mysterious beam meant and where it went, whether the planet's headed for another world war, and what more might be found on Antarctica, keep your shoulder straps fastened.

The first two chapters of ICE GENESIS, the next in the series are available at the end of the book! Hope to see you back for more Jack and Leah adventure.

ACKNOWLEDGMENTS

Producing a (readable) novel without a professional editor is like trying to make an Olympic team without a coach. Ed Stackler is the best. There are plenty of editors who can correct messy English. Ed took ownership of my characters and plot lines, and guided me along throughout the twists and turns of ICE, many times, over a period of nearly TEN years. Without Ed's guidance and professional help, ICE wouldn't exist. Thanks, Ed! www.fictioneditor.com

DEDICATION

This book is dedicated to you, dear reader. Thank you for taking the journey with Leah, Jackson, and crew. I sincerely hope ICE gave you the thrill ride that I intended. This is not the end, but just the beginning for the ICE crew. I hope you come back for more!

I would also like to thank the following individuals for guiding me along the way: Ken Atchity, Story Merchant, extraordinaire. Mic Grandfield for his eagle eye and knowledge of all things mechanical. Patrick Walraven, Samantha Parent, Kelly Houston, Sandie Brown, Jim and Janice Tinto, for wading through early drafts and still finding something to like. My wife Laurie for allowing me the freedom to risk my neck pursuing a plethora of hazardous activities, and for her unending support. Any tech-related mistakes in ICE may or may not be deliberate artistic choices. If you do catch something embarrassing, please drop me an email and let me know. I will be grateful.

Kevin@writingthrillers.com www.writingthrillers.com

Ice Genesis

Dr. Leah Andrews crouched at the top at the cliff, looking down at the mix of Native American peoples, speaking different languages and trying to adapt to life after the trauma of their abduction experience. Not to mention being suddenly thrust 800 years into the future and slammed down into the 21st century. This following their removal from stasis, "rescued" from a situation that, to Leah, still seemed surreal.

The sad reality was, her plan to return the cliff dwellers back to their normal lives prior to the abduction was already in deep trouble. Despite her best efforts, including wearing traditional deerskin clothing and working alongside the tribal women day and night, she knew they were not adapting well. In fact, the "Ancients" (or Anasazi), as they were known, had completely refused to embrace her goal of restoring their peaceful existence on the tops of the mesas.

Leah hadn't harbored any illusions of creating an ancient utopia here; still, it was a shock to any modern person to see how people survived in a thousand-year-old culture, especially when they subsisted in constant fear.

Leah, along with native-speaking tribal leaders from a plethora of tribes and cultures, had tried to assure them that the Holy People, or Angry Gods, wouldn't return. But the twenty-seven survivors did not feel reassured. In fact, they had been terrified when offered an opportunity live on the open mesa. Leah had agreed to allow them to return to the claustrophobic cliff dwellings in Gila National Monument. Huddled within the cliffs, they were at first, reluctant to leave the security of the cliff dwellings, except at night, when the occasional hunting party ventured out, so quiet and swift, even the modern-day tribal trackers couldn't keep up with them.

Thanks to the stasis systems—an alien technology still not fully understood—twenty-seven Native Americans had been preserved under Antarctic ice for more than 800 years, and the current theory was, there still might be more, a lot more, elsewhere under the ice, living in stasis in yet-to-be-discovered alien stations.

Dr. Alfred Gordon—"Big Al" or "Gordo," depending upon Leah's mood—and his growing team of medical doctors, geneticists, and physicists had made one amazing discovery after another. The biggest so far was that the Ancients had been genetically modified while in stasis. They were seemingly immune to disease, hardly affected by changes in temperature and climate, and, if so inclined, could set world records in any Olympic track event of choice, even on a bad day.

Leah shaded her eyes, in order to make out individuals from the top of the mesa, looking down at the green valley below. She had more than a soft spot for the first of the Ancients revived, a ten- or twelve-year-old girl named K'aalógii. A warm smile spread across her face, when she saw K'aalógii with Garrett Moon. Garrett was Leah's archeological sidekick and a full-blooded Navajo, whose easy and relaxed methodology stood in stark contrast to Leah's bull-in-a-china-shop approach to archaeology, science, and well everything. Garrett and K'aalógii walked side by side, chatting as usual in an ancient Navajo dialect that Garrett had mastered in a matter of days.

K'aalógii had had the most exposure to modern culture and technology, including aircraft, helicopters, and more. Still, she asked repeatedly why they couldn't live with the Bégochiddy, the mythical, fair-haired, blue-eyed god of goodwill. She'd come to believe that Leah was the daughter of Bégochiddy.

In other words: 'Why do we have to live like this, when we could live with the gods, in safety and warmth? With real clothes, hamburgers, a pink iPod, and more?'

It was a question that Leah had begun to ask herself. While her husband Jack Hobson would be content living on a life-long campout, eating pine-nuts and relieving oneself in a hole-in-the-ground commode, the reality of primitive life was hitting Leah hard. Speaking of the communal commode, she literarily did deep breathing before entering, and held her breath the entire time. The facts of ancient Native American life as taught in the classroom seemed like a laughable fantasy compared to the real thing.

"Diyin Dine'é! Diyin Dine'é!"

"What now?" she said, scanning the village below. Diyin Dine'é translated, roughly, in Navajo as "Angry Gods." It was a cry she'd heard often in the ten days of Anasazi habitation.

Leah scanned the skies. Each time before, the panicked cry had been in response to Blackhawk helicopters flying routine patrols over the monument. An understandable cause for panic among the Native Americans.

As usual, Leah saw and heard nothing. The Ancients had hearing far more sensitive than the average person's, seemingly another genetic boost that had been introduced into their physiology.

When the sounds of rotor blades echoed off the sandstone at a level Leah could detect, she knew another Blackhawk was closing in. Irritating, because she'd asked the brass overseeing the security detail to keep their choppers out along the park perimeter.

Leah shaded her eyes and saw the sleek silhouette of an army Blackhawk coming in from the south at low altitude. She knew where it was headed: a landing zone, or LZ, that she'd authorized a few miles north on the mesa. But only to be used in case of *extreme emergency, with the agreed* approach only from the north!

She hadn't called for a helicopter, so she wondered what this jackass thought he was doing. She instinctively felt for the satellite phone she was *supposed* to have on her person at all times, but didn't. She glanced down to the mesa top, where the Ancients climbed over each other, trying to get up their ladders and into the dwelling.

Leah spun and sprinted away from the mesa cliff, feeling every pebble under the thin soles of the deerskin moccasins she wore, matching the rest of her native attire. The LZ was more than five miles away, so she'd had the military deliver a deadly quiet, special-ops electric quad runner. With the help of the perimeter security crew, they'd built a camouflaged "hide" about a mile north of the village, on the way toward the LZ, deep within the forest.

Leah was breathing hard from the combination of altitude and the sprint when she arrived at the hide. She dug at the base, knowing exactly where to find the knife she needed to free the quad. Once in hand, she cut the nearly invisible nylon fishing-style line that held the pine-tree-bough-woven "door" in place, regardless of the weather. It was less a door, actually, and more a one-sided lean-to propped at a 45-degree angle.

She reached in and grabbed the handle bars, leaned back and let all of her 120 pounds lever the quad out of its hiding spot. After several cuss words worthy of her mechanic friend Mac Ridley, and despite her promise to Jack to watch her language, she pulled it clear. Leah grabbed the helmet off the seat and, without a second thought, tossed it back into the hide. She couldn't see shit through that thing, despite the coaching she'd gotten from the security crew.

Leah secured the pine door back in place without the line, tossed a leg over the quad, and pushed the red power button center-left of the display. When everything lit up and the LED lights flashed green, she rolled on the throttle, just enough to get the quad moving. The last thing she needed was digging two big tire divots right next to the hide.

Several hundred meters away from the hide, the quad rolled down into a wash solid sandstone. Leah "put the spurs to it," as the Texas-born security tech had shown her. Unfortunately, she didn't take into account the incline, and the front tires wheeled skyward and the quad nearly flipped over backward. Leah cut the throttle, and the quad came down so hard on the front wheels, she banged her forehead into the control panel.

"Whoa, Nellie," she whispered. "Okay, note to self: helmet a good idea."

Despite the near disaster, Leah twisted open the throttle until the quad nearly flew over the rocks on the way to the LZ.

CHAPTER 2

The chopper had already landed on the grass pad and powered down by the time Leah rolled into the LZ, fifteen minutes later.

She was nearly spitting bullets. The death-ride at higher than recommended speeds and seeing the Ancients running for the safety of the cliff dwellings had her ready to issue a military-grade, extra venti-sized can of whoop-ass on the dipshit who'd ordered an overflight right above one of the most sensitive and secure locations on the planet.

She glanced around and spotted movement at the tree line. Two men dressed in flight suits were clearing the forest. Even before Leah could open her mouth, they both raised their hands.

"Hold fire, Dr. Andrews! Please! It's not our fault!"

The fear on the faces of these hardened Iraq and Afghanistan combat veterans disarmed Leah, and although she gave it her best effort, she couldn't withhold the grin.

"What the hell is wrong with you guys?" she said, feeling the anger return as she spoke. "You know damn well if you approach from the south, you're gonna send my people running for their lives." She placed hands on hips. "Not to mention this is an *EMERGENCY ONLY*, LZ, to be used upon my order via the sat phone."

"Yes, ma'am. You've briefed us many times...as you know." The pilots looked at each other, then took two steps back as she approached within arm's reach.

"What?" Leah asked, as both pilots, wrinkled their noses, while trying their best to hold a professional face. "As much as I'd like to, kicking your asses isn't my style, boys. Relax."

"I don't think that's why they're backing up, dear."

Leah spun. Out of the cover of the pine trees, walked Jack Hobson.

"Ha! Jack!" Leah sprinted toward the handsome mountain climber and was ready to throw her arms around him, when he too backed up, holding his arms out.

"Is this the kind of greeting I get?" she said, more hurt than angry.

Jack glanced over toward the flight crew, and started to laugh. Leah turned, and found them trying to hold back laughter themselves.

"What?"

"And you thought my climbing gear stank after six weeks on Everest? Damn, girl, you are downright…well, put it this way: the smell coming off those skins is enough to gag a maggot."

It suddenly occurred to Leah that she had been living and working in the cliffs with the Ancients without a bath for more than ten days, in native-appropriate costume that hadn't been all that clean to begin with.

She'd been gutting and cleaning deer, squirrel, and fish along with the rest of the women; cooking while choking on a damp-wood fire inside the dwellings; gathering wood until her hands bled and she was soaked in sweat. She'd gotten to the point where she didn't even notice it.

Now, though, she realized how bad she must smell. She reached up and touched her stringy, dirty hair. She looked at her hands. Her nails were rarely manicured during the best of times. Now her hands were dirty and covered in cuts, scrapes, and burns, the nails jagged, broken and dirty. "Oh yeah…well, you know, I've been busy…and…sorry," she said, unusually meek for Leah Andrews.

Jack suddenly and without warning, reached out and despite the near gagging odor, picked his wife up and hugged her tight. He then leaned over and gave her a deep kiss.

"Wow, she said, wiping at her mouth, now more embarrassed than anything.

"We've been trying to call you for at least 48 hours," Jack said. "Nada."

"I can't be a slave to that thing. I'm working to save these people. Sooner or later, they're gonna catch me with it."

"Leah, these Indians have been abducted by aliens, sent to Antarctica for an 800-year-old big sleep, woken, poked at with a variety of high-tech equipment, eaten foods they never dreamed of, and you're worried about the sat phone?"

She visibly winced.

"How is it going, by the way?" he asked.

"So far, not so good, for all of the above and more."

"How does Marko put it?" he asked. "The Prime Directive "Dude, you can't mess with the Prime Directive."

Leah chuckled. "Yeah. Mr. Star Trek, always with the one-liner. I'm beginning to wonder if he isn't right. Mixing cultures and technology thousands of years apart in development is always a disaster, no matter how well-intentioned.

"Perhaps a lesson our alien visitors learned themselves," said Jack.

"Well, at least they had the good sense to put them to sleep. It's like herding cats over there."

Leah glanced over at the air crew, as they seemed ready to start the helicopter.

"So what's going on? I must have missed any message. Last we spoke, you were in Washington with Paulson in top secret meetings with members of congress, the military, and just about everyone else who has a clearance."

Jack nodded, the expression on his face telegraphing bad news.

"What is it, Climber? After what we've been through, how bad can it be?"

"There is news, Leah. Some you'll find distasteful."

"Yeah. Tell me something I don't know."

"Okay. First, the President."

"All right." Leah rubbed her hands together. "This is gonna be good. So, have you had a chance to water-board that SOB yet?"

"No." He drew a breath. "In fact, the President isn't going anywhere. He is continuing on as President, with his entire staff intact, including Fischer, like Antarctica never happened."

"Are you kidding me?"

Jack sighed. "Let me give it to you straight. "We're in a world of shit right now. A world of shit that you, and most people, know nothing about. Antarctica is a free-for-all killing zone, with Russian, American, Chinese, British, French, Israeli, Koreans, and more going at it. We're talking every-thing from hand-to-hand combat to ships and planes being shot down and sunk. Frankly, it's a miracle this hasn't escalated into full-on nuclear war... yet. It's a good bet the North Koreans are on the verge of invading South Korea, and China looks ready to take on Taiwan, as the 'superpowers' seem otherwise indisposed. The thinking, and I agree, is that more instability may well provoke one or more of the above."

Leah grimaced. "Thanks for the cheery update. I hope you brought along the anti-depressants I did not request, but now need." She took a deep breath and closed her eyes for a moment, trying to absorb it all. "Okay, this probably sounds ridiculous, but what's the good news?"

"We're headed back to Antarctica," Jack replied, a twinkle in his eye. "To save a friend."

Thanks, Readers and Fans of ICE!

CPSIA information can be obtained
at www.ICGtesting.com
Printed in the USA
LVOW13s0631240517
535631LV00007B/108/P